BRIARS,

The House of Heirs

By

Ann Gray

*To John Couch
Thanks,
Ann Gray*

Christmas, '03

© 1998, 2002 by Ann Gray. All rights reserved.

No part of this book may be reproduced, stored in a retrieval system, or transmitted by any means, electronic, mechanical, photocopying, recording, or otherwise, without written permission from the author.

ISBN: 0-7596-9513-X e-book
ISBN: 0-7596-9514-8 softcover

This book is printed on acid free paper.

1stBooks - rev. 06/28/02

*This book is dedicated to Norman,
my husband of over fifty years.*

Darling, I STILL love you...MOST!

Acknowledgments

It was my husband Norman's constant reassurance that I would succeed when I doubted my own ability that encouraged me to begin this novel. It was his often repeated advice: "Just tell the story" which lifted me up again each time I stumbled and wondered if I could finish it. Without his never-ending patience, tending to all life's necessary daily duties so that I could spend my time, all day every day and sometimes half the nights, weaving other people's lives—this book would never have been.

I want to thank my wonderful children, Steven and Claudia Gray, for their constant faith in my ability. Claudia, our family artist, designed the cover for this book. Steven is our reliable business advisor. First cousins, Barbara Newman, Sarah Fulton, Betty Standard, and dependable lifelong friends, Elizabeth and Cooper Smith contributed their encouragement early on after reading original drafts. Thanks to my cousin Barbara White Hambrick for genealogy searches and family backgrounds. Debby Harris, Ramona Feliciano, Joan Marulli, Allen Olson, Helen Kautz, Jim Lynch, Mary Milo and Jane Storms were valued proof readers. To all those who have been interested enough to ask to read the story from diskette without waiting for publication of *BRIARS, The House of Heirs,* I thank you, one and all.

Without the Internet's endless availability of reference books on—and maps of—Atlanta, Georgia and Petersburg, Virginia in the 1800s, compiling this information would have been a much longer, more tedious and difficult undertaking. Thanks to Microsoft for the wonders of Word and the ease of using it in the accomplishment of my purpose; and for Encarta, which put a world of information within reach of my keyboard.

And for her innumerable contributions to the intricate detailing and accuracy of historical events depicted within these pages, I wish to acknowledge in loving memory, my second cousin, Leonelle Baker Bullard, who passed away on April 24, 2000.

Ponder the capriciousness of human nature,
which allows momentary appetites and fleeting attitudes
to set the courses for entire lives and future responsibilities.
—Author—

References:

"Guns of the Old West" by Charles Edward Chapel;
"Atlanta, It's Lore, Legends, and Laughter" by Elise Reid Boylston;
"White Columns In Georgia" by Medora Field Perkerson;
Microsoft Encarta - 1996, 1998; University of Georgia Libraries.

x

CHAPTER ONE ~ LILLIAN

2:55 p.m., November 15, 1864 ~ Briars, Atlanta, Georgia

Yankees

Heavyhearted, Lillian Heirs, Mistress of *Briars*, peered out her parlor window at what ordinarily would have been a picture perfect November day but on this particular Tuesday afternoon her panoramic view was shrouded in leaden shades. In the distance, billowing clouds of dense black smoke had gathered into great angry mountains silhouetted against a limitless crimson sky. Lillian counted her blessings for little more than ten miles to the south, by order of Union Army General William Tecumseh Sherman, the city of Atlanta's celebrated heritage and beauty were being transformed into sooty ash and fed to voracious winds of a raging fire storm visible from four states.

Ten miles was not a comfortable margin for safety. The Heirs family should have evacuated with their neighbors, but their scheduled leave-taking had been interrupted by Morgan Heirs' last impetuous, self-indulgent temper tantrum at the *Spike and Rail* tavern two days earlier, precipitating his own senseless and inconsiderate demise.

Now *Briars* was the only occupied house for miles around, and Lillian understood only too well that meant there would be no dependable help available from outside should the need arise. Now, with Sherman's 'burning teams' striking first in one then another area of Atlanta's surrounding communities, Lillian feared for *Briars* as well as for the neighboring estate of *Greenleaf* and other properties in their *Briarwood* section but, mercifully, so far they had all been spared.

Yet within *Briars,* Lillian observed, peering over her shoulder in response to a burst of laughter from the young people sharing the room with her, despite the uncertainty of the times and their own recent loss, youth could not contain its fervor. Her daughters and son, Sarah, Morgana, and Wil, along with daughter-in-law, Laura Lee, sat altogether on the floor playing a game of Whist. Wil, youngest and least tutored in the game, teased and meddled good-naturedly in his sisters' game playing.

Turning back to the window Lillian's pulse quickened as she watched, fearfully, the gradual appearance of a blue-uniformed rider on the rising road then another and another until a column of ten riders had come into view. Approaching from Atlanta, at the intersection of Briarwood Road and Northside Drive, they had chosen a left turn over a right, which would have taken them downhill towards an evacuated *Greenleaf*. Instead, they were riding slowly up the hill towards *Briars*.

Lillian hesitated before saying anything to the family on the chance that the Union soldiers would continue on. But when she saw the leader of the column stop and raise his hand, looking long and hard at the Heirs' residence, then turn his mount to study the view, she knew they would not ride on. Once he had noticed her home and its sweeping vista, choosing *Briars* for whatever purpose useful to their cause would be a logical choice for the officer. But, Lillian dared to hope, surely, not for burning!

Observed from any distance, *Briars* was truly an imposing sight. There were few *Briarwood* estates to rival its tranquil beauty with its iron-barred entry gates, neatly groomed prickly hedges, gently rising lawns, and majestic oak to compliment the stately gray stone residence.

The column paused at *Briars'* entry gates only long enough for the leader to reach through the bars and lift the latch. From their saddles, two men pushed the gates open and the detail rode straight up the long ascending driveway, their horses hooves crunching noisily on the white gravel until they reached the hitching post beside the steps to the verandah.

The tall, slender Lieutenant in charge—Lillian would have called him 'handsome' in a Confederate uniform—dismounted and stepped lightly across the wide porch to the front door. Removing his gloves, he tapped the heavy door-knocker summoning anyone from inside.

In only moments before his arrival at her door, while the alarmed younger women had rushed upstairs to their individual bedrooms, Lillian had sent Wil scurrying to the library on an important errand. Then, willing her heart to stop pounding, she walked briskly into the front hallway where she watched the Union officer's approach through the oval glass of her front door.

Lillian quickly breathed a prayer for guidance, smoothed her skirts, stretched to her most regal height, set her expression to one of calculated arrogance and, at his knock, promptly flung open the door. "Yes, young man, who are you and what is your business here?" she asked bluntly. She purposely neglected to acknowledge his uniform and rank.

The Lieutenant, grinning subtly at her patronizing attitude, removed his hat and addressed her politely. "Madam, I am Shane Alexander Moss, First Lieutenant, Army of the United States of America."

Lillian raised an eyebrow. Any fool could see that! However casting aspersions now would, most surely, generate regret later. She remained silent, her green eyes reflecting his image, impatient for him to get on with it!

In turn, he recognized that here was a woman unaccustomed to catering to imposed authority. "May I inquire whom I have the honor of addressing, ma'am?"

"My name is Mistress Lillian Heirs and I am head of this household, sir, in my husband's absence." She saw to it that her voice never quavered.

"Mistress Heirs, ma'am, I truly regret this imposition—" His earnest blue eyes said he didn't lie. "—but I must inform you that I am compelled to commandeer your house overnight." He mentioned General Sherman and told her he had "important orders and maps to be studied," and that he and his men required "a place of reasonable comfort, quiet, and security for tonight's lodging. *Briars—*" he said, because of its lofty perch atop the knoll, "—suits that need." He went on to say, "I further regret, ma'am, that it will be necessary for supplies and animals to be peaceably confiscated from your household stores and stables when we leave."

Having heard his intent, Lillian asked, her voice deceptively calm, "And in return for my *hospitality,* sir?"

"In return, Mistress Heirs, we will not disturb your household any more than is absolutely necessary. We will be on our way tomorrow as soon as is reasonably possible since we have an important rendezvous to keep."

"Though it will not cause me to accept your presence in my home with grace, sir—" She eyed him, tentatively. "—if you are saying my home will not be burned when you leave, I can truthfully say I am grateful for that clemency."

"I am, ma'am. Then, shall we call it an agreement?"

"Agreed." Lillian felt a surge of relief tingle out to her fingertips and down to her toes.

He nodded to the sergeant, who spoke to two of the horsemen in muted tones, then turned back to her. "May I ask how many are in your household at this time, ma'am?"

"My two daughters and daughter-in-law are in residence with me, now. I've two household servants. Also, my groom and gardener share quarters in the stable." She stood squarely in the entry.

"While we are here, ma'am, we will confine our business to your lower floor. Therefore, with the exception of meals at table, your family will not be disturbed. They will sleep in their own beds tonight, as usual, and tomorrow this detachment will withdraw— on my honor as an officer and a gentleman."

Lillian frowned. "I don't care for—nor understand, precisely—your reference to my family's sleeping arrangements, sir. However, I won't ask you to explain, as I expect I might value your explanation even less." She moved aside.

"My husband's library is on your right," Lillian said, walking beside him down the wide center hall.

Seven riders dismounted and followed the lieutenant inside, their heavy boots echoing on the polished hardwood floor. The eighth and ninth soldiers to whom the sergeant had spoken led the horses away to the stables.

An impeccably dressed, lean and tall, gray-haired Negro man emerged from the library as the assemblage approached. He nodded slightly to Mistress Heirs then stepped away, eyes respectfully downcast, making way for the uniformed intruders.

The lieutenant gestured for the sergeant to lead the others of their unit into the room while he continued conversing with Mistress Heirs in the hall.

Lillian nodded towards the Negro man. "Lieutenant, Henry, here, is trusted caretaker of this Heirs estate. He will see to all of your company's requirements."

Turning her back on the unwelcome sight of the Yankees passing, one by one, into Morgan Heirs' library, she looked up into Henry's worried face and he lifted his gaze to meet hers. "Henry, Lieutenant Moss and his men are to be our overnight guests. Tell Rachel there will be ten more for supper. The Lieutenant and his party will dine at table this evening. The family will take our evening meal in our rooms."

She addressed Lieutenant Moss again. "Henry is my most valued servant of twenty-one years. His wife, Rachel, is an excellent cook as you shall soon learn for yourself." And, Lillian thought, when Henry speaks to Rachel in the kitchen as instructed, she will either quake with fear or seethe with anger at the altered state of her plans for supper. Lillian tended to favor the second choice, knowing Rachel's high strung temperament.

Earlier, Henry had built a crackling fire in the library fireplace where a snarling, black bearskin rug lay guarding the broad granite hearth. The fierce-fanged rug immediately attracted the soldiers' admiration and attention.

Morgan, himself, had chosen most of the furnishings for the room: A deep red brocade sofa before the massive stone fireplace, a handsome mahogany collector's weapons cabinet off to one side of Morgan's favorite cordovan leather easy chair, ottoman and small service table. Under the single window, a rich chestnut leather-topped mahogany desk, upholstered chair and matching side chair. Floor to ceiling book shelves fronted by two fawn colored wing chairs nestled on the far wall.

Concern etched two narrow lines between Lillian's brows as she watched the men's inquisitive exploration of Morgan's inviolate personal lair where they would find barely adequate seating.

An undisclosed feature of the room—and a closely guarded secret of the household—was the wall of bookshelves which, when folded away, disclosed the entrance to Morgan Heirs' private liquor closet. Without doubt, the hidden locker's library shelves, graced by a plethora of historical volumes, poetry and fiction would be its best defense.

Lillian had carefully avoided any mention to the lieutenant of Willow, her servants' seventeen year old daughter. For Willow's very existence and whereabouts, as Wil's, would certainly serve themselves and the family better, undisclosed. Nor had she seen reason to mentioned Laura Lee's and Drew's four years old twins, napping upstairs in the nursery.

Immediately upon Lillian's dismissal of Henry, Lieutenant Shane Alexander Moss—Lillian already knew she would never forget that name—began walking his hostess towards the front stairs. Though she considered protesting his going to the upper floor, better judgment prevailed and, silently, she relented to his company.

As they ascended the stairs, the Lieutenant turned his pleasant smile on her. "I hope you don't mind my saying so, ma'am, but being once more in the company of a refined lady such as yourself reminds me of my own mother back in Virginia."

Lillian, her gaze riveted to the multicolored floral design of the carpeted steps just ahead, answered, "I'm sure even Union soldiers must have mothers, sir, but quite frankly the thought that I might be old enough to be yours would never have occurred to me had you not brought it up." She stopped halfway up the long staircase and fastened her fierce gaze onto his. "Being a Virginian, Lieutenant, how does it happen that you are here in the uniform of our opposing army?"

"I was in military school in Lexington, ma'am, when the war commenced. Naturally, we were required to respond to President Lincoln's order." His sheathed sword rattled between two posts of the staircase banisters' highly polished carved wood and he quickly retrieved it. Attempting casual conversation again, he grinned. "I'm sure your daughters must be most charming young ladies if they take after you, ma'am. May I ask—what are their ages?"

Lillian spoke firmly. "My daughters' ages are immaterial to this arrangement." Her face clouded. "Lieutenant, I want you to give me your word of honor my girls won't be molested—nor will they be disturbed in any manner! Is that understood?"

A strained silence prevailed until they stepped onto the pale blue carpet at the top of the stairs. He seemed terribly nervous and insecure, and he had as much as admitted to her by his awkwardness that this foray was his first command.

Lillian said, "The first three rooms to our left, sir, are those of my daughters. My room is here on our right. Will you speak to them, individually, or shall I call them all out into the hall?"

"That won't be necessary. After you, ma'am," he said, gesturing for her to lead the way to her own door. Then he added, "I shall rely on your good judgment in informing the other ladies of the house of the new and temporary rules. Also, Mistress Heirs, in return for your generous cooperation, I promise to see to it that you and your daughters are afforded the complete privacy of this upstairs floor." Then his voice took on a far more serious note. "Frankly, ma'am," his open gaze penetrated her troubled frown, "although I have never yet had cause for concern over my men's behavior, they have had many long weeks of fighting, strict discipline, and short rations, and now that it's all but over—" Lillian's green eyes flashed sharply in his direction at those provocative words. "That is—" he continued, "under the present unavoidable circumstances—especially if there's liquor about—I do strongly advise that all your womenfolk remain behind locked doors, quietly occupied. As soon as I leave you, I shall expect you to immediately advise the other ladies of the household, the same. I assure you, ma'am, that I will do my utmost to spare your family any impropriety." His guileless blue eyes, circled with weariness, spoke honestly enough to her.

"You see to it, Lieutenant, you see to it!" she said, powerless, watching as he removed her key from its inside lock and placed it firmly in the palm of her hand. Comforting words and a noble intention, Lillian thought, as she watched him returning downstairs. But she didn't believe for one minute that the well-meaning and solicitous Union officer would be able to control his clutch of rugged fighting men once they were rested and full of meat and bread. She hoped she was wrong.

She called her daughters into Laura Lee's room where, with appropriate replies to their myriad questions and concerns, she delivered the lieutenant's edict.

After her daughter-in-law's concern for her own children demanded it, Lillian accompanied her on a short visit to the nursery in the back hall where the twins had awakened and were playing quietly in Willow's care. Laura Lee held and kissed her children, and promised to see them again as soon as time and circumstances would permit.

Willow was cautioned to stay out of sight and to keep the children's enthusiasm subdued until the enemy had left Briars' premises. All their needs, overnight, would be met right there in the nursery by either Rachel or Henry.

Willow did not require telling twice.

Laura Lee, on returning to her room, closed and locked her door.

Weary from the escalating tensions of the afternoon, after Lillian locked her own bedroom door, she moved directly to her dressing table, took down and began unraveling her heavy red braids, lately blighted by random strands of gray. She spoke to the woman in the mirror. "'Spare your family any impropriety—' he said!" Irish eyes shone brighter, anger blazing anew, as she pulled the brush, over and over, through cascading waves. "'I'm sure your daughters must be most charming young ladies if they take after you, ma'am.' In a pig's eye!" She laid the brush aside and traced deepening lines at the corners of her mouth. "As for you—you're old!" she said to the still attractive, but careworn face scowling back at her. "Used up! Widowed! Half—where you used to be whole!"

But the enemy entrenched in her house at this very moment didn't know that, did they? The handsome young Lieutenant Moss and his nine horse soldiers didn't know her Morgan was lying dead, right now, in a nearby cave filled with every imaginable supply those plundering Yankee thieves could possibly have need of!

For two days now, before the unexpected arrival of the Yankees on this—the third, she'd been damning her husband for dying. For leaving her. Damning him for his time consuming business interests. His drinking and gambling. For all the empty nighttime hours through the years he'd left her alone tossing, restless, in her bed while he drank the nights away in that filthy tavern, discussing politics and business with his cronies. That was how he'd cheated her—not with other women! He'd used her all up with unfulfilled promises of times he'd sworn to be there but never was. Wasted her urgent desires and ungratified longings for days, months, years. Until, finally, it didn't matter any more. In truth, she asked herself, hadn't he always been that way? Hadn't she always known of his weaknesses for gab and drink, his love of male companionship, even before they escaped

Richmond and Morgan's antagonistic father and fled to Terminus?

Here in the silence of her bedroom, painfully aware of the offensive Yankees' presence downstairs, Lillian moved back and forth from the dresser to her bed to her boudoir chair, sitting only moments in each place then rising, too restless to be still. Looking about at the luxury Morgan had provided, Lillian asked herself: Had business, drink, and gambling truly been the sum and substance of the man, Morgan Heirs? No, she told herself. She wasn't being altogether fair when she spoke disparagingly of her so recently departed husband. Later, when all the good and bad about the man was counted up, Lillian knew the pain of losing him would go much deeper. Why did she torture herself with anger towards this man whom she had loved when there were now more deserving targets for her damnation. Yankees! And, right here within Morgan Andrew Heirs' beloved *Briars*.

Afternoon shadows deepened into evening and finally dissolved into a moonless night. And as she paced, Lillian thought of her young son, Wil. Despite her intense mood, a wry smile forced its way across her weary face. Poor Wilson! At fifteen, all elbows and knees, he had certainly been an unwilling pawn in this hopeless game of war. Aching to join in the fray, even now, as his older brother Drew had done at the war's beginning, Wil's wish had been denied by his mother's selfish fears and his father's unquestioned authority and political influence. Well, the Yankee's wouldn't find *him,* thank God! Nor would they find the Heirs' root cellar! Lillian knew that if they should find either, she'd soon hear about it!

Earlier, at the sound of the first hoof beat on the driveway, Lillian had sent Wil hightailing it to the root cellar with every weapon in his father's gun cabinet. She certainly had no intention of allowing the soldiers now occupying her home to make off with Morgan Heirs' prized firearms collection. More importantly, she would have been concerned for any youngster who, like her son, was tall for his age and still at home with his family rather than lying dead in some meadow after the bluecoats had passed through. God only knew what would likely have happened if the Yankees had found him in the house on their arrival. Besides, she had calculated in those first critical moments, some member of the household had to be on the outside.

The Root Cellar

The soldiers hadn't seen, hadn't heard, couldn't know that young Wil Heirs had left the root cellar to pay his mother a visit barely four hours after they had taken over *Briars*. After their parley, Lillian admired Wil's courage, for by sneaking back into the house, he had played out his own private game of intrigue and with very good cause.

The root cellar, which had been used by the Heirs family for safe shelter in stormy weather and for cold storage for years, was always cold and damp. In corners where ground water had seeped through the low ceiling and run in rivulets down it's slick clay walls, mucky pools had formed on the straw strewn clay floor. Potatoes, turnips and other root vegetables were stored in the chilly room year round. Over the years, too, other provisions requiring cold storage for preservation had come to be stored there. Cider barrels, earthen milk jugs and butter crocks; sacks of hard tack biscuits, and jars of jams, jellies and fruit preserves lined the floor to ceiling shelves. Aging meats and cheeses hung from hooks in the rafters, along with horns of gunpowder and bags of shot, safe from children's curious hands and convenient for the Heirs mens' hunting expeditions. Short tightly sealed kegs of flour and corn meal offered fairly comfortable seating whenever the need presented itself for safety from storms or cyclones.

In fact, during his imposed vigil, Michael Wilson Heirs had not lacked for nourishment. But his appetite was somewhat put off by present company. He stepped closer to the makeshift bier, consisting of three wide boards stretched across two sawhorses, and by the light of two enormous imported German candles—one situated at Morgan Andrew Heirs' head and one at his feet—Wil stared down on his father's waxen features.

In the flickering light from the candles, now spiraling ribbons of feathery smoke toward the earthen ceiling, the corpse didn't look too bad for having been dead these last three days. His high forehead was adorned by an enviable heavy thatch of jet black hair with silver temples and sideburns, not red nor thin like Wil's own, an unwelcome trait his mother attributed to his Irish grandfather. And there was, oddly enough, the hint of a smile on his father's cold tightly closed lips. Wil was glad the Colonel had not died with his mouth open in some grotesquely distorted fashion so that he would have been required to close it appropriately. He leaned over and gently smoothed the blue silk lapels of his father's favorite velvet dress coat his sister Sarah had so lovingly hand sewn for their father's forty-eighth birthday, his last. Yes, Wil had to say that his father's attire was impeccable, even if he did do the washing and dressing of the corpse, himself. His mother would not be put off when she came, at last, to view her deceased husband.

Having laid in a goodly supply of spirits for his own use before the war shortage commenced, Morgan Heirs had graciously sold back to the tavern owner who favored the locals with fair prices but sold at twice the cost to the occupying army. Morgan had collapsed and died, suddenly and fiery-faced, at the *Spike and Rail* tavern surrounded by his cronies while arguing battle strategies which the defeated South should have used. Wil's father had spent long hours in such useless arguments with other unfit men while drowning persistent frustrations in bourbon and ale.

"To pacify a guilty conscience," Pa often growled in disgust, tapping his cane against his crippled leg, "while young men fight and fall."

Pa's oldest and closest friends, Jeremiah Baker and Tom Garrett had brought Wil's father's body home draped across his saddle and—by Wil's mother's instruction—directly to the earthy room where, the deceased would await in cold storage the time of interment.

It wasn't as if they weren't going to give the Colonel a proper burial when Wil's older brother, Drew, got home from the Confederate Army. They had appealed for a family death leave, but such appeals moved slowly through the military. Wil wished his brother would hurry though—he wouldn't want to guess how long the remains would hold scent-less, even in the dank chill of the root cellar.

Actually, stealing in and out of the enemy-occupied house had been easy. Wil had made a cloak and dagger game of his secret entry and surreptitious performance of his mission.

While the troopers were behind closed dining room doors, eating *his* supper, Wil entered the kitchen by the outside pantry door. Behind Rachel's generous back, he picked up three hot biscuits from the pan on the stove and, eating the biscuits, sneaked up the servant's staircase to the upper hallways. Tiptoeing past the twins' nursery, he paused at the corner junction of the back and center corridors to look and listen.

Around the corner, Wil caught a glimpse of Henry going from bedroom to bedroom picking up the family's dirty supper dishes. Henry knocked at Sarah's door and as the servant entered the room with his big round service tray, satisfied it was safe enough, Wil sprinted past his own door and entered his father's room. There, he quickly gathered the Colonel's best attire, laying it out carefully on the bed. He also bundled and knotted into the Colonel's favorite ascot, a razor and toiletries his father regularly used. Getting it all to the root cellar would be an almighty task. He needed a satchel. But where—? After a few minutes of groping through his father's wardrobe, he tapped softly on his mother's door. "Ma? Ma, it's me, Wil!"

The door opened a crack and Lillian, catching her breath, peered into her son's face. "What in Sam Hill are you doing back in this house?"

"Sh, Ma, not so loud!" he pleaded.

Immediately, she flung open the door, reached through and crushed him to her bosom. "Don't you realize the danger you're in—coming back here?"

"I need a satchel, Ma, I can't carry all this stuff like it is!" He pointed to the array of items on Morgan Heirs' bed. "I'm going to fix Pa up, you know, make him look nice for the burial, but I got to have—"

Pleased with his pluck, his smiling mother interrupted, "Now, that's a mighty worthy task." She released him and went directly to her husband's clothes closet from whence she magically produced a fine leather satchel.

"I looked there," Wil sighed. "Why could you find it and I couldn't?" Wil asked, stuffing items into the satchel. The compliment had obviously been pleasing to his mother as her face suddenly looked years younger.

"Because I knew right where to look and you didn't," Lillian said, fingering a stray red lock out of his eyes. She pushed him gently to one side and folded and rolled and carefully tucked until the satchel was full and the bed, clear. "Now, hurry, get on back to your father and be careful doing it!" She kissed him soundly on his lips and pushed him towards the door.

Wilson stopped, his hand on the door knob, and looked back over his shoulder. "Ma, you seen old Storm around? He ain't going to understand me not being up here at the house, and he ain't going to be able to find me in the root cellar. I worry about them Yankees shooting him. You know how he don't like strangers messing 'round."

"I'll tell Henry to keep an eye out for him." She watched his frown soften. "Storm's probably put off by all this activity and strange new people. Son, don't you worry, he'll come home at feeding time, and don't worry about the Yankees hurting him.

They're not likely to see enough of Storm to do him harm." She smiled, loving him for his courage. "God go with you, son."

Retracing his route, Wil returned with the satchel to the root cellar.

Yep, Wil thought, looking down at his handiwork a while later, no doubt about it, Colonel Morgan Andrew Heirs looked every bit the Southern gentleman most everyone knew him to be. After all, he got the "Colonel" moniker in the first place being honored by the state of Georgia for what they called "his civic and charitable contributions". Well, that was just the way Pa'd always been.

Wil yawned and stretched out on a pallet of straw he'd gathered from the cold, clay floor. The need never occurred to him when he was up at the house, or he'd have brought back a goose down quilt from his own bed. He was just glad he'd seen his mother for the few minutes they had shared. Sleeping beside his revered dead father's bier would be easier now, having reassured himself of his mother's continuing existence by sharing her embrace and kiss tonight. He brushed away hot tears that rolled, unbidden, down his cheeks. How he hated it when such lingering boyhood traits unexpectedly reminded him of his immaturity. With the damn Yankees in residence, tomorrow would no doubt offer yet other trials for him to overcome on his journey into manhood.

The Contest Begins

After Wil's surprise visit, the remainder of the night had passed uneventfully for Lillian. She had heard Henry walking the upstairs halls all night, and each time he'd passed her door, though she knew his step and he passed hourly, she would listen to be sure that it was not some one of the intruders approaching the family's sleeping quarters. Finally she had given up all thoughts of rest and began pacing back and forth like a caged lion, alternately praying to God for guidance and cursing Morgan Heirs for dying. She stopped at the East window on each turn to measure the new dawn in the eastern sky, apart from the glow of Atlanta.

Even the old house creaked and groaned more than usual and seemed to recognize the strained difference with the Union soldiers' unbidden presence. With the subtle tint of dawn on the horizon came muted voices and bumping noises of the intruders' awakening and moving around downstairs, the hubbub growing louder and more irksome because Lillian couldn't know what was afoot. Then she heard a faint scratching on her door, and Henry's unmistakable low-pitched voice whispering, "Miz Lillian, it's Henry."

Lillian opened the door wide enough to examine the aging servant's anxious, haggard face. "Henry, you look just awful."

"Yes'm, I been awake th' whole night, listenin' and walkin' these halls from stairs t' stairs. I's th' only man in th' house, and I feels responsible fo' y'all."

"Thank you, Henry." She clasped his large work-worn hand. "What would we do without you?" She could tell by Henry's furrowed brows, that wasn't all.

"An', Miz Lillian, I gots to say it. You an' th' other ladies'd be better off getting' on down t' th' root cellar—right now! Them men 'as quiet enough las' night after they et Rachel's collards an' ham supper, 'cause then they 'as all done in, an' they all piled into th' guest rooms, 'cept fo' th' Lieuten't. He slep' in th' lib'ary on Mister Morgan's couch."

"Guarding Mister Morgan's liquor closet!" Lillian had already guessed. "Oh, my God, Henry, they haven't—?"

"Yes'm. I never heard a whisper from down there 'til 'bout a half hour ago. I thought maybe that lieutenant might of had a tight enough rein on 'em but, Miz Lillian, they must of woke up at five o'clock all full of mustard! Anyways, they done found an' broke down th' door t' Mister Morgan's liquor closet, ma'am. They down there ahoopin' an' ahollerin' an' aspillin' all that fine whiskey all over th' place an'—an', Miz Lillian, what they ain't drinkin' an' spillin' they's pourin' down that young lieutenant fella's th'oat! An' he ain't got a chance again' all o' them."

Lillian nodded and quickly took a deep breath. Then her words began tumbling out one over another. "For now, Henry, you go on back down and take Rachel to y'all's room and stay right there 'til things simmer down. Give them some time to sleep off their drunk. Then, tell Rachel I said for her to make them a big meal. I want them full and sluggish. I don't want them nosing around the grounds any more than they already have. They'll probably be gone soon enough, but I'm going to warn my girls to go to the root cellar just the same. Now, Henry, the root cellar is much too far for Laura Lee's twins to run, so I'm going to send Willow with the twins to the briar cave."

Henry's long face grew longer. "Yes'm."

Lillian tried to appear calm. "Now, don't worry, Henry! Tell Rachel I said, 'if those men should discover Willow here in the house—her not being truly white—they might mistreat her'. Better to keep her safely out of sight. She'll protect the twins! Now, let's hurry!"

Jonathan's Return

Shaking with chills and fever and dragging his swollen, blood encrusted right leg, discharged Confederate soldier Jonathan Baker made his way cautiously through Atlanta's congested streets. He had entered Atlanta from the Southwest quarter and was working his way through to the Northeast and, ultimately, home. Some distance out from the city he had been aware when the thunder of Sherman's cannons had finally ceased, but reverberating explosions still rocked the city. Victorious Union troops were burning rampantly and fast spreading fires continued to destroy building after crumbling building, sending flames leaping skyward.

Jonathan had found this appalling defeat easier to bear when he saw where withdrawing Confederate soldiers had destroyed munitions storage sites as well as municipal facilities which might have benefited Union troops. But, here, in the railroading capitol of the South, while taking control, Sherman's Army had ripped up large sections of railroad tracks, crippling lifelines into and out of the city.

He felt compassion for the injured and dying who lay, head to toe, along the tracks in the rail yard downtown, their cries of pain and despair echoing and re-echoing against the dirty sky. Doctors, insufficient in numbers, worked unceasingly in the makeshift open air hospital against mounting odds, moving past the dead and dying to minister to those who appeared likely to survive. Jonathan considered stopping to ask for treatment but having survived this long, rather than wait his turn after the more seriously injured were doctored, he determined to try to complete his mission to reach *Briars* first, then home, if possible. Dodging wild-eyed horses under the whips of frenzied wagon drivers, he joined other citizens in edging along fire-gutted buildings as they sought safe passage from the maelstrom.

Finally, unable to walk further, Jonathan crawled into the comparable safety of a small niche formed by a toppled brick wall of the Thomas Warren building. Fire had eaten away its very heart and the empty shell had fallen in on itself. Hot bricks burned his hands as he tossed them aside, widening his refuge. Exhausted, watery-eyed and coughing, he sat down and leaned against a charred timber, gulping in tainted air, his fevered mind racing wildly.

Four years ago he'd helped erect the building lying in shambles around him now. He would have sworn, back then, that it would have stood for decades past his expected life span—and he'd turned twenty-five only nine months ago on the fifteenth of February—but war had not been taken into account. War changed everything.

Pain forced his attention to the throbbing blue-black thigh exposed below the tattered cut-off pants leg of his gray Confederate uniform. The wound was oozing again and hurting more than ever. It would have been easier to bear if it had been a war wound, but he had gotten it three days earlier when an Alabama farmer somewhere near the Georgia line had objected to the freeing of one of his layers from his chicken yard. Jonathan had dug out the shot when it was safe to stop running, and washed the wound in a stream. He had sought aid as he traveled homeward, but it seemed every doctor had been dispatched to help behind battle lines, and there had been no medicine readily available for a stranger in the back roads of the farmlands that he traveled. People had to look out for their own. He understood.

Walking, he had left from Fort Morgan, Alabama, on the morning of August sixth. Farrogut had entered the bay about six o'clock the morning of the day before with four armored warships and fourteen wooden vessels, and Fort Morgan had fired on the advancing ships. The Yankee's *Tecumseh* was sunk but the other vessels chased after the Confederate warship *Tennessee,* and she surrendered by ten o'clock. The fort was conquered, but the official surrender hadn't yet been made when his ragged little troop was discharged.

There at Mobile Bay, Jonny Baker and Drew Heirs, best friends and next door neighbors since they were born five days apart, had made a pact. They had sworn that if either of them didn't survive the battle, the other would take word back to their families as to how, and how well he had died. If they both died, then so be it.

He had given his word, and he was bringing the hateful news to Drew Heirs' family at *Briars* that though he was sure Drew would have fought bravely in the battle given the chance, he had been blown to smithereens by the first volley from Farrogut's own guns. Not that he had actually seen Drew blown up. But he'd had it on good authority that nobody at Drew's site had survived the fusillade and he'd never reported back. If Drew'd been alive, Jonathan would have found him because after the battle he volunteered for bringing in the wounded, but Drew Heirs wasn't among them.

Now the way Jonathan figured, counting today he'd been on the road traveling Northeast three months and nine days and he still had a ways to go before he'd see either *Greenleaf* or *Briars*. He had been on foot most of the way, but he'd gotten a few rides, hitching on rough carts and trade wagons from travelers moving in his direction. Once, in a stolen racing surrey as far as the Chattahoochee river, where the heartless driver had dumped the expensive vehicle and rode the horse on, leaving him walking again.

This morning, he'd hoped to reach *Briars* by sundown, but now it had to be nearing three o'clock, and he didn't see how he was going to get there at all, let alone by sundown. The fiery lesion was hurting him a lot and it had a sickening sweet smell rising from it and he felt pretty sure rot was setting in. He knew that if he didn't find medical attention soon, he would surely die.

Jonathan thought if he had ever believed there really was a God, he'd have asked Him for help right now, but that was one of Hamita Baker's teachings that had slipped off him like water from a duck's back when he was growing up at *Greenleaf*, and he'd never had time enough since to contemplate such weighty, conscience baring thoughts. He laid his head back against the warm wood and let his troubled mind rest on Sarah Heirs. Lying amid the ashes and rubble of the burned out building, Jonathan realized that on this fifteenth day of November in 1864, Sarah would be thirteen days into her twentieth year, and her sister Morgana would be seventeen.

Unlike these poor frenzied souls in Atlanta's dangerous streets, if Sarah and her family had not earlier fled to sanctuary along with his own parents, she would still be back at *Briars* and, no doubt, overcome by paralyzing fear. Gentle, beautiful, golden haired Sarah. Skin, pale as fine china and eyes, bluer than summer skies. But even after four long years, just the thought of her re-opened the old ragged wound, his puzzlement and disappointment at her sudden and unexplained rejection of his proposal of an earlier marriage than they had originally planned. It was Sarah's decision, alone, to send Jonathan away to war—still unwed.

Stunned, ashen and shaken, he'd asked her then, "Why, Sarah? Tell me—why?"

She had kissed his icy fingers and held them against her soft, warm cheek, and said, with tearful honesty, her short and obviously well practiced piece: "I'm so sorry, Jonny, truly I am. But I simply can't marry you, now. Not just now. You know we'd planned our wedding for next year and I've still to finish my wedding dress. Why, it's—it's not even half done."

"That's no reason, Sarah. I'd marry you in sackcloth. You should know that!" Jonathan said, his voice even, controlled.

But she released his hand and grasping her skirts, turned quickly away from his pleading, searching gaze.

Angry and confused, hurt and demanding, he'd reached for her trim waist and quickly spun her around, feeling the fervor of his emotions rising, barely in check. He held her fast and prompted hoarsely, "Tell me the truth, now, Sarah? You owe me that!"

Drawing away from him, Sarah shook her head and frowned. "Don't be so rough, Jonny. You know I don't like that!" She smoothed her skirts and added resolutely, "When you return, s*afely*, then, we'll marry. Please, try to understand. I do love you, Jonny, honestly I do but I just can't marry you—n*ow!*"

Jonathan would not soon forget the withering smile on his own mother's face nor the disappointment in Lillian Heirs' green eyes when he had reluctantly joined Sarah in announcing to their families that there would be no wedding until his return.

In a daze of confusion and humiliation, he'd inquired of Drew, and then Drew's wife, Laura Lee, Sarah's sensible sister-in-law, if they knew what could possibly have caused her sudden rebuff of him. However, they had expressed their own disbelief and shock at Sarah's behavior and had no more knowledge of her thinking than he had. But he never approached Sarah's mother with his query. If Sarah had spoken to her mother of this decision, he would not embarrass both himself and Lillian by compelling her to deny him in order to protect her daughter's confidence.

Sarah's younger sister, Morgana, who had been watching Jonathan's every move from a distance, dashed across the porch, and in a burst of youthful unladylike passion, startled him by throwing her arms around his neck and kissing his cheek, as she exclaimed, "My *own* sister! How could she be so cruel? *I'd* never disappoint you like that, Jonny. *Never!*" But Morgana was only fourteen, and Jonathan had already knowingly abided Morgana's childish infatuation for several years.

Shamefaced, and with trembling lips, Sarah had kissed him tenderly and stood watching from the top of the verandah's tall steps as Jonathan and Drew hurried down the driveway. Looking back over his shoulder, that was one puzzling picture Jonathan would ever hold in his memory: Sarah weeping bitter tears, waving her handkerchief, and calling after him, "Jonny, I'll wait for you—I swear I will!"

At the end of the driveway, each man paused, shaking hands with twelve year old Wil Heirs, who busied himself by swinging back and forth on one of the open iron gates. Wordlessly and admirably, young Wil had contained his urge to cry as his brother shook his hand and tousled his hair, reminding him to behave himself. As they fell in step with the troop, Jonathan looked back to see Wil close the gates, knowing the boy would watch through the iron bars until they were out of sight.

Over the first wartime year, bedding down with his unit in open fields and abandoned barns, grabbing what little sleep he could, Jonathan often awakened from unsettling dreams of Sarah. Once after a bloody, violent day on the battlefield, wondering at his own good fortune, he'd cried out to the black night sky, "See, Sarah, I'm still alive!" As time and war wore on, realizing the danger of such preoccupation, he'd made a conscious effort to abolish such thoughts until the war was ended.

Throbbing, grinding pain in his thigh shocked him back to the present. He still desperately needed medical attention and release from the savage delirium that ruthlessly pursued him. Yet without means of travel and burning up with fever there was nothing more he could do this day to hasten his journey. He had no choice but to wait out the turmoil in the frenzied city. This decided, he breathed deeply and closed his eyes inviting sleep, hopefully to drive away those relentless apparitions of 1861.

The Briar Cave

Watching the first pink glow of morning light creep beneath the window shade in their bedroom opposite Mother Heirs', Confederate soldier Drew Heirs' young wife, Laura Lee breathed a sigh of pure relief. She had lain across her bed all night, wide awake and fully clothed, listening to the sounds of the house, anxious in this whirlpool of disruption for her children's safety though she knew they were with Willow in the nursery at the opposite end of the long hall. Eager for their company, yet another worry wrinkled her brow. Drew should be on his way home to attend his father's funeral by now but, God willing, he mustn't arrive until after the enemy now defiling *Briars* with their raucous presence had departed.

Laura Lee had listened to Henry's reassuring slowly paced gait outside her door at every passing hour, which gave her encouragement that all was well with the family. But a short time ago, a little before daybreak, she had heard a racket begin in

Ann Gray

the library downstairs. She was sure Mother Heirs would have awakened to it, too, if she had slept at all.

But then, all at once, Laura Lee heard Mother Heirs' plaintive whisper as she rapped sharply on the door. "Laura Lee, let me in!"

Laura Lee rushed to crank the key in the lock, allowing Lillian to slip inside. Then just as quickly, she turned the key again.

Mother Heirs hurried to Laura Lee's front facing window. "Come here, and watch with me. Hurry!"

Tall, thin, and stately, Laura Lee rushed to join Lillian, her long, honey colored hair spreading like a silken shawl over her broad shoulders. "What is it?"

"Look! There, along the hedges—see them?"

"Oh, my God! It's Willow with the twins!" Laura Lee's ordinarily mellow brown eyes hardened into bullets of disbelief aimed at Lillian's decisively set expression.

"I've sent them to the briar cave. I wanted you to know they were there—"

"No! You had no right!" Laura Lee's resentment flared as she faced her mother-in-law defiantly. "How dare you send them out without first consulting me! They belong with me!"

Mother Heirs clasped Laura Lee's trembling, clammy hands. "I'm sorry, my dear. But you must realize they'll be safer there than anywhere else if this situation gets out of control with the Yankees. I didn't want them to hear—" She squeezed the younger woman's hands tightly. "The Yankees have broken into Father Heirs' liquor closet. Quickly, now, while they're occupied with their drinking—hurry, go straight to the root cellar. That's the one place, thank the Lord, they haven't found. Go by the back stairs and pantry—and hurry."

"But, Mother Heirs, you shouldn't have—I *need* to be with my children!" Laura Lee insisted, pulling away to return to the window.

"You must know they could never make it as far as the root cellar," Lillian contended, still. "None of us could carry them that far but you must go there—and now! It's the only safe place! Wilson's there with Father Heirs. Hurry—go now! I've got to warn the others. But, Laura Lee, if you don't make it, that is, if they should catch you—God forbid—regardless of what happens—Laura Lee, you know Drew will always love you." She kissed Laura Lee on her flushed cheek. "Keep your strength up, dearest, your children will still need a mother when this nightmare is all over."

Laura Lee wasn't altogether sure exactly what Mother Heirs expected of her, but as she slipped from her room and ran down the hall to the back stairs she knew that, as usual, Mother Heirs was right about one thing—for her to come through this day mentally whole if the enemy did catch her, it would be her children's need for her that would sustain her.

Sarah

In the early morning duskiness, Sarah had opened her door to her mother only after Lillian had shoved her wedding band under the door and sworn as God was her witness that she was alone. Scared as a rabbit seeking its burrow Sarah had rushed into her mother's arms.

"Oh, Mama, I'm so afraid. How many are there? What if they— what's to happen to us? Will they kill us? Oh, Mama, I don't want to die!"

"Sh, quiet, sweet, nothing bad's happened to you so far, has it?" Lillian stroked Sarah's soft, pale hair. "The lieutenant is looking out for you—for all of us! But they've gotten into your papa's liquor, and that's distressing. Right now, I want you to go—"

"Oh, no, Mama!" Sarah's face grew ashen and she started to shake violently.

Ann Gray

"Listen to me, Sarah," Lillian grasped her shoulders and looked squarely into Sarah's frightened eyes. "Make sure the way is clear down the back stairs, go through the pantry and hedges straight to the root cellar. Wilson's there with your father. I've sent Laura Lee on ahead. Morgana and I will follow you. I think if you girls can all get out of here before they're full of spirits—if you can get away from the house—you'll be safe."

Sarah stopped sobbing and sat, quaking, on her bed holding onto her mother's hand. "I'm sorry, Mama, I guess I'm just not strong like Heirs women are supposed to be." Sarah shook from head to toe and her eyes were like blue crystal saucers. Even in this state, Lillian secretly held Sarah, barely twenty, fair and petite, always modest in dress and conduct and certainly of a milder nature than Morgana, to be the more likable of her girls. That was why everyone had called her, "Sweet Sarah" since she was only two and toddling about before Morgana ever drew her first mischievous breath.

"Think of Jonathan," Lillian soothed, "who loves you, and who's coming back to marry you one day soon. Why, you'll go on to have daughters of your own, you'll see. But, Sarah, darling, you must stay calm, and if the Yankee devils *should* catch you when you're on your way—be brave. Where's your faith?" Lillian asked. "You've always put your faith in God, now, haven't you? Whatever happens, if your faith is strong enough, everything will be all right, I promise you." Lillian smoothed Sarah's silken hair. "Now, do as I've said, Sarah."

"Oh, I'll try, Mama, I'll try!" Sarah smiled gallantly at her mother.

Lillian embraced her and kissed Sarah's trembling lips and, after checking the hallway, moved quickly to Morgana's room behind Sarah's, and Sarah could hear their voices through the wall.

Morgana

"Morgana, open the door, it's Mama!" Lillian whispered, tapping lightly.

"Mama? Are you alone?" Morgana asked, imagining her mother with a gun to her head. After all, what if someone did have a gun to her mother's head? She had no way of knowing what means the enemy might employ to gain entry into the bedrooms of the Heirs women.

"Of course, I'm alone. Would I escort the damn Yankees right into your bedroom?" Lillian whispered, hoarse with impatience after dealing with Sarah's reticence.

"No, Mama, you wouldn't," Morgana said, opening the door a crack and peering out before swinging it wider, "—at least, not willingly, I should hope."

Lillian stepped inside and holding her younger daughter at arm's length, looked seriously into Morgana's flawless dark beauty. "Listen to me, now! They've broken into your father's liquor closet. I've sent Willow with the twins to the briar cave. You must go straight to the root cellar. Wil's there with your father. Laura Lee and Sarah have gone on ahead of you. That's the one place—thanks be to God—the Yankees haven't found yet! Go by the back stairs and pantry through the hedge tunnel. Be quick, now!"

"But, Mama, what's going on down—?" Morgana began asking for details.

"There's no time for talking now!" her mother admonished. "I want you safely out of this house as soon as possible! Go straight to the root cellar—now!"

The late Morgan Heirs' glinting black eyes, framed by a waterfall of bobbing jet ringlets, spat silently back at her, but Lillian cupped Morgana's dimpled chin in her hand and kissed her pink lips.

"Morgana, Morgana! You are your father's child, though I fear you'll be the death of me, yet!" She sighed, pleading, "If you've ever once obeyed me in your seventeen years, Morgana, let it be now!"

"Oh, Mama, you do exaggerate so!" Morgana's eyes flashed with excitement and anticipated disobedience.

Moments later, from the junction of the upstairs halls, she paused long enough to blow a kiss back to her mother, who stood watching from the doorway to her own bedroom. The girl padded softly down the quiet back corridor past the empty nursery and descended the servants' stairs, stopping at the foot to listen. Rachel's and Henry's muffled voices were coming from their room on the right of the stairs. She edged along the back downstairs hallway, peering into the vacant kitchen before venturing down the center hall that divided the large house, east and west, with kitchen, dining room, and Mama's parlor on the front west and Papa's library on the front east, backed by three small guest bedrooms. Morgana paused halfway down the wide center hall and listened again. She heard nothing.

Lillian's flight

Lillian knew she had to give Morgana time enough to reach the vacant lot before she went charging out. Pacing back and forth from the front window to the door, she thought how chancy it was for one person passing the distance from the house to the side yard's tall hedges without being seen from the house, the stables, or the barn, but this morning there'd have been a veritable parade stealing across the space. Once beyond the hedges, the weedy path to the root cellar was fairly safe from view except from the barren garden where—now in mid-November only dried corn stalks stood, skeletal guardians. The pasture beyond the garden and the copse of sycamores along the back path to neighboring *Greenleaf* were bare-boned for fall as well, and would offer no cover for anyone traveling along that route.

Briars
The House of Heirs

Lillian stopped pacing long enough to gaze out her front window. Still falling softly as snowflakes, delicate white ash from the flaming city had collected silently overnight atop the dense hawthorn hedges that lined the iron-barred fence fronting the Heirs estate. In the increasing light, she was aware of multiplying columns of black smoke rising against Atlanta's fiery skyline, but she concentrated more intently on the shadowy entrance to the hawthorn hedge's secret cranny and the newly posted enemy sentries, easily visible from her second story front window. The guards, contentedly chewing their cud and spitting brown tobacco juice all over the once white gravel entry to the driveway, leaned against the east pillar supporting the heavy double gates where a brass nameplate engraved *Briars, 1838* had been embedded.

What a fool she had been to send Willow with the children to the briar cave! It was simply the first hiding place that came to mind! Now she watched with fearful apprehension as the soldiers began pacing back and forth across the driveway's access, holding her breath each time they paused. So close. Too close to Willow and the twins. But she hadn't thought! Hadn't guessed there'd be guards posted at the entrance!

With her accustomed eye, she detected a slight movement in the hedge row. The occupants of the hidden nest had to be growing weary of their confinement and silent vigil, and Willow would be despairing of ever being bidden to leave. If only the girl could find the fortitude to disobey! Just once! If only she would watch for an opportunity while the soldiers were turned the other way to make a break for the root cellar. How Lillian wished she had chanced sending them there away from the vicinity of the house, entirely. It would have been better if all the family were as far away from the house as possible until the undisciplined drinking ended and the men settled down for a binge-ending nap and repast of Rachel's invention before taking to the road again.

The children had discovered the hedgehog lair in the hawthorn hedge when they were only toddlers. Wil's old shepherd bitch, Daisy, had evicted the spiny inhabitants and dug the cavity even deeper for her own comfort. Then one day the curious twins followed the big dog into it and, until she died, she'd shared her shady retreat with them. Nowadays, Daisy's offspring, Storm—Wilson called him Storm because he was whelped during a bad one—sometimes shared the space with the children when he wasn't down at the stables courting one of the groom's fox hounds. While the briar cave was not easily detectable to the unaccustomed eye, Lillian reassured herself one last time that the three occupants were secure before checking the Seth Thomas clock on her mantelpiece.

Morgana had been gone a good four minutes when Lillian tossed a shawl around her shoulders and hurried from her room, attuning her hearing to listen for any vague sound that might imply that one of her own had fallen into enemy hands. Hearing no sound at all, she crept down the back stairs, using care to avoid the squeaking treads she knew so well. She passed Rachel's and Henry's room and moved into the unoccupied kitchen listening at the open pantry's outside door before dashing out, through the hedges, and along the weed-choked path to sanctuary. Lack of sleep, worry, and anxiety were taking their toll on her. Her burning eyes and aching body cried out for rest, but she would relax better in the bosom of her family when she, too, reached the root cellar. Thank God, the girls had done her bidding and were safely away. Laura Lee, Sarah, Morgana, and Wil would be waiting for her with her dear, dead Morgan. Oh, how he would have loved being engaged in this game of conniving!

Willow

Twenty feet west of the iron gates, concealed beneath sheltering boughs of *Briars'* dense hawthorn hedges in a small, prickly hollow, the twins huddled against their young Mulatto nursemaid. Dried tears had left tracks down their cold-kissed rosy cheeks and their anxious faces were upturned to Willow's as she cooed soothing words. When Miz Lillian sent them out there she couldn't have known there'd be guards posted at the entry gates within the hour. Now, Willow's legs were numb from being tucked tightly beneath her in the small enclosure, the children's playtime hideaway and her arms tingled, from being so tightly wrapped around her charges. Still, she dared not release the children for fear one of them might make a sudden move or a loud outcry and attract the attention of either of the two uniformed men staggering back and forth beyond the barred entrance.

Though warmly dressed against the cold, they had not eaten since last night. Hunger and thirst gnawed away at Willow's own insides and she feared the rumblings of all their empty stomachs must soon give them away. Nature's unanswered urges had left them, all three, soiled and ashamed.

How things changed! Yesterday had started out a pretty average, crisp and clear November day for everybody until about three in the afternoon. While the children napped upstairs in the nursery, Willow's other duties had her downstairs in the dining room, polishing Miz Lillian's good silver, just like there wasn't even a war on. That was when she'd heard the sound of many horses' hooves on the gravel drive and, fearful of what wartime horror these new arrivals to *Briars* might bring, she'd hurried out the dining room side door onto the west verandah. Tiptoeing to the front corner and peeking round, Willow had watched, panic-stricken, while a young Union officer led his detachment of nine horse soldiers right up to the hitching post at the verandah steps and dismounted, climbing the steps to the porch. Her heart pounding with fear and apprehension, she had run quickly to take word back to the kitchen that the damn Yankees were here—right here, knocking at *Briars'* front door!

Even with the Yankees taking over the lower floor, everything had seemed quiet enough last night when Willow had put the children down and crawled into her own snug bed in the alcove of the nursery. Naturally, she knew she would never sleep a wink with the enemy actually inside *Briars* but at dawn Miz Lillian had come racing into the nursery in a "tizzy".

"Willow," Miz Lillian spoke sharply, "wake up! They're in the library and they've found Mister Morgan's liquor closet! They'll all be falling down drunk within the hour and all hell's going to break loose." She shook Willow until her head bobbed back and forth. "Do you hear me, girl? Look alive!"

"Yes'm, I'm awake," Willow replied, grasping the meaning of Miz Lillian's words through a sleep fogged daze.

"Quickly, now, dress." Miz Lillian nodded towards the canopied beds where the children slept. "The children, too! I don't want them in this house a minute longer than necessary. The Yankees are all together in the library! Take the children out by the pantry door. Run along the hedges to the briar cave." She frowned, worry creasing her brow. "Their short little legs would never make it to the root cellar and I don't know where else to send you. Don't make a sound, you hear? And don't budge from there 'til I call you out, either— no matter what you see or hear—you understand?"

Willow was afraid she did.

It had been a little over an hour since the changing of the guards and now, a tense silence rested over the majestic old house, as the new team at the gates relaxed, chewing their tobacco, laughing, and talking quietly. Earlier, from within the gray stone walls of the manor house, she had heard a discordant symphony of ribald laughter mingled with cries of fury and fright that floated down the long driveway, prompting the first shift of Union Army guards then leaning against the closed gates to chuckle and wink knowingly at one another. Now in full daylight, Willow judged by the position of the sun it must be nearing nine o'clock.

Here in the protection of the thorny grotto shielded and unobserved, looking down at her precious charges Willow felt absolutely no guilt in having left the others to deal with the Yankees because she'd had no say in leaving. She had, though, grasped completely the fact that it was for the children's sake that she, too, had been spared from witnessing and possibly falling victim to the wrathful passions of the unruly men from the North. Willow knew Miz Lillian couldn't have guessed they'd post soldiers at the gates when she sent them out. Still, time had crept by and it seemed to Willow they had been in the burrow for days, though she knew it couldn't have been longer than three or four hours. She just thanked God for Miz Lillian's concern for her grandchildren. The heart wrenching cries the children and she had heard from the house had only served to re-enforce her fear and loathing of the 'Yankee devils' and to make her blood run cold.

"Willow, oh, Willow, was that my mama I heard?" the wan, carrot-topped boy whispered so as not to be overheard as he moved one briar-scratched hand from a small ear. "I just can't stand to hear yelling like that, Willow!" His wide blue eyes, deep-set and circled, searched her face.

"'Course it wasn't Mama!" his sister hissed back softly, snatching angrily at the hand still covering the ear nearest her, and shaking her curly red head. "Mama would never let any old 'damn Yankee' make her yell like that. You ought to know better!"

"Sh, Alice! No, Andy, it wasn't your mama! Now, y'all be quiet!" Willow could recognize the voices of all the Heirs women, and she knew painfully well what had been going on inside *Briars*. Since before good daylight, the ash-laden, prickly hedges under which they huddled had surrounded sinfulness and corruption as had never been imagined by such gentlefolk as the family, Heirs.

She'd had one terribly troublesome turn around breakfast time when she'd seen her own papa walking towards the guards at the gates, balancing that heavy round tray on one broad hand above his shoulder just like he was serving the ladies tea on the verandah. She had clasped her hands over both children's mouths, fearful they might call out to him. Then she had caught the sidelong glance, the slight nod of his head when he had seen them there, safe and secure. He had ambled back to the house in the same manner he had come, as if he had all day.

While Thomas, the groom, and Grady, the gardener, shared quarters in the stables, Willow, herself, took a great deal of satisfaction in being an integral part of the Heirs family household along with her parents. Rachel and Henry had spent the better part of their lives looking after the Heirs family. They knew, too, that when they died they'd be buried right out there in the back pasture in a corner of the Heirs' cemetery with the rest of the family.

Yes, and Willow, above all, as nursemaid to Miz Lillian's grandchildren and as household maid when called upon for other chores, took her responsibilities most seriously, too.

But who would ever dream the things that happen?

Alice was right about one thing. It hadn't been their mother's voice the children had heard. Miz Laura Lee, being a married woman, would have knowledge of such matters. Miz Laura Lee would hold out.

But it was when the children's Aunt Sarah, four years promised to Jonathan Baker, had screamed, "No more! Please, God, please take me, now!" that Willow had silently wept. It was Sarah's outcry that had upset the boy. Willow knew from experience how brutal drunken men could be. They might not have killed Sarah but they had made her pray for death.

Actually, Willow felt more compassion for the fragile Sarah than for Morgana. Though the Heirs daughters were not prepared to deal with the filth and vulgarities that this sad day would have forced on them, Willow knew Morgana would survive. It hadn't been that long ago—

'Gana had been horrified when she'd discovered Willow at the stream that ran between their property and the Johnson's place. Weeping silently, Willow had been attempting to wash away the blood, and heat, and sticky leavings right after the drunken, no-good older Johnson brothers, Milton and Curtis, had brought the youngest, Daniel, to lie in wait for her on the back path between *Briars* and Bakers' *Greenleaf*. They had dragged her off into their cane field where the older two had each shown young Danny how to 'do her'. Then it was Daniel's turn to 'do her' while they stood and watched. Scared and ashamed, she'd begged 'Gana not to tell her Papa, lest he'd go after those boys with his shotgun, and she didn't want to be the one to start a big stink with the Johnsons. In the bargaining, Morgana had demanded to know exactly what had happened in every gruesome detail. Well, Willow thought, if I've been able to get on with my life, 'Gana will just have to do the same.

She squeezed the twins closer to her bosom and hummed *"Amazing Grace"* over and over until she could see their long-lashed lids twitching in sleep. It was past time for their morning naps, and their small bodies and minds were beyond weariness.

Lillian's Fear

In answer to Lillian's four sharp knocks as agreed upon, and her dear voice, whispering, "Wil, open up! It's me!" the heavy door groaned open and a stream of cold, damp air escaped and wrapped itself around her. There was no odor of death from the cave, just the clean fresh smell of stored apples.

"Ma, I sure am glad you're here!" Wil's slender face, eyes circled from worry, looked for the first time ever that Lillian had seen it, exactly like his father's.

Ann Gray

Breathing hard from her trek, Lillian attempted a smile, kissed Wil's lips, and moved past him searching the silent shadows expectantly.

Her horrified expression jarred Wil's relief at her arrival. "What's wrong, Ma?"

"The girls? They're not here?" She paled and felt strength flow from her legs as they gave way under her. "Oh, God, Son, what's happened?"

Wil reached to catch his mother. "Come on, Ma, sit down, you're white as Pa."

Lillian allowed him to lead her to a flour barrel where she sank down, gesturing towards the door. "I sent them on down here..." She ran her fingers through her unpinned hair—no time today for morning rituals— "...a while back." She got up and paced the straw-littered clay floor—three steps away, three steps back. "What could have happened to them—all? I didn't hear a sound nor see a soul on my way."

"They just never got here, Ma," Wilson patted her shoulder awkwardly. Then he moved into the shadows at the rear of the cave and brought out his rifle. Stepping past her towards the door, Wil said, "You stay here, Ma, I'm going back up to the house and see if I can find—"

But Lillian wrapped her arms around his narrow waist, pulling him back. "Oh, no! God, no! I'll not give you to them, too!" Her red-rimmed eyes finally overflowed, and she stood, reaching up—for he had grown a full head taller than she was—to pat his peach-fuzz cheek. "We don't want to do something rash now we're scared and not sure what's going on. We don't want to get somebody killed." Then she looked past him towards the bier. "Wil, I need to talk to him—alone, I think."

Wil laid the rifle aside. "Yes'm, I'll just go stretch my legs. Maybe I'll see old Storm around."

"You'll not go further than the hedges!" Lillian said, half-telling, half-asking.

"Yes'm." He slid a sympathizing kiss across her damp cheek, lumbered out and closed the heavy oaken door behind him.

The Conversation

Lillian moved to the crude and hastily devised bier and in the pale, spiraling candlelight looked down on her husband. Her silent, dead Morgan, lying there so still. Though she'd never expected they'd live forever, she'd counted on him for a few more good years. How unlike him to be so neglectful of his duties; dying and leaving her alone at a time like this. But judging from what Jeremiah Baker had said when they'd brought Morgan home from the tavern, he'd died just like he'd always lived, dauntless to the end, and with fiery passion.

She reached out to stroke Morgan Heirs' alabaster cheek, so cold to her touch. "Old man, who's going to tell me what to do, now? If only I hadn't sent them out! If they'd stayed in their rooms they might have been all right, after all. Now, because of me, it looks like the enemy's gotten hold of our daughters, and they may kill us all before they're gone. Oh, Morrey, now when I need you most—your keen mind, your good judgment, your eagle's eye for details—you've left me to think through this whole muddled scheme, all alone." She rolled the flour barrel up close beside the bier and sat back down on it. "What would you do? Oh, Morrey, what shall I do?"

Wil had done a good job of preparing his father for her visit. Morgan was always at his handsomest in this favorite blue dress coat. And in the flickering candles' light, she could almost see him smiling. She would not have been surprised to see him turn to wink at her any minute now, and say he was only fooling. Dead though he was, she found a kind of soothing comfort in his closeness, and she laid her cheek upon the soft silken sleeve and breathed in the well-remembered smell of him that lingered in the garment. Physically and emotionally exhausted, she closed her eyes just for a tender moment...

CHAPTER TWO ~ MORGAN

11:30 p.m., Saturday, July 7, 1838 ~ Terminus, Georgia

The Land

Morgan Heirs braced his foot on the bar rail in the sweat-reeking *Spike and Rail* tavern and grimaced in absolute agony. He curled his fingers through the handle of a pewter mug spilling foam on the counter before him and, lifting it for all to see, forced a wry grin. "And now, gentlemen, here's yet another!" In one long draught, he drained the cup and slammed it to the counter, wiping his mouth on the back of his hand.

Aside to his best friends, he snapped, "Either of you damn barflies keeping count?"

In answer, Tom Garrett doubled over in a spasm of cackles holding his sides, but Jeremiah Baker grabbed Morgan's finished tankard and, making a show of it for onlookers, shook it upside down to make sure it was completely drained. Then grinning ear to ear and staggering in the doing, he let out a "Wahoo!" and sent the lot of emptied mugs in quick succession skating down the sodden counter to the barkeeper at the other end.

Catching each one in turn, the tapster wiped it's rim with a damp bar rag and hung it with a rhythmic clink on an overhead hook while spectators counted, "Five!—Six!—Seven!"

Jeremiah's hazel eyes sparkled, his contagious laugh assurance of good will. "That's only seven! You've two and a half to go! Nine and a half was the bet—one tankard, each ten acres—with half a mug for the seven! That half less, my floating friend, is a gift from me!" Reeling with laughter, he slapped the bar and shifted his gaze to Morgan's awkward stance focusing on his best friend's obvious discomfort. "You'll never make it! You'll be wetting us all down soon enough, but mind you, piss yourself more room and you've lost the bet!" Then pointing to the pained expression on Morgan's face, he doubled over in a spasm of laughter. "God, Morrey, give it up!"

Morgan Andrew Heirs had accepted Jeremiah's wager silently gloating. He knew for a positive fact that his horse, Ambler, one of the finest sorrel Tennessee Walkers this side of Chattanooga, could out-rack the other two men's five-gaited horses any day in any weather. His mixed breed bird dog, Freckles, could out-sniff their pure-bred hunting dogs in any field. Why, four times before, based on his superior judgment of fine animals he'd bested these same two favorite companions in similar competitions. The horse and the dog were Morgan's stake in the wager under way at this precise moment and he figured he'd never made a safer bet. Standing shoulder to shoulder drinking with his two best friends all afternoon, it was his turn to protect his established winner's status by performing well himself. But judging from the expressions on the faces of these previous losers, his friends were determined this time to even the odds. All that would be required of him to prevail was untried endurance, an unyielding resolve, and a bladder that would stretch to the size of a bull elephant's. Yep, Morgan Heirs determined he'd win this bet or burst—wetting down the whole of Terminus—trying.

Although Morgan gambled and drank too much every Saturday after work, swapping witty stories and lies, he was usually quite dependable the rest of the week. Especially when it came to his responsibilities, which he'd succeeded so far in limiting to a manageable few. First and most cherished was his pretty young bride, Lillian, who required nothing of him save loving, a roof over their heads, and food for their bellies. Second was his job with the Western and Atlantic Railroad in this isolated little village called Terminus. It barely paid a living wage but it was insurance against having to return to Richmond and more confrontations with Glenn Arthur Heirs, his estranged father. Then there was Ambler, purchased with his first week's pay after arriving in Terminus. Last and least was Freckles, a speckled brown and white mixed breed bird dog that had followed him from work at the railhead one evening months ago and now, fattened and loyal, shared quarters with Ambler in the shabby village stables behind the boarding house where Morgan and Lillian lived.

Taller and thinner than the other two men, Morgan's restless black eyes, above a day's shadowy growth of heavy beard, glowed with the intensity of a man in the throes of physical torture. Frowning, he ran his fingers through the mane of jet locks that swept his forehead and concentrated on the task remaining as the good-natured bartender set three more frothy mugs of warm ale before him.

Jeremiah

Sporting a neatly groomed narrow mustache, Jeremiah Baker was almost as tall, almost as dark, almost as good looking and twice as smart as Morgan—by Morgan's own measure—when sober. But at the moment, Morgan recognized that in his present condition Jeremiah had lost every ounce of judgment he'd ever possessed. Twenty minutes before he'd as much as offered to make Morgan a gift of the most desirable piece of property in the North Georgia wilds—ninety-seven wooded acres atop the rise overlooking Terminus.

True, Jeremiah had just won that land off Tom Garrett not thirty minutes before, but Jeremiah craved the applause of the tavern's patrons to a daring wager as much as the next man. Maybe, even more!

Tom Garrett, pug-nosed and blond, heavyset and muscular, whose only genuine interest lay in the study of law rather then railroading, was tipsier than either of the other two. Being the younger of the trio by two years and still unmarried, he'd received the land along with signed papers less than forty-five minutes before in exchange for a small cash loan from one Ezra

Clark, a skinny, pallid fellow about his own age, a regular *Spike and Rail* corner hugger.

Recently arrived from Pulaski, Tennessee with Althea, his fourteen year old wife, Clark professed to have come by the property from an uncle who had fled the Georgia wilderness to return to Tennessee. Tom had been skeptical of Clark's story of ownership until the man produced the signed deed naming himself as the land's legal owner. Truthfully, Tom had absolutely no use for the land, so signed paper in hand, he bet Jeremiah that he couldn't keep his nervous fingers off his mustache for ten minutes. Jeremiah resisted wiping foam from his upper lip for eleven full minutes and Tom passed along Clark's land to him. Clark's desperate plea for ready cash was the unfortunate basis for the high-spirited on-going contest now between Jeremiah Baker and Morgan Heirs. It was obvious, too, that merriment of dozens of patrons at his expense was thoroughly irritating to Clark.

Knowing well the tract of land in question, Morgan believed he would have been a fool not to have taken Jeremiah's playful wager. No matter that the three of them had been holed up in the dark and disreputable tavern since quitting time six hours earlier. No matter that they had not eaten since noontime. No matter that it was nearing midnight on another hot and muggy July Saturday night. Nor that two very pregnant and probably very angry wives awaited Morgan and Jeremiah back at the boarding house, knowing full well their whereabouts. At the moment Morgan honestly couldn't have cared less! There was much more at stake here for Morgan Heirs than retaining the ownership of the two fine animals he had wagered. What mattered—the only thing that really mattered—was that valuable land was being offered as a stake in a foolish bet and he was determined to win it. Once he'd finished this painful pursuit and the land was his, Morgan would build a proper home on it for his Lilly. The aching knot in his belly cried out for relief, but if

Morgan could ignore the agony, suffer it five minutes more —two tankards and a half of ale—he'd be a landowner!

The public house echoed with raucous laughter and garrulous voices of encouragement until Morgan slammed the very last of the ten empty tankards to the counter. He bowed to the howling bystanders, all known to him, then turned his attention to his favorite drinking buddy.

"Now, sign the damn paper!" Morgan ordered Jeremiah Baker, pounding the countertop and scowling. "Sign it, quick!"

Minutes later, having tucked the valuable legal document into his shirt pocket, Morgan Heirs stormed out the tavern door and relieved himself in the dark shadows beside the shanty.

Hurriedly tucking an unwrapped sweet roll into his vest pocket and licking his fingers, Jeremiah followed him out. Grumbling, Jeremiah watered a few weeds alongside the structure, himself.

Lacking so much as another word to Jeremiah, Morgan immediately slung his musket's strap over his shoulder, buried his hands in his pants pockets and without pausing to pick up a torch, stomped away down the road at a fast pace leaving his reliable friend to tend to details.

Jeremiah frowned at Morgan's back, fastened his musket between his knees, and grabbed one of the unlit rough wood torches from the row leaning against the shanty's coarse siding. He touched the torch's wadding to the flaming pot of pitch the tavern keeper filled each evening for that purpose then, shouldering his un-slung weapon, hurried to catch up.

Raising the hissing flame above their heads so that he could see Morgan's face, Jeremiah puffed less than kindly, "Dammit, Morrey, I almost didn't even have time to pick up Hamita's sweet roll!" He looked angrily at his friend. "I know you had to piss—so did I—but why did you have to black Clark's eye? What on God's green earth made you do that?"

"I didn't have time to argue," Morgan shot back. "Besides, I don't trust him! He's walking bad luck! He's an insipid, gray-eyed snake-in the-grass—you can tell by that slouching, belly-crawling way he has about him. And, hell, we had to bet on something! That bet was good as anything else."

"Right," Jeremiah agreed. "Besides, it was Tom won it from Clark! I was the one won it from Tom!" Jeremiah stepped lively to keep up with Morgan. "You won it from me! It's going to be very valuable land someday and knowing that, Clark was looking for a loophole to discredit the signing of the paper. Aw, Morrey, you should have guessed he was just trying to get a rise out of you."

"Well he got it, didn't he?" Morgan frowned. "No man calls me a cheat and gets away with it—so I punched him—! And I'll do it again if he gives me half a chance." His jet black eyes flashed in the torch's flaring light. "You and Tom are supposed to be my friends, Jere. You ought to be taking my part—not his!" His irritable voice echoed up and down the sleeping street, but he didn't break his pace.

"Don't be a damn fool stupid ass, Morrey, we weren't taking his part!" Jeremiah countered with exasperation, jogging to keep up. "We were trying to stop you doing something you'd regret tomorrow. And lower your voice. People are trying to sleep."

"Now, I'm a damn fool and a stupid ass, am I?" Morgan set his jaw and quickened his pace, stepping out again ahead of Jeremiah.

"Come on, Morrey!" Jeremiah called. "Don't charge ahead like that—wait!"

Morgan's Blunder

Morgan fumed as he stomped away down the empty red clay road. The acreage was his! *His!* The best piece of land to be had in the hilly wilderness surrounding the village of Terminus belonged to him, Morgan Andrew Heirs. He'd won it fair and square and he would fight any man who said he hadn't!

Briars
The House of Heirs

Tomorrow when Tom Garrett was sober again he'd regret having gambled away the land, but a bet was a bet and Jeremiah was right, it hadn't been Tom who'd lost the land to him but Jeremiah, himself. What fools they were, the both of them, not to realize the value of their losses.

He'd learned much about Georgia land values in the short time he'd been living and working in Terminus. Mostly during hours after work in the *Spike and Rail*, listening to tales from old timers who'd been there for the laying of the rails. And he'd heard about the Cherokee and Creek Indians, who had suffered for years through long and hard times to keep their rights to this land called Georgia but in the end they'd lost it to the white man.

Then last year, in 1837, barely ten years after the birth of railroading in America with the establishment of the Baltimore and Ohio Railroad, surveyors for the Western and Atlantic Railroad moved into this wilderness territory with work gangs. They cleared and prepared a bed for their tracks, but just seven miles short of the Chattahoochee river, which meandered off to the southwest, they laid down their tools.

At the time, Surveyor Stephen Long declared the staked out site at the end of the line to be good for "a tavern, a blacksmith's shop, a general store, and nothing else."

Chopped from the green and granite hills, a settlement did spring up. It was the end of the line and they called it Terminus. It was a destination that beckoned to the discontent and to the adventurous. Young men, like Morgan Heirs, looking for asylum from distant critical relatives. Or, seeking relief from all-too-familiar and boring big city societies, they traveled into this southern upland back country seeking adventure, with or without the company of their own women. Finding employment to sustain themselves day to day, they worked the slender web of tracks building brawn and slowly accumulating capital from wages earned with few places to spend them. Conveniently, the tavern faced the railhead.

Ann Gray

A meager few pioneering families came bravely into the wilds on their own, building their one room shacks on the outskirts of the Terminus clearing. But where the crossing red clay roads marked the center of the little colony, the railroad had provided a roughly constructed boarding house with two out-houses for their newly arrived workers. Before long, to quell the men's loneliness and unruly behavior in their off hours, a bawdy-house with five full bosomed women and lumpy beds soon appeared a ways off from the village proper. While nobody actually knew anything of its origins, it was rumored the railroad's local boss had sponsored it—no, required it—for his disorderly men's improved comportment, and the path out to the brothel was well worn. Tom Garrett was a regular, who sang the praises of the buxom ladies but then, Tom was a bachelor still, while Morgan and Jeremiah had their own women to comfort them.

The coming of the noisy railroad trains with screaming whistles, sooty fumes, and rowdy crews disturbed the sanctity of the region's wildlife. Wild boars, lured from the forest by pleasingly puzzling smells, explored dark passages between the settlement structures, snorting out garbage and feeding on it at night. Morgan knew as well as anyone else in town that in such a small settlement as Terminus, recently carved out of the forest, there were even more dangerous scavengers—black bears, regularly prowling the dark streets and narrow alleys. But at the moment, none of that mattered to a peeved and petulant Morgan as he always was after a bout of drinking.

Few lanterns burned along the deserted street. Most were reserved for the several posts near housing and at out-houses. Anyone sensible moving about after dark knew to carry a torch to discourage prowling animals. Alone on foot at night, a man's life was worth as much, or as little, as the faith he put in his aim and his firearm.

Still half a mile from the small boarding house they'd called home during the past year, Morgan stretched out his long legs, striding faster and faster, straight up the middle of the street until the faint glow from Jeremiah's torch vanished and the full moon, scudding in and out behind a line of dark clouds, disappeared completely. Sensing more than seeing his route, he heard the all too familiar sounds of night foragers echoing against the sparse structures and beyond. As the night air cleared his thinking, he realized that without a torch he should have already had his weapon at the ready. It was good he was heading into the wind, sending his scent back towards Jeremiah and not forward into the unseen.

His fingers had barely closed around the musket's leather strap when, without warning, an ominous roar burst through his head, a vile smell enveloped him, and he stumbled, falling blindly against a thigh high, unyielding hairy wall. In the next moment, searing pain burned a path down his right leg and an unseen force battered him about before squeezing the breath out of him in a hug of death. Then he was falling—falling into oblivion.

Morgan's agonizing screams combined with the scavenging bear's grisly roar and the dreadful sounds reached Jeremiah, bringing him in a run towards the gruesome scene.

In the torch's light, Jeremiah saw the brute standing over the motionless, bloody form of his hot-headed friend. The savage turned to look with glowing eyes into the approaching light.

At Morgan's feet lay the remnants of a partially gnawed rotted ham, discarded garbage. Yet booty enough to cause the foraging vagrant to defend his prize.

Jeremiah couldn't be sure if Morgan was dead or alive, but he swung the torch in a fiery circle flailing away at the slavering beast and moved closer to the man, forcing the beast's retreat from the flame. The animal stood down and swaggered away a few feet making a wide circle, swinging his rugged body in a rhythmic dance, away and back, in and out of the torch light, edging ever closer to the partially devoured ham and to the unconscious Morgan.

Jeremiah, spinning to keep the fiery brand in the bear's face, looked for an opportunity to drop the torch in favor of his weapon but the wary creature kept him unsure. Finally, it seemed to Jeremiah that if the ham were allowed to remain on the ground, untouched, and he could remove Morgan from the proximity of it, the bear would lose interest in both men. Holding the torch aloft, he slung his weapon back over his shoulder and reached with his free hand, grasping Morgan's collar and slowly started hauling him away from the bear's prize. Soon he had moved Morgan far enough away from the scene of the attack to feel more secure in releasing him.

The bear retreated, making another wide circle, nose tilted to the wind. Something else had gone wrong. Terribly wrong! The animal, sniffing the air, pranced back to within fifteen feet of the men and stopped, huffing forcefully and champing his teeth—a warning.

Expecting the bear to circle again, Jeremiah quickly jabbed the pointed end of the torch into the yielding clay of the road. He stepped away from the fiery wadding that flared towards him in the changing wind, it's brilliant light half-blinding him. Then swinging his musket into firing position, he stood over Morgan, stealing a moment to look down at him for any sign of life.

But the wary creature changed course, heaving forward in that unguarded moment to slash the side of Jeremiah's head with one massive clawed paw, knocking him to the ground and sending his weapon spinning out of reach.

Hard as it had always been for him to believe what he'd been told was the only positive action to take in a bear encounter if one wanted to come out of it alive, he had no choice but to put the advice to the test. He lay motionless while the hulk rolled him over with a broad paw, hovered over him—its foul smelling breath in his nostrils, nuzzled him—hot drool wetting down his clothing. Finally the brute rooted his long, wet snout into Jeremiah's vest pocket and brought out Hamita's sweet roll.

Sitting back on his haunches, he ate the morsel, finally licking the sweetness from his padded paws. Then he scurried away.

Jeremiah looked up into the cloud-strewn night sky and said a silent prayer of thanks for his own survival before seeing to his friend.

Heroes

Cursing the ambivalent moon, Lillian Heirs, dressed for bed, sat anxiously watching the poorly lit red clay road from their boarding house window as she had on so many nights. It was long past midnight, and though she had told Morgan how she worried when he and Jeremiah stopped after work on these late Saturday nights to drink with Tom Garrett at the *Spike and Rail* tavern, tonight they were out even later than usual. It was particularly hot in their little room, and for almost four hours she had been nervously braiding and unbraiding her waist long red hair while sitting, barefoot, on the uncomfortable sill of the open window, her thin bed pillow tucked beneath her.

It would be a month yet before her eighteenth birthday and, after a secure and comfortable life with her parents in Richmond, here she sat in the middle of nowhere, a bride of only four months, undoubtedly pregnant since her first coupling, and deathly nauseated daily. Acutely aware of the firm, cabbage-sized swelling beneath her thin summer night gown, right now she was also fiercely angry and almighty indignant that her new husband could think so little of her as to leave her for such long periods of time in her condition while he caroused with his railroad cronies.

Charming though he was, without a doubt when he had been drinking, Lillian knew Morgan Heirs could be the most aggravating man who ever drew breath! Perhaps he exhibited a tendency towards over-doing on all accounts. He worked harder, drank heavier, loved and hated with deeper passion than most men and, often, he became argumentative, even antagonistic, when over his limit in ale. He had absolutely no sense of time when he was involved with his cohorts at the tavern, but since it was the men's only recreation when they'd finished their week's work in the rail yard, Lillian and Hamita Baker, Jeremiah's wife, had agreed to be understanding regarding their husbands' choices of relaxation. Indeed, she had no doubt that Hamita Baker was sleeping soundly in the room next door and that she was the only person in the rickety boardinghouse wide awake at this ungodly hour.

It had rained in the afternoon but the night sky had cleared, leaving a scattering of dark clouds that skittered across the full moon from time to time, making the night moonlit and bright one minute, black as a well the next. Because of the hour, even the lantern hanging from the nail on the post at the street corner opposite the boarding house began to flicker and sputter; its supply of oil running low.

Knowing the men's tendencies to over-imbibe, Lillian was hoping to—and prepared to—see Morgan and Jeremiah reeling under the lantern's dying light, at any moment. Of course, Morgan had told her time after time that she and Hamita should never worry about Jeremiah and him, since both were excellent shots and always armed at night. But the very fact of their being out there somewhere on the poorly lit street and impaired by drink so late at night when there were known to be wild animals about—well, such things fed her worry.

Lillian thought for a moment that she saw something—there, in the shadows! Why was it that the obstinate moon chose to retire behind dark clouds at the very moment it was most needed? She listened intently. There! What was that? Perhaps what she sensed moving out in the shadows was a loose pig or some poor family's un-tethered dog which by tomorrow would be gone, repast for a wild predator.

Yes, there was something out there! And as she felt her heartbeat quicken, she tried to tell herself there was no need to become unduly fearful for Morgan and Jeremiah if they were this near home.

All at once, the moon glided into view and in its pale silvery light, she made out the shape of a man with a weapon strung across his back, arms stretched behind him, bent almost double from the effort of dragging something extremely burdensome after him. Calling out to him would surely awaken every sleeper in the boarding house. And if, indeed, it were Morgan and Jeremiah with one so besotted he had to be, literally, dragged home and she cried out for assistance, would that not wake everyone within hearing and make Morgan and Jeremiah the town's laughing stock? Lillian had no desire to be party to such shame, herself.

Swinging her bare feet and legs through the open window, she dropped the short distance to the ground and ran into the street towards the slowly advancing figure of Jeremiah Baker. She knew then that the burden he dragged was surely her husband, Morgan.

When she reached them, Jeremiah loosened his grasp on Morgan's wrists and smiled faintly, whispering, "I *did* make it!" before he collapsed, unconscious, crimson flowing from a series of gashes on the left side of his head.

Dressed for bed, standing alone in the middle of the street in the wee hours of the morning with two unconscious men lying wounded at her feet, Lillian squatted between them. Once she had examined them in the inconstant moonlight, she realized that Morgan's wounds were far more serious than Jeremiah's. Actually, she viewed it a blessing that her husband was unconscious. The remains of his tattered shirt were soaked with blood from gaping bloody gashes on his back, and there were long deep scratches on both arms. His trousers were ripped to shreds. But more grisly, his bared right leg was a bloody mass of raw meat and exposed broken bones. The ferocious attack must have come suddenly and unexpectedly because, although his musket hung in its accustomed place, as Lillian carefully

Ann Gray

slipped the strap over his arm and laid the weapon aside, there was no smell of burnt powder about it. The musket had not even been fired. She dared not turn him over to see his face, fearing the worst.

Cupping her hands to call out, to bring someone from the boarding house to help get the injured men inside, she saw Jeremiah coming round again.

But Jeremiah, a look of terror disfiguring his usually pleasant features, gazed beyond her. "He's back!" Jeremiah whispered, hoarsely. "Run, Lilly, run!"

Following his gaze, Lillian turned and saw the rumbling black bear, not more than thirty feet away, stand and begin walking upright towards them in the deserted street. Jeremiah's eyes closed, and he fell back again—unconscious.

Morgan's musket lay less than an arm's length from Lillian and the slavering, sauntering animal couldn't be more than twenty feet away. But when she tried to reach out to grasp the weapon, Lillian realized her arm refused to move.

As the beast waddled towards them, he could have been moving in three-quarter time. A guttural roar from deep inside rose and fell with each stride, and Lillian watched the heavy fur coat ripple and bounce with each earth-shaking step. The bear was no more than ten feet away, now, and closing on them when she heard Morgan's shout from behind her.

"Lilly, you've got to do this! Pick up the gun, now, Lilly, now! Shoot him, Lilly! Shoot the bear, Lilly!"

The musket's report split the silence of the night like a clap of thunder. Lillian had aimed for the bear's open mouth but the shot had found yet another lethal mark, penetrating his right eye, lodging within his brain and killing him instantly. Looking at the size of the felled beast, Lillian realized there must have been an all-powerful struggle by Jeremiah for Morgan's deliverance on the road back that night.

One of the first to arrive in response to Lillian's gun shot was the railroad's Doctor Daniel Goddard. He would have amputated Morgan's mutilated leg on the spot but for Lillian's protests. "No, please, not now! Later—if it doesn't heal," she pleaded.

"It's sure to rot off!" Doc said, shaking his head at the woman's foolish plea. But, because she pleaded with such feeling, he set the bones, dressed Morgan's and Jeremiah's wounds and, after the men were safely delivered, went back to bed.

Distressed as she was over Morgan's critical condition, Lillian still breathed a sigh of relief when she saw his handsome face was unscathed, his more serious wounds being confined to his leg. And, though Lillian swore it had been her husband's voice that prompted her to act, Morgan had not actually regained consciousness for two full days after the bear attack and even then he had no recollection of the events of that terrible July night.

After watching Doc Goddard work over her husband, Lillian vowed to learn all she could about treating wounds and injuries. When Morgan was better, she would borrow Doctor Goddard's well-preserved old medical books, one by one, and read them late into each night, making a reference notebook for herself.

The next day when Jeremiah went to feed Morgan's animals, he found Morgan's faithful hunting dog Freckles, his throat slashed, lying dead outside the stable doors. Knowing a challenged boar's sharp tusk could make such a wound as cleanly as a hunting knife, he took Freckles out into the deep woods and buried him. Luckily, no one spoke of hearing a ruckus, so he told Lillian Freckles must have run away. Lillian had enough to worry about right now without bearing that added grief.

It wasn't until the following Tuesday that Lillian finally gathered enough courage to ask Jeremiah what had happened and to thank him for his bravery. He sat her down on the boardinghouse steps and, sprawling out alongside her, smoothed

Ann Gray

his trim mustache—a sure sign he was enjoying himself—and told her the story in detail, for Jeremiah loved storytelling.

"Well," Jeremiah began, "Morgan had a set-to in the *Spike and Rail* over the bets we'd been making back and forth for the land."

"Land? What land?" Lillian asked.

"I'll get to that later," Jeremiah said. "Anyways, this fellow, Ezra Clark suggested Morgan might have cheated some. Well, one word led to another and Morrey's short temper got out of hand. You've probably guessed! He punched Clark! Well, we left the *Spike and Rail,* and he marched away, simmering like he does, without even picking up a torch." Jeremiah's frank, amiable eyes searched her face for understanding and finding it there, he blurted out, "Aw, Lilly, you know as well as I do, what happened that night was Morrey's own damn fault!"

"Of course, I know it, Jere!" Lillian agreed, adding, "Morgan *knew better,* too. I hate to think what would have happened if it hadn't been for you!"

Jeremiah patted Lillian's folded hands. "That's what being best friends is all about, Lilly—saving each other's rear end when the need's there."

After he'd finished telling her about the bear fight and she had expressed her boundless admiration, Lillian remembered to ask, "Earlier, you mentioned some land had caused the argument at the *Spike and Rail*—?"

"Oh, that'd be that ninety-seven acres up in the hills north of Terminus. I swear to you, Lilly, Morrey won it fair and square off me after I won it off Tom. Tom came by the property in payment of a debt owed him by Ezra Clark and neither had any use for the land." Jeremiah looked away. "There was some mighty heavy ale drinking going on, Lilly, so please don't ask me to explain any more because it might prove a mite embarrassing." Sheepishly, he added, "Promise me you won't tell Hamita that it was her sweet roll that saved our butts when the bear came after us. I kind of like being a hero, don't you?"

Lillian laughed and agreed to keep Jeremiah's secret.

That very same evening after Lillian's conversation with Jeremiah on the boardinghouse steps, his petite, yellow haired wife, Hamita, with her sprightly brown eyes twinkling, had speculated to her closest friend.

"I tell you, Lilly, more 'monkey business' is conducted in that tavern over mugs of ale than 'true business' ever was conducted in the railroad office. Imagine! Three grown men gambling for that prize property by seeing which one could hold the most ale without having to pee?"

Lillian burst out laughing at the revelation Jeremiah had so scrupulously avoided while Hamita persisted, "Take Morrey's win with a grain of salt, Lilly! As soon as he's himself again, it will likely be somebody else's property."

But the land had not changed hands again.

As heroes will, Lillian and Jeremiah basked in glorious notoriety. They fed the entire boarding house for two weeks on the bear's meat, and Jeremiah dried and tanned the beast's hide, saving the fierce head intact with agate marbles where the eyes had been. When it was thoroughly cured, he brought the skin to Lillian and Morgan in their cramped room in the boarding house.

He cleared his throat and said, ceremoniously, "According to the Bible, God gave man dominion over the animals. Now, Lilly, He didn't say anything about 'women'. Probably because He hadn't laid plans for you yet but, well, since you bagged this one, you deserve the trophy."

Lillian ran her hand over the thick, shiny black hair of the hide Jeremiah held in his arms and thought of the warmth the pelt would provide on the cold, hard wooden floor when her expected baby began to crawl. Still, remembering the pain and crippling Morgan had suffered as a result of the near fatal attack, Lillian worried that keeping the bear's skin—having it under foot as a constant reminder, would be too depressing for Morgan. She looked to her husband for a hint of what he was feeling.

"What do *you* think?" she asked, mildly.

Morgan tugged the heavy pelt from Jeremiah's grasp, flung it open onto the floor at their feet, and squatted down, eye to marble eye with his late tormentor. "So, Bruin, you're the cause of this?" he said, rubbing his lame leg, thoughtfully. After a moment's consideration, wagging his head at Jeremiah's offer of help and struggling to his feet again, Morgan rapped his cane against the bear's toothy head and winked at Lillian. "He's yours!" he said, "Do with him as you like."

Lillian thought that the bearskin rug would do nicely in front of their parlor's fireplace when her dream home became a reality.

After the crippling bear attack, Morgan remained with the Western and Atlantic Railroad and, in view of his outstanding work record and his knowledge of numbers, a result of his years of clerking in his father's grocery stores, he was readily promoted into a starting managerial position. The new post required less of his time and paid better wages, allowing him to increase his railroad stocks, which he added to whenever possible.

The Survey

It was not until mid-August, that Morgan finally brought Lillian to their rolling hills property for the first time. Riding a borrowed horse, she was to choose the spot on which he would build their house. She had packed a blanket and lunch of bread and cheese into her saddle bags and they had drawn clear, cool water from a swift flowing stream adjacent to a red clay cliff, where they had enjoyed their picnic under the broad umbrella of a whispering willow tree. There, they had loved until both were exhausted and, lingering in the afterglow, they rested in the willow's appealing shade until, laughing lightheartedly, Lillian got to her feet and buttoned her bodice while Morgan watched with unquenchable desire.

She rode beside him, then, hour after wondrous hour, marveling at the fact of his good fortune, and though they had covered only a small portion of it, she was overwhelmed by the realization that all this land was theirs. They topped a familiar rolling hill, and she reached to capture a flaming tendril of flyaway hair that had escaped her heavy red braid and was whipping about her face in the freshening breeze.

"When I married that young railroad worker in Richmond, I never realized I was going to become a land baron's wife," Lillian said, a serious note in her voice. "Tell me again," she urged him, watching intently, his changing expressions of pride and satisfaction, "how you came by all this land?"

"Business deals, my love, *important* business deals!" With one hand on the back of her saddle, he leaned across from astride Ambler to press his lips tenderly on hers. "You mustn't bother your pretty head with such weighty matters. Just tell me where you want your house."

Trying valiantly to keep a solemn expression, and recognizing the tell-tale glint in her husband's flashing black eyes when they both knew he was lying, Lillian pointed. "There—up there where that giant oak is—on that hilltop, that's where I want our house. I've known all day, I just wanted to see how long it would take you to bring me back to it."

He grinned at her uncanny ability to read him. "Do you want it to face South overlooking Terminus with the warmth of the sun on your parlor all day or do you want it facing East into the rising sun?"

"The house should face South, I think. We'll like watching Terminus grow from our front porch."

"Ah, already you're adding to our house and it isn't even on paper yet," he chided, gently.

"I can wait for our front porch as long as I know it's coming some day," she declared. "Won't it be wonderful, Morrey? Our own house! And so soon! I can hardly believe it."

Ann Gray

"The house will be only the beginning, Lilly! I'm going to give you *everything!* Everything you'll ever desire!"

"But I don't desire *'everything'*, darling! Just you and our baby and our house. Our very own house."

When they reached the favored hilltop, they dismounted to appreciate the view. Morgan stood behind Lillian, wrapping her in his arms—shielding her from the rising wind.

Secure in the power of his embrace, Lillian felt the sleeping child awaken within her, and she marveled at the miracle of their happiness and gave thanks to God in silent prayer.

Morgan believed himself to be, without a doubt, the happiest man in Georgia. He lured strong and able-bodied railroad friends to help in the carefully managed partial clearing of his newly acquired land—good-natured, industrious men, who worked on weekends and on long Summer evenings in exchange for an acre of land and the promise of enough wood to build his own house when the Heirs' project was done. Word spread, and in the little village of no more than forty families, Morgan had more volunteers than the job required, but he never turned away a man in need of work.

Morgan sold the hardwood from the land to the railroad for ties, the pine to settlers for the building of homes around the fringes of the village, and to new businesses which soon began springing up—the general store, the shoemaker's shop, the smithy's. He gave away odd wood scraps to all takers for fireplaces and the stoking of cookstoves.

While he convalesced, Morgan scouted and mapped sections of the cleared land and laid out parcels to be sold in due time when the property would have grown in value as he knew it would. He continued to help Jeremiah Baker where he could, admiring the slowly on-going progress of the building of their house. Jeremiah Baker showed great promise as a builder, working their crew of volunteers in his spare time away from the railroad's demands. Noting Jeremiah's skill and precision,

Morgan had no doubt the house would be finished next year in time for their expected baby's first Christmas.

Each train's arrival into Terminus brought a few more adventuresome immigrants eager to try their luck at living on the outer limits of civilization; the next day puffing away North again, hauling back the vulnerable, the home-sick, and the disillusioned.

Tracking down disappointed state land buyers' distant addresses, Morgan wrote letters and used accrued bank funds to buy adjacent acreage to the East, South, and West of his land. He looked ahead, believing that because of the coming of the railroad—soon, maybe in one year, surely in two—Terminus would become a thriving town, and he wanted a stake in its future. Morgan found the newly acquired role of land owner rewarding and intriguing.

He knew, also, that Lillian never noticed the cane that accompanied him now wherever he went. Actually, she had even said she gave much of the credit for his speedy recovery to his determination to see the building project finished so that he could get on with his primary interest, his real estate venture. That business, merely a sideline to his railroad job in the beginning, had begun demanding more and more of Morgan's attention and promised to bring in more money than either Lillian or he had ever imagined possible.

After winning the land from Jeremiah Baker, when he lay awake nights beside his sleeping Lillian, making plans for the future he often swore to himself that he would rise above his antagonistic father, Glenn Heirs. S*ecretly,* his greatest desire in life was to hear the imperious patriarch *acknowledge* that his disobedient and ungrateful son was, in fact, a better businessman than he had *ever* been. Someday—he vowed—*someday!*

Ann Gray

Drew and Jonathan

Terminus' two story boarding house, a roughly constructed assemblage of small rooms and hallways with rickety stairs at front and back, offered little comfort as far as living conditions went but every occupant of the shabby building, mostly other railroad men, knew that Morgan's and Jeremiah's wives, the only two women in residence, were both nearing full term by the New Year. The men tipped their hats and spoke solicitously to them whenever they passed in the halls or on the streets.

Circumstances being what they were, it seemed only natural that the two women would welcome each other's company. Acting as mid-wives to one another, they each gave birth to sons within the same week. Lillian's child was the first to be born.

The February weather outside being intolerable for even the hardiest of humankind on that early Sunday morning, an imminently expectant Morgan with his friend Jeremiah striding beside him for moral support were seen pacing the lower hallway together.

A small knot of interested boarders soon gathered to wait with them. The railroad doctor, Daniel Gossard, had even brought a comfortable chair from his own room down the hall, to sit by the door so as to be near just in case his services might be needed. And it had been at Doc Goddard's insistence that a wash pot of water had been set to boil over a fire out back to be available when needed. Actually he had even brought along forceps in his deep pocket just in case unforeseen problems developed!

He could have saved himself the trouble though, as Hamita Baker closed the door to Lillian's room and set about bringing forth Morgan Heirs' firstborn. Neither Hamita nor Lillian knew exactly what would be required of them but in the twelve hours that followed nature educated them in the act of delivering a child.

While the harsh wind whistled around corners of the drafty building, more chairs, several small tables, cards, and a keg of beer appeared magically in the corridor. And with the addition of a guitar and song, the wait became somewhat better than tolerable for the cluster of interested men.

At sundown on that bitterly cold tenth day of February in 1839, Morgan Andrew Heirs II, bawling loudly, made his presence known to the listening satisfaction of those who eagerly awaited his arrival. According to the scales which Tom Garrett ran to borrow from the general store for the occasion, the healthy eight pounds, five ounce boy won Morgan the jackpot of three dollars since his prediction of the child's birth weight came closest by one and a half ounces, well within the three ounce allowance.

The following equally frosty Friday while Hamita gave birth to Jeremiah's eight pounds, four ounce boy, Jonathan Jeremiah Baker II, with Lillian's assistance, the festivities in the drafty hall resumed. The second gathering evidenced more conviviality than the one before with the addition of a mouth organ and set of musical spoons.

To Lillian's and Hamita's utter surprise, the sex of the unborn babes had not been viewed by the men as a worthwhile wagering issue. Indeed, that detail had never been in doubt—not even for one instant!

The Hawthorn Hedges

Lillian thought for some time trying to decide what worthwhile pastime she might undertake to spend her unused energy without taking attention away from her motherly duties. Then on the thirteenth day in May, when Drew was almost three months old, she announced to Hamita that she had decided to plant a hedge to surround and enhance the new home now under construction.

She had seen thick thorny hawthorn bushes along the paths through the woods in every season and had determined to use them for her hedge. A hawthorn hedge would be green all year long bearing white flowers in spring and red berries in winter. Its needle-like thorns would discourage trespassers—be they human or otherwise.

It was a beautiful Sunday morning in late May, when Morgan saw Lillian at a distance hammering stakes into the hard red clay and stringing cotton lines, he stopped measuring and sawing and walked to where she stood. Listening patiently, he smiled his engaging smile while she explained her plan to him. Immediately, as she'd known he would, Morgan offered to have the hedge planted for her but she steadfastly refused.

"No," she said. "This is something I want to do—I, myself. Let's say it's my own small version of your determination to buy up all this land," she said, with a sweeping gesture. "You can understand that, now can't you, Morrey?"

He shook his head at her stubborn determination though his eyes told her that he understood.

And so she busied herself taking cuttings from the wild hawthorns that grew in the woods below the clearing. She trimmed and placed them in pails of water. Then following the cotton cord from stake to stake, she lined up the pails containing the cuttings around the entire perimeter of the hilltop area that was to encompass the Heirs' house and lawns. Weeks passed while she waited impatiently for the twigs to root until finally she was satisfied the future shrubs were sturdy enough for planting. When they began to bud, she summoned Morgan to climb the great oak tree and hang a swing—fashioned of her laundry basket, pillow lined and goose down soft—from its lowest limb so young Drew could watch her at her work.

"He might as well learn early," she said, "what life's all about."

Day after fatiguing day, hand-carrying water pails from rain barrels Morgan and his helpers had loaded onto their wagon for her, she squatted and bent to her labor, planting the spindly budding sticks. She was compelled to take frequent breaks from her labor to rest under the sheltering oak to soothe and coddle the infant, to change and suckle him. Each day by dusk, when she gathered the baby's things to return with the men in the wagon to the boarding house, her back ached and her hands and arms were scratched and rough, but the satisfaction that she felt was wholly gratifying.

There were also, of course, the regularly expected letters yet to be written in the evenings when she arrived back at their furnished room in the boarding house. She often wondered what her parents and Morgan's mother back in Richmond would think if she wrote to them of the way things really were rather than the vivid stories she invented about living in Terminus? She found it so much simpler to write as she envisioned it when the houses were all finished—and the church, and a mercantile store, and a school—a school for Drew and Jonny Baker and all the other little future citizens of Terminus. Yes, in time, Terminus would become a grand city like Richmond, and New Orleans, and Savannah.

When the planting of the hedge was finally finished on an evening in late June, Lillian stood at a front corner of the boundary, gazing with pride at the thin green spikes marching in two straight lines away from her on the slope forming a perfect right angle to the hilltop. Today they look puny, she thought, but when the house is finished and the hedge has grown—how grand it all will be.

She walked back to Baby Drew, swinging and cooing in his cradle beneath the regal old oak and sat on a soft, cool bed of clover. Reaching into the muslin bag that held the baby's fresh linens, she brought out her worn and faded Bible. "You see this big book, Son? This is the book you'll be raised by. Your papa's not what you'd call a praying man, but he's a good Christian at heart and he'll bring you up right and honest in your business with the world, but it's your mama who's going to try to guide you in your dealings with Heaven."

She looked away towards the hammering and the sawing, then turned back to explain to the cooing child, "All that land as far as you can see—well, it's all Heirs' land and it's going to be yours someday. Now, the Lord knows your papa's real busy right now building us our house so it's up to you and me to dedicate this ground." When Drew cooed his understanding, she looked down at her callused, rough, and briar-scratched hands, and smiled. "We're going to call this 'estate' of ours, *Briars*. And we're going to ask the Lord to look out for it's owner, your papa, and all that's his. You pay attention, now, Drew, to what I'm saying." She opened the Bible and read from Job 1:10: "Hast not Thou made an hedge about him, and about his house, and about all that he hath on every side? Thou hast blessed the work of his hands, and his substance is increased in the land." Then she knelt and prayed for God's blessings on the prickly hedge, that it would grow strong and hardy. And for His blessings on all the people that it would encircle. And on all the land that bore the name of Heirs.

Over time, when challenged as to her questionable taste in ornamental shrubbery because of its unattractive, prickly nature, she would simply smile and answer, "It suits me."

Progress

Up North, the Baltimore and Ohio Railroad had introduced a passenger coach that would carry up to sixty people. The Southern companies, still in their infancy, were striving to catch up. The Central Railroad had already linked Savannah with Macon and there were rumblings of extending it on northward to Terminus. The Georgia Railroad was in the planning stages for the same destination by 1845, in six years.

Briars
The House of Heirs

Already in Terminus, the railroad's iron web was reaching out in all directions from the central hub, swallowing up the settlement by degrees, stimulating the village's outward growth into the surrounding forest.

Time passed, and Morgan grew amazed and proud of his accomplishments. The most outstanding example of his eye for planning and design was *Briars*, itself. Early on, in discussing their house, Lillian had declared firmly to Morgan that regardless of what was 'done or not done' according to tradition, she preferred having her kitchen inside her house, declaring that having to go into a separate building in all kinds of weather to prepare meals was an unnecessary, unappealing requirement she had never understood, and while an out-house for toilet was obligatory; for cooking, it was nothing short of ridiculous! Morgan had smiled and indulged her. Jeremiah had seen to sturdy construction from the beginning, the original five room house having been comprised of a south facing parlor, a dining room, and a kitchen at the back, divided by a wide hallway from a small room designated a nursery, behind a large south facing front bedroom.

"Someday," Morgan had promised Lillian, as they had stood together watching the last stroke of the painter's brush, "when we are wealthy, there'll be two floors."

Whenever Morgan's plans to enlarge *Briars* in the future came under discussion, Lillian always laughed and said, "I'll be happy with whatever we have."

But the very next year after they had settled into the house, Lillian had requested that Morgan add a large pantry off the kitchen, with an outside door accessible for stocking from the wagon or the garden, as well as a small back porch, a shady place on the North side, for sitting with her lady friends and stringing beans and shelling peas in the late Summer months when the sun was boring holes in everything it touched. Morgan had relented and seen to both additions, even though they jutted out from the house proper, ruining the lines of his design when viewed from the rear.

In 1843, the burgeoning settlement of Terminus was renamed by Georgia state authorities, and Morgan being less than pleased at the name change, had led a contingent of local property owners in fighting it—and lost. His political interests having grown along with his real estate activities, Morgan had taken great pleasure in speaking out against the proposed new name in a town meeting.

"Terminus means just that—it's a terminal, the end of the line! It's fitting. Therefore, it's asinine—," he had exploded when pleading their case in the new town hall, "—that Terminus' name should be changed to 'Marthasville'! And why? Why, to humor Governor William Lumpkin's whims, of course! Marthasville—to be named after his daughter! *Marthasville—for God's sake!* Now, gentlemen, I ask you—?" But the name change had been enacted. The fuss causing hurt feelings all around.

Immediately thereafter, one incensed real estate businessman, Morgan Heirs, along with his best friend, eminent builder, Jeremiah Baker; Tom Garrett, his banker; Stewart Farley, Heirs' new next door neighbor to the west; and other purchasers of property from Heirs made it their urgent business to prevail upon Marthasville's malleable mayor to reinstate their political support by authorizing the cutting of a proper road to replace an existing double rutted track from the town limits through the new outlying community of eligible voters. Ultimately, Morgan had snubbed state authorities by suggesting to the town fathers without objection that the small but somewhat separate community of small estates be called *Briarwood*.

Lillian, undismayed by Morgan's penchant for politics, ignored the whole fracas and concentrated on domestic matters, of much greater interest to her. But secretly she took pride in the fact that, thanks to his astute business sense, Morgan Heirs'

Briars
The House of Heirs

parceled out properties were blossoming with attractive houses all around and the new community of homeowners was winning praise for the beautification of Marthasville's suburban area. Morgan, too, had given Lillian and Hamita and their new circle of lady friends his word that he would head up a committee of gentlemen to begin making plans for the building of a church in *Briarwood,* and he swore there would be no taverns, mercantile or other business establishments to mar the quietude of their neighborhood, even though it would mean still traveling some distance for needed supplies into Marthasville.

With the cutting of the new road, Morgan's remaining unsold parcels leapt skyward in price but they, too, were snapped up by eager buyers and by Fall, a *Briarwood* address had become the most desirable, the most prestigious of all locations within a twenty-five mile radius of Marthasville.

In truth, the house on the hilltop was taking on a personality of its own. The hawthorn hedges Lillian had planted to surround the house and grounds proper, had grown thick as Lillian had expected they would, and Morgan found time to keep them neatly trimmed. The bushes in the front facing the road were kept to a formal three feet, but the sides and rear hedges were allowed growth to a height of ten feet or better.

Already last Summer, *Briars* had been enhanced by the addition of a wide verandah, stretching from the pantry wall at the dining room all the way forward, across the front, and around past the nursery on the other side. Morgan said it gave the house individuality, and he liked sitting out there afternoons with his newspaper, and evenings with Lillian and Drew, enjoying the breezes and watching the fireflies dance.

Morgan had scouted around *Briars'* expansive grounds and found a location suitable for a storm cellar. It lay at the foot of the vacant lot between *Briars* and Farley's place where the stream flowed past the bare-faced red clay cliff and lone weeping willow. A familiar picnic spot, fondly remembered.

Ann Gray

When time came to start the hard labor, Morgan borrowed three Negro slaves to accomplish the burrowing out of the cave from Charles Watson Davis, a wealthy cotton plantation owner from down by Savannah. Davis, in town at the time of the town's name change, had sympathized with Morgan's argument, and during their several conversations, had broached the subject of slave ownership to Morgan. But Morgan suspected that Charley Davis was in Marthasville in the first place, not on legal business, but rather strictly for the resale of slaves. Further, from the beginning of their association, Morgan had theorized that Davis bought extra slaves from the slave runners and after they'd been cleaned up and civilized some, culled out and sold off the lazy, undesirable ones, or the married ones before they could breed, to inland buyers at a profit.

According to Charley Davis, Morgan Heirs had made the biggest mistake of his life by parceling out his acreage instead of laying in a plantation. However, not one to turn away from good fortune, when Charley offered to loan him three slaves on approval, Morgan thought of the proposed cave to be dug and took the loan of the slaves with the understanding that if he liked their work he'd consider buying one or more of them. No papers, no strings. No money would change hands until the deal, if there was to be a deal, was firm.

The truth of Davis' statement concerning plantation ownership, Morgan had to admit, was reflected in the emergence of Georgia as a leader in cotton production. The Savannah Cotton Exchange was now setting the world price for cotton and cotton was on almost every Southern gentleman's mind as more and more Georgia plantations switched from growing rice, tobacco, and hemp to the more lucrative product.

Nonetheless, Morgan and Jeremiah working together had done quite well. Morgan had the land and timber to sell and Jeremiah had recently left the railroad and put his saved money into a saw mill, reasoning that working with timber off the land would be more to his liking and certainly more financially beneficial to him and Hamita. He had even bought Hamita two slaves to help around the grounds while he was away working every day.

Unaccustomed to the role of slave ownership, and fearful lest he overwork the other man's slaves, Morgan restricted the men to eight hours of hard labor daily, but he was getting accustomed to seeing all three of them moving about the place as they found additional tasks to fill their otherwise empty hours.

Grady, the youngest of the three, busied himself until dark, after putting in his hours of digging, by weeding around the hedges, trimming the lawns, raking and keeping the long rock driveway weed-free.

Thomas, the slight one, found time every evening to curry Ambler and clean his stall, piling all the dung which Grady used around the plants and hedges, into a mound behind the stables.

CHAPTER THREE ~ TWO JOURNEYS
8:00 a.m., September 6, 1843 ~ Marthasville, Georgia

Henry's Problem

And, Henry. Henry had proven himself invaluable, over and over again. Before his labor in the cave began each morning, unbidden, he chopped and stacked enough firewood to see Lillian through the day, and kept the kindling box in the kitchen filled to capacity. Sometimes, in the evenings he entertained Drew on the back porch steps with stories while Lillian finished her work in the kitchen.

Morgan held that in the absence of his own physical soundness, if *Briars* was to thrive, it would require brawn. It was about the beginning of September, the root cellar being finished, that Morgan decided to make Charley Davis an offer for the three borrowed slaves. There'd be more than enough work to keep the three Negroes busy in the Winter months ahead, clearing the back lot for a pasture, chopping posts and building fences. And when Spring came, along with the necessity of garden plowing, there would be the digging of foundations for the planned barn now that Lillian, expecting another child, wanted a second cow. And he shouldn't forget to count the expansion of the stables for the new mare and foal he was getting from Homer Johnson in trade for the strip of property across the stream backing *Briars*. While they were adding to the stables, too, he'd include a room for *Briars*' three new permanent residents, who were now bedding down in the wood shed.

Though Charley Davis was a cheat, unscrupulous, unprincipled and, doubtless, corrupt, Morgan had to admit he had demonstrated he was a hell of a salesman! Davis had beamed when Morgan admitted to him that the slaves had performed well and he would, henceforth, be pleased to count them as assets of the *Briars'* estate. At that point, Davis gave Morgan a hand-written copy of his new slaves' legal rights.

Morgan was amazed at the content of the contract, which stipulated the owner's responsibility for the slave's support in old age and/or sickness, a right to limited religious instruction, and the right to bring suit and give evidence in special legal cases. Custom, it read, also decreed they could exercise the rights of owning private property, marriage, earning free time or making contracts. Females were allowed domestic or lighter labor than men, only if the owners so dictated, as they were not bound by law to respect the latter stipulation. There were also laws forbidding mutilation, branding, chaining, and even murder. Morgan certainly knew that instances of such cruelty were not unheard of.

After he had read, understood, and signed the paper, Morgan declared that its clearly drawn requirements were, appropriately, rights that should be afforded any human being. Morgan paid Charley Davis for the three slaves and though he considered the price outrageous, he was proud of the fine work his new slaves had done.

One could get to the root cellar from the house and grounds proper by passing through a narrow tunnel in Lillian's hedge and taking a good long walk down a winding, weedy pathway in the vacant lot next door. The cave, approximately twelve feet square, had been carved out of the belly of the red clay cliff facing the stream, a natural sentinel discouraging trespassers. Together, the borrowed slaves had painstakingly fitted tall rough hewn oak timbers at appropriate intervals into horizontal overhead beams for support. Its sturdy oak door had been framed into the high clay bank. Cold and damp inside, the room smelled of fresh earth.

Undeterred by the stream, no more than five feet from the cave's entrance, Henry, Thomas, and Grady had trudged in and out, day after humid day, hauling out wheelbarrows full of the heavy rock laden clay and dumping it up and down the water's edge to be gradually washed downstream. Indeed, having the fresh cool water at hand for drinking, and for pouring bucketsful over their heads and shoulders in the heat of the day lifted their spirits, and resting while they ate their meal under the nearby willow tree kept them working steadily throughout the Spring and Summer months until the work was finally accomplished.

That fateful day, indirectly, brought about another brow-wrinkling problem for Morgan Heirs. It was early one September morning after the completion of the root cellar that Henry came knocking at the back door, asking for Mister Heirs.

Lillian had opened the door to him. "Wipe your feet and come on in, Henry, I'm in the middle of something." Hurriedly, she put the last plump, pale biscuit into a pan and popped it into the oven. "Mister Heirs will be in presently. Is there something I can help you with?" She wiped her brow with the back of a floury hand, and examined his sad expression.

Henry removed his crumpled hat and stepped into the kitchen, carefully avoiding the braided rug at the entrance. "No, ma'am, I don't rightly 'spect Mister Heirs would 'prove if I brung it up wit'out him bein' here."

"Oh, well, in that case, I certainly won't insist," Lillian said, busying herself with setting the small breakfast table situated against the kitchen wall between the pantry and dining room doors.

"Would you like a warmed over pork chop, Henry? I've warmed some from last night's supper for Mister Heirs' breakfast and he never eats more than one."

Henry eyed the platter of chops. "That 'as a right generous breakfast you already fixed us this mornin', Miz Heirs, but I reckon I could squeeze one in, if'n you is sure."

Lillian took the chop from the platter and placed it alongside two jam tarts on a cotton napkin and handed it to him. "Come, Henry, it's such a nice morning, let's go sit on the back porch while my biscuits bake. We can wait for Mr. Heirs just as well out there."

So as not to embarrass Henry by watching him eat, Lillian turned her cane-backed bent wood rocker at an angle away from the porch steps and sat down, while Henry settled on the top step with his back to her.

"My, it's such a beautiful day, isn't it? It'll be getting cooler now Summer's almost gone." Lillian watched a graceful black and yellow swallowtail butterfly glide past and pause to drink from a blue morning glory blossom on the twining vine that crept over the porch railing. "It's hard for me to realize, Henry, that you and Grady and Thomas have been with us for a year!" The butterfly moved on to another blossom, lingering over the sweetness of it. "In all that time, neither Mister Heirs nor I have ever even inquired about how you like being here with us at *Briars*. I do hope you're happy here, Henry. We've come to depend on you, so." The butterfly swooped down on another blossom only to flit away as a honey bee emerged from the flower's throat, its legs heavy with pollen. When there was no answer forthcoming immediately, Lillian turned to pin her gaze on Henry's broad back, shaking now with silent sobs. "Henry!" she said, rushing to stand over the stricken man, her hands buried deep in the pockets of her apron to keep from reaching out to him. "What in Heaven's name is wrong?"

"It be my Rachel, Miz Heirs." Henry bowed his head and examined his dusty toes, peeking out from the worn leather shoes that Mister Heirs had given him, their too-short toes cut away. "I ain't seen my Rachel in this whole year, now, and I gots me a terrible ache t' be wit' her."

"Henry, you're married! Rachel is *your wife!*" Lillian was, at once, astounded and ashamed. She couldn't imagine living even a week without Morgan, a year was unthinkable. "All this time you've had a wife living somewhere else?"

Henry got to his feet and stepped back up onto the porch. "Yes'm. She be back yonder at Cotton Creek." He folded the

Ann Gray

napkin into a neat square and handed it back to her. "I don't mean no bother askin' time off, but Mister Davis, he promise he'd talk t' Mister Heirs 'bout sendin' her on if'n I 'as t' stay. I don't reckon he tol' Mister Heirs 'bout Rachel an' me."

"Why, of all things! Are there children, Henry?"

"No'm. And not likely t' be none, neither." Unsmiling, Henry dabbed at a leaky nostril with the back of a long, slender finger.

"Thomas and Grady, Henry, are they married, too?" Lillian breathed a sigh of relief when Henry shook his head, no. "All this time!" she sympathized. "You poor man, of course, Mister Heirs will allow you to go get your wife. If you'd only spoken up sooner, Mister Heirs would have seen to all that months ago."

"What would I have seen to months ago?" Morgan's voice came from the kitchen. "And what's burning, Lilly?"

"Oh, my biscuits!" Lillian exclaimed, barely able to brush past Morgan in the doorway, and calling back. "Morrey, please talk to Henry. We need to buy his wife, Rachel, from Cotton Creek and he needs your permission to go for her as soon as possible."

Joyous over the prospects of having help in the kitchen, Lillian had insisted that the woman, Rachel, whom she dared to hope would be a good cook, couldn't be expected to share a room in the stables with her husband and two other men.

Morgan, on the other hand, had grumbled that the necessity of adding still another room to the back of the house would call for a hallway, too. But knowing Henry's situation required remedying, immediately he put a crew from Jeremiah's saw mill to work on the new addition and sent Henry on his way to Cotton Creek with a bank draft made out to Charles Davis for an outrageously high, though agreed upon price for Henry's woman, Rachel.

It was the first week in November of 1844. The finished room sat unoccupied, and Henry hadn't been seen nor heard from since he'd left in early September. They had been expecting the two slaves back for weeks and the bank draft had already been cashed by Charles Davis.

Morgan cursed himself for not having taken the responsibility of handling the transaction, himself, for having depended on the Negro.

Lillian, too, was terribly disappointed in Henry. Somehow, she could not have imagined he would run away. Henry was so dependable it just didn't seem to be in his nature to do something like this. Nevertheless, Lillian felt responsible for the loss of the valuable slave and the money since it had been at her suggestion that Morgan had sent Henry to bring his woman back.

Undoubtedly, the two slaves had been inspired by all the talk of abolitionism to break for freedom while on their unsupervised return. Thankfully, Thomas and Grady were apparently still content with their circumstances.

A Good-sized Turnip

Hamita's Jeremiah, with his crew of workmen—and to Morgan's profit, also—had cleared most of the tall trees on their adjoining properties for timber so that now Lillian could sit at her bedroom window with her sewing, quilting or rug braiding, and watch Drew and Jonathan, bundled up warmly against the November chill, scampering about the yards at *Greenleaf.* Hamita Baker, knowing that Lillian' pregnancy was not going well, had proven to be a most faithful and caring friend, often welcoming the energetic and rambunctious Drew next door for hours at a time. Watching Drew, Lillian could not fathom how in the world the five year old could be in so many places at once. The child never stopped, and it was all she could do just to get around in her state, let alone chase after a whirlwind.

How she looked forward to Spring when she would be able once more to enjoy the out-of-doors, planting her flower garden and relaxing on the wide verandah without the awkwardness of pregnancy. Should this second child be a girl, she wondered how long the two children would be compatible sharing a room. When it came to planning ahead, without a doubt Morgan was more far-sighted than she would ever be, therefore she had no intention of bringing up the subject of adding even more rooms.

This had not been an easy pregnancy, and there had been weeks when she'd gone to bed to arrest the spotty bleeding, a sure sign things were not as they should be. The child wasn't due until the end of December and every day since the first of October, Lillian had prayed that with all the trouble she'd had maintaining the pregnancy, she would be able to deliver another ripe, healthy child like Drew.

Morgan was in town with Jeremiah on that cold Saturday afternoon when Lillian, sitting at her window sewing and watching the children at play, had recognized the first sharp stabbing labor pain.

Now, after timing the thrusts of pain as they came closer together, warning of imminent childbirth, there was no doubt that the child was definitely about to make its debut—a full month early. Fearfulness and anticipation battled for supremacy in her mind as Lillian prepared for the inevitable. She went to the pantry and took down a large metal wash tub from a hook, stopped in the kitchen, added wood to the stove and set a large kettle of water on it to boil. Then, on her way back to the bedroom, she stopped by the cabinet nearest the stove and removed a large ladle from the top drawer.

Between *Briars* and *Greenleaf*—Lillian and Hamita—a signal had been devised so that either woman might summon the other in time of need though until now it had never been tested. Bracing the upright tub on the open window sill in the bedroom, she dealt it a series of mighty blows with the large ladle, producing deep resounding gongs. Then she watched and waited. Moments later, in mounting urgency, she was relieved to see Hamita Baker—shawl, apron and skirts flying—racing up the slope with two small figures in tow. Fearing she might have waited too long to summon Hamita, Lillian sank to the floor and spread her knees.

"It's a girl!" Hamita said, an hour later, her small brown eyes crinkling at the corners as she held up the squalling, premature child for Lillian to admire. Quickly, she pulled off her clean, white apron and wrapped it about the infant, making a small bundle which she placed in the crook of Lillian's left arm. "Here, you hold her while I bring water to clean you, both, up." And in her next breath, "Listen to those boys in that room back there, would you? They're going to tear the whole house down in a minute if I don't speak to them." Hamita turned on her heel and stepped lively, pausing in the doorway to ask, "What have you and Morrey decided to call the girl?"

"Actually," Lillian said, "we haven't decided on a girl's name at all—yet."

"Just as I thought! Men are always so busy thinking about manly things, they seldom find time to think of family things, even names! I've always been partial to Sarah for a girl, myself. Of course, I'll probably never have a girl! Jeremiah's sure he's got nothing but boys stored in his jewels! Here, you hold Sarah 'til I get back and don't drop her or that little head'll crack like a pecan." With that Hamita Baker disappeared into the hallway.

Lillian lifted the child and looked up into the tiny wrinkled red face. "Sarah!" she said, weighing the name, as well as the child. The fragile, too-small package couldn't weigh more than a good-sized turnip. After a moment's consideration, she said, decisively, "Sarah. Yes, Sarah, you'll do fine, once I've fed you some!"

It was very late when, reeking of whiskey, Morgan slipped into the room. He stopped short when he saw the oil lamp burning on the table and Hamita, nodding, under a quilt in the chair near the window. Tip-toeing across to the bed, he looked down on his sleeping child for the first time, not knowing if it was a boy or a girl. Unsteadily, he leaned over Lillian, hesitant to wake her. In the lamplight, he saw the shimmer of a tear as it rolled down her cheek, followed by another and another.

Morgan knelt beside the bed, then, and reached out to take her hand. "I didn't know," he whispered. "I'm sorry. Are you all right?"

"Now, I am," she answered in hushed tones. She pulled back the soft flannel blanket. "Say 'hello' to Sarah."

Awkwardly, Morgan touched the newborn's cheek with a finger and the child yawned. "I'm afraid of her" he said, "she's so little."

"She'll grow," Lillian said. She looked across at Hamita, slumped in the chair, snoring softly. "Jonathan's in with Drew. I wonder what Jeremiah thought when he got home and found them missing?"

There came a pounding on the front door, shaking the house to it's very foundations, and Jeremiah's anxious voice, calling, "Hello, inside! Come to the door!"

"We'll ask him." Morgan said, quickly getting up to go.

Hamita's head snapped up at the sound and, put out by Jeremiah's perpetual lateness, she yelled after Morgan, "Let *that scoundrel* worry for a change!"

On his way, Morgan yelled back, "Peace, woman! He's brought you a sweet roll. What more do you want?"

Rachel

In the next several weeks, Lillian found herself wondering how she could have been so wrong in her judgment of Henry's dependability. She would have sworn that he'd still be there when the others, faithful though they were, had been long gone.

On this blustery November day, she found herself taking the time to look often down the red clay road, wishing Henry would suddenly appear climbing the hill to *Briars* in the company of his woman. With the new baby, Lillian could certainly use the woman, Rachel's help around the house.

Meanwhile, near Macon, the Heirs' servants were being herded out from a slave holding shack into the cold November rain and ordered into a rickety wagon with twelve other Negroes. Henry hoped for two places at the back because he had quickly hatched a plan to leap from the wagon at the first opportunity after it was rolling, and to drag Rachel down with him. A few scratches would be a small price to pay if it would get them away from the demons with the whips and guns, and safely on their way back home to *Briars*. But Henry had hoped for much too much.

The short, well endowed, young mulatto woman, Rachel, cried "Henry!" in pain and fear as, hands tied, she was roughly lifted aboard and pushed along to a seat halfway down the rough wooden bench in the canvas covered wagon. "Please, suh, let me sit wit' my hus'ban'!" she pleaded with one of her captors, as five more females were packed in after her, lining both sides of the wagon. Her reply was the flat of the man's hand against her cheek, throwing her head back against the wooden side panel.

Henry seethed with anger when he heard her cry of surprise and pain, but his countenance remained unchanged.

"Easy, there, Frank, don't mess her up!" The driver called back through the curtained opening, "They ain't worth much damaged, you know! And that one will bring a good price. Hell, she's white as my own mother!"

"Yeah, well, she just rubbed me the wrong way, is all. Come on, get a move on, there!" He pushed the last woman into a cramped space and picked his way back through the intermingling legs of the women from both sides of the wagon's benches. Jumping down from the wagon, he poked eight men along as they swung up. Henry was the last to be loaded, folding his long legs so as to fit the narrow space remaining.

Along the wagon's length, two stout ropes were threaded through the knotted hemp bindings that held each prisoner's wrists together, and tied to big iron rings mounted at the back of the driver's bench and on the closed tail gate of the wagon. When the last knot was tied at his knee, Henry guessed that short of a miracle, there'd be no way out of their situation. Henry heard the cloaked driver click "Gitty-yup!" to the team of horses as his companion swung up beside him.

Thunder rumbled and heavy rain pelted the wagon as it squeaked out of the deep mire in front of the holding shack, finally rumbling out of the woods and onto the rutted back road in the dead of night. The pounding rain beat on the holey canvas overhead and with rain trickling down his back, Henry looked down the bench to where Rachel sat, shivering, and was grateful that, at least, there were no holes over her head.

The malevolent slave dealers' attention had fallen upon Henry and Rachel in Macon after they had gotten off the train from Savannah, and during the time they were waiting at the station for public conveyance to Marthasville. While it was not unheard of for slaves to travel from point to point with their owners' permission as long as they carried papers of identification should they be questioned by authorities, it was most unusual to see a Negro man coupled with a mulatto woman, and both moving about with as obvious a sense of assurance as these two showed.

The men loitering nearby were up to no good of that Henry had no doubt. And as the area began to empty of other travelers, Henry became increasing uneasy over the men's growing interest in him and Rachel. Calling on his memorized instructions from Mister Heirs, as well using as his own good judgment, Henry could come up with no quick solutions to this disturbing situation. Henry and Rachel, waiting for the Marthasville coach, were finally the only ones left.

"More uppity Negroes looking for Underground Railroad connections!" one of the men had spit into Henry's face, as he purposely bumped him. "Going to New York or Canada, are you?"

Henry had avoided the man's eyes, stepped back and answered, respectfully, "No, suh! Jus' goin' t' Marthasville." Once in a while, Henry thought, that approach prob'ly worked—provokin' a Negro into a fight he would surely lose t' th' end of a rope, a knife or a bullet. But wit' all their papers bein' in order, Henry saw no reason t' tempt th' devils, especially with Rachel along.

It was the sudden thrust of cold metal against his ribs which convinced Henry that they needed to go with the men. Rachel, always so timid and easily frightened, gripped his arm with trembling fingers. As Henry reached to pick up her small valise, it fell open and Henry hurried to push its contents back inside as the closest man ripped the case from his grasp. Recovering one small item he'd almost missed that lay at his feet, Henry hurriedly stuffed it into his pocket.

That had been two months ago at the end of September. Since then, they had languished in the abandoned shack. As the weather worsened, each long, torturous week brought—maybe one, maybe two— additional captives to share the bread and water and wait out the cold with them until a wagon-load had been assembled for movement to some unethical plantation owner known to the kidnappers, who refused to pay legal value.

The cold rain had continued the whole night through, and as the dreary morning light blinked through the closed canvas slit at the rear of the wagon, Henry had glimpsed something that had awakened hope in him. The road had forked and though the driver had taken the right fork, off to the left behind them, Henry had seen a familiar sight. He couldn't read the letters B-A-K-E-R-S, but he knew the saw mill belonged to Mister Jeremiah Baker, all right, and that meant they were being delivered somewhere in the vicinity of Marthasville.

Henry watched and counted other familiar landmarks through his private little slit of a window as the wagon traveled on into the hilly countryside. When they were approaching

Ann Gray

Briarwood Road, Henry suddenly began foaming at the mouth, howling, and biting at his bindings like a mad dog.

Taken by surprise, other occupants of the wagon pulled at their wrist bindings, slipping them along the length of anchor rope until they were all sitting one on top of another, jam-packed at the front end of the wagon with Rachel caught up in the pile of humanity.

Henry raged at the back of the wagon, convulsing and heaving against the wagon's wooden sides, against the benches and the floor, against the heavy ropes that bound them altogether.

When the driver stopped the wagon, everyone heard the one called Frank, shouting from the back as he threw the wagon's rear-curtains open, "Hell, Woody, we got us a mad dog nigger! Quick," he urged, "you hold onto the rope at that end and be ready to pull when I untie it back here! We got to get him out of there before he ruins the lot of them!" Henry whooped and slobbered froth while Frank worked feverishly to untie the knot. Then the rope spun through the bindings of half the wagon-load of Negroes, who sat frozen while waiting for the stricken Henry to be removed.

As soon as the anchor rope was withdrawn, a slobbering Henry fell from the wagon to the ground writhing, as in agony. Five more prisoners slid their bindings down and off the loose end of the rope and leapt from the back of the wagon, running in all directions. Rachel jumped down, too, rushing to Henry only to have him clamp his teeth into her extended hand, bringing forth a sharp yelp of pain.

"Hellfire! He's bit the woman! Leave 'em—leave 'em all go! Seven niggers ain't worth worryin' about, Woody! Let's get out of here!" Frank sang out as he raced back to the safety of the wagon's seat. And the wagon began to slowly pull away, leaving Henry and Rachel alone in the rain on the road.

Henry sat up and spat the sliver of soap into his hand. "Here," he said, handing it to Rachel, "When we gets t' *Briars*,

Briars
The House of Heirs

you tell Miz Heirs how yo' lavender soap saved us from th' slave devils."

"*Saved us?*" Rachel asked, yanking on his hand to help him to his feet, "We's still slaves, ain't we?" Her throat hurt, her chest ached, and she burned with fever, but she'd not tell Henry, lest he'd see her as sickly and fragile.

Though the merciless cold rain continued to beat down on them, Henry's face lit up as he drew her closer, draping his arm around her shoulder, which reached slightly higher than his waist. "There be slaves and there be *Heirs'* servants," Henry grinned, proudly. "You and me, Rachel, we's *Heirs'* servants."

Henry rinsed his mouth with rain water caught up in his cupped hands and continued spitting on the roadway until the taste of soap was gone. Soaked to the skin, they climbed the sloping, slippery clay road towards *Briars* at the top of the hill.

Lillian, had not been prepared for her meeting with Henry's Rachel. The short, attractive woman, slightly on the plump side, was as white as Lillian, herself.

Her every move being followed by tawny eyes, Lillian stepped quietly about the small, sparsely furnished room. She added a thick stick of pine to the small fireplace. Adjusted a window covering to keep out the morning sunlight. Removed a large jam jar filled with stems of red and orange Fall leaves from the yet-to-be-painted chest of drawers long enough to wipe where it had sat with the hem of her apron. And finally settled in a straight chair beside the bed to adjust the counterpane over the woman lying, uncomfortably, there.

"How much longer you goin' make me stay in 'is here bed, Miz Heirs? I tol' you, yeste'day, I 'as all well." Rachel sat upright and, in frustration, flapped the coverlet with her open hand. "I can be a he'p t' you, if'n you'll only let me."

"I'm sure you'll be worth your weight in gold, Rachel," Lillian answered the uneasy woman, whom she judged to be about five to six years her junior, "when you are well enough to try your hand at cooking. It may be that you'll have to make some adjustments in your methods of preparing certain dishes in order to satisfy the tastes of Mister Heirs and our boy, Drew, since they are accustomed to the way I've always prepared our favorite dishes. But once that's accomplished you won't have any problems, I'm sure." Lillian looked concerned. "Are you sure you're well enough to be up for a little while? It's only been a week and we don't want you having a relapse, now, do we?"

Rachel showed a pretty row of even teeth when she grinned. "Yes'm, I's plenty well 'nough." Then, she swung her legs over the side of the bed and sat there for a moment. "Miz Heirs—"

Lillian, at the door with her hand on the knob, looked back. "Yes, Rachel?"

"What might they be— y'all's favorite dishes?"

"Oh, fried chicken, of course. And banana pudding. Oh, and potato salad!" Somewhat self-conscious, she added, "Mister Heirs says nobody can make potato salad as good as mine! I'll show you all my secrets!"

"Yes'm," Rachel said, scrambling out of the bed and hurriedly making it up. "I can tell you, ma'am, I's sure goin' t' be glad t' get back in a kitchen, again! Had me pickin' cotton 'fore I come here!"

"Well, then, when you're dressed why don't you go on into the kitchen and look around," Lillian suggested. "I'm sure you can find something to do to keep busy. The baby's just been fed and changed and is sleeping, so before it gets any later, I've got to run down to Mistress Baker's for a few minutes. She's down with a fever like you've had, and I want to see about her. But I'm sure I'll be back in plenty of time to cook dinner." She started to leave but turned back. "If I should get held up, I usually serve dinner about noon or a little after. There's fresh milk and some cooked potatoes and greens out on the back porch banister. I sure hope they haven't frozen. It got mighty cold last night.

Briars
The House of Heirs

"And since Mister Heirs is seldom here during the day, there'll only be Drew, me, and you, here, but remember Henry, Grady, and Thomas are working in the back pasture. We'll have to see they get something warm and tasty to keep them going. You feel free to help yourself before I get back, Rachel."

Lillian stepped through Rachel's bedroom doorway, disappearing into the new back hallway that stretched from the kitchen door beyond the center corridor and past Rachel's and Henry's new bedroom to the large storage closet on the East wall of the house. Morgan had said there'd probably have to be a staircase to another floor there soon if Lillian kept adding people to the household. The hallway still smelled of fresh paint.

Hamita's Fever

When Lillian reached *Greenleaf*, Hamita, wrapped in a warm woolen lap robe, had greeted her from the comfort of her rocking chair before a roaring fire. "Come in! Come in!" she'd croaked when Lillian knocked.

"What in this world are you doing sitting up?" Lillian asked the red-nosed, agitated woman, immediately on her arrival.

"I haven't been to bed all night," Hamita answered, testily. "Can't breathe if I lie down." She coughed, and her chest rattled.

"I don't like the sound of that!" Lillian said, reaching out to feel Hamita's forehead. "Why, Hamita, you're burning up!"

"No, I'm not!" Hamita snapped, "I'm freezing"

"Why didn't you send Jeremiah up to the house for me before he left this morning?"

"We're not speaking!" Hamita said flatly, not inviting inquiry.

Lillian didn't waste her breath delving into the cause of Hamita's petty quarrel with Jeremiah, but busied herself for the next five hours preparing and applying, timing and turning mustard plasters to break up the congestion in Hamita's chest until her labored breathing eased and she dozed.

Vinegar

It was nearing one o'clock when Lillian hurried up *Briars'* front steps to the verandah and into the house. The spicy smell of fried chicken still lingered in the center hall as she raced down it and burst into the kitchen to find Morgan bouncing Sarah on his knee, and Drew seated at the small morning table while Rachel hovered over them with a bowl of potato salad in one hand and a serving spoon in the other.

"Lilly, how's Hamita?" Morgan asked, when he saw the worried frown on her face.

"Hamita's doing better," she answered, raking Rachel with a scowl. "How's your dinner?"

"Delicious!" Morgan answered. "I had to have some papers from home, so I decided to surprise you!"

"Oh, I'm surprised, all right," Lillian admitted, tossing another look of aggravation in Rachel's direction, before pulling her chair up to the table. "I'd like some of your potato salad, if you please, Rachel, and maybe one little piece of that chicken." Lillian realized she was famished when she bit into the crisp, juicy chicken breast. And the potato salad fairly melted in her mouth.

"Rachel, I like you!" Drew cried, rushing to wrap his arms around the new cook's generous waist. "Mama, Rachel cooks good just like you do! And she's got banana puddin' coolin' on the back porch, too!"

"Oh?" Without looking up, Lillian said, "The potato salad needs a touch more cider vinegar, Rachel."

Rachel's Trek

Summer's heat having shown no mercy, seeking the slightest breeze, Morgan settled into his favorite rocker on the verandah late in the afternoon of Friday, August 6, 1847, the latest issue of his Penny Press in hand. The air moved around him and the corners of the newspaper fluttered. Delightful! On the front page of the newspaper he read with interest a detailed article on the continuing activities of Abolitionists, having now split into two groups, "the radicals and the graduals". More fodder for him and his associates at the *Spike and Rail* to grind, as if the vexing Abolitionists hadn't stirred up enough trouble when they were united!

Having the cook, Rachel, pregnant and short tempered at the same time as Lillian made life within *Briars* a challenge. There were times when the women's combined temperaments became unbearable, causing the children to take to the yards, Henry to seek the safety of the back porch and Morgan, himself, to seek refuge on the verandah. Today's high humidity had set the children to whining, intensified Rachel's crankiness, tested everyone's temper, and added to Lillian's discomfort, which she described as feeling like a pea pod about to pop. Morgan felt he had practically allowed his business to run itself these last few days.

Hamita and Jeremiah had traveled to Macon for Hamita's younger sister, Samantha's long anticipated marriage. And though Lillian's latest pregnancy had been easy compared to the last one, without Hamita Baker nearby, Morgan had watched over her like an old broody hen. He could sense Lillian's uneasiness, too, though they had all laughed when Hamita had left from the station with the admonition, "Now, Lilly, don't you dare have that baby without me!" Morgan was half afraid she might.

Hamita had never had more children in the eight years since Jonathan's birth and Morgan sometimes wondered if the failure had been Jeremiah's. Some failings could be blessings! Indeed, after Lillian's difficult second pregnancy, he should never have gotten her pregnant again. But, wrapped in the euphoria of a little bourbon, with reckless abandon and without thought to consequences, he'd often foolishly allowed his passion to hold sway over his better judgment. But no more. After many years of running his own successful business, Morgan had come to believe that, like everything else rewarding in life, a sensible man's passions required constant control until given release, meticulous preparation, and proper performance. Impetuousness was for the young and foolish! He had left Lillian's bed for the benefit of both.

This latest unwanted pregnancy had, however, propelled Morgan into another building frenzy. He had purposely seen to it in his plans that *every* member of the Heirs family would have his or her own bedroom. *Especially* Lillian and himself.

The addition of *Briars'* second story had gone flawlessly. Jeremiah had sent Morgan his best work crew and they had followed his plans, exactly. Besides the new bedroom for the expected baby, keeping the building's symmetry had required including the addition of a spare room behind his own bedroom. The extra room hadn't gone unused as he was now keeping his old business records, fishing gear and hunting trophies stored there.

Downstairs, the wall between the original oversized bedroom and nursery had been removed. Morgan's new floor plans called for dividing the area into a cozy library on the front for himself and behind that, three small guest bedrooms; each guest room having its own entrance onto the East verandah for the convenience of early and late arrivals and departures. The addition of stairs to the second floor at the end of the back hall had completed the building package nicely, leaving only the first floor pantry, back porch, and servant's bedroom to jar the rear visual symmetry of the house.

Briars
The House of Heirs

The sun was already riding low in the Western sky as Morgan folded his newspaper, picked up his cane, and stood for a moment admiring the beautiful view of Atlanta. *Atlanta!* In several hours the gas lights would start blinking on below. From here it would look like a thousand glowing fireflies.

It was hard to imagine that two whole years had passed since the town father's had come to their senses at last and decided to drop the name, Marthasville, in favor of one more fitting. Though it had been rumored that Atlanta was so named to retain Governor Lumpkin's daughter, Martha's middle name, Atalanta, Morgan doubted the rumor's truth. The Western and Atlantic Railroad having been first to lay track into the region, the name seemed to Morgan inherently suitable. Fast becoming a rail center and seat of industry, Atlanta was being incorporated into a city. The year 1847 would, indeed, be remembered in Georgia as an auspicious one.

Ten minutes later, promptly at five o'clock, Lillian, Morgan and the children sat at the dining room table in their accustomed places while Rachel trudged back and forth from the kitchen to the dining room, serving dishes in hand. Catching the door on the fly, she would give it a shove with her shoulder, letting it flap back and forth with each entrance and exit.

"Rachel," Lillian said, mildly, "Why isn't Henry serving tonight? I hate to see you doing all this extra work right now. You've cooked us a lovely supper. Now you should have your own then go rest for a while. I'll call you when we're finished."

"Henry ain't about." Rachel frowned, trying anxiously to catch Morgan's eye. "Ain't seen him since mid-afternoon. Other chores ain't finished, neither." Rachel slid a platter with a steaming roast of beef surrounded by small potatoes, carrots, and onions onto the table before Morgan's place. Then she disappeared into the kitchen.

Lillian looked at Morgan, who was looking at the roast beef and potatoes. "Morrey, where do you suppose Henry's gotten to?" Worry crept into her voice. "It's not like him to take off in the middle of the day and leave his chores undone."

"He's around somewhere, Lilly, don't worry," Morrey said, picking up the carving knife and fork, the aroma of beef wrapping itself around his nostrils.

"Papa, you forgot the blessing!" Sarah reminded her father from her place atop three books of varying thickness. "Jesus said—"

Carving knife and fork poised in mid-air, Morgan swept Lillian with a withering glance. "The child is carrying this praying thing too far, Lillian. It's all she talks about. We go to church on Sundays, that should be enough. Need we bring it to the table with us at every meal, too?"

"Is a small prayer before partaking of the Lord's bounty too much to ask?" Lillian pursed her lips and a faint smile curled the corners of her mouth as she looked from Morgan's face to Drew's to Sarah's. "I shouldn't think so, dear."

All eyes were on Morgan, and he laid the implements on the platter before he began: "Lord, please bless us and make us thankful for these and all Thy many other blessings. Amen."

After a little while, when everyone was about finished with their peach cobbler, the door swung open a little, and Rachel's head popped through. "I's goin' to look fo' Henry, now, 'fore it gets too dark. If'n he be down with a broke leg or somethin'—somewhere," she cast a reproachful glance at Morgan, "—he goin' need he'p!"

When Rachel went back into the kitchen, Lillian turned pleading eyes on her husband. "She doesn't have any business going out on a hunting expedition in her condition, does she, Morrey? She's as far along as I am."

Hunger appeased, a more congenial Morgan got to his feet, wiping his mouth with his napkin. "All right, I'll go. I'll send Thomas and Grady out, too." He picked up his cane and hurried into the kitchen past Rachel, thrusting the rumpled napkin into her open palm. "It was a delicious dinner, Rachel, in spite of all your efforts to spoil it!"

"Now, Mister Heirs," she called after him, "Henry done promised me, an' he ain't touched a drop in all these years!"

"If I find him drunk somewhere, Rachel, I promise you'll never hear a word about it! I'll gladly join him and we'll run away together and find us some young, skinny, and sweet tempered women!"

"Miz Heirs, she goin' whomp you, she hear you talkin' thataway, Mister Heirs!" Rachel shook her head, chuckling. That Mister Heirs, he did have a way about him!

Back in the empty dining room, she began stacking supper dishes. She felt a lot better now, knowing Mister Heirs was on Henry's trail.

The old scary feeling came over her so all of a sudden, it took her wholly by surprise. But then, it always did! It rarely happened—except when she was almighty scared or almighty worried, and it was happening, now! Understanding had come early in her lifetime that she had been gifted by her mammy with an awesome power inherited from her mammy's mammy and her mammy before her, and so on for generations back, but whenever it happened, Rachel continued to resent its command over her. It was "the sign" and it was always the same! Just before one of her "spells", she'd have an awful spinning in her head! When she nearly dropped a plate, she grabbed the table's edge to steady herself.

An' then—she 'as standin' outside th' root cellar, and beside th' cellar door 'as a wooden block wit' a nail fo' a pivot, an' it 'as turned cross-ways, barrin' th' door from openin'. That door 'as always propped open wit' a big heavy rock when somebody 'as in there! An' that same rock 'as leanin' up against that closed cellar door!

Rachel came awake from the vision and as she did, she heard herself yelling out to Henry through the cellar door, "I's here, Henry, I's here, now!"

When she arrived at the blunt face of the carved out hill, her heavy breasts heaving from the effort of the hike, she saw the weighty rock propped against the cellar door and the wooden block turned just as she had seen them in her vision. Rachel set down her unlit lantern and beat her fists against the door, calling, "Henry? Henry, is you in there, answer me!"

From inside, a raspy-voiced Henry proclaimed, "Yes, yes, sweet Jesus! The Lord done sent my Rachel t' deliver me from th' deeds of th' ungodly!"

Rachel felt her abdomen convulse, and her water broke and ran down her legs. The baby would be coming soon. Using the last ounce of her strength, she rolled the massive rock aside and twisted the wooden block straight up and down on it's nail, allowing the cellar door to burst open and Henry to leap forward from his prison.

Henry caught Rachel up in his arms, and lifted her off the ground, whirling her round and round in his joy and thankfulness. But his joy was short-lived as Rachel cried out, "It be comin'! Put me down, it gots to come, now!"

Minutes later, as soon as the slick child slid from her body, Henry held the silent, limber little form in his large, rough hands for Rachel to see.

"It ain't cryin', is it dead?" he asked, his voice trembling.

"Smack it on its bottom," Rachel advised, catching her breath. Henry did, but the baby didn't cry.

Rachel struggled to her feet. "Give it to me!" she cried, snatching the limp child from his hands and swatting it several times in quick succession on its tiny wrinkled rump. Then, she commanded it, "Cry, cry!"

Henry turned away. The child—his child, was dead!

He had walked only a few paces when he heard the newborn's wail. Spinning around, he saw Rachel up to her knees in the cold artesian stream, lifting the hitherto silent mulatto infant by its heels from the water. The child kicking and squirming in her grip, loudly complained of the harsh, new world it had entered.

Henry produced a piece of string, which had been the drawstring on his tobacco pouch, and a knife from his pocket for Rachel to use on the cord, and tore off his light cotton shirt for her to dry and wrap the child in. A broad grin beamed where a sad frown had resided only moments before. "Now, tell me, wife," he asked tenderly, when she was standing with him on the pebbled shore beside the rushing waters, "did you bring me a girl child or a boy child?"

"Oh!" Rachel laughed, and folding back the cotton wrappings, she noticed for the first time, answering, "We done made us a girl child! I wants to call her after that willow tree yonder, Henry, 'cause when she come out'n me, she be limber as that weeping willow's boughs."

Henry reached down into the stream and brought up a handful of water and, allowing it to trickle through his fingers onto the child's forehead, he said, "I names this child 'Willow' 'cause it make her mammy happy." Then he kissed Rachel.

Lighting and carrying the lantern in one hand because the twilight was fading, Henry wrapped his other arm around Rachel with the baby, and half-led, half-carried them back up the path to *Briars*.

There'd be so much happiness, Henry thought, when they reached home an' th' Heirs saw th' new addition to th' family. Tomorrow would be soon enough t' tell Mister Heirs about th' three white men he'd come upon raidin' th' root cellar and what they'd done t' him. Henry knew, too, when Mister Heirs counted th' losses from their thievery, it wouldn't be long before th' root cellar'd have proper locks and bolts.

Ann Gray

Morgan's Image

Earlier in the evening, after Rachel's delicious cobbler pie, Lillian had ushered the children upstairs for their evening rituals. Sarah's room, behind Drew's, was noticeably warmer. Lillian bathed Sarah at the wash basin and helped her into fresh underwear.

"You certainly won't be needing this tonight. There's not a breath of air stirring." She turned back the primrose patterned coverlet and folded it neatly at the foot of Sarah's narrow four poster bed, which fit perfectly between the open windows. The lace curtains were tied back so as not to impede even the faintest movement of air.

Lillian sat on the side of Sarah's bed and listened patiently to Sarah's long and detailed prayer, which finally wound down, "—and bless our new baby, and—and— and—!"

"Don't you think that's enough 'ands' for now, Sweet?" Lillian smiled. "I'm sure God knows all the prayers that are still in your heart. Just say 'Amen' and close your sleepy eyes."

Sarah yawned and said. "Amen."

Lillian kissed Sarah's rosy lips and, lifting the lamp from the table, tiptoed from the room, leaving the door ajar.

Drew had long since refused to be tucked in, but every night after leaving Sarah, Lillian held her lamp high, and peeked into his room. Worn to complete exhaustion by his active day, he was already sound asleep, stretched out across the bed corner to corner in only his underwear. Both the west and south windows were open wide, but no air moved between them.

She walked down the hall and entered the third bedroom on the west side, the one that would belong to the new baby when he or she was old enough to sleep unattended. Until then, the small crib Drew and Sarah had used would serve the child beside Lillian's bed in her own bedroom. Lillian appreciated the fact that the child's room was already in 'apple pie order'. She indulged in the luxury of pride, for once. How circumstances change, she thought, remembering Drew's birth back in the austere days of the boarding house when Atlanta was still called Terminus.

Yes, all the charming bedroom required was the presence of one who resided, still, within her. Lillian ran her hands over her swollen belly, and spoke to the active occupant: "Baby, there's a very nice room waiting for you, here. Won't you, please, come soon?" Almost in answer, a griping pang came and lingered, causing Lillian to catch her breath.

Already having delivered two children, Lillian anticipated a fast delivery once the process was begun. She hurried to the top of the back stairs and called down to Rachel in her room at the foot of the stairs, "Rachel, I think it's getting ready to come!" After a moment when there was no reply, she called again, "Rachel, are you down there?"

Silence.

Where was the woman? Looking down the flight of stairs, Lillian determined she could make it down, but getting back up might pose a problem. However, there was no way around the fact that the tub and hot water would be needed, and both were to be found downstairs. Hesitating now might make the descent more difficult later. "Rachel?" she called, more urgently. When no answer came, Lillian determined that if the birth were to take place in the kitchen, so be it! There was little else she could do, so she began her slow, tedious descent to the lower hall, halting midway to allow a pain to pass, then going on. Once she was downstairs, moving came much easier.

Holding her lamp higher, she opened the door to Rachel's and Henry's empty room. "Rachel, I need you—are you sleeping?" she asked softly. Stepping inside, shadows melted in the lamplight. The spotless room smelled of wisteria. Atop the still unpainted chest of drawers, the large jam jar Lillian had filled with colorful autumn leaves when Rachel first arrived sat filled to overflowing with cascading fragrant lavender blossoms plucked from the verandah's abundant vines. The chest's bottom drawer, a makeshift bassinet lined with soft cotton batting and clean white flour sacking, rested on the floor beside their bed. Hastily, Lillian closed the door.

A lantern was missing from the shelf by the back door which meant that without telling her Rachel had left the house. Now, when she was needed most! Peeking into the dining room through the swinging doors, she saw that the dining table remained un-cleared. Something terribly important had to have drawn Rachel away. It was not like her to leave her duties half done, any more than it was for Henry to disappear in the middle of the afternoon.

Lillian set her lamp on the table and checked the water level in the heated kettle on the stove. She picked out a large, clean towel from the supply of fresh linens on the lower shelf in the pantry and laid it in the bottom of their largest wash tub. Then, staring at the collection of necessary paraphernalia, she sat uncomfortably in her straight chair beside the breakfast table to wait. To wait for the next pain. To wait for someone—anyone—to come. The wall clock's ticking was the only sound in the house. Lillian counted time between labor pains and they were consistent. The room grew hotter, stifling.

Fifteen minutes between. The intensity of cramps increased along with Lillian's anxiety. Was she to be left to birth this child, alone? Had the search for Henry been so widespread and so terribly demanding as to take away all *her* available help? Shouldn't someone have considered *her* condition, *her* possible need? Where was everybody? Now—when *she* needed them most?

Ten minutes between. Twilight faded into darkness and the clock read eight-thirty. Why was Morgan never home when there was a child to be birthed? Why was Morgan seldom at home any more *for anything!* Why was his precious business so much more important than her concerns? Wrong! *Wrong!* What was wrong with her thinking? Hadn't she, herself, persuaded him at supper to go look for the missing Henry? How long ago was supper? What could have happened to Henry? Where *was* Rachel? Morgan?

Five minutes between. Less? She wasn't sure. She'd lost count of time. It seemed she'd been staring at the waiting tub, pushing against the griping pains for an eternity. The clock's hands were racing ahead of time. Could it really be nine fifteen? *Call Hamita Baker!* Foolish woman, Hamita's in Macon! Where are they, *all?*

Lillian knotted her skirts under her bosom, took a firm grip on opposite edges of the tub and lowered herself onto the heavy towel. Her face, her hair and clothing were soon wet with sweat. Her mouth and lips, bone dry. Her breathing came in shallow gasps. It was as if the unborn child were squeezing every life giving breath from her.

Slipping in and out of consciousness? *She must be!* It was impossible, she knew, that she should be hearing the child's cry from her womb but there it was again, the newborn's cry. Lillian's head bobbed forward and she dreamed she was astride an airborne horse riding at full gallop across a star-strewn sky.

Rachel and babe in tow, Henry pushed open the kitchen door.

At once, Rachel screamed, "Oh, my God, Miz Heirs!" She handed their own newborn to Henry. "Put this chil' in her drawer, Henry, an' go fetch Mister Heirs. You knows where you'll likely find him! Miz Heirs be in trouble, here! I can see she been at this birthin' a long time, now!"

Henry turned away from the scene of his mistress's distress, running down the hall with the squalling baby, he called back over his shoulder, "Miz Heirs goin' be all right, ain't she, Hon?"

"I don't know how bad it be yet. Hurry! Go, Henry! Fetch him!"

"Rachel, you're here! Thank goodness!" Lillian said, weakly, looking up into the worried servant's face. *"It won't come, Rachel!"*

Ann Gray

It didn't take Rachel long to determine, by feeling the firm, round hardness of the small skull beneath Lillian's ribs, that the child in Lillian's belly was sitting upright. When she ran her palms over the panting woman's lower abdomen, she felt the quick erratic movements of tiny limbs.

"Oh, Lordy, Miz Heirs," Rachel complained loudly, "we gots t' turn this baby 'fore it can be birthed—'else it goin' t' come out back'ards an' tangled up, fo' sure! I's goin' push down on yo' belly an' I wants you t' grunt. Grunt hard fo' me, you hear?"

"Of course, I hear, Rachel, I'm not deaf!" Lillian declared between shallow breaths. "Where in the world were you? I've called and called!" Lillian chattered on, despite the contractions that came quicker now. "Wouldn't you know this taciturn child would decide to come when there was nobody about but me, and after being all of three weeks late, at that! Oh! Rachel, you're hurting me!"

"Not nearly so much as it goin' hurt, that baby don't turn over soon! Push, *Miz Lillian*, push!"

Rachel continued massaging the roundness of Lillian's belly, pushing, prodding—compelling movement.

The child leapt.

Lillian felt the baby turn, and she cried out, angrily, "Come on! Come on, if you're coming!" Then she gave herself over to the uncontrollable involuntary rhythmic thrustings of her body which were constant now.

Rachel massaged, stroked, encouraged. "Push, Miz Lillian, push! It be gettin' here, now. You goin' be fine."

The child had chosen the day, the hour, and the minute, and had entered the world at exactly twelve minutes to midnight on Friday, August 6, 1847.

"It be a beautiful baby girl, Miz Heirs," Rachel said, holding the perfect kicking and squalling child out for Lillian's inspection. "She sure be full of spirit!"

Briars
The House of Heirs

"She's Morgan Heirs, born anew," Lillian said, through cracked and bleeding lips, admiring her latest accomplishment. "Will you look at all that black hair, Rachel? And look here, she's even got his long fingers and his dimpled chin! I don't see anything of me in the whole bundle, do you? How can that be, Rachel? How can such a tiny female appear so exactly like a grown male in all respects—save one?"

"Lordy, Miz Heirs, I can't rightly say! But she sho' do favor Mister Heirs, all right, don't she?" Rachel lifted her head to listen. "I hears my baby girl callin' me. You hold your'n while I goes t' see t' my Willow. I be right back an' we goin' get you all cleaned up then fo' Mister Heirs."

Contrite for her inappropriate self-indulgence, Lillian apologized, "Oh, Rachel, shame on me! I hadn't noticed! You've had your child, too! Then it was your baby I heard squalling? My, my, I'm glad to know that. I thought this one was crying out for notice before she'd even gotten here. And you've named your girl 'Willow'. That's a mighty pretty name. Go on, Rachel, go see to your child. I'm naming this one right now, and I'm calling her after her father, since she's the image of him, anyway. Miss Morgana Heirs and I will get acquainted while we're waiting your return."

"Yes'm, Miz Heirs."

When the other woman turned to leave, Lillian grasped her hand. "But, Rachel—Rachel, I found it most comforting when you called me, 'Miz Lillian' a while ago. I don't want you ever to call me 'Miz Heirs' again—not after all we've been through together here tonight. Actually, Rachel, I don't ever want to be without you—not ever again."

"God willin', Miz Lillian, I don't reckon you goin' ever need t' be," Rachel said, tears filling her soft, tawny eyes.

Ann Gray

Politics

Lillian's first outing following Morgana's traumatic birth took place on Sunday of the following week. Back from Macon the day after all the excitement and somewhat jealous of Lillian's Rachel for having usurped her birthing duty, Hamita had invited the entire Heirs family next door for a Sunday afternoon of "purely relaxing". Jeremiah had chosen the largest, yellow-bottomed, bee-stung, red meat melon in the entire garden and left it to chill overnight in the deepest part of the stream that ran behind their adjoining properties. Now, under the watchful eyes of the young'uns, Jeremiah stood at the round wicker table on the verandah at *Greenleaf*, slicing the giant melon into smiling crescents while the other adults, chatting amiably, seated themselves comfortably in squeaking rockers scattered about *Greenleaf*'s wide porch. Even the weather had cooperated. The temperature had not soared into the nineties, but remained in the lower eighties, while a gentle breeze moved Hamita's fragrant jasmine tendrils on the columns of *Greenleaf's* verandah.

From her chair near the banisters, Lillian looked up the hill to where afternoon shadows were shading her new bedroom window on the second floor of *Briars'* East side. She had been there when Morgan had arrived home that night after Morgana's traumatic birth, but she had not spoken because Morgan's joy at finding such serenity and beauty had been almost tangible to her when he leaned down to wake her with his kiss, whispering his love. If he had arrived sooner, wouldn't she have been mortified to have him see her in such unflattering straits as she had experienced? Relieved of her burden at last, tired beyond belief, and thankful that her ordeal was finally over, she immediately drifted back into restful sleep. It would be the next day before Morgan learned this new girl child was his namesake.

Not until then, either, would Morgan explain to Lillian how in his search for Henry, he had stopped first at *Greenleaf* where Jeremiah Baker, suffering the pangs of loneliness in Hamita's absence had diverted him to the *Spike and Rail* for a short refreshment. But when Henry arrived at the tavern on one of the Heirs' horses, Morgan had hurried home again to find Lillian, resplendent in blue silk and lace, asleep against a mound of pillows, cradling his third child.

But there would be no more babies in the Heirs' household. She and Morgan were agreed on that and she was wholly relieved. However, Lillian knew that Morgan's solution, separate bedrooms, would only achieve their mutual goal if they remained separated, and Lillian knew, without doubt, there would continue to be ungoverned times when the door between their bedrooms would open to cravings for intimacy, mutual or otherwise.

"More watermelon, Lilly?" Jeremiah asked, his words jarring her from her daydream.

"Good Heavens, no! Thank you, Jeremiah, though I think our children would finish all the rest, if you offered it," Lillian said, noting their interest.

Morgan sat across from Lillian, cooing to the child he held so tenderly, watching the changing expressions of delight in her eyes.

Contrite over his second consecutive absence at the hour of a child's birth, and forgiven as soon as the words of regret were spoken, Morgan had fairly beamed with his proper introduction to the newborn, Morgana, a small female edition of himself.

Lillian knew it would have been nothing short of conceit had Morgan named her so, but having it be Lillian's own choice had relieved him of reproach and left him only to acknowledge, proudly, her uncommon resemblance and to glory in her cherished presence. Yes, Lillian realized, she had paid her husband the highest compliment possible in naming the girl child after him.

"Isn't that so, Lillian—?" Hamita was somewhat red of face and though she was attempting to remain calm, her brown eyes were beginning to flash, a sure sign of Hamita's displeasure. Obviously, Lillian had missed something in the conversation of

Ann Gray

some importance to Hamita, who was now seeking Lillian's endorsement.

"What?" Lillian looked at her quizzically, turning from watching the boys lay aside their dishes of scooped out rinds and bound down the steps with Sarah at their heels. Lillian knew the boys wouldn't wait for Sarah, they never did. "I'm sorry, I'm afraid my mind was wandering. What did you say?"

"This 'Slavery issue'! These *Abolitionists!*" Hamita spat the word. "They're running this Underground Railroad and sponsoring the writing of these Negro journals like the *North Star*, just stirring up trouble. People like that Birney, those Tappans, Douglass! They've even talked innocent Negroes—Negro women, at that—into spewing their ridiculous maliciousness. What I said, Lilly, was that our Southern slaves are not unhappy with their living conditions any more than we are. They work hard, yes, but they certainly don't lack for anything necessary to good health, do they? You know it's so! They eat the same food we eat. Heavens, yours live right in the same house with you."

"Yes, yes, they do," Lillian nodded. "They're more family than slaves, anyway—"

"My dear wife," Jeremiah broke in, "forgets that all slaves are not treated so kindly. You take Charley Davis's down at Cotton Creek. For years, he's been running a brutal slavery mill." Jeremiah took Hamita's hand, kissed and patted it, prior to divulging his knowledge to her. "Some of the horror tales Henry's told to us men about that place would curl your pretty yellow hair. Why, I wouldn't want you to even hear them, they're that bad."

The relaxed atmosphere of the visit having dissolved into a political discussion, Lillian stood to leave.. When the others followed her lead, she smiled, and offered a calming voice to cool the heated conversation. "I'm sure Time will take care of these issues, my dears. But we'd better be getting ourselves back up the hill before Rachel comes looking for the children.

Their naps are way overdue." She reached out and embraced her dearest friend. "Thank you, Hamita dear, for having us. It's always enjoyable when our two families get together and—" she whispered, "—Heaven knows, it's never boring."

By November, despite the twists and turns of national politics—the controversy over slavery and other issues that separated the South from the North—everyday life had once more settled into quiet routine for the family Heirs.

With Rachel in charge of Morgana and Sarah for allotted play time and naps, and Drew away at least five hours each weekday going to and coming from school, Lillian finally came into some free time of her own.

The Letter

Because there were people of various faiths living together harmoniously in their community, as promised Morgan had led the way in founding and funding a nondenominational church in *Briarwood*, and Lillian's ladies' circle spent their free hours almost daily in "doing good works" as a service of that Briarwood Community Church. They fed the hungry, clothed the poor, and held bazaars and bake sales for the benefit of the indigent. It was rewarding work which also offered opportunities at their gatherings to keep up with scandalous events of the week just passed.

For the second time in this week Lillian had carried groceries to a pitifully abused woman named Althea Clark, often victimized by a brutal husband. The couple's only child, Carla, a little girl not much older than Sarah, also showed signs of physical abuse. Lillian feared for the woman's and the child's welfare but she had been told there were, after all, boundaries over which even volunteer church workers could not step.

She was just arriving home from that errand, when she was met by Henry on the steps to the verandah, waving an envelope.

"This here letter done come while'st you 'as gone, Miz Lillian. Rachel, she took ahold o' it an' she drop' it like it 'as afire. She say it got nothin' but bad news in it. I sho' hopes it ain't bad news, Miz Lillian." He handed the letter to her.

"So do I, Henry, so do I," Lillian answered thoughtfully, taking the envelope and examining it. As she had expected, it was from Constance Heirs. In the last two months, because the two women corresponded regularly, Morgan's mother had written letter after letter pleading with Lillian to convince Morgan to return to Virginia if only for a few weeks. Each time such a letter had arrived, Lillian had attempted to talk to Morgan about it, but because they concerned his father, Morgan refused even to listen.

Constance gave progressive accounts in her letters of Morgan's father being slowly consumed by an unknown malady that had at first cost him only his pride and independence in that he required a hired boy to push him in a wheeled chair wherever he went. Now months later, the disease had advanced to a stage making him helplessly dependent on Constance, even to moving food from his plate to his mouth. His mouth, she characterized as being contorted into a disagreeable smirk, though his ability to speak was still intact. Indeed, he frequently gave vent to angry bellowing at his inability to manage for himself. Mercifully, Constance wrote, most of his ranting remained restricted to her ears.

Lillian determined that this time, she would not be put off by Morgan.

Rachel's supper of succulent stewed chicken with dumplings, candied sweet potatoes, green beans and sliced tomatoes from the fall garden had not softened Morgan's austere mood.

"Hard day, darling?" Lillian asked, looking down the dining table past the children on either side.

"Extremely hard." Morgan watched Drew building a teepee on his dinner plate out of cleaned chicken drumstick bones while he waited for Rachel to bring the banana pudding. "Don't do that, Drew," Morgan said, sternly. The boy dropped the greasy bones onto his plate and sat back rigidly in his chair.

Sarah, her entire serving of green beans completely untouched, conversed loudly with the doll currently in favor perched on her lap. "Put the doll down, Sarah, and eat your beans," Morgan said, pointing to the mound of cold vegetables, his voice harsh.

"Her name is Margaret, Papa," Sarah said, walking the doll towards him on the linen tablecloth.

"That's fine, then put *Margaret* away," Morgan said, pointedly, looking past the child to Lillian. "Why is it, I must come home every day that passes and discipline the children? They should know how to behave at the table by now."

"I'm sorry, dear, perhaps it's because they see so little of you, they seek your attention any way they can get it."

Silence fell like a hammer around the dining table as Morgan inspected each solemn face, in turn.

Henry brought in Rachel's scrumptious banana pudding and everyone finished their meal in subdued silence.

After the children had been seen to, Lillian joined Morgan, who had retired to the verandah after supper. When she thought enough time had passed, Lillian withdrew Constance's latest letter from her pocket and offered it to Morgan. "It's from your mother."

Morgan pushed her hand away. "You know how I feel about my mother's letters, Lilly. Put it away."

"No, Morrey, not this time. I can't. It's important that you know—"

He had sworn never to return to Richmond. Now, this! "All right! You read it—please." Morgan locked his gaze onto the oak tree and listened as Lillian read the letter aloud.

As he listened, long-buried memories awakened and, against his will, Morgan relived them. Back in Richmond, the elder Heirs, once an humble English merchant-man had managed through frugality and iron-handed practices to become a self-made, if insufferable, grocer with a chain of small emporiums in Virginia and Maryland, decorously called *The Grocery*. The man from whom Morgan had inherited his dark good looks, his sharp mind—and according to his mother, his quick acerbic wit—that man was in Morgan's eyes in a single word, "dictatorial". That man was the parent he'd never been allowed to call "father" or "daddy" even as a child. Only, "sir". The taskmaster who, when Morgan's schooling was finished, kept him fettered by filial obligation to the storerooms and counters of *The Grocery* nearest home on a fixed salary —measly for the work he did— controlling him like a puppet with the family purse strings.

His mother, Constance, whom he adored, the oldest daughter of the wealthy and respected Virginia Courtlands, whose family roots entwined the very foundations of Richmond, shared his unhappy situation. The elder Courtlands had found the upstart, Glenn Arthur Heirs, far removed from desirable gentry material for their cherished progeny but Constance, irretrievably charmed by the witty, handsome young Heirs, and in open defiance of her family's wishes, allowed herself to be swept away in an impromptu elopement which within the year produced Morgan Andrew.

When Morgan matured to an age of awareness marked by his own grievous experience, he understood his mother's gradual transformation from a beautiful and vivacious woman into the depressed, nervous shadow of her former self he kissed "good morning" at breakfast every day. Morgan often wondered if his father regulated her thoughts as well.

It had happened on Morgan's twenty-first birthday, January 5, 1838, that final argument when he had spoken his well-rehearsed piece to his father. Years of stored up grievances had poured forth, first condemning, ultimately disavowing the rigidity of Glenn Arthur Heirs' invincible domination.

He had been ordered out.

Briars
The House of Heirs

Gratified, at last, by the self-satisfaction of having stood up to his father, Morgan packed a satchel, kissed his mother, and left home with four dollars in his pocket.

Taking a room in a shabby hotel on the lower side of town, Morgan breathed freely for the first time in his life. Three days later he found a job at the Richmond railroad yard and because he showed an aptitude for figures, he was placed in a position dealing with measurements, calculations and computations. But having much to learn about railroading, his first month was spent learning the fundamentals—hauling heavy rails, laying track, driving spikes—stretching lax muscles, aching.

The railroad paid Morgan Heirs his first truly fair wage. On Saturday, his first payday, he laid aside the portion he calculated would be required for his next week's expenses and, taking the rest, went straight to the nearest tavern where upon encountering several well-seasoned railroad men another first occurred and he got deliciously drunk to celebrate his newly claimed freedom.

That was also the momentous day that Morgan Heirs first heard talk about a place so remote that the Western and Atlantic Railroad ended there. It was a God forsaken place in the Georgia wilderness called Terminus. Far from Richmond and Glenn Arthur Heirs, it was as remote a refuge as Morgan could have imagined.

Early the following Monday morning when he stepped from the roundhouse with his notebook in hand, his mind awash with figures, an attractive young woman wrapped in a heavy cloak against the harsh Winter wind appeared without warning at his elbow, swinging a lunch bucket by her side.

Smiling above a tartan scarf, emerald eyes dancing, cheeks flushed from running, and with her loose red hair whipping in the wind, she greeted him. "Hello! I'm Lillian O'Donnell. Would you happen to know where my father, Michael O'Donnell might be found by any chance? He left in such a rush this morning, he walked right out the door without his lunch bucket!"

Morgan grinned, stunned by her winning smile and confident attitude. "Morgan Heirs, ma'am. Michael O'Donnell is my supervisor, and he's working a crew a mile's walk away down these tracks, which is exactly where I'm headed."

"And are you, sir, a man of 'airs' as your name implies?" she asked, her smile warming the bitter chill of the day.

"Not at all." Morgan executed a deep bow. "I am but your humble servant, ma'am, and I'd be pleased to take the bucket to him for you."

She laughed and her green eyes sparkled. "Now, that's very gentlemanly of you, Mister Heirs, and I thank you for offering. But I'll just walk along with you if you don't mind. It would be a shame for me to have come this far without my father's kiss as my reward."

She danced along beside him down the tracks, talking excitedly about all manner of things from the chilliness of the present Winter when compared to last year's to the senselessness of the latest in ladies' fashionable headgear, which she seldom bothered wearing anyway.

Unknowingly, the entertaining and beautiful Lillian O'Donnell, as she chattered on and on, was spinning Morgan Heirs into a silken cocoon of wonderment: How could it be that such an exquisite creature could possibly have evolved from the less than attractive personage of that scrappy Irishman called Michael Wilson O'Donnell, who stood ahead on the tracks, waving to them?

After that chance meeting, Morgan Heirs and Lillian O'Donnell became constant companions in his off hours and in little more than two months, with the final determination that he would, indeed, leave soon for Terminus, came the shocking realization that he shouldn't go—indeed, that he absolutely *couldn't go*—without the light-hearted, adorable Lillian O'Donnell by his side. Morgan Heirs proposed marriage and Lillian O'Donnell, unhesitatingly, said "yes" with her father's and mother's sincere, if concerned, blessings since the young couple was soon to leave for the wilderness. They were married by a Justice of the Peace on Wednesday, March 21, 1838.

Glenn Arthur Heirs, on hearing from his uneasy wife, of his daft son's hasty marriage had declared, "A marital union so soon established is doomed to failure from the start. Now that you see what your constant catering to the boy has accomplished, are you satisfied?"

Soon after, when Morgan saw his mother for the last time in their lavish brownstone home in the most desirable residential section of Richmond, it was to introduce the two women in his life, Constance Heirs, the consummate woman of breeding, and the spirited, nervous, and unpretentious Lillian O'Donnell Heirs, whose father worked for the Virginia Railroad as a supervisor of work crews.

Much that needed saying between Morgan and his mother was left unsaid in that meeting but it was evident to him at once that the women were in harmony.

"My dear Lillian," Constance Heirs said after they had talked for a while, "your beauty is surpassed only by your intelligence. My son is a very lucky man!" Before they parted, the gracious Constance Heirs had embraced her new daughter, eliciting a promise from her to write faithfully of their activities.

The Oak

Now ten years later, after reading the letter to Morgan, Lillian sat with it open in her hand watching his profile because he would not turn to face her.

"Lilly, the only two good things I recall from my past in Richmond were my mother's love and finding you. Do you realize what you're asking of me?"

"Yes," she replied softly. Then she put the question to him, gently, "When shall we leave? Hamita has agreed to take the older children, and I feel perfectly confident putting Morgana in

Rachel's charge. She cares for Morgana as lovingly as she does her own Willow." She sighed. "And the way we've been bickering lately, it would be good for us, too. We should get away from Atlanta for a little while." In the faint, flickering light of the porch's oil lamp, Lillian watched Morgan's lips form a thin line and his jaw tighten as the inner battle between conscience and obstinacy raged.

"There's really nothing to keep us from going, Morrey, and your mother needs you—now. Tell me how soon we can go and I'll write her tonight."

"I can't leave the business—!" Morgan countered. "Not right now. I'm engaged in some very delicate bargaining!" He stood and walked quickly to the banister, leaning against the white railing, looking up at the star-studded night sky, out on a shimmering sea of street lamps—looking everywhere, anywhere—except into Lillian's eyes. "I need to be here. I can't leave, right now. I just can't. Maybe in a week or two—! You wouldn't understand."

"I *do* understand," she said to his back. "I understand that your father is probably dying, and your mother needs you. A week or two may be too late, Morgan. And Morgan, you need to see your father—*now*. To repair your relationship *now*—before it's too late. Morgan, if nothing else, you must give *him* the opportunity to make amends." Lillian moved to stand beside him. "Please, Morrey, look at me. If you don't go—later, after—I'm afraid you'll never forgive yourself."

When Morgan turned to face her, dark shadows had carved deep circles beneath his hard, defiant eyes and plainly etched across his troubled countenance, haphazardly buried these past ten years, she saw soul-deep grievous pain and injured pride. Freshly unearthed and still un-dead, they haunted him along with unresolved anger, rivalry, and inborn love—long unacknowledged between father and son.

"Nothing could possibly be more important than being with your mother right now, could it?" She paused, then she said,

"Morrey, look around you. You can afford to lose a few dollars! We've much, much more than we'll ever need." Her voice, pleading, "You *can* leave your business for a fortnight, darling, it will survive. Glenn Arthur Heirs won't," she whispered, her eyes desperately seeking his. "Morgan, don't *become* your father."

Morgan reached out and caught her arms, roughly crushing her to him, embracing her with a dark and unfamiliar fury. "Don't say that! Don't *ever* say that again!" He kissed her, then — harshly. His grim lips hard on hers. But before the kiss was ended, anger's passion had exploded into fiery, urgent desire too long denied.

Suddenly caught up in abandoned responses, Lillian trembled and she cried out softly, excitement burning a path of desire through her, setting her body aflame. This desire, this passion, was the emotion that a young and vital Morgan Heirs had first awakened in her. This was the all consuming excitement that had been theirs when they first married. This insistence! This need! This sensuality, so long ignored, so well shrouded, on reawakening was overwhelming, breath-taking in impact.

Ignoring his nearby cane, Morgan swept Lillian off her feet and carried her down the broad front steps and across the lawn to the foot of the giant old oak tree where in the dark and silent night on a bed of grass they loved again.

Unconditionally, Morgan gave himself over to the demands of his body—stronger now than anger; stronger than pride; stronger, even, than the obscure and obligatory filial grief that tugged at his very marrow. Without moving his lips far from hers, Morgan said, "Tomorrow! I'll send a telegram tomorrow."

After so long a time, as Lillian lay spent in the arms of her lover, aware of the oak tree's softly whispered melody, she was convinced that trees do, in fact, read the hearts of those they shelter, and she cherished the great old oak tree all the more.

Ann Gray

CHAPTER FOUR ~ VIRGINIA HEIRS' HOUSE

11:45 a.m., October 2, 1848 ~ Richmond, Virginia

Reunion

Richmond was nothing at all like Lillian remembered it. Wide-eyed, as they rode through the heavily trafficked city streets, Lillian was glad that they had been met promptly at the railroad station by the Heirs' driver and whisked immediately into the open carriage for the ride to *Heirs House*. Shoppers dressed in latest fashions bustled along the crowded sidewalks past broad store windows crammed with goods for sale at outrageous prices. Considering the fact that they were wearing the very latest in couture Atlanta had to offer and it was so utterly out of style, Lillian concluded a shopping excursion would certainly be a must while they were there.

Looking at Morgan, uncomfortable after so long a trip in his starched collar, confining vest, and dress-coat, Lillian thought she sensed the anxiety he was feeling. After ten years away from his mother, to whom he had looked for all things good and encouraging and whom he had, no doubt, loved with disproportionate devotion, wouldn't he unquestionably find comfort in this return? Or, having gained ten years of maturity, marriage and children of his own, would their relationship have modified into one less substantial?

Also, would his father be only the shell of the overbearing man Morgan remembered so bitterly? The man he had clashed with repeatedly, and hated with such fury? What new insights and emotions would this meeting bring for them? Was there still hope for closure of the breach that separated father and son? Or would Glenn Heirs' lack of desire to communicate deny it?

Never having met the man, Lillian would have few preconceived ideas to shade her opinion of the man. To be fair she must attribute those unflattering remarks she had heard from Morgan to the complaints of a very young man in the throes of maturation, rebelling against authority. Still, she would have to guard against allowing the sympathy she expected she would soon be feeling for the poor dying man to shade her thinking.

"Darling," Lillian said suddenly, startling Morgan whose attention had been focused on the route their driver was taking, "sad though our mission is, you must admit to feeling some excitement coming back to Richmond after all these years." Squeezing his hand, she added, "Isn't it exhilarating? The fast pace, the modern look of everything."

Having had his concentration abruptly interrupted, Morgan picked a white fleck from his dark blue sleeve and frowned, obviously annoyed by the driver's dawdling. He was taking the long way round. Must it always be mandatory for visiting guests to *Heirs House*, hot and tired from their journeys, to take a drive through the entire affluent section of town?

"Presentation," he could still hear his father, the grocer, insisting, "is the most important part of selling any product as it should be—not only in our stores—but in our home, as well. Presentation, boy! We show our guests our best side, whether it be for a week's visit or for an evening meal."

Morgan used his cane to tap the driver's bench for attention. He spoke curtly. "Turn here, Carl, we'll forego the tour this time."

"Yessuh!" Following his blunt instructions, Carl swung the horses and carriage in a wide turn around the next corner and plowed his way back into the flow of traffic on the busy avenue.

Morgan sat erect, looking with intense disapproval at the passing scenery. So much had changed, and not for the better. Having swallowed up every former residential property they passed nearing the Heirs' estate, a business district had invaded the once serenely quiet community, peppering the broad avenue with two and three story buildings, all of them either whitewashed or displaying gaudily painted signs. A few blocks farther on they turned onto the familiar gravel driveway. *Heirs House*, the residence, stood alone in what had once been an area of expensive and handsome homes.

"Stop here," Morgan exclaimed to Carl once they had passed beyond the entrance to the rough drive which formed a half circle before the brownstone house and reentered the avenue several hundred feet farther on. Edged by unkempt juniper bushes, rutted and weed invaded, the sparsely graveled drive appeared to be seldom used and less often maintained. The once broad lawn and azalea gardens it bounded, overgrown and blighted, showed utter disregard. Even the front doors of the house flaked paint.

"What's happened here, Carl?" Morgan asked, kinder in tone, as he leaned forward in his seat. The white-haired old man deserved better. He'd been loyal to Morgan's father and mother through the years, when others of the household staff had defected and gone North seeking what they could never have found in Richmond—freedom to choose their own futures. Bad choices or good, nevertheless, their own.

"Don't reckon it hurt much, I tell you that, suh!" Carl said, turning on the driver's bench to face Morgan. "Miz Heirs, she just been trying t' hold things together long 'nough 'til you got back, suh! Mister Heirs' bus'ness bein' gone an' all, they be hard up. Not long fo' he be gone, too, I reckon."

"I see," Morgan said, sitting back. "Thank you, Carl. You may drive on, now." He turned searching eyes on Lillian. His hands, resting on his knees, formed white knuckled fists. "Did my mother ever tell you about this in any of her letters?"

"Never," Lillian said, reaching out to place a hand over his. "I'm so sorry. It must come as a terrible shock to you seeing things in such terrible circumstances. I'm as bewildered by all this as you are, truly I am."

Briars
The House of Heirs

Before the carriage stopped, the wide double doors suddenly were flung open and a frail white-haired woman swept through them and stood impatiently waiting at the top of the steps.

"My God, it can't be!" Morgan cried out. "Tell me it's not her, Lilly! It's not, is it?" He turned to Lillian as the carriage drew nearer, avoiding eye contact with the woman on the steps, putting off the inevitable. "Have I changed so much, too, Lilly? Tell me, now! Have I?"

"Of course, you've changed, Morrey. We've all changed. Nobody stays young forever." She watched the phenomenon of transformation as he quickly disguised his wretchedness, cloaking it in smiles and a warm and tender tone as he turned back to greet his mother.

"Mother," he shouted, bounding down from the carriage the moment it stopped. Two steps up to the stoop, and the fragile lady was in his arms, and he was whirling her round and round.

"Oh, Morgan, put me down," she cried, "my head is spinning." When her feet were once again planted firmly, she embraced him and stretched to kiss his cheek. "You have grown more handsome with the years, my dearest," she said. "More handsome, even than I imagined you to be." Then she reached out her hand to Lillian. "My dear Lillian, you have remained more beautiful than I remember you. How have you done it? I would think that my three grandchildren would have worn you into a state of sheer exhaustion, by now."

"They have," Lillian answered, smiling, "but you are kind not to notice."

"Well, now, let's not stand out here talking when I've a fine supper in the kitchen just waiting upon your arrival. She spoke to Carl who had been busily unloading luggage from the carriage. "Carl, just leave all the luggage in the hall outside Mister Morgan's door." She slipped her arms through both of theirs and walked them in through the wide double doors, leaving them open.

Once inside, joyousness dissolved.

The dreadful bellow echoed through the essentially empty hall, penetrating the warmth and lightness of the moment as the three stopped still, listening, until the howl gradually died away. The sounds of their arrival had reached Glenn Heirs' ears.

Constance whispered, "I've had your father brought down to the study. It will make it easier for him. I think he would have welcomed death before having you see him abed. I think it advisable that we give him a while to adjust to your being in the house before bursting in upon him. After supper will be soon enough. Following these ten years apart, a few more minutes won't add noticeably to his disagreeable mood, I'm sure."

She led the way into the parlor, a friendly room, her room. Heavy tapestries adorned the walls and well-worn, fading brocade sofas welcomed them. Gesturing to a couch as she sat in her dainty Duncan Phyfe arm chair, Constance smiled. "I know you're anxious to refresh yourselves and eat a bite, and I won't keep you but a moment." She sat taller in her chair. "First of all, since this is the only room in the house which I have kept respectable, I must explain so that you won't be dismayed by what you find beyond it. I have sold most of the furnishings to provide for us under the sad conditions that exist here.

"Secondly, I know that you are shocked by what I'm saying and are wondering why I have not informed you before now of our circumstances." Her gaze shifted for a moment to Lillian's face, then back to rest on Morgan's. "However, Morgan, considering both yours and your father's attitudes at the time of your departure, I knew that neither of you would find a face to face meeting tolerable. Therefore, until your father's condition deteriorated to its present stage where arrogance has finally been subjugated by utter helplessness—and that only within the last few months as I've written to Lillian of late—only since then, has he sickened to a point where I felt this meeting might possibly serve a useful purpose. I apologize for keeping you uninformed for so long, but it was as much for the preservation my own sanity as for anything else. As you heard upon your arrival, his displeasure concerning you remains with us. He had been told you were coming and reacted as I expected he would to your arrival.

"The business, I'm afraid, went quickly. Having no knowledge of such matters, I relied too heavily on our solicitors' advice. They advised me badly and although they, themselves, profited through fat commissions, our continuing operational losses were substantial enough to force my selling."

When Morgan attempted to speak she raised a hand and continued, "I know. I know. You think I should have called on you to return at the time. I've no doubt you could have saved your father's business but to what end? You hated it all your young life. You have built your own business and have your own interests, elsewhere. And I must admit, I was rather exhilarated by the sudden impact of possessing such power.

"However, I am still in authority here, and the decisions that have been made, rightly or wrongly, have been my decisions." Her eyes softened. "There, now, I feel much better." For a stunned moment, she questioned Morgan's reaction to her words for he was laughing softly.

"Well, our little caged bird has found her wings at last," Morgan grinned broadly at his mother. "I am proud of you for what you've done! He reached across and took her hands in his. "It can't have been easy, Mother, all this time. But your choices in this matter have given you back what nobody else could— your ability to cope and, I believe, your self-respect."

Smoothing the fullness of her skirts, Constance blinked back tears as she stood and changed the subject. "I'm so pleased to see you both looking so well. Later, you'll tell me all about my grandchildren, won't you?" Without waiting for an answer she added, "As I've said, supper will be waiting in the dining room by the time you're ready for it. Come, now, I'll show you to your rooms."

Morgan stood and helped Lillian to her feet, his eyes meeting hers. "One room will be sufficient, Mother," he said. Lillian felt her cheeks color at his words.

"Oh?" Constance said, lifting an eyebrow and smiling mischievously at Lillian. "How pleasing to learn that after ten years in a marriage 'doomed to failure' as described by my husband, our son and his wife's conjugality still endures."

Lillian tucked her chin in embarrassment and shared a sly grin with Morgan as they fell in step and followed Constance up the stairs.

Though he should probably feel guilty for it under the circumstances, Morgan's long buried youthful disposition was enjoying rejuvenation by his mother's very presence. She had rediscovered herself, virtually come back to life in a decaying house, and under the reproachful eye of a dying tyrannical patriarch. Even if there wasn't another stick of furniture in the entire house and they sat upon the floor to devour their supper, nothing could take away from Constance Heirs' triumph.

Glenn Arthur Heirs

After supper, leaving the ladies in the parlor, absorbed in conversation about the grandchildren, Morgan faced the inevitability of the purpose of their trip and slipped away, walking down the dimly lit hallway to his father's study.

The door stood ajar against a roomful of dark shadows. One small pool of lamplight defined a tabletop, the curved wheel of a narrow-armed wooden wheelchair, and part of a red and black plaid lap robe that appeared to tailor itself to an insubstantial and shadowy form seated in the wheelchair.

As he tapped on the door he experienced the all too familiar sensitivity he had always endured on approaching his father, the same quickening heartbeat, the same leaden weight in the pit of his stomach. "Sir?" came, unbidden. Even after ten long years away, utterance of the forbidden word "Father" would not come. It was as it had always been. "Sir, I've come back for a visit. May I come in?"

"No." The barely audible voice, once so ominous, quavered. A bony, wrinkled hand trembled as it moved from the chair's arm rest into the circle of lamplight and took hold of the lap robe upon one knee, clasping it tightly.

Pretending a cheerfulness he did not feel, Morgan sidestepped the rebuff. "Sir, I've brought my wife. You would like to meet the mother of your grandchildren, wouldn't you?" He entered the room slowly, allowing his eyes to become adjusted to the darkness. Moving to within arm's length of the table and wheel chair, he waited in the shadows outside the circle of light for an overlong minute, while hateful eyes examined him.

"No, no! Go away!" the voice bellowed loudly—unnecessarily. "No, I said! Damn you, have you grown deaf as well as overly bold and impertinent in these past ten years? I said, 'go away!' and I meant it! I want no part of you! Nor of the woman you call your wife! I have no grandchildren—none! Do you hear that! Go, now, go away!"

"Now, look here, *Father*, rant at me as you will, but I will not stand here and listen to your raging against my family. *Do you hear me?*" The fury that arose in Morgan was so strong, so demanding, he reached out and turned the lamp up bright. The shocking sight of his father's condition caused him to lower his voice and continue, "Whatever you may think of me, you don't know them—any of them!" Morgan placed his hands on both arms of the wheel chair and leaned down to face the ill, shriveled, and boisterous old man, eye to eye. "Do you know what I see? I see a sick, bitter old man, ranting and raving, and using his illness to hold others in his power. But, Father, whether you like it or not, you no longer hold power over me! I've made my own way. I've gained success. I have money and power of my own and I accomplished it with the loyalty, encouragement and compassion I received —first from my mother, and then from my wife and family. Also, I might add, with the mental prowess I inherited from you, Father. With or without your love and understanding, you contributed to who I am, and I am proud to be the man standing before you." Looking deep into the intense eyes, Morgan watched a tear form and run down the hollow cheek.

The skinny hand released the knot of plaid wool and attempted to reach up to wipe away the tear, but the jerking motion stopped short and the hand fell back, useless, into the narrow lap. "Every coin has two sides," the old man said, and the tear rolled down to his chin and formed a droplet, hanging there.

Morgan felt some wicked satisfaction in watching the escaped tear roll uninterrupted the full course of the furrowed countenance, but he withdrew his handkerchief and gently dabbed at the old man's chin. It was the first tear he had ever known his father to shed a tear.

"Never believe that I didn't feel affection for you!" The rheumy eyes filled again. "But for *her* smothering love for you, I could have shown more affection. *Somebody* had to uphold authority. *Somebody* had to teach you duties and labors necessary to earn a livelihood. *Somebody* had to bear the brunt of your youthful aggression. I taught the way I was taught. Maybe, it wasn't the best way, but it was the only way I knew." The rejection in Morgan's eyes prompted him to add, "I might well have given my blessing on your wedding, too, if you'd waited to tell me but, no, you chose to steal into my house in my absence with the woman, to kiss your mother 'good-bye', and to steal out again like thieves in the night!" The old man, blinking back more tears, whispered, "Hell, I'm no good at this! Even now, I flinch—" He looked away towards the open door. "I'm embarrassed speaking to you of such things. I've said far more than I'd intended. It's too late, now, to mend our ways. Too late for both of us, I see that in you."

Briars
The House of Heirs

"No, Father, what you see in me now is —is amazement! Shock, even—if you prefer—that we're actually speaking to one another, here and now, like two human beings. You always made me feel so worthless, so undeserving! I tried to please you all my young life and all I ever got from you was impatience, excessive discipline, and unabashed contempt."

"Impatience, yes, I confess to that. Discipline, yes. Discipline is the backbone of learning. Without discipline, without direction, no amount of instruction would have stuck in your excitable, exploring mind." He shook his head. "But contempt, *no!* Never contempt! Contempt I saved for the lawyers and worthless advisors your mother hired after my illness commenced." Heavy frown lines on the old man's brow folded tighter. "Tell me, Morgan, would you willingly turn your business over to your wife?"

"Certainly not," Morgan sneered, pulling up a chair close to his father's knees so that the two men faced each other. "She knows nothing about my business. I've shielded her purposely from the complexities of such enterprise—" He watched a crooked smile creep slowly across his father's face lightening, to some degree, the aspect of it.

"Your mother refused my council; even refused to send for you until it was too late. You see the results. We are destroyed." His fingers suddenly began plucking at the lap robe and his breath came forth in whistling gasps.

Morgan got to his feet. "I'll get Mother."

"Wait—!" Glenn Heirs hissed.

Morgan waited, as he was bidden. His hand clasped his father's claw-like fingers plucking away at the plaid design, stilling them. "Here! What do you think you're doing?" he asked. "You're not going to die on me now, are you? I've only just found you!" He talked faster and louder to counter the wheezing sounds emanating from the ill man. "You've yet to meet my Lillian. You'll love her, Father, I know you will. She's beautiful. She's witty. She's practical, but smart, too. Our children are all small wonders within themselves. Drew is nine, now. He favors you. Sweet Sarah is four, and a fair skinned beauty like her mother except her hair is blonde not red, and she has beautiful blue eyes. Mother has told you, hasn't she, that my Lillian has green, green eyes and fiery red hair? And the temper to go with it, I can tell you! Our baby, Morgana—my namesake—is barely fourteen months old."

"Too excited," his father sighed, finally. "I hate it, but it happens." Exhausted, he leaned his head back against his cushioned chair. "Well, go and bring your woman to me before it's too late! By now, your carping mother has probably worn away your beautiful Lillian's ears with her bellyaching."

At last, Morgan had penetrated the facade, and recognized himself in his father. Despite the old man's terminal infirmities, he understood the deep sensitivity disguised by a flaring temper. He read the whimsical humor; identified with the stern manner of expression used by the frail man, unquestionably his sire and his mentor. Mirrored in his father's sorrowful eyes, he had defined the long lost contest between the once arrogant and ambitious young businessman and the sheltered, lonely and possessive woman. The prize—their only son—the boy called Morgan. Gone, dissolved overnight, in reciprocal candor, the underlying tensions generated by a lifetime of latent rivalry between father and son for the affections of the woman who stood, knowingly, between them. Under his mother's discreetly calculated influence he had not perceived the truth—heads, she won—tails, his father lost.

Later, Morgan had explained the revelation to Lillian in great detail so baffled was he by this sudden discovery.

Atlanta Bound

Lillian breathed a sigh of relief. The activity and excitement of four weeks in Richmond had ended and she and Morgan were actually, finally, on a train bound for Atlanta. Thinking back on their time there, much had been accomplished! So very, *very much!* She smiled across the compartment at her sleeping husband, slouched on the opposite seat, his head propped against the window, rolling with the motion of the train. The graying at his temples, she determined, only added to his startling good looks. At last his tormented spirit rested at ease. How long, she wondered, had it been since he had relaxed so completely?

Beyond the windows, the bleak Winter terrain rushed by as the transport wound its way through desolate back country, reminding Lillian of the dreary wooded cemetery where Morgan's father had been laid to rest with only the grave diggers, a hired preacher, three family members, and Carl, the Heirs' loyal driver, in attendance. They had laid a single wreath of white chrysanthemums on his grave.

When they returned to *Heirs House* after the burial, not unexpectedly, Carl had been given a small bonus out of Morgan's own pocket, and an admirable letter of recommendation, written the day before in Constance's small precise hand. Head bowed, Carl solemnly walked away to freedom with his meager bundle of belongings never once looking back. Watching until he was out of sight, Constance Heirs stood up to his departure resolutely calm and tearless hoping he would be better off.

Lillian had purchased a Richmond newspaper and would carry it home to Atlanta. There had been no detailed newspaper account of the rise and fall of the man responsible for numerous, now defunct, grocery stores called *The Grocery*, which once had peppered the states of Maryland and Virginia. Morgan had authorized only a short obituary notice: *"Glenn Arthur Heirs, born October 2, 1794, in Richmond, died Sunday, October 29, 1848 after a long illness. Mr. Heirs leaves his wife, the former Constance Marie Courtland, also of Richmond; a son, Morgan Andrew, of Atlanta, Georgia, and three grandchildren."*

Ann Gray

Following the funeral, the week long visit with her own parents had gone smoothly enough, though Lillian was astonished at how very little outside of the children they had to talk about. Lillian soon tired of reminiscences and Morgan, restless to finish family business and get home, declared five days into their visit, and truthfully so, that they were needed back at *Heirs House*. They returned to see the Widow Heirs comfortably settled in residence with her sister, Winifred, before leaving Richmond.

The sale of the house had been immediate. Prospective buyers of the valuable property were practically nesting like vultures on the *Heirs House* doorstep the morning after the funeral announcement was published. Soon enough, the avenue would have yet another whitewashed store front and the last vestige of the Heirs family of Richmond would have been swallowed up by progress.

Lillian and Morgan, under her unyielding persuasion, had spent the entirety of the last two days shopping. They had made all their purchases in Richmond's newest, most modern emporium on the avenue. Lillian could never have imagined in her wildest fantasies anything like it, much less thought to experience such a multitude of choices in merchandise at any one location. She had selected the very newest designs in apparel for herself and a fidgeting Morgan; the most durable of clothing and toys for the children; several pieces of exquisite personal finery for Hamita, who had adamantly insisted on absolutely nothing; a Swiss pocket watch for Jeremiah; various other souvenirs, trinkets and gifts galore for everyone else, all wrapped and packed neatly into her own new cedar lined steamer trunk with hammered copper corners, lock and trim.

Before long she would be greeting her brood. She smiled at the thought. She had not honestly expected to miss her children. In truth, she had been happy over the prospects of a respite from all the quarreling, the whining, the nose blowing, and the noise. But she *had* missed them, terribly. Far more than she had expected to—especially when the busy days wound down into quiet nights and there were no prayers to hear nor sweet wet goodnight kisses.

Sweet, wet goodnight kisses! Thoughts of the children brought to mind an uneasiness Lillian had tried to ignore for the past week. Morgan would not be pleased when she told him what she feared their own sweet, wet kisses had accomplished!

Morgan's chin bobbed onto his chest, startling him into wakefulness! Lifting his head, he opened his eyes long enough to deliver a sleepy wink as he repositioned himself against the seat, drifting off again into easy slumber.

Lillian smiled, savoring delicious memories of recent nights in Richmond too intimate to be shared with Hamita. Moreover, she'd never again look upon the beloved old oak tree on *Briars'* front lawn without reliving the joy and bewilderment of that wondrous night of rediscovery. Morgan's release of passion had rekindled flames in her long since banked and, in so doing, he had lit a bonfire of eager anticipation and responses. She wasn't ready to relinquish the recaptured intimacy of these past few weeks to Morgan's business ambitions.

Soon, they'd be home. Wouldn't it be wonderful if he would set aside the enterprising, precise and uncompromising man who was his other self? Why should it be that his more pleasant nature must give way to the all-consuming pursuits of the very political world of business? Why was it so very imperative that every month's ledger sheet must show an increase in profits for Morgan to display that wide happy smile of his? When he was wholly occupied with his business dealings, he seemed to find gratification enough in a well turned "deal" to offset their personal lack of intimacy, and she believed that was taking business matters much too far.

Perhaps, she was more passionate than was comely. Nevertheless, she would wait a while before mentioning her present situation to Morgan. Besides, when she got back to

Briars and her regular routine, the problem would probably right itself. Why worry him until she was absolutely sure?

As the rhythmic clickity-clack of the rails soothed her, too, into drowsiness, Lillian pondered the capriciousness of human nature, which allowed momentary appetites and fleeting attitudes to set the courses of entire lives and future responsibilities.

CHAPTER FIVE ~ APPETITES AND ATTITUDES

10:00 a.m., Friday, July 27, 1849 ~ Briars, Atlanta, Georgia

A Room of Her Own

The hot and humid days of July had set the children to squabbling among themselves trying adult patience and setting everyone's tempers on edge.

"Miz Lillian," Rachel howled, as she stomped down the back hallway to the kitchen, "you jus' gots t' do somethin' 'bout that child, Morgana! She be up there totin' clothes all th' way down th' hall, spillin' 'em all over."

"Um-hum! In a minute, Rachel." Lillian, immersed up to her elbows in a small round tub of water, lifted a dripping lace trimmed batiste christening gown for Rachel to inspect. "Can you still see the yellow cast, Rachel? Is it going to do? Or am I going to have to bleach it again? I'm not at all sure it'll stand bleaching again. It's done for the first three and I really want to use it again, but I don't want it to look —you know —used."

"You ain't heard a word I's said, is you?" Rachel took the garment in her hands and rubbed the delicate lace between her wrists, then held it out to look at it from a different point of view. "It look fine 't' me!" she said, gently squeezing the water from the garment and wrapping it in a towel as she talked. "Now, you goin' come see what I's talkin' 'bout?"

Lillian dried her hands on the rolled-up towel and started for the back stairs. "Tell me again, Rachel. Morgana's doing what?"

"She be draggin' clothes out'n your dresser drawers an' totin' 'em all th' way down th' hall t' that room y'all fixed up 'fore she 'as borned." Rachel grabbed her skirts and followed Lillian up the back stairs.

"I was going to move her into it when the baby came," Lillian puffed as she climbed, "but that's at least a week or two away. I've been a little worried about sending her off to that room all by herself so far down the hall from me, anyway. I thought that we could call it a birthday present. It wouldn't be fair to the other children to move them around after all this time," Lillian wheezed, as they hurried along the back hallway. "How do you suppose she got it into her head to do it now, and all by herself?"

"It 'as prob'ly Drew put that idea there, Miz Lillian. He be gettin' t' that age, now! I wouldn't be surprised he tol' her it be th' new baby's fault she soon goin' be sent out'n yo' room!" Rachel shook her bandanna wrapped head. "If'n it ain't one problem wit' that boy, lately, it be 'nother."

"Oh? I know Drew is getting difficult, Rachel, but I don't think he would say anything to Morgana that would cause her to do something like this." Lillian turned the corner where the two passages joined and stopped still. "Well, I do declare!" They had arrived just in time to see Morgana, her arms overloaded, dragging clothing along the floor, and toddling past Sarah's bedroom door towards the last, unoccupied bedroom on the West side of the upper floor.

Lillian rushed the short distance to her daughter, hands out. "Here, darling, let Mama help. That's a lot for such a little girl to carry."

Morgana dropped the armload of miniature pantaloons and petticoats into Lillian's open arms, her perfect face pleading, "Nobody else is using it, Mama, please!" And seeing Lillian's soft expression, she added, "All right! You carry these, Mama, 'Gana will get Mary, Annie, and Teddy." She turned her black eyes up to Rachel's tawny ones. "Rachel, you didn't need to go get Mama, 'Gana could do it by herself!" She turned on her heel and marched back to the front of the house and into the bedroom she'd shared with Lillian since the day she was born.

Watching her go, Lillian carried the batch of clothing through the open doorway and deposited it onto the canopied bed's bluebell patterned coverlet along with Morgana's other assorted belongings. "You'd better call Henry to come up later and move the rest of Morgana's playthings in here. You know, sometimes I wonder if I'm really suited for motherhood, Rachel." When Morgana had disappeared through the far doorway, Lillian said, "Well, now, Rachel, suppose you tell me why you think Drew may be at fault."

Together they began folding and layering clothing into the drawers of the empty dresser.

"I loves that boy, Miz Lillian, an' you knows that be so but, sometimes, I senses a mean streak in him. There be somethin' else, too. Sunday school ain't doin' him a lot o' good. I means, Drew need his papa 'round sometimes to show him right from wrong —an' talk t' him 'bout women."

"About women? Rachel, what in the world do you mean—?"

"Well, him and Jonathan, they been sneakin' 'round down behind th' barn, lately, wit' that Johnson boy, Milton, smokin' rabbit tobacco from th' West field. Henry, he been tryin' t' keep a eye on 'em t' see they don't get in no real trouble, but if'n they's out runnin' all day long wit' that no good Johnson boy ain't no tellin' what kinda mischief they's gettin' into."

"My goodness, Drew seems perfectly normal to me."

"'Course, he do! He ain't no dummy, that boy! If'n he can charm th' bloomers off that Farley girl —an' her bein' thirteen, he can keep us, all, guessin'!"

"He didn't!" Lillian's eyes grew wide with amazement. "Stella?"

"Um-hum! Henry heard it from Thomas, who heard it from th' Farley's groom, Linus. Them chil'ren 'as up in Farley's hayloft when her bloomers come flying down and land right on

Linus' head. Linus say he hangs 'em up on a nail an' leaves. When he comes back twenty minutes later, they be gone an' Drew's hand'chief— one of them wit' M.A.H. like you embroiders on one corner— it 'as on that nail. Linus give th' hand'chief t' Thomas and Thomas, he give it back t' Henry, and I done washed and ironed it and put it away." Rachel, hands on hips, eyed her mistress. "You don't look too surprised, Miz Lillian. You looks somethin' more like *proud!*"

Lillian bit her lip to halt the smile creeping across her face. "Of course, I'm shocked, Rachel! The boy's only ten! He's maturing very fast, though, wouldn't you say? It's also pretty obvious he wanted it known he'd been the one up there with Stella. I'd think he'd want to keep something like that to himself, wouldn't you?" She laid the last of the folded petticoats into the drawer and shoved it closed. "I'll certainly see that Mister Morgan gets this news tonight."

Later in the afternoon, when Henry had finished his task according to Lillian's instructions, Lillian and Rachel stood looking into the newly occupied bedroom at Morgana. Lillian smiled—a somewhat sad smile. "My goodness, just think of the space and privacy I'm going to have, now. Though I wasn't quite prepared for this move right now, it seems to have been made according to Morgana's agenda rather than my own. We all have to adjust to changes, Rachel!"

"Yes'm!" Rachel said. "Yes'm, we sho' does! Another room t' keep clean is what I sees in it fo' me!"

Wil

Seeking even the slightest breeze, Lillian and Morgan retired to the verandah after an early, cold supper. It was the first time Lillian had been really comfortable all day, and much as she hated to pass on unpleasant or disturbing news to Morgan, he needed to know of the day's events.

Rockers side by side, she looked across at her husband behind his newspaper and summarized the day including Morgana's move and the discussion with Rachel concerning Drew's reportedly shameful behavior. When Morgan made no comment on her news, she finally admonished him. "At least, tell me you will speak to Drew, Morrey."

"For what?" He crumpled the pages into his lap. "For what, for goodness sake? For being a boy? Really, Lilly, I think you're making too much of the entire episode. Everybody knows the Farley girl's reputation. Boys always learn about women by experimenting with the local harlot. I did."

She stopped rocking to look at him. "Morrey, I don't think you should call Stella Farley a 'harlot'. Her mother is very active in charity work within my ladies' church circle."

She rocked back and forth. "Don't harlots do it for money?"

Morgan shook out his crumpled newspaper and prepared to resume reading.

Lillian stopped rocking. "Good Heavens! Drew wouldn't spend his allowance on *that* at his tender age, would he?"

"Lilly, please, this appears to me to have been simply a case of adolescent curiosity. Quite frankly, I'd forget it. I think drawing attention to it by discussion would embarrass Drew, acutely." Morgan went back to reading.

"Very well, dear, if you really believe that's the way to handle it." After a moment, Lillian said, thoughtfully. "Dear, *who* was the 'harlot' you learned from? Was it someone I knew?"

From behind open pages, Morgan answered, "Certainly not. It was long before we met."

"Was she pretty?"

"Very."

"Prettier than me?"

"Much!"

"Oh, Morrey!"

Lillian snatched at the newspaper just as Morgan lowered the pages, laughing. "I might add she was *very* talented. I learned a lot from her."

"Oh, I can attest to that," Lillian said, stroking her ample belly, "I can *certainly* attest to that!" She reached for the arms of her rocker and pushed against them to stand erect. "You may have to help me tonight, Morrey, I don't think I'll be able to manage those stairs alone. I'm a bit frazzled, too, what with the day's activities, the heat, and all."

Morgan dropped his newspaper and sprang up. Laying aside his cane, he clasped his arm around her broadened waist. "Lilly, you're all right, aren't you? Shall I call Hamita? Or Rachel?"

"No, no, I'm sure I'll be fine. Just help me up to my room, please, dear."

The stairs had been challenge enough, but by the time they reached Lillian's bedroom, birth pangs came upon her suddenly, and she began sweating profusely.

Morgan carried her to her bed.

"I'll get somebody," he said, turning to leave the room.

"No! That flannel blanket on top of my cedar chest, hurry, fold it four times and force it under my hips!" When that was done, she grasped his arm with both hands, pulling him down beside her.

"Oh, Morrey, dear, I'm sorry to do this to you," she panted, "but I'm afraid you're going to have to help me through this birth. After all, three have already led the way, so this one will come quickly enough!"

"I can't do this! I'm going for Rachel, Lilly," Morgan said, paling, as he stumbled to his feet, his voice shaking, but Lillian's impulsive oath brought him back.

"*Damn you*, Morgan Heirs, don't you dare leave me, now! Four times, you've planted a child in here." She guided his hands to her round belly. "Now, the least you can do is to help me get one of them out!" Straining to expel the lump, as her hips rose and fell with each contraction, she continued softly, her words following in rhythm. "I'm sorry! I sound like a fishwife!" She panted. "*Morrey* —I think it's coming —it's coming —*now!*"

Morgan caught the slippery child in his strong hands.

All flailing arms and legs, the baby wailed loudly at such an abrupt eviction.

"Ha, ha! I *did* do it! It's here, Lilly! Look! It's here." Morrey held the baby up for Lillian to see. "It's a boy, Lilly, a little old redheaded man! He looks just like your papa. I swear he does, Lilly, just like Michael Wilson O'Donnell."

The pride in Morgan's voice so delighted Lillian, she laughed. "Here, now, don't go thinking they've all been this easy." She tucked the squalling child into her petticoat and laid him against her breast. "There, there, baby, Mama and Papa are here!"

She felt Morgan's adoring eyes on her and when he sat beside her and leaned down to kiss her, she reached to caress his cheek.

"My God, Lilly," he whispered, tears shimmering in his eyes. "I've just been part of a miracle, and I'm still shaking from it. Lilly, I do love you *so!* It's easy to say, I know, and I don't show it most of the time but I do, Lilly, *I really do.*"

"I know, darling, I know, but don't be talking to me like this, now, or you'll have me bawling." She pulled away the cover to inspect the squirming bundle on her bosom. "Oh, Morrey, see how long he is."

"Twenty-five inches, at least! Eight pounds—nine, maybe!" Morgan smiled. "This one's mine to name, Lilly, and Michael Wilson Heirs, it is!"

"My father will be pleased to know our second son's been named for him. Just look at that! My red hair, and my father's. Poor child, he'll hate it. I always did." But she could see that Morgan wasn't listening, so intent was he in thought as his finger traced a contour of the tiny face. "Actually, dear—," Lillian added, "*now* would be a good time to get Rachel. There are still a few details to be taken care of."

"Wil." Morgan said, out of nowhere. "We're going to call him 'Wil'."

Then he went to call Rachel.

Growing Up

Season after season, Lillian's hawthorn hedges grew stronger and more luxuriant, putting down deeper roots, encircling her personal sanctuary. According to her faith, Lillian had planted the unbroken line of hedges believing that all they encompassed would be protected by God. Earnestly believing God's blessing was truly bestowed on *Briars'* prickly hedges, over the years Lillian had come to measure time and the growth of her family in the strength of her hedges.

But when Morgan expressed his determination to expand *Briars'* grounds, a worried Lillian consulted Reverend Wiley who read to her from Collossians 3:18 in his Bible: "Wives, submit to your husbands, as is fitting in the Lord." And, accepting Reverend Wiley's theological qualifications, Lillian laid aside her fear of having disobeyed God by allowing *Briars'* surrounding hedges to be divided. As proof, knowing that her husband, over time, had ordered the hedges interrupted in several places, she had seen that *Briars* continued to thrive.

Drew, moderately handsome at twenty-one, properly schooled and educated in all facets of conduct and citizenship, having reached a dubious state of adulthood, Lillian left to the sterner authority of his father. He had shown no interest in following his father into business and he had ignored suggestions as to ways he might get started in a business of his own choosing. Rather, having expressed no interests, no inclinations towards any worthy occupation of his time, he lolled around town night and day, gambling, wenching, and spinning yarns with wastrels for companions. Tales of his indiscretions were constantly reaching Lillian's ears through social contacts, but she chose to ignore them, openly branding them 'idle gossip', while her intuition gave credence to the disheartening scandals.

Sarah, petite and blonde, would be sixteen in November. She was onto Lillian constantly about making plans for her debut into society though she still had eight months to go. Her childhood affection for Jonathan Baker, the boy next door, happily, was returned and as soon as she had 'come out' their engagement was to be announced, their pairing having been nurtured by both families. Deeply absorbed in her religious teachings, Sarah kept her Bible handy and was forever reciting chapter and verse to define the faults of less temperate mortals, which, according to her sister, Morgana, included just about everybody on Earth.

Raven haired Morgana, who would be thirteen in August, sassy, and already half a head taller than Sarah, had formed a probationary alliance with her brother, Wil, two years her junior, sharing with him a love of animals and associated outdoor activities just so long as she could be in charge. Rachel's Willow, more companion to Morgana than servant, shared Morgana's birth date and her schooling classes, and found a niche in all Morgana's schemes. Though such an arrangement, doubtless, appeared strange to outside observers, it seemed perfectly logical to Lillian. When regular study became required of Morgana at age six, Lillian decided to school Willow, too, to quell Morgana's jealousy of Willow's continuing freedom. They formed a mutual regard for each other more solid than Morgana's for her sister, Sarah.

Wil, the lanky red-haired child nearing eleven, thoughtful and eager to please, was already being molded into the gentleman his brother would never become. His aptitude for figures put him in good standing with his father, who had already begun teaching him the 'ins and outs' of money management. When he was only ten, he started doing afternoon chores after school at his father's office for pay and saved enough to purchase the horse of his choice, a Tennessee Walker he called "Pal".

Morgan saw Lillian's hedge as a living shield, shutting out the view of the vacant weedy field to the West, which he insisted on holding in its present condition as a buffer zone between *Briars* and their neighbors the Farleys, Stewart and Margaret, and their disreputable daughter, Stella. Morgan not only found the Farleys socially unacceptable but, in addition, Stewart Farley's politics were disgustingly inappropriate for a Southern gentleman, favoring the deportation of all Negroes back to Africa.

He held the Farley's occupancy of the land next door partly responsible for Drew's unacceptable behavior. Morgan saw Drew as a handsome, preening and egotistical fellow, who was not one to hold his amorous adventures confidential, proclaiming that he had found his manhood with Stella Farley during one of his many early escapades in the loft of Farley's barn. To Morgan's private embarrassment, as evidence of his sexual prowess, Drew had taken to leaving his monogrammed handkerchiefs at prestigious addresses throughout the general area.

It was not at all unusual for servants from other well-known families to come knocking at Rachel's' kitchen door delivering handkerchiefs belonging to the younger Mister Heirs. Rachel had no doubt there had been many others *never* returned! She had sent word to Mister Morgan by Henry innumerable times that another grievance had occurred. Grievances that would break his mother's heart, "if'n she knew".

Drew's promiscuous activities had finally come to an end when Morgan had actually encountered his eldest son on a Saturday night in the *Spike and Rail*, drunk and disheveled, boisterously proclaiming his most recent impropriety with Stella Farley, whom he unabashedly named as his all-time favorite whore. Immediately after that worrisome event, a private meeting had been called between father and son in the library at *Briars* in which Morgan informed Drew that nothing short of a forthcoming announcement of his betrothal to the daughter —any daughter—of an upstanding Southern family—any upstanding Southern family—would insure his anticipated birthright at Morgan Heir's demise. As a matter of fact, Morgan mentioned the names of several business friends' daughters on the spot.

So it had been that on Saturday, March 3, 1860, eight months before Sarah's participation in her own debutante ball, *Briars* was the site of a most extravagant gathering for the wedding and reception of Morgan Andrew Heirs, II, to Miss Laura Lee Hill, only daughter of a prominent Atlanta family, her father being a well-known real estate attorney and business cohort of the senior Morgan Andrew Heirs.

"Well, they're gone—!" Morgana said to Sarah, as they stood looking out the open dining room doors onto the West verandah while the reception wound down. "They'll be enjoying Savannah soon! Wasn't Laura Lee positively the prettiest bride you ever saw?"

"Well, of course, she was," Sarah agreed. "All brides are beautiful. But why Drew and Laura Lee would choose to honeymoon in Savannah I simply can't imagine. Savannah's so mundane. I shall choose some place big and exciting like Richmond or New Orleans when Jonny and I marry. Besides, they'll be at the seashore! Can you imagine actually walking out into that huge ocean every day? I've heard it's tides can be extremely dangerous, even to carrying one away!"

"You're scared of horses! You're scared of dogs! Now, the ocean? God, Sarah!" Morgana replied, rolling her eyes, "—you're scared of everything!"

"There! You did it again. That's the third time today you've taken the Lord's name in vain. Don't you learn anything from our Bible studies?" Sarah demanded.

Morgana spun on her heel, donned her pained expression and looked skyward beyond Sarah, beyond the overhanging verandah roof, even beyond the fleecy clouds in the perfect March afternoon sky, and directed her words into the ether. "I'm sorry, God!" she shouted, turning heads. Then she smiled at Sarah, who turned up her pretty nose and went to join their mother.

Morgana estimated by how many people still lingered, the time she would have to remain in her good clothes including her newly required and patently resented confining corselet. Little knots of finely clad ladies and gentlemen, reticent to leave, still congregated on the verandah, spilling over into the garden and onto the rolling lawn. Earlier, fancy carriages had lined the street as far as one could see, but now that the bride and groom had departed they were being brought up quickly by Henry, Grady and Thomas, and the guests were disappearing inside them to join in the slow parade down the hill towards town.

Morgana advanced on Rachel, busy clearing the long dining table. She hugged the plump woman around her ample waist. "Rachel, you are the very best cook in the whole of Georgia. Your white cake is positively lighter than those pretty white clouds floating by out there, and your fluffy white icing is delectable. I shan't be able to move soon if you keep forcing such delicacies on me."

"Now, you done had all th' cake you goin' get, Miss Morgana! So jus' you quit hoverin' over them remains. They's fo' Miss Sarah t' put under her pillow tonight."

"Sarah doesn't need such a big piece of cake to dream of Jonny Baker, Rachel! She does that all the time anyway. She told me so!" God! Hadn't she, too, always loved Jonny, *really* loved Jonny Baker? But Sarah, almost three years her senior, had forever had him groveling at her feet. Morgana suspected that after Sarah and Jonny were married, if she still survived, hers would be a sad and lonely spinster's life. But suffering, after all, was the nobler part of sacrificial love. She ran a finger along the plate at the bottom of the remaining chunk of cake leaving a small vacant groove and licked the finger clean.

"Where's Willow? I'll bet you didn't save her any, did you? Here, I'll cut this piece in half and take her some. That will still leave plenty for Sarah to mash into mush tonight." Morgana sliced the chunk of cake into equal portions and placed one half onto a napkin.

"Willow be in th' kitchen. Tha's where she be! Washin' up all them dirty dishes, an' don't you go in there gettin' her mind off'n what she's about, neither."

Morgana found Willow singing a gospel hymn softly to herself in her pleasing soprano voice as she washed and piled dishes upon dishes on the drain-board. "Look what I've brought us," Morgana said, holding out the cake and napkin. "Here, I'll slice it." She picked up a clean knife to cut the cake into halves while Willow looked on, her mouth fairly watering at the sight of it. But when Morgana saw Willow's anticipation, she put aside her former selfish plan and said, "My goodness, I am positively so full I could not eat another bite! Here, you have it all."

"Are you sure?" Willow asked, her eyes on the cake.

"Of course," Morgana assured her, fibbing, as she pushed the cake and napkin into Willow's eager, open hands. "I have to watch my figure from now on, anyway. In no time at all, I'll be coming out, and I must be slim if I'm to catch a handsome husband."

Morgana watched as Willow devoured the lighter than clouds white wedding cake with the delectable fluffy white icing.

Twins

It was nearly nine months later, Thursday, the twentieth of December, 1860, and in Rachel's eyes, everybody was in a "tizzy". Either they were too busy with their own activities to bother listening to her complaints or being just plain hard to get along with. What with the additional work of having Drew and Laura Lee and their new twin babies in the house, and with the Christmas holidays right around the corner, Rachel was already at the end of her patience, and now there was the additional nerve-shattering noise of more construction going on upstairs as Mister Morgan hurried to finish the twins' new nursery over the servant's bedroom in time for Christmas.

Although the two women were standing not three feet apart in the kitchen, Rachel shouted over the hammering, "Miz Lillian, I's tryin' t' hear what you is sayin' but that hammerin' is goin' right through my head!"

"Of course, it is, Rachel! It's going through mine, too. But we just have to bear with it for a little while longer and it'll be all done." The noise ceased for the moment, and Lillian lowered her voice. "Mister Morgan and Mister Baker are doing a wonderful job on the nursery and we wouldn't want to say anything to cause them to stop working, now would we?"

"No'm, but I could've tol' him 'fore them young'uns left fo' th' 'shore, there was goin' t' be a need fo' it. If'n you'd of let me tol' him then, we wouldn't have t' be listenin' to th' buildin' all day, an' them babies all night, now!"

Rachel had whispered her "second sight" discernment of Laura Lee's secret to Lillian the week before the wedding and Lillian had, by design, kept it just between the two of them all this time, and Lillian intended it to remain so. Therefore, she deliberately ignored Rachel's latest reference to the supernatural occurrence and inquired, "Oh? Can you hear the twins all the way downstairs at night, Rachel?"

"Yes'm. They's jus' bein' colicky. If'n Miz Laura Lee'd jus' let me give them babies a taste o' my peppermint tea, they'd quit they squallin' right now."

"Well, Rachel, it's her decision to make and I suppose she doesn't put much stock in folk medicine. The doctor's told her there's nothing seriously wrong with the twins."

"Yes'm!" Rachel said. "That young lady, she be plumb tuckered out wit' two o' them pullin' on her, and one o' them's a boy." Then, shaking her head, "She ain't complained once, though, is she?"

"Not once, Rachel. Drew has found himself a gem in Laura Lee." Her eyes saddened, and she confided, "I only wish I felt she'd done as well."

"Mister Drew been on his good behavior, Miz Lillian. I ain't got even one hand'chief since they been married."

"Oh, I hope so, Rachel, I hope so," Lillian said, draping her shawl around her shoulders as she left the room to climb the back stairs.

In the back upstairs hallway, Lillian pulled the shawl closer around her shoulders, stepped through the newly framed doorway and looked around the practically finished nursery. Two narrow East facing windows framed a small fireplace that shared the chimney with Rachel's and Henry's room below, and on the North wall a pleasant alcove allowed the sloping ceiling to follow the gabled roof line.

Lillian waited until the hammering stopped before attempting to greet her husband and Jeremiah. "Well, now, you two seem to be making great progress in here, today. How soon before it will be ready?"

"Not soon enough!" Morgan answered, mopping his brow, though the room felt extremely cold to Lillian. "If I lose much more sleep because of that chorus coming from Drew's room every night, I'm going to start sleeping down in the root cellar!"

Lillian laughed. "Oh, you will not!" Then she said with a sigh, "You're not the only one disturbed by the babies, dear, and as I've tried to explain to you, they do have colic. Be patient. I'm sure in a day or two they'll quiet down."

"I don't doubt Jeremiah and Hamita can hear them on cold, clear nights." He looked to Jeremiah for confirmation, but his friend turned both palms out in a gesture of declining comment. "Well, then, Lilly," Morgan continued, "since Jeremiah withholds comment, have you asked Henry and Rachel how they feel about having the twins directly overhead? I'm quite sure Rachel would have some rather pointed comments."

"Certainly not! But, Willow is terribly excited that she's to have the title of "nursemaid" and a real bed in this nice big alcove in the children's room as opposed to that cot in the cubbyhole under the back stairs she's occupied most of her life. That was very thoughtful of you, dear!"

"Not at all! When the twins cry, she'll be handy to shut them up." He leaned against the unpainted wall. "I don't know what we'll do though, Lilly, if anybody else wants a room at *Briars*, we've plumb run out of space to build on more."

"It's such a shame you wouldn't allow Drew to build a home of their own on that lot next door," Lillian said, thoughtfully. "I still can't understand why you'd rather have them here at *Briars* with us than in their own place next door."

"I've told you, Lilly, as long as Drew's family is in this house, he'll have to live by our rules. I want to be sure that little lady and those babies are well cared for, and until I see some indication that he's ready to assume responsibility for their welfare, that's the way it's to be. He hasn't said anything to you otherwise, has he?"

"No, dear. That's the sad part, isn't it?" Then she turned to Jeremiah. "I do so wish Drew could be more like your Jonathan."

Jeremiah grinned at Lillian. "Jonny's not all that innocent! But he does love and respect Sarah, and rightly so. Drew'll be all right. He's just late growing up, is all. I expect they'll all start leaving the nest before long, though, and then what'll you do with all these empty rooms, Morrey?"

"Open a hotel, I suppose!" Morgan grinned. He placed his arm around his wife's shoulders and pulled her close. "Will you be lonely, Lilly, when it's only the two of us, again?"

Remembering long, endless nights she'd waited up for him over the years, she smiled patiently and replied, "Lonely? Why, how could I ever be lonely with you, Morgan Heirs?" A shiver ran through her and she asked, "Why don't you use that fireplace? It's cold as a tomb up here." When she turned to leave, she looked back over her shoulder. "I've had Rachel leave you a platter of fried chicken and some biscuits on top of the stove so you can help yourselves when you're ready. The girls and I have some last minute Christmas shopping to do so Henry's driving us into town, and I'm taking Rachel along, too. The girls are dead set on my not being present while they're shopping. Is there anything in particular I can bring back for either of you?"

"Two fingers of bourbon would be nice!" Morgan said, straight-faced, and when Lillian frowned, he offered, "I just thought it would warm up our insides, Lilly."

"Oh? I suppose the hoard you keep in your library closet is strictly for medicinal purposes?" Lillian suggested.

"After the morning he's put in, the walk downstairs would probably do him in." Jeremiah said, reaching into his hip pocket and bringing forth a small flask, which he handed to Morgan. When Lillian frowned again, Jeremiah shrugged. "What are friends for?"

Grinning like small boys caught raiding the cookie jar, they watched as Lillian flounced resolutely back down the hall to the back stairs.

Morgan turned up the flask and took a long draught of the warming liquid, then he handed it back to Jeremiah, who wiped the small bottle's mouth and drank, too.

"I couldn't tell her!" Morgan frowned. "I haven't the guts to tell her that her reckless and self-serving eldest son is probably going to be called off to war soon and that's why his family needs to be here with us. At least, he's promised me that when the call does come, he won't run away to get out of it. I tell you, Jere, if the war doesn't kill him, maybe it'll make a man out of him. I've certainly failed at it. He'd never held a job more than a month or two at most before his mother convinced me to take him into the company but, I swear, if I'd kept him on he'd probably have ruined me. He was helping himself to company funds. I tell you, I hate to think of the money he's squandered. If only I'd kept a closer eye on him—listened to my accountant! Since I let him go, I've set up a small annuity for him just to keep him from pestering his mother for cash."

"Now, Morrey," Jeremiah said, tucking the flask back into his pocket. "Drew's been accustomed to people catering to him his whole life. You can't expect him to change now simply because he's gotten older. There's still hope that the army will change him. In any event, Jonny's raring to go! He's seeing visions of the two of them swaggering around in fancy uniforms with swords and shiny brass buttons."

Morgan looked away, then he said, "There's something else, Jere. Mischief down at the office. When I got there yesterday morning, I found that overnight some rascal had smashed the front window, dumped and scattered files, broken into my wall safe, and left a dead weasel on my desk. Thank God I'd made the deposit the day before! No note, nothing! Just a damn dead, smelly old weasel. What do you make of that?"

Concerned, Jeremiah asked, "Any idea who it could have been?"

Morgan shook his head. "Not a clue. I just know I don't want Lilly to know about this, Jere. It's bad enough she has to worry about Drew's family and future."

Stella

Later in the afternoon of the same day, in front of the Carlton Arms Hotel near the corner of Peachtree and Ellis streets, a handsome young man and a curvaceous blonde woman in a green velvet coat and matching plumed hat stood curbside before a hansom cab's open door. Crowds of cheerful Christmas shoppers laughed their way around the fashionably dressed

Briars
The House of Heirs

figures. The pair addressed one another with considerably less kindness than even their whispered words might imply—were they discernible.

Her eyes lacked sparkle, and she appeared older than her twenty-four years as she asked him urgently, "Why must you always do this on the street, Drew? I'd much prefer you to pay upstairs."

"Well, I prefer doing it right here. Besides, there's no reason professional fees shouldn't be paid openly. There's nothing personal going on here, is there, Stella?" He was holding out several folded bills. "Do you want it or not?"

"You're absolutely right! Nothing personal, at all!" She snatched the money from his hand and hurriedly tucked it into the ample bosom that graced her low cut neckline beneath the open coat. But she looked up quickly, as he suddenly reached out and twirled her around so that their positions were reversed.

"Oh, God!" he whispered. "Of all people to happen along—my mother and sisters! I can't let them see me here with you."

Peering over his shoulder, she wrestled free of him and lifted her skirts in preparation to mount the carriage step. "Why, Drew, darling, you'd better be careful," she said with a sarcastic grin, "or you'll hurt my feelings! Maybe I should just shout 'hello' and wave to them. After all, we used to be neighbors, didn't we? Humph! My own family doesn't recognize me, anymore! But God knows, I see more of you, now, than I ever did before I tired of being a little old homebody and moved into town."

"All right, Stella! I think you've said quite enough on that subject. Please just get in, now." Drew watched over his shoulder and was visibly relieved when his family members disappeared through the ornate doors of the Peachtree Bazaar several shops away.

"Well, of course, my darling!" she continued, evenly, as she stepped into the cab, finally allowing Drew to close the door. "Anything you say, my darling Drew!" She kissed a gloved finger, reached out through the coach's open window and touched it to his lips. "Oh, I understand perfectly, my sweet. I've always been good enough for you, but not for your family, isn't that it? Otherwise, why would you have sneaked around behind their backs all these years to keep on seeing me?" She lowered her gloved hand and gently caught hold of his brown silk lapel. "Don't let it end, now, Drew? You know you'll never get from her—that proper little wife of yours— what you've gotten from me all these years. I know—because you're back again, today! It'll always be that way, Drew, you needing me and me wanting you. Nothing's going to change that!"

He pulled away. "You're not going to make a scene, are you, Stella? Any obligation I may have had to you was just settled. Don't try to make it seem like there's more to it than that!" He looked back at the shoppers rushing by and lowered his voice. "I was hoping we could settle our business, once and for all, on a friendly note today. Don't complicate it, now, by acting hurt."

"But, Drew, you could have skipped going upstairs altogether —and owed me nothing!" She smiled. "Oh, yes, dear heart, you'll be aching for Stella again before long. You can't live without me—and what I do for you. Haven't you learned that yet, Drew?" Her pleading eyes reflected an anguish Drew had never thought her capable of feeling. "We could have been happy together. You know we could. I would have been a good wife, too. What was it, Drew, the Heirs' name or the Heirs' money?" She searched his face. "You picked the money over me, didn't you, Drew? And now, look at us! Do you really love her, Drew? Just tell me that you do and I'll go away. Heaven help us, I can ply my trade in any town or city! I'll leave Atlanta tomorrow, if you'll just say it's true. Tell me that you love her. Tell me that it's like it's always been with us."

Drew leaned down to gaze through the small window squarely into Stella's teary eyes. "Like it's always been? With us? *Yes, I do love her.* And you, Stella—? For years, you've been an overly expensive indulgence, a futile addiction, a dissipating convenience —nothing more! Now go on to wherever you please. Go to Hell for all I care!"

Ignored, futile tears rolled down Stella's painted cheeks while she searched Drew's hard eyes. "I guess I should have known, shouldn't I, Drew? Why is it, where I'm concerned you always say the thing that's going to cut closest to the bone? You're really cruel, Drew, do you know that? You're like an old stray Tom cat toying with a mouse before he eats it. I've been your mouse all these years, and now, finally —"

"Oh, Stella, please!" Drew pleaded. "Spare me!"

She removed a handkerchief from her purse and wiped her eyes. "Well, all right, I'm going, now, but before I go—" she looked down at the handkerchief in her gloved hand, the initials M.A.H. embroidered in one corner, clearly visible. "I kept this one, Drew, as a keepsake. Here, you take it back and put it with your collection of memories." Then she handed the handkerchief to him. "Oh, and one other thing," she added finally, smiling clear-eyed. "My, my, how forgetful of me—! I haven't congratulated you, yet, on those adorable twin babies. Now, what are their names? Let's see? Martha Alice and Morgan Andrew—the third, isn't it? And they've got that flaming red hair just like your mother's."

"How do you know that?" Drew paled slightly. "You haven't been spying on me at home?"

"Certainly not, darling, nothing so mean as all that! I went to their christening. It was all right, my being there, wasn't it? Since I stayed in the balcony of the church with all the other slaves?" She formed a kiss with her ruby lips. "Good-bye, Drew. When the longing comes so strong you hurt, just tell your little kitten of a wife what you need. Or feel free to come looking for me in Natchez. It's far enough away, and I know somebody there. Oh, and Drew, Merry Christmas!" Quickly, then, she looked away, calling loudly to the driver. "Take me down Pryor Street. I'll recognize the house."

Ann Gray

The View

Knowing everything she'd said was true, Drew dropped the handkerchief into the gutter and spat on it as he watched the cab edge slowly into traffic. Then he walked briskly across the street and down the block towards the *Spike and Rail*. Perhaps he'd run into someone there he could drink with and talk to, and for a short while, lose those damnable feelings of guilt and worthlessness that constantly haunted him. He *would* change! This time, he'd stand by his resolve. God, how he wanted to! He'd always wanted to but, over and again, he found himself seeking the solace only Stella provided when the prurient urges were uncontrollable and he needed desperately to satisfy his cravings.

The wind picked up and blew, icy cold, into his troubled face, bringing water to his smarting eyes. He turned his collar up and walked, heedlessly, into it.

"Drew! Drew, wait!" The voice was Morgana's. She and Sarah, working their way through the sidewalk traffic, ran quickly up to him. Poor Rachel, loaded down with the girls' purchases, trailed behind. "We've been trying to catch up to you—" Morgana said, between breaths, "—since we saw you cross the street back there."

"We're on our way over to see Jonny," Sarah added, equally breathless. "He's working on the new Thomas Warren building."

Morgana reached out and took her brother's hand, pulling him along, excitedly. "Come on, go with us. Jonathan says it's very impressive. It's going to be one of the tallest buildings in Atlanta. Look there—," she said, pointing with a gloved finger, "—you can see it right over the tops of the other buildings. It's not even finished, yet and I've never seen a building that high! Have you, Drew?" The liveliness of the young dark eyed beauty spilled over into everything she said and did. "Come on, let's hurry! It's getting so cold, can you believe it?"

"Well, actually, 'no' to both questions," Drew answered, setting aside his low spirits for the moment and returning her smile.

When Jonathan saw them approaching from his perch on the skeletal fourth floor of the building, he held onto a piece of wood framing and waved his hammer. "Come see the view from up here," he urged. "There are stairs inside. Just be wary of loose boards and brick hods."

"Oh, Jonny, be careful!" Sarah shouted up to him. "Must you stand so close to the edge?"

"Come on, Sarah," Morgana implored, already stepping out towards the building's entrance. "Let's race."

"I'll do nothing of the kind!" Sarah answered, standing firm. "I have no desire to go climbing about in any old unfinished building, especially one so high." She cupped her hands around her mouth and spoke rather louder than usual. "Come down, Jonny, so that we can talk. We only have a few minutes. Mama will be waiting for us back downtown. It's getting so much colder, you must be freezing way up there." He waved again, and disappeared from view.

"Oh, Sarah! Why don't you just admit it?" Morgana said, annoyed with her older sister. "You're scared to go up there. Well, I'm going! I'm not going to let you keep me from seeing the view. Come on, Drew, let's go. We'll leave her down here to wait for Jonny, so they can kiss. That's what you're hoping for, isn't it, Sarah?"

"Morgana, you're such a child!" Sarah replied, reversing the censure. "Go or stay, it makes no difference to me." Then she turned to Rachel. "Rachel, hand me the sack with the material for my wedding gown. I want to show it to Jonny when he gets here."

"Am I missing something here?" Drew smiled down at his fair and proper sister. "You and Jonny were only formally engaged last month. When's the wedding to be?" A heaviness settled into his midsection. Was he also about to lose his drinking, gambling, carousing companion, now? First, Stella. Now, Jonny?

"Oh, gracious, not for another year, at least. I shall make my own dress and train though, and that will take quite a spell. You see, it must be perfect and I shall stitch it inch by inch by perfect inch. After all, it's for my wedding." Sarah looked reverently skyward. "Revelations 19:8 says of holy marriage: 'And to her was granted that she should be arrayed in fine linen, clean and white: for the fine linen is the righteousness of saints.' I shall be married in fine white linen."

Sarah's words impaled Drew like the swift thrust of a sword and he felt himself sliding back down, down into the abyss of self-hate.

"Ye Gods!" Morgana exclaimed, drawing attention away from Sarah's pious remarks. "Come on, Drew, if we're to see the view, we must hurry. Look how low the clouds are getting. It will soon be raining!"

"Or snowin'—" Rachel said, between chattering teeth, producing the large sack Sarah had requested. "Y'all jus' go on an' do it, if'n you goin' to, 'cause I's goin' back t' th' carriage in a few minutes, wit' or wit'out any o' y'all."

Drew allowed Morgana to haul him off into the hollow building, her laughter echoing back. Minutes later, Morgana's sharp cry of delight punctuated the cold damp air, and Sarah and Rachel looked up to see her standing far above them with Jonny and Drew on either side holding onto her hands. "Look, Sarah!" Morgana shouted down, "We're almost to Heaven! See what you missed!"

"What's going on over there?" Drew asked Jonny, pointing off towards the front of the telegraph office where they could see a man in the doorway reading from a sheet of paper in his hands to a large gathering of citizens.

Briars
The House of Heirs

"I've been noticing him for the past five minutes or so. Must be some important news just came in. People been congregating and listening and then running away in all directions. Maybe you'd best get on down there and find out what it's all about. Tell Sarah, I'm sorry I couldn't come down, but much as I'd like to, I've got to finish up this section of framing before it starts to rain. Or at least, I've got to try. If I quit now, I'll be sure to catch hell from the boss."

"The boss? That's your Papa!" Morgana stated, disbelieving his words.

"You bet it is, and a harder man to work for, I never met!" Jonathan laughed.

"See, Drew! Jonny's always worked for his Papa." Morgana laughed. "Why in the world can't you work for Papa, too?" Then she turned and fixed her brother with insolent, inquiring eyes. "Papa's always saying that you never did an honest day's work in your whole life! Well, looks to me like if Jonny and Jeremiah Baker can work together—!"

"Morgana!" Drew interrupted in a rude, sharp voice, squeezing her hand until it hurt. "Mind your own damned business! I don't care to discuss my work habits— or lack of them— with a thirteen year old 'know-it-all', and particularly from the top of the tallest building in Atlanta. The temptation may just get to be too great!"

"Well, I declare!" She pulled free of his grip and Jonathan's. "Drew Heirs, you are just plain mean! I'm going down now and if you don't want me to tell Laura Lee that I just saw you with that Farley woman, you'd better be home in time for supper, too." With that, she turned and carefully picked her way back out of the building, leaving the two men together on the open shelf overlooking the city.

Holding onto the raw wood strut closest at hand and looking out past Jonathan, Drew said, "Stella's leaving. I'm through with her for good and all."

"I hope so, Drew." Jonathan looked down and waved to Sarah when he saw that Morgana had reached the street and spoken to her. He watched as the three figures hurried away retracing their steps, then he picked up his hammer and gave a half-driven nail a sharp blow, pounding it into the wood up to the head.

"It's only fair to Laura Lee," Drew said. "I really intend it to be done with this time." How many times before had he heard himself saying those words?

"Yep, I know you do," Jonathan said, patiently. "You need to talk?"

"I need a drink. How long before you'll be done here?"

Almost as if on command, the rain began pelting down in big round drops. "Guess I'm finished now," Jonathan grinned. "Let's go!" He picked up his tools, and led the way back down into the bowels of the building.

The rain settled in, pelting down finer and colder until it became a harsh, stinging hail. They reached the tavern door just as Milton Johnson came rushing out. Flushed with ale and excitement, he gripped each man's broad, wet shoulder while fairly jumping up and down. "Y'all heard the news—?" Looking from face to face, he announced, "South Carolina's just seceded from the Union!"

War

Lillian stood at her bedroom window and watched the commotion in the road below. Coming together from homes all over *Briarwood*, youthful Confederate army volunteers had arrived, loud and rambunctious, outside *Briars*' open entry gates at the appointed hour and called out, good-naturedly, for Drew Heirs and Jonathan Baker to hurry out and join their ranks so that they could be on their way. A war was waiting to be won!

Briars
The House of Heirs

War! It had always seemed so distant to Lillian, an interesting topic of conversation whenever they discussed the possibility of it at social affairs and at table with guests. It had been all newspaper print and rumors, nothing at all having to do with the Heirs family until Jonathan Baker, in his eagerness, had convinced Drew they should join up without waiting to be called. By that time, it seemed the war "itch" had spread like poison ivy to all the sons of neighboring families. The whole frightening reality had come about much too quickly for Lillian to prepare herself for the worst news of her life: her eldest son was actually going away from home to join the Confederate army, to fight a war, possibly to die.

It had come on insidiously, this war-mentality of the youth in the South, affecting rich and poor alike. It had gained strength when Lincoln was inaugurated President of the United States of America. By that time six other states: Texas, Mississippi, Louisiana, Alabama, Florida, and Georgia had joined South Carolina in secession. As Morgan had predicted, Lincoln had held firm to his belief that secession was an illegal act and declared he had no intention of relinquishing federal holdings in the South.

Circumstances had escalated rapidly after that. On April 12, 1861 when Lincoln had ordered an attempt be made to re-supply Fort Sumpter at Charleston's harbor in South Carolina, resistant Southern artillery opened fire. Then Lincoln called for additional troops to put down that rebellion, and four other states—Virginia, Arkansas, North Carolina, and Tennessee joined with the other seceding Confederates, and Jefferson Davis was chosen to head the new Confederate States of America. Thus, consecutive retaliatory events had quickly changed the map of the nation, cutting it in two.

It was all too much for Lillian. She had stolen away from the Heirs and Baker families' buffet gathering on the verandah for the departing soldiers-to-be shortly after Drew had pulled her aside and kissed her, promising to say his prayers, to take care of himself, to watch after Jonathan as best he could, and to come home safely. She had no desire to witness the actual leave-taking from the crowded porch, particularly with Morgan and Jeremiah, both deep in their cups, slapping their sons' backs and filling their minds—sad and fearful as they must be—with inappropriate wartime slogans and battle strategies, as older men are wont to do.

Leaving Drew alone with Laura Lee for their last few minutes together, she had sought out Hamita, wretched in her own misery at Jonathan's leaving, and excused herself supposedly to check on Willow and the twins. In truth, choosing to watch the final leave-taking, alone from her upstairs front bedroom window where she would be free to cry aloud.

Earlier, Laura Lee and Drew had spent the last precious few minutes he would share with their twins until his return. As the time for Drew's departure neared, Lillian watched Laura Lee in her own quiet and courageous way accept Drew's leave-taking as a requirement of the times. Lillian knew Laura Lee would display no emotional outbursts, make no tearful scenes. Staunchly, she would stand atop the front steps on *Briars'* broad verandah, and wave her departing husband on his way.

On the other hand, Sarah, whom Lillian had left standing rigidly at Jonathan's side, had dissolved into fitful spasms of sobbing by the time Lillian decided to retreat to her room. Watching her fiancé walk down the long driveway with Drew to join the others waiting in the street, would have to be the most painful experience of Sarah's spoiled and sheltered life. While it had been Sarah's decision to send Jonathan away still unwed, the opportunity had presented itself several days before with both family's blessings. But she had chosen to put him off. Lillian would not soon forget the look of disappointment on Jonathan's face when he had reluctantly joined Sarah in announcing to the families that there would be no wedding until his return.

Wil, not being one for gushiness, had escaped from the tearful bosom of his family and ventured close to the road with a purpose, swinging back and forth on one of the heavy iron-barred entry gates. Lillian understood his need to be last to shake the hands of his brother and Jonathan, who would be passing through the gates soon. It wouldn't be fitting for any one back up at the house to see tears in his eyes. Not at twelve.

At one point halfway down the long driveway Drew turned, his gaze seeking the face of the woman who smiled down on him from the second floor window and he lifted a flying kiss to her. That was all it took to bring heartrending sobs from his mother's trembling lips, and she wept copious tears as she watched the two young men stride away.

When the troupe had passed from view down the curving road, Lillian dabbed at her eyes with a dainty lace-trimmed handkerchief. Her eldest son was a most impressive figure of a man. By all outward appearances, though he'd had his share of problems reaching maturity, Drew had finally settled down and become a devoted husband and responsible father. He'd make an fine soldier.

After a quiet knock, Sarah opened Lillian's door a little and called softly, "Mama, they've all gone. Papa said I should tell you he and Jeremiah have gone to the *Spike and Rail*. He said you'd understand."

Lillian nodded. They would return home reeking of whiskey, but she had learned over the years that while women cried away their woes and grief, men customarily drowned theirs in mind-numbing spirits.

Sarah's nose was red and her eyes swollen from the deluge of tears she had shed. "May I come in, Mama?"

"Of course, Sweet." They must have been a sorry sight, the two of them, Lillian thought, as she motioned her daughter into the room. Smiling through her own pain, and taking into consideration the mix of emotions Sarah must be suffering, she explained unnecessarily, "I felt the need to be alone for a while." She patted a spot beside her on the bed. "Sit here, darling."

Sarah sat down, resting her head on Lillian's shoulder. Then she pulled away and looked wide-eyed into Lillian's face. "Oh, Mama, I feel so guilty! I'm just a horrible person, I know, but Mama I couldn't marry Jonny and have him go off to war and leave me—maybe pregnant—and tied to a man I hadn't slept with more than once or maybe twice in my whole life. What if I found somebody else I loved more while he was gone? What if he got killed and there I was—a widow with a child I was afraid to have and didn't want in the first place? Who'd want to marry me, then?"

"Well, now," Lillian raised her eyebrows and gazed into Sarah's weepy, reddened eyes. "I don't hear words of concern for Jonny's safety coming from those rosy lips, do I? Maybe it's a good thing for all concerned there was no marriage before he left. Maybe it would have been better for Jonny if there had been no prolonged engagement, either. Jonny deserves better than that, Sarah. Does he know the depth or extent of your doubtful feelings concerning your future with him?"

"Of course not! I wouldn't tell him all that, Mama! Not just before he marched off to war, for goodness sake. I only figured it out myself last week when he really started to rush me. I don't think I even want to be married, Mama. I know I don't want to have any babies! I remember when Laura Lee had the twins, for goodness sake! I also remember hearing you tell Hamita all about Morgana's being born."

"Then you would have heard me say, too, that Morgana's was not a normal birth."

"Nothing about Morgana is normal," Sarah asserted.

"Sarah, it sounds like you've been terribly confused these last few weeks. You should have come to me if you had doubts and questions. Why didn't you come and talk to me?"

Sarah got up from the bed and strode to the window, looking out for a moment before allowing her eyes to stray back to her mother's face. "Because I was afraid you'd try to 'talk some sense into me' and I didn't want to hear what you might call 'sense'. My mind's made up. I just have to wait until he gets back home to tell him, is all."

"Sarah, that's not fair to Jonny. You know that, don't you?"

"Yes, ma'am, I guess I do," Sarah agreed, turning to walk back again to her place beside her mother. "But the whole idea of marriage, the responsibilities —and babies— is so awesome, I'm not sure I'll ever be ready for all that, Mama, really."

Lillian smiled. "Oh, you'll change your mind when you're able to take things in their own good time and count them up in proper order. Then you will realize all the good things that marriage brings as well as the less appealing duties. It's this war! It makes us see things in a whole different light. But be patient, Sarah, the war won't last forever. Get on with making that beautiful wedding dress. Soon enough, everything will change for the better again, you'll see."

"Oh, Mama," Sarah kissed her mother's lips. "I do love you so! You make all kinds of scary things seem so very ordinary."

"Never forget, Sweet Sarah, you are not alone in your fear. Everybody fears something. But how we respond to that fear is within each of us, alone, to choose. Fear can either work for us or against us, depending on how we react to it. I was never so frightened in my whole life as when that big black bear was charging Jeremiah, your father, and me. I either had to reach for Papa's weapon and kill that bear or wait frozen in my tracks for him to charge! Nobody could have been more frightened than I was when I saw that ferocious beast coming straight for us. But I chose to shoot, Sarah. If I hadn't, neither you nor I would be sitting here, now. Choose to stand up to your fears and you'll always be victorious."

"Like Daniel in the lion's den," Sarah said, positively. "Or David with Goliath."

"Exactly like Daniel or David," Lillian agreed, smoothing Sarah's pale hair from her forehead. "I believe that courage in the face of danger is the most admirable trait any of us ever comes by. If we face our fears courageously, putting our faith in God, we will overcome whatever obstacles life puts before us."

"Mama, will you pray with me for Jonny and Drew?" Sarah asked fervently, moving to kneel beside Lillian's bed.

"I will pray with you, darling, for us all," Lillian said, slipping to her knees and clasping her daughter's hand firmly on the bed in front of them.

Outside the partially open door to her mother's room, Morgana stopped short of entering when she recognized the intimacy of the moment. Having heard only Sarah's request for prayer and her mother's earnest reply, when Lillian and Sarah bowed their heads, even though she remained unconvinced anyone was 'up there' listening, Morgana knelt in the cold, dark hallway and prayed to Mama's and Sarah's God to look after the new Confederacy and departing friends and neighbors, to protect her older brother, Drew, and especially, Jonny Baker; and for the protection of all who dwelt within *Briars'* gray stone walls.

Spike and Rail

Heartfelt and reverently rendered, though strident and sorrowfully off key, the tones of "Dixie" greeted Morgan and Jeremiah when they pushed their way through the door of their accustomed old lair. Raw stench from un-emptied cuspidors, smoke, sweat and coarse spirits assailed their nostrils. The patriotic song ended to a grave silence, punctuated by nose blowing and unashamed snorting and sniffling before the room, filled with tangible emotion, began humming with unreserved declarations of loyalty.

Morgan and Jeremiah, squeezing in at the rail, greeted old and faithful friends, companions from that generation of men unwilling to surrender allegiance to the antiquated old tavern for the newer, fancier bars that had sprung up in urbanized Atlanta over the twenty-three years since they had arrived in Terminus, among the first to patronize the *Spike and Rail* while working for the Western and Atlantic Railroad.

Morgan rapped on the counter and lifted the tankard of ale that had just been placed before him, addressing all those present: "Gentlemen, a toast to our sons and other men's, who have this day pledged their very lives to defend the sovereignty of this newly established Confederacy."

"To our sons!" The toast was raised and echoed throughout the assembly.

Morgan lowered his mug and, across the room, his eyes met those of Ezra Clark who had no sons. In spite of worthy credentials as a successful cotton merchant, Clark was still an unsavory fellow whose nightly presence in the *Spike and Rail* was barely tolerated by most of the tavern's regular patrons. He had a habit of making unwarranted remarks belittling anyone's opinion save his own.

Morgan went on for he had the attention of the public house: "Gentlemen, I believe there's been more going on between the North and South than merely disagreement on the rights and wrongs of slavery. We've grown further and further apart on many issues. The national government has been growing too fast, adding new territories—New Mexico just last year. There have not been enough federal funds to sustain such growth."

"Then there's the question of authority!" Tom Garrett interjected. "Where's the proper division of power between the states and the federal government?"

Morgan declared, "It's always been my belief that the North was more concerned with preserving the Union than fighting slavery in the South. This final separation has only sped the war's beginning."

"Well," Doc Goddard shook his head, "there was hope that a recognized, legal and orderly secession of the Southern slave states would avoid an all out war. But now that's failed. And nobody has any notion of what an internal war will do to this disjoined country."

Ann Gray

Jeremiah said, "I hate to think of what's coming, myself. Worst of all, I hate to think that my boy's going into the conflict and I'm too damned old and stove up to volunteer, let alone be called!"

"I know the feeling, my friend," Morgan said, looking down at his cane. Then he gazed about at the aging and haunted faces of the other men left behind like him, and said, "There will be much blood spilled on both sides before this conflict ends, I'm afraid. Unfortunately, secession alone would never have guaranteed our right to preserve our heritage. Not with Lincoln in the presidency."

Clap. Clap. Clap. The clapping of hands came from Ezra Clark who staggered from his corner and commanded the attention of the crowd by approaching Morgan at the bar.

Beginning mid-sentence, as if he'd been talking for some time, Clark said, "—and I'll tell y'all somethin' else." Puffy bags hung below his blood-shot gray eyes as Clark flashed a steely glance at Morgan, spitting into the sawdust that covered the dirt floor. "Them was damn pretty words! From all of you! Well, I come from Tennessee and I know Northerners got to blame the need for this war on something purely Southern! Ownin' slaves is about the only likely thing they got to hang it on. I got several niggers, myself. But what Southern gentleman of character would ever allow one of his niggers to sleep in the same room with part of his family?"

"You're straying from the subject, Clark," Morgan barked, "but I take it those words were meant for me!" Suddenly, he felt recently well-controlled anger awaken within him. Morgan grabbed Ezra Clark by his open collar and pulled him close, eyeing him face to face while tightening his grip against Clark's Adam's apple. Holding onto the startled man and looking around at his companions, Morgan snarled, "I've been insulted. What should I do about it?"

Laughter and ribald suggestions followed, but Jeremiah grasped his friend's shoulder and worry lines creased his brow.

"Remember what Doc told you about that temper now," he whispered in Morgan's ear.

Grinning, Morgan rasped back to Jeremiah, "Hell, Jere, I just want to rearrange his face a little, you know, for old time's sake?" But Morgan loosened his hold on the irritating Ezra Clark's collar and said evenly to the paunchy, sallow man, "It's true. My grandchildren's nursemaid does sleep in their nursery, and two married servants have a room inside my house. I have two others who sleep in my stables. If I had a plantation—*and slaves*—they'd sleep in slaves' quarters, but I *don't own* a plantation. Neither do you, Ezra Clark. But you call your two servants 'slaves'. I hear tell you beat your good wife and disgrace her regularly by spending most nights in your female slave's quarters in the loft of your barn. Tell these gentlemen, Ezra, do you beat your wife and spend most nights in your barn where your favorite she-slave sleeps?"

Taken aback by Morgan's pointed censure, Clark smoothed his collar then reached to finger the hunting knife on his belt. Thinking better of that move, he wiped wet palms against his britches. "Where I sleep is my own damn business, Heirs." The irksome fellow slouched away quickly to his table. From there, he stared back at Morgan much too long before silently downing another full tankard of ale in one long draught.

Morgan asked Jeremiah privately, "Jere, what would you have done if I'd actually punched him?"

"Ducked and run like hell," Jeremiah answered quietly, wiping his mouth on the back of his hand and smoothing his neat mustache while examining the noxious cloud of smoke that rested against the ceiling. "I learned that lesson the hard way a long time ago by having to fight a damn black bear."

Morgan wrinkled his forehead. "I'm a little fuzzy on the time around that bear fight, but didn't you tell me it was a tangle over our little pissing bet for the ninety-seven acres back in thirty-eight that caused my first set-to with Ezra Clark?"

"Yep." Jeremiah nodded, watching Morgan's brow wrinkle as he struggled in vain once again to remember. Morgan had no memory of that entire July day and night. Jeremiah was always patient, because several weeks after the vicious bear attack when Morgan had begun to heal from his injuries, he'd had to tell Morgan of that first clash with Clark all over again. It happened every so often.

Finally, accepting his unalterable past, Morgan draped an arm loosely around Jeremiah's shoulder. "Did I ever thank you for saving my ass?"

"Not that I recall," Jeremiah answered, coolly.

"Damn, that was a mighty big oversight on my part, I reckon," Morgan admitted, when their eyes met again. He squeezed Jeremiah's shoulder. "Old friend, let me thank you, now, for saving me from certain death—back then."

"I always wondered if I'd ever hear those words from you," Jeremiah confessed in muted tones. "Well, now that I have, I'm a mite disappointed."

"Disappointed?" Morgan repeated, his expression reflecting complete dismay.

"Yeah, disappointed!" A peevish Jeremiah turned to look Morgan squarely in the face. "Now that you've finally remembered to say it, you're welcome—" Jeremiah's eyes shone, anticipating the gibe. "—but I was kind of hoping for a nice, big sloppy kiss!" Morgan jerked his arm away, a look of pure disgust etched on his reddening face. Jeremiah declared, "Well, hell, if you're going to make another ugly bar scene, just forget it!" Bouncing with laughter, he lifted his mug and buried his jovial face in it.

Morgan stifled a belly laugh; frowned instead, and growled, "All right, then!" They drank to their long, genuine friendship; to their dedicated sons serving the South's cause in their stead, to the young Confederacy, and finally to their faithful and patient women waiting even now for their return. Afternoon faded into evening. Evening darkened into night. The men arrived home late, as usual.

CHAPTER SIX ~ PRINCIPLES

10:30 a.m., Wednesday, November 16, 1864 ~ Briars, Atlanta, Georgia

Discovery

In the cold silence of the cave, Lillian became aware of her surroundings again and with a sharp stab of guilt she realized she had been sleeping. How long, she dared not guess. It was as if they'd had a conversation, she and her husband, because when she was fully awake she knew exactly what she was going to do. If she found her girls had been molested as she feared they had been, she was prepared to confront the enemy. Morgan's words from long ago—twisted and yet suitable, echoed in her mind: "*Lilly, you've got to do this!* Pick up the guns, now, Lilly, *now!* Shoot them, Lilly! *Shoot the enemy, Lilly!*"

Crises demanded action, and this crisis was of particular consequence to the Heirs family. Lillian went into the shadows at the back of the undiscovered cave and started taking inventory of the weapons and munitions stored there. If circumstances within *Briars* were as she feared she would have to decide now exactly which weapons they'd make use of and the course of action they'd follow.

When Lillian emerged from the cold damp hillside a short time later, she glanced up at movement from the rough cut embankment above her head. There was the dog, Storm, his great plumed tail beating a tattoo on the hard red earth, leaning against Wil—a gratified Wil—who sat with one arm wrapped around the big shepherd dog's neck. They sat alongside a delinquent Henry, chores still unfinished, with Wil sharing puffs on Henry's corn cob pipe. All three of them grinned sheepishly down at her.

Briars
The House of Heirs

"I see your dog came back." Lillian smiled up at Wil. The boy was maturing faster than she'd wanted him to, and he was proving to be a stronger person than she'd ever thought of him becoming at such a tender age. He'd taken the sudden death of his father better than either of his older sisters, and he was soberly dealing with the Yankees' invasion by showing a sensibility far beyond his years. Lillian didn't bother scolding him for smoking; nor Henry for letting him. No, not anymore. It would only be a waste of breath.

"You feeling better, Ma?" the boy asked, looking down at her, possibly hoping for a faint hint of what she'd been up to so long in the root cellar.

"I think so. Your Pa and me, we had a nice talk. I'm afraid I fell asleep."

"You needed it," Wil said, matter-of-factly. "You're going back, aren't you?" Then, getting up. "I'm going, too."

Lillian then turned to go, lifting her skirts to mount the craggy path as she said to Wil over her shoulder, "You stay down here, now, you hear? Henry, you stay here and keep him company as long as you can. I'm going back up to find my girls."

"Let me go wit' you, Miz Lillian," Henry pleaded, climbing down from the prominence. "Ain't no tellin' what them devils is up to by now."

"No, Henry, stay here and keep Wil company as long as you can. I'll feel better about him, knowing you're down here looking after him. I'll tell Rachel where you are."

Trudging back up the long hill, her shadow tailed along beside her. It had to be nearing ten o'clock. She'd been gone much too long, and guilt chewed at her conscience for the nap that had forced itself upon her, but she did feel stronger for it, and better prepared to deal with whatever she might find up at the house. Besides, if something untoward had happened to her girls, it had happened hours ago and hurrying now wouldn't undo it.

Depravity

Acting according to Mother Heirs' bidding, Laura Lee had gotten down the back stairs, past Rachel's and Henry's room and as far as the kitchen. She had barely entered the room when two Yankee intruders pushed open the partially closed pantry door from inside, where they had been pilfering supplies. Leering suggestively at her, each burly man dangled a jug of Father Heirs' best scuppernong wine from a bent forefinger. The sweet liquid still dribbled down their chins.

"Well, looky-here what we got!" the beefy, mustached sergeant croaked, showing his yellow-green teeth.

"A honey-haired, chocolate-eyed queen, I'd say!" the lanky corporal observed over the sergeant's shoulder, licking his thin lips.

"Hey, Sarge, it ain't Christmas, is it?" a third unkempt soldier asked, pushing his way through.

"Come on, Fowler—Jenkins—move over! Let's see what're you taking on so over—!" A fourth voice came from a private trapped behind the other three.

"Easy, Burgess, we saw her first!" the sergeant warned.

"My, my!" a fifth man exclaimed, peering over shoulders, "I do declare! Christmas—it must be! Now you know, boys, there's got to be enough sweet stuff there for all of us!"

As one, they advance on her.

Laura Lee turned and ran fast as she could, retracing her steps, towards the back stairs. But she couldn't outrun the soldiers, and as they dragged her off to the back guest bedroom, one of the three rooms they had used for billet, she pleaded for them to release her, knowing even as she did, it was futile. Shortly after they dragged her into the room and her ordeal began, she heard Sarah's heart-wrenching screams echoing through the house.

Briars
The House of Heirs

The best she could judge —possibly two torturous hours later—gathering her clothes, she had crawled off the foot of the bed and stolen from the room, leaving the five soldiers in drunken stupors. On the rumpled bed, the sergeant and the corporal snored loudly. One short private had commandeered the child's cot in the corner. Another slept, fitfully, legs dangling over one arm of a pink lounge chair; the tallest of the lot sprawled on a lavender velvet chaise lounge.

Naked, struggling up the back stairs, Laura Lee realized that she could never have anticipated the full impact of the pain and fury she had experienced at the hands of the five drunken Union soldiers. Her knowledge of sexual gratification had always—and only—been with her husband and had been so gentle and satisfying that she could never have imagined such vileness as she had just endured existed. Still, she had not granted them the satisfaction of crying out, nor in any way given expression to the cold, dark terror and loathing that filled her. No, she had worn a mask of impassive indifference.

Her aching body still drenched in sweat, teeth chattering with cold and shock, she hurried to her own bedroom and straight to the front window, to reassure herself of the briar cave's continued security.

Nothing moved, save for the two guards placidly pacing back and forth across the gated entry. Nothing outside of *Briars* had changed; inside, nothing was the same! Once she was certain the children were still safe, she went to the wash stand and poured a basin of cold water from the pitcher to wash herself.

Had Mother Heirs not sent her directly to the pantry, she might have been spared humiliation and pain, but Mother Heirs could never have guessed they'd be in there pilfering the pantry's goods. In fact, Laura Lee had gained courage from Mother Heirs' words in that few minutes before the assailants had captured and raped her so brutally. No, Laura Lee's children had not heard her voice. But she feared the children and Willow must have also heard Sarah's pitiful cries from upstairs. When she was clean again and dressed she would go and find her sister-in-law.

Choices

Sarah had not attempted to leave the house as she had been bidden to do, but had quickly closed and locked her bedroom door behind her mother. Standing with her ear pressed against the locked door, she had heard every sound from the hall. She heard Mama and Morgana's voices clearly as they stepped outside Morgana's room, Mama urging Morgana to 'hurry and follow Sarah'. If only she'd had the courage to fling open the door and show herself then she, too, could have gotten out of the house and safely away. Once, she'd even reached for the door knob to join Morgana, but the quickened beating of her heart grew so fierce it frightened her and she pulled her hand back as if the knob were a snake that might bite.

It was only minutes later that she heard Mama's own familiar footsteps heading towards the back stairs. She should have gone then, too. Mama would have held onto her and they would have gone together, but she couldn't. The sound of Mama's tread, too, quickly faded and too frightened to move from her stance behind the locked door, Sarah remained behind, alone.

Her ear to the door, and with legs shaking so intensely they could hardly support her, she continued listening. Within moments, boisterous laughter echoed up the stairwell, announcing the arrival of Union soldiers on the family's floor. Any number would have been too many, but when they reached the landing, it sounded like there were at least four of them! Loud as they were, couldn't the Lieutenant downstairs hear them? Couldn't anybody in the whole world hear them besides her?

Briars
The House of Heirs

"Hey, hey! Here we are on the forbidden floor," a high pitched voice announced loudly.

Then over his companions' gravel laughs, another voice added, "Right, Burgess, and ain't nobody sober enough to call us back down, neither!"

A third companion sang out, "Ta-ta-ta, ta-ta-ta!" mocking the sounds of a fox hunting horn, "Let the hunt begin! My, my, look at all them foxholes!"

It was to be a game of fox and hounds.

Sarah's stomach heaved, and she was nauseous with fear. Her heart was beginning to pound so hard and fast it was losing rhythm.

They were outside her mother's and Laura Lee's opposing doors. "Left or right?" Burgess' high voice chuckled, "Loomis, you choose!"

"I choose left!" the thickest, deepest voice said, obligingly.

"Left, it is!" came a slurred reply. "Hey, wait, it's open! Did this little fox desert her hole?"

There followed the squeak of hinges as Sarah heard the door to Laura Lee's room swing open.

"Aw, you're right, Slade, nobody's home here. Now, Burgess, where could our little fox be?" asked voice number four.

They were back out in the hall again outside Mama's room.

"Maybe they'll all be together in this next one!"

"Aw, damn, Black! It's empty, too,"

They were coming down the hallway room by room. "My turn!" High Voice insisted. "I choose—that one!"

As she knew they would, they chose her door next, twisting the door knob, then pounding away. "Ho, ho, ho! Got us a fox in the hole, here!"

Sarah heard the urgency of lewd anticipation in the besotted, chortling voices.

"Time to meet the boys, girlie! Open up!" the coarse voice coaxed.

They were getting impatient, louder. "You'll be glad you did! We got something for you!"

Sarah went into her closet and, pushing aside her shoes, crawled in behind the closely packed curtain of long frivolous gowns and heavy cloaks, but she could still hear the hunting dog voices, howling discovery of their prey.

In the darkness of the closet, Sarah whispered, "Mama, oh, Mama, I'm so sorry! Oh, God, forgive me! I was too afraid! Please, God, give me strength to endure this ordeal!"

Then she heard them chanting in unison, "Here we come! Ready or not! One! Two! Three!"

The door's hinges sprang to the men's assault, and knowing she was somewhere inside because her key was still in the lock when they broke open the door, they quickly found her.

Defiance

As Morgana moved stealthily along the long center hallway downstairs, unintelligible sounds floated down both stairwells and out from the back downstairs bedroom so she hurried past that door. She knew that each of the downstairs guest bedrooms contained a double bed, seating of some kind, and cots used primarily for guests' children. The rooms opened, conveniently, onto the east verandah making it possible for early arrivals and departures of relatives and other invited overnight guests. Hurrying along the hallway towards the front of the house, she peered into the unoccupied dining room, Mama's empty parlor, and last of all, Papa's library. There was certainly no one moving about in any quarter of the house that she could determine.

Moreover, the Yankee soldiers seemed to have evaporated right into thin air, but the stench of whiskey emanating from Papa's library was appalling. Morgana tip-toed in, hands on hips, scornful of the presumption of the Northern intruders, in having reduced to ruins the richly decorated sanctuary of her beloved, too recently departed father.

It was then that she heard the low moaning sound like the wind whistling down the chimney. It came from the sofa facing the wide granite fireplace with the bearskin rug before it. When a man staggered clumsily to his feet, Morgana stood like a statue just inside the doorway, too shocked to speak.

Slowly, the lieutenant turned towards her as he sought to balance himself against the sofa. He managed to bring his bloodshot blue eyes into focus, gazing down on Morgana Heirs' flawless beauty for the first time ever. "Uh, excuse me, ma'am," he said, taken completely by surprise in seeing her there. "Lieutenant Shane Alexander Moss, ma'am, at your service."

"At my service, indeed, sir!" Morgana blurted out, recovering her wits. "What a nerve you Yankees have—coming right into a perfectly respectable family's home and making an absolute shambles of it. I suppose you also aim to rape all the women and kill all the men—as I've heard you *Yankees* do?"

His union-shirt, disheveled and unbuttoned to the waist, revealed an old crescent shaped scar over his breastbone, which could well have been the price paid for standing too close to an angry or untrained horse. As a courtesy to Morgana, he quickly began fumbling the buttons on the shirt as he spoke. "You'd be the younger Miss Heirs, I presume."

"You presume correctly, sir," she answered, defiantly moving to stand directly behind the sofa, looking across it and up into his sun-bronzed face. "Is there some problem, Lieutenant, with me walking through my own house?"

"The problem being, Miss Heirs—," He reached for his tunic and, searching behind his back for a sleeve, attempted to pull it on. "—my instructions to your mother regarding yourself, as well as the other ladies, were that you were all to stay in your rooms behind locked doors. For your own safety, I might add."

Morgana folded her arms. "Lieutenant, if I am in any danger as you suggest I may be, then it must be from you, alone! It appears your drunken, boisterous and unruly men have completely deserted you! For I swear I have yet to see a living soul that does not belong in this house—*save you*, and I have walked it from top to bottom and back to front."

The moment Morgana finished speaking, she heard Sarah's pitiful wail from the room upstairs and it was like a skeletal hand clutching at her heart—reminding her—warning her. She suspected Willow must have made just such a fuss that horrible day last summer in the Johnson's cane field.

Lieutenant Shane Alexander Moss chose that moment to drop his tunic, reach across the sofa and catch her wrist, twisting it and flinging her, even as she flailed out at him with her other fist, onto the soft plush brocade of Papa's couch.

"Sir, you are drunk!" Morgana protested, fighting him with every ounce of strength she possessed.

"Yes, ma'am, I am that!" he answered, and ever so gently, he wrapped his wet, warm mouth around her tight, hard lips.

Had she not badgered him, probably nothing would have come of their meeting save a scolding and her being sent back to her room. But she had badgered him, and she hadn't been sent back to her room. Instead, after he was spent and had fallen back asleep, Morgana stood looking down at him in utter amazement while adjusting her clothing. On the one hand, she couldn't believe what had just happened had actually, truly, happened. On the other hand, despite the stench of liquor about him, despite her losing struggle to fend him off, how tenderly, how pleasingly, this handsome stranger had ultimately brought her along with him to that previously unknown summit. There, they had blended into one motion, one breath, one being. How could anyone, after tasting such ecstasy, ever willingly depart from it?

Why bother going to the root cellar, now? Morgana retraced her steps through the quiet house, and climbed the back stairs to her room. A smile found its way to her lips. The warmth of her first sexual encounter did not fade with the washing of her body.

The lingering thrill of it still tingled deep within her, reminding her of the exhilaration she had experienced. Morgana knew she should hate Shane Moss for the Yankee he was and the crime he had committed against her. The tussle she'd put up before surrendering had served to give her reason to feel she had tried to avert the act, and she had stolen from his arms at the first opportunity. But hidden away in her heart was the truth she would never, never tell of the perfect oneness they had shared. If it was rape which had caused Sarah to raise such an ungodly ruckus, it had surely not been the same pure pleasure that hers had been. Morgana was certain Mama had instructed them both the same. Why hadn't Mama's obedient and perfect little Sweet Sarah gone to the root cellar? Setting aside her own gnawing guilt, she would go look for Sarah.

Ann Gray

CHAPTER SEVEN ~ JONATHAN'S RIDE

7:30 a.m., Wednesday, November 16, 1864 ~ Downtown, Atlanta, Georgia

The Johnson Boys

With nothing between him and the blue skies above, Jonathan awakened the next morning to the brilliance of sunshine in his eyes. It wasn't until he tried to stand that the numbness in his wounded leg subsided and wrenching pain reminded him of his impairment.

The strident sounds of panic in the streets had tempered since yesterday, though there were still occasional loud voices and the grinding of wagon and carriage wheels in the street outside his lair. It was only then that he heard the labored breathing. His fevered and pain numbed mind fancied it might be some thief out to rob him of what few possessions he still carried. Or, might it be, perhaps, a late leaving Union soldier seeking personal vengeance against any Confederate uniform he should encounter?

Long since having abandoned his rifle in painful and exhausting travel, tentatively, he reached for a weapon—a brick, and leaned forward, peeking around the crumbled remains of wall through which he'd crawled inside.

Down the side of the standing wall—legs trembling, flanks striped by lash welts and bleeding, a lathered copper stallion stood puffing and blowing out against the girth of a fine leather saddle. Oblivious to scurrying crowds that hurried along giving him wide berth, the frightened horse had stopped not ten feet away, too spent to run farther with his cumbersome burden.

Briars
The House of Heirs

The Confederate cavalry officer whose limp body, battered and bruised, hung awkwardly from the saddle—his booted foot twisted awry in the stirrup—would never whip this fine animal again, Jonathan thought. No telling how far the steed had run, dragging his dead rider. But the horse's presence was a natural fact, Jonathan theorized, not providence. He stepped slowly through the niche, stretching out his hand towards the frightened mount as he moved. "Easy, boy, easy! I'm not going to hurt you." The stallion, unable to run farther, lowered his head and submitted to Jonathan's gentle persuasion.

Tying the nervous stallion's reins to a gaslight pole, Jonathan saw to the luckless rider. Disengaging the man's twisted foot broken at the ankle from the stirrup, he laid the crumpled body on the hot pavement, using the officer's own coat to cover his bloody grimacing features and upper torso. That was the least he could do seeing he was in no condition himself to remove the corpse completely from harm's way. He didn't bother to search the remains for identification, though he felt sympathy for the family of any man who would beat his horse as mercilessly as this man had done. They, too, had doubtless felt his heavy cruel hand.

Well now, he thought, tucking the ill-fated officer's loaded forty-four caliber pistol into his belt and swinging up into the saddle by the pommel, he'd make it to *Briars* and Sweet Sarah sooner than he'd figured, after all, and Lillian Heirs would use her medical knowledge to treat his infected wound—if it wasn't already too late. If they were gone but *Greenleaf* still stood, at least, he would have the comfort of dying at home.

Away from the chaos of the inner city Jonathan urged his mount along at a faster clip, and even though ash still rained from the turbulent clouds overhead the air was breathable. Traffic had thinned to a mere trickle and those wagons and riders he did see were headed south to Macon or east to Savannah, all hurrying away from his destination.

As he rode he was overwhelmed by the totality of destruction. Areas he remembered as exceptionally beautiful—majestic homes with columns and balconies, immaculate rolling lawns with dogwood trees—were no more; every site razed to a smoldering bed of ashes and rubble. Losses, when counted, would be staggering. Looters would find little to scavenge here. He could only hope that the same fate had not befallen *Greenleaf* or *Briars*.

He had decided to call the dead Confederate officer's horse "Spirit" because the stallion was so all-fired full of it. Well trained, Spirit responded to the slightest twitch of the rein or lean in the saddle. They moved as one and Jonathan counted himself fortunate in having been able to liberate the elegant steed from his luckless owner. Perhaps he should have taken time to search the poor bugger's body for identification so that by-and-by, at least, he could return the animal to his rightful owner's family. Yes—perhaps!

As Spirit stretched out his long legs and laid down a trail of red dust behind them, Jonathan relaxed and allowed himself to be temporarily soothed by the simple pleasure of the smoothness in the horse's rack.

His leg was paining him less though it still throbbed with every heartbeat, and the swelling seemed to have diminished somewhat now that he had been resting it. Hopefully, it wouldn't be long before he would receive the help he needed from Lillian Heirs. Her understanding and ministrations of first aid had brought broken bones and various other injuries to her door for years. Moreover, she had seldom seen the need to send one off to a doctor for treatment. He felt satisfied that if she got to it soon enough, he'd be just fine.

Coming slowly from the opposite direction, a wagon being pulled by a team of mules caught his eye even at a distance. Jutting out from the jumble of furnishings piled haphazardly into it was a floor lamp with a wine and ivory colored octagonal fringed lamp shade bobbing and dancing with each bump in the road. Yes, there was something intimately familiar about that lamp and lampshade!

Jonathan inspected the faces of the three young men on the driver's bench. The driver, bearded and narrow of countenance, looked for the world like a neighbor, Milton Johnson. The Johnson family had lucked into buying a parcel of land on the back side if *Briars* and *Greenleaf* from Morgan Heirs years ago when he decided to pare down on the size of his personal land holdings. Homer and Mistress Johnson were as nice an old couple as anybody could know, but the unfortunate Mister Johnson suffered with a palsy, and those boys of theirs, all three of them, lacking the strict upbringing of a strong authority figure, had been in trouble with the law more than once. Mostly petty theft, but enough to cause one to keep them at a friendly distance rather than inviting them for dinner when the good silver was in use.

The nearer the wagon advanced, the surer Jonathan became that it was the Johnson boys, all three of them. Milton, eldest at twenty-four, thin and wiry, was a little younger than himself. Seated in the middle, Curtis, nineteen, had always seemed a mite beefy. Daniel, youngest and skinniest, was the same age as Sarah's brother, Wil. With every yard that closed between the wagon and himself, that lamp shade looked more and more like one from his mother's parlor.

The youngest boy, Dan, on the outside of the wagon seat threw up his hand and called, "That you, Jonny?" All three were grinning so, they looked like they'd be busting their jaws any minute.

Jonathan didn't smile nor throw up his hand but as the wagon ground to a stop up ahead of him, he eased his mount down gradually to a walk and approached them. How in blazes would they handle this meeting? Imagine, Jonathan thought, the bad luck of bumping into somebody whose house you've just robbed with the booty to prove your guilt right there in your hands, so to speak. That should make for quite a predicament!

He doubted there'd be any plausible explanation for them to be riding right up to him, grins over all their faces, with his mother's sitting room lamp in their wagon. But then, wasn't that also his mother's own pastel pink Queen Anne chair, her favorite, turned up on its side and tied down with a length of wine colored drapery cord from the very same room? Jonathan laid Spirit's reins gently across his neck and leaned heavily on his saddle's pommel as he pulled up even with the driver's bench.

"Jonny, what a crying shame!" Milt's smile fell off into an expression of sincere concern. "Managed to get yourself shot, I see!"

"Yeah," added his youngest brother, Dan, with admiration shining in his eyes, "But I bet you got the other fellow, too, huh?" Maybe he was just making a lame attempt to divert attention from the apparent theft, but he, too, sounded genuine enough.

Guessing it wouldn't sound too exciting to say he was stealing a chicken when he got shot, he just evaded answering the part about getting the other fellow. "Yep, I'm shot up a little, all right."

"Good to see you riding' back, anyways," Milton said, earnestly. "At least, you're all in one piece." His eyes moved quickly from Jonathan's face to the horse and gear. "You went away walking but I see you're coming back in style. That's some fine stallion!"

Jonathan restrained himself from bringing up the stolen property. "Yep, found him running amok back there in town; wasn't anything to be done for his rider." He would parry with the Johnson boys as long as it took. "It'll be good to be back home." Spirit moved impatiently under him. "How long you been home, Milt?"

"Three days. Learned me a trade in the army, too." He smiled with pride. "Going to set me up a smithy shop in town soon's I can find a likely place still standing." He hesitated.

Briars
The House of Heirs

"Jonny, I was wondering—" Milton went on, "—about Drew Heirs, seeing he ain't with you." He slung the reins back and forth over the mules' hind quarters, stirring up a batch of bloodsucking flies that resettled, immediately.

Spirit, too, snorted and pawed the ground, anxious to be moving.

"Drew won't be coming back," Jonny said, shortening his reins. "I'm on my way to tell his family, then I'm going on home to *Greenleaf*." He watched Milt's face closely at the mention of *Greenleaf*, but there was not the slightest hint of guilt, only sympathy.

"I'm sorry to be the one to have to tell you this, Jonny." Milt sounded honest. He paused, mulling over what he was going to say and it was obvious to Jonathan that it was not going to be good news. "You'll find *Briars* still standing, but *Greenleaf*'s likely gone by now! Your pa and ma let everybody that wanted to—go! Then they left *Greenleaf*, themselves, day before yesterday on the train to Macon. Your ma told my ma they was going to her sister, Samantha's." He took a new breath. "Sons of bitches have probably torched our place by now, too! Ma got Pa out in the chaise first thing yesterday morning. Didn't want him to have to watch it burning, you know. We're to meet them at a cousin's house in Savannah. Then later on, we'll make plans about coming back and rebuilding." He looked plain worn down. "Pa's not too strong, these days."

Curt leaned forward, picking up the story, "Damned Yankees are working out of *Briars*. A small squad. About nine or ten. Guards on the front gate. Got there yesterday mid-afternoon."

Dan, who'd just used his open hand to swat a blue fly sucking blood from the hind end of the mule in front of him, took over. "Don't reckon they'll leave *Briars* standing, neither, once they get ready to pull out. They ain't apt to leave nothing standin'!"

Suddenly, the purloined lamp, the chair, and whatever else of *Greenleaf*'s the wagon contained, held no interest for Jonathan Baker. He could see no earthly reason to require the Johnson boys' confession for absconding with furnishings from *Greenleaf* after Ma had left, knowing the house was going to be burned anyway. It really didn't matter a hill of beans—not anymore.

"I appreciate y'all telling me all this, Milton, I really do," Jonathan said, extending his hand. "And I wish y'all the very best."

"There's something else you ought to know," Dan spoke up again. "Colonel Heirs is dead! Died three or four days ago. I run into Wil this morning down at the creek, and he told me they got him stored right there under the Yankees' noses in the root cellar."

"Damn!" Jonny said, Spirit dancing under him. "The way things work out!" He wouldn't have known the facts if he hadn't run into the thieving Johnson boys. The thing that mattered right now was that the enemy was occupying *Briars* and the Heirs women were in a gravely dangerous predicament. "Alone in that house with only the boy and the servants? God only knows what treatment those ladies may be suffering!"

"What you aim on doing?" It was Milton, again, his somber expression beginning to brighten, sparked by anticipation.

"Well, just now, I'm thinking that there's a bunch of Yankees holding my future wife and her mother and sisters captive, and I'm thinking, nine or ten more dead Yankees may not change the outcome of the war one damn bit but if I can get there before they leave, I do plan to see to that deed done, one way or another."

"Reckoned you might," Milton smiled. He looked over his shoulder at the newly acquired treasures. "Guess we got a small debt to even, anyways, now that we've met up. We got no timetable so tight we can't put off travel for a little while. Right, boys?"

There was agreement, in general, that a fight was a far better use of one's time, any day, than a long, dull journey. And an act of gallantry—well, that was to be admired.

Yep, Jonathan thought, assured of their collaboration, there's safety in numbers and nothing better than a wagon load of old, used, heavy, out-dated furniture for cover when shots start flying. He waited while Milt Johnson turned the wagon and in the next minute they were riding along together planning their strategy.

CHAPTER EIGHT ~ QUESTIONS

10:30 a.m., November 16, 1864 ~ Briars, Atlanta, Georgia

Treachery

Lieutenant Moss awakened to Sergeant Crane's prodding and gingerly got to his feet, massaging his throbbing temples. "What time is it, Sergeant?"

"I make it ten-thirty, sir." Crane answered, looking down at a recently confiscated gold pocket watch, a souvenir from a past foray.

"Damn, Crane!" Moss used the tall weapons cabinet standing against the library wall to steady himself. "How much whiskey did you boys pour down me, anyway? My Pa always told me, 'Never drink in the morning unless it's the hair o' the dog that bit you the night before'. Hell, we got to be on the road again before long, and not one of us is going to be worth killing for the rest of the day. That was a real stupid prank, Crane! When my head gets back down to it's rightful size, remind me to reprimand you for allowing things to get so far out of hand. Look at this place—I swear the last thing I remember is you pouring a quart of liquor down me!"

The wily Sergeant Crane smiled, watching Lieutenant Moss' struggle to stand erect.

The younger man ran his hand over the polished mahogany of the weapons cabinet doors and snapped them open. For a few moments he examined the vacant interior. There were deep imprints in the green velvet footing and backing of the cabinet.

Crane could tell that Lieutenant Shane Moss had admired the weapons cabinet yesterday by the way his face lit up when he first noticed it. Crane could see he had an appreciation for nice things, coming from a genteel Virginia family as he did. But not everybody born in Virginia came from such good stock, he knew that, too, first hand.

"Does it strike you, Sergeant Crane," Moss asked, "that there should still be weapons in these racks? I count two revolver impressions and six long guns. How do you count?"

"The same, sir." The Sergeant touched the dents one after the other. "This, here's a Springfield Cadet. Notice the narrow stock. There's another one. That one, there, looks for the world like an old Flintlock Musket. The pistol that fits there's an Ethan Allen Pepperbox—see how deep the print is?"

"Very good, Sergeant." Lieutenant Moss patted the sturdy man's back, then grabbed the cabinet door once more for support.

"Thank you, sir." Sergeant Crane smiled, baring his yellow-green teeth.

"Would you say the owner of all these weapons was, possibly, a collector, Sergeant?" the lieutenant asked, closing the cabinet doors and examining the un-tampered lock.

"I would, sir," the sergeant agreed. "Also a man of means."

"Where would you say the contents of that cabinet might have gotten to, Sergeant?" Moss raised an eyebrow, inquiring, "Were they there when you boys rescued the liquor from that closet this morning?"

"No, sir!" Crane stiffened. "If the lieutenant is suggesting my men took the arms, sir, I can assure you—"

"Never mind, Sergeant." Moss walked unsteadily towards the door. "Just get this room cleaned up! I'm going to find a pot of coffee."

"Yes, sir, right away, sir." Sergeant Crane snapped a smart salute.

Moss paused in the doorway and a frown burrowed into his forehead when he focused again on his sergeant. "Oh, and, Sergeant, the ladies of the house?"

Crane held his salute and stared straight ahead, not allowing their eyes to meet. "Still secure in their rooms, sir."

"That's good." Moss nodded, turning away.

A smile played at the corners of Crane's mouth as he watched Moss leave. "Yes, sir!" he muttered under his breath. The young ninny didn't remember a thing about this morning, it was obvious. The liquor monkeyshines was a major stroke of genius and even though he'd never laid a finger on young Moss, personally, God, how he loved teaching that brat the way they did things in the ranks. Besides, there wasn't a chance in hell any man of them was going to admit to anything that happened while Moss was sleeping it off. There'd be a dead man among them if anybody even hinted at it. Let the two women tell if they dared! Hell, they'd be scared to open their mouths for fear they'd get worse than what they got before. Too bad about the boys upstairs though. They couldn't have guessed their little banging session would end up like that! He was glad he'd sent them all out after they'd told him about the injured woman. No need to complicate matters, now, with confessions of disobedience. Better to keep it the way it was. No admission of insubordination—no discipline. Crane stood in the middle of the room looking after his superior officer.

Moss stopped to look back before he proceeded down the long hall to the kitchen. "Sergeant, was there something else you wanted to say?" He never felt comfortable with the sergeant. Never believed the man was trustworthy.

"Me, sir? No, sir." Then Crane began picking up empty bottles from the floor.

Coffee

When Moss reached the kitchen, he found a large pot of lukewarm coffee steeping on the side of the unattended wood stove. He reached into the wood box and brought out a slender splinter of pine, which he used to remove one of the stove's hot eyes. He fed the pine kindling pieces into the stove one after another until flames licked up through the opening. He grated it closed, placed the pot on the center of the eye, and walked out onto the back porch to wait in the crisp morning air for the coffee to re-heat.

If the guns were not in the cabinet, and the sergeant was telling the truth, they'd probably been removed by the men of the house when answering the call to arms. Most every able bodied man or boy, civilian or slave, had been pressed into service at the last and they had fought barefoot and threadbare until they couldn't hold out any longer. At least, he knew the weapons weren't on the grounds. His men had made a thorough search of the stables, barns and sheds when they'd first arrived, but it was a fact that the Confederate Army in and around Atlanta had been worn down and dispersed weeks ago.

In fact, after Kennesaw Mountain's ugly defeat, an angered General Sherman had led them straight into Atlanta where, starting in July, torch-bearing men had burned over thirty-six hundred homes. The Battle of Atlanta had culminated in the defeat and scattering of General John Bell Hood's Confederate forces with his official surrender on September 2, and during these past months occupying Yankee troops had cut telegraph lines, blown up trains and ripped out rail lines, isolating Atlanta and strangling the city's supply lines from Savannah and other port cities. They had held the city hostage until today and when they were finished with the last phase, the burning of Atlanta in it's entirety, according to his orders and timetable, they were to rejoin Sherman for a march to the sea. Shane Moss didn't always like his orders but he was obliged to carry them out, tempering them with reason where possible.

Here in this house, for instance, there were only four white women, along with an old Negro man and his wife. Moss would not be so insensitive as to ask Mistress Heirs what had happened to their men folks. Puzzling though, that with the presence of five women, there were no children about. No children, at all. Sent away to safer lodgings? Probably. With the city under siege, that would have been logical. Macon, he'd heard, was overflowing with refugees from Atlanta. Lucky, too, the ones who had chosen Macon over Covington or McDonough. According to his maps and the confidential information he'd been privy to, once they rejoined General Sherman, those towns would be directly on their route and were also doomed to a fiery destruction. Concerning Atlanta, the General had been plain spoken: "They may not be made to love us but they can be made to fear us." While Shane Moss believed Sherman to be a born leader and a man of many commendable accomplishments, he found it difficult to accept that such a highly respected man would deliberately plan to burn a trail right through the state of Georgia all the way to the sea. As the smell of burnt wood reached his nostrils, he found it even harder to accept the fact that he was duty bound to carry out such crimes.

As a boy, at his father's bidding, Shane Moss had begun schooling at Virginia Military Institute in Lexington, Virginia, but he was never a warrior at heart; and although he knew a Springfield Cadet rifle from a Cavalry Muskatoon he'd been sent out into the field, untested. He proudly joined with Mr. Lincoln, though, on his moral principle that no man should own another.

His older brother, Luke, had chosen the Southern cause. That was the way things had been back home in Virginia—the war splitting families right down the middle. Breeding and training horses—that was the very core of his life, and just about the only thing he and Luke had ever seen eye to eye on.

He sighed, rubbing his aching temples. The fresh air was helping a little to clear his thoughts. Yes, it would take a war to make enemies of families like the Heirs and Mosses. They'd probably have gotten along fine under different circumstances.

Mistress Heirs had said, "I'm sure *even* Yankees have mothers—" His own mother, in *Moss Hall*, would surely be missing him now just as she'd be missing her older Rebel son, Luke.

Briars
The House of Heirs

"This war is Hell," General Sherman had said just before he ordered the burning of Atlanta. But, by God, Shane Alexander Moss had no intention of doing battle with gentle ladies of the South!

There came a rattling of pots and pans and loud voices from the kitchen, interrupting his musing. A woman's high-pitched voice shrilled, "you better see t' them—"

"Hush, woman, somebody goin' hear—"

Moss recognized Henry's slow drawl, scolding, softly. His mulatto wife was obviously upset over something.

The woman's voice suddenly took on a scornful pitch. "Who been messin' wit' my stove?"

"Now, Rachel, hon, you goin' get yo'self all het up over nothin'."

Moss stepped back into the kitchen and upon seeing him, the Negro woman, in a frenzied state, dropped the folded towel she was about to use to remove the spewing coffee pot from the stove top.

The lieutenant caught her arm. "Careful, don't burn yourself! That pot's boiling over!"

She recoiled, quickly pulling her hand away and stepping back.

He bent and picked up the towel, handing it to her. "I'm afraid it was my fault. I stoked the stove and then went out onto the porch to wait for the coffee to boil—"

"I don't boil my coffee!" the woman said, reproachfully. Folding the towel around the pot's handle, she carried it through the back door and poured its contents onto the ground beyond the railing.

There was more weighing on this woman's mind than a ruined pot of coffee.

Henry, his forehead bunched into a frown, spoke up. "Lieuten't, I's sorry my woman done spoke improper t' you. She don't mean no harm. It's jus' she ain't used t' bein' touched—I mean—" Henry looked like he'd spoken out of turn.

"—that is, suh, she's scared t' death o' all o' y'all." Rachel stood subdued, watching, listening, half in-half out of the room; the partially closed back door resting against her ample backside. Henry smiled a broad smile. "She 'bout t' start makin' y'all some dinner. My Rachel's one fine cook. Um-um! Come on in here, woman, what yo' waitin' fo'?"

It was a good rescue, but Moss knew there was more left unsaid than said by the tall black man and the round Mulatto woman. He checked his pocket watch, a 'going away' gift from his father. Almost eleven. Sergeant Crane would make quite a point of the fact that while he was sleeping off the whiskey they'd half-drowned him in last night, Crane had gone ahead and, according to plan, sent out men earlier on General Sherman's standing order to burn as they went. Crane would want extra credit for covering for the Lieutenant while he slept off the prank, too, no doubt. The men should finish their assignments and be back by noon. Properties surrounding *Briars* would have been reduced to rubble by the time they ate and got on their way. Crane knew as well as Moss did, the unit had to be on the road by two o'clock at the latest to rendezvous with Sherman at the appointed time.

"I'll leave your kitchen to you—Rachel, is it?" the lieutenant said. "Send my coffee to the library when it's ready." She'd be more comfortable taking orders from him.

Oaths and Prayers

Peeking through the break in the hedges, Lillian paused to get her breath. She could see the pantry entrance on the side of the house and the back porch. She smiled, remembering Morgan's concern for the porch's protrusion ruining the lines of the house when she asked him to build it years ago. Now, she was glad for the porch's prominence, for she saw the lieutenant standing there, and he would surely have seen her, too, had she headed out across the yard without checking first. She waited behind the hedges until the soldier re-entered the kitchen before proceeding to the pantry entrance.

From within the pantry, she thanked God for Henry's logical and sensible approach to each problem as it emerged within his range of responsibility. She had heard their voices from her hiding place, and Henry's show of angry authority in hushing Rachel when she spoke out of turn had been about as out of character for Henry as Rachel's asking the soldier to join them for a cup of coffee would have been, but Henry's ruse had worked all the same.

Lillian worried about Rachel should both Henry and she become casualties of the battle that lay ahead. She felt the knot of anxiety—anxiety concerning her own Sarah, Morgana and Wil, and Rachel's Willow—tighten and grow larger and her heart ached for what new tragedy might come, but there could be no turning back now.

She listened to make sure that the lieutenant had gone and when there was no one in the kitchen but Rachel, she stepped from the pantry into the room. The cook jumped like she'd seen a ghost. "Oh, Miz Lillian, you done give me such a turn!"

"I'm sorry if I startled you, Rachel." Then trying to appear unruffled, Lillian asked, "Do you know where the girls have gone? They weren't in the root cellar when I got there."

Rachel's answer was evasive. "I ain't seen nobody but that Yankee lieuten't." Her gaze shifted to the frying pan she held in her hand. "I's about t' make some Vittles, like you said, now things is quieted down. I hopes them girls is all right when you finds 'em, Miz Lillian. They's been such goings on!"

Rachel's words sent shocks of dread through Lillian. "Goings on? What kind of 'goings on', Rachel? What are you talking about?"

"Good thing you 'as down at th' root cellar, Miz Lillian! It would've broke your heart, you'd been here."

"What, Rachel—what! For Heaven's sake, woman, what did you hear?"

"It 'as Sweet Sarah—!" Rachel started, "That child—"

Terrified, Lillian hurried up the back stairs.

She raced along the upstairs hall from the back stairs towards her eldest daughter's door. This morning, she'd spoken first to Willow, next to Laura Lee, then to Sarah, and from Sarah's room she'd gone directly to Morgana's. She'd even watched Morgana leave, following her sisters to safety—following Laura Lee *and Sarah* to the root cellar.

She stopped outside Sarah's closed door, a silent prayer on her lips.

They had stood Sarah's door back up, fitting it's pin-less hinges together so that when Lillian turned the knob and pushed, the door swung open. Without even stepping inside, Lillian could see that Sarah was dead. Poor Sweet Sarah, too frightened even to run as she'd been warned to do.

She was lying crumpled on the Prussian blue carpet at the foot of her bed, her slim and dainty body, nude, in a pool of her own blood. From the quantity of blood, there was no doubt she'd bled to death. It must have taken a very long time, and the look of horror etched on her face said that she'd died in terror.

"Oh, God, why?" Lillian lamented, quickly gathering her lifeless daughter to her breast and covering the young woman's nakedness with her own ample skirts. Oh, God!" she whispered, "Oh, my Sarah, I'm so sorry. I didn't know you stayed behind! I would've died in your place—!" Lillian wept, and cradled Sarah's dead body until there were no more tears. Sarah had always had trouble with her monthlies, and she'd worried about having babies. But, Lillian thought, if Sarah hadn't been raped, she would still be alive and well.

Lillian cried out, raising her clenched fist to God, and swearing in a harsh voice unlike her own, "On my oath, these Yankee soldiers—these rapists—in my house are good as dead as of this very moment."

It would be hate, anger, resolve, that would keep her on her feet, now. There'd be time for grief later, after.

Against the Lieutenant's promise, Sarah had been accosted in her room. But what of Morgana and Laura Lee? She had watched Morgana leave. God willing, they had found safety outside the house.

Lillian went quickly to Laura Lee's door. Married, older and more mature than Sarah or Morgana, if Laura Lee had also been attacked, she would have been able to withstand the grievance better than either of her younger sisters-in-law. Fearfully, she rapped softly on Laura Lee's door, but got no answer. Quietly, she turned the knob, holding her breath as the door swung open.

At the door's opening, Laura Lee, clean and clothed, turned from looking out the window and with apparent apathy, said, "Oh, it's you, Mother Heirs, come in. I've been watching the briar cave."

Lillian's heart ached as she hurried to embrace her daughter-in-law. The story of her encounter was etched on Laura Lee's finely carved features. "Laura Lee, I'm so sorry!"

"It's not your fault." Laura Lee let herself be held for a moment then pushed away to turn back to the window. "I'll be all right. My babies are still safe. That's all I care about."

Slowly, Lillian turned Laura Lee to face her again. "Laura Lee, it's Sarah! Sarah, you don't know—" The expression on the younger woman's face said she did know. "Tell, me!" Lillian urged, shaking her gently, though she could see how terribly painful it was for Laura Lee to talk about the events of the morning. "I'm sorry, dear, but I have to know?"

"They caught me downstairs. They were in the pantry."

"Oh, dear God, no! I sent you there—all of you!"

"You couldn't have known." Laura Lee's gaze went back to the window. "I heard Sarah cry out. She's somewhere in the house."

Lillian prompted, softly, "And Morgana? What about Morgana, dear?"

Laura Lee's apathetic expression gave way to one of bewilderment. "I don't know. I thought she'd gotten out somehow!"

Lillian led Laura Lee, obviously in a state of shock, away from the lure of the window. "Your babies are safe in Willow's care." Then, she told Laura Lee about finding Sarah, and they returned to Sarah's room. Together, they lifted Sarah's body onto her bed and bathed her and dressed her. Still pained and indignant from her own loathsome experience, Laura Lee released pent-up tears and wept at their loss, but knowing Sarah's delicate nature, she was not, altogether, surprised by the outcome of Sarah's attack.

Lillian left Laura Lee with Sarah while she went searching for Morgana. She approached Morgana's door just as Morgana, freshly bathed and dressed, opened it.

Could Mama tell? Morgana wondered. Did it show that she was no longer virgin?

"Mama, I was about to come looking for y'all." Then, Morgana saw the paleness of her mother's face and saw Laura Lee looking out from Sarah's room, and she rushed into her sister's room.

Laura Lee slipped quietly away and returned to keep vigil at her own bedroom window.

"Sarah! Oh, no, Sarah!" Morgana wept with anguish when she saw her sister was dead. Lillian tried to hold her and comfort her but Morgana pushed her away. "Leave me alone!" she howled. Seeing Sarah like this, Morgana's own guilt for her offense in discovering sexual pleasure took refuge under the cloak of righteous indignation. "I'm going back down there right now—," She stroked Sarah's pale cheek. "—and demand that that raping lieutenant— *oh, yes, Mama, me, too!*" She was glad for the chance to confess it, now. *Her* wantonness. *Her* sin. *Her* shame. Laughing, and crying, and shrill, Morgana exclaimed, "*He raped me, Mama! But they killed my sister!* Now, I'm going to see that those murdering demons responsible for my sister's death are stood up against a wall and shot down by a firing squad! No—," she declared, "a firing squad is too humane." She'd demand to kill them, herself, each guilty man in turn with his own weapon while the others watched and quaked. "You think I couldn't do it, Mama?" she cried. "Oh, you just watch me! Killing in war isn't murder— not killing like in the Bible! War is different! This is war, Mama, and *we're right in the damn middle of it!*"

It was at that point that Lillian interrupted her and asked, quietly, "Morgana, where were you when you were assaulted?"

Morgana's voice wavered, "What difference does that make? I was raped, Mama, isn't that what counts?"

"You were in the library, weren't you? I specifically instructed you to go to the root cellar, but you chose to disobey me."

"Mama, that's all you ever do!" Morgana's liquid black eyes shimmered with the sudden release of long contained anger. "You order me about like I am one of the servants! You treat me like I don't have a brain in my head! I can think, Mama, and I would think for myself, too, if you ever gave me the chance! But, no, it's always been, 'Do this, Morgana! Don't do that, Morgana!' I'm seventeen, and most of my friends are married. Some already even have babies! But you, Mama, you won't let me grow up! Well, I *am* grown up, now, Mama, and nothing you can do will ever change that. What's more, if I want to kill Yankees, now, I'll kill damn Yankees!"

Lillian shook her head. "You're too impulsive for your own good, Morgana, and if you don't strive to overcome that trait, some day it will be your undoing. Be quiet for one split second—" Lillian admonished Morgana, still deep within her wild tirade of how she, personally, would eliminate the enemy. "—and, listen to me!" Lillian waited calmly until Morgana hushed and paid attention to her.

Lillian carefully explained how, by the family's all working together, they would exact vengeance against the savage, murdering, raping band of Yankees. She prayed God, in His infinite mercy, would decree it 'an act of war' and that He would forgive her for leading her household into mortal sin. "Oh, darling girl," Lillian assured her only living daughter. "Those Yankee scoundrels will never leave *Briars* alive after the outrage they've perpetrated on this house of Heirs today!"

Composed at last, Morgana looked down on Sarah's pale silent beauty and feeling the weight of her own passion and guilt said, "My sister was too good to live in this evil world, Mama."

Lillian kissed her dead daughter's cold lips, embraced Morgana, and went to tell Wilson of his sister's death.

Entering the kitchen, Lillian raised a finger to her lips when Rachel looked up from her cooking. Stepping into the pantry, she gestured for Rachel to join her, and when the cook was there, she told her about Sarah, and held the small, round woman while she wept softly.

"I knowed it, Miz Lillian, I knowed it! That child's prayer 'as th' dying kind!"

Then Lillian left a lamenting Rachel to her duties, swearing to her that all their sacrifices, heartaches and suffering would soon be at an end and scores would be settled. Once more, Lillian paused beside the outside pantry door—looking, listening. She thought of Morgan's propensity for gambling. What would he say the odds were that sooner or later she would be seen making one of these excursions?

The stables showed no activity and probably wouldn't until the Yankees' mounts, and the fine Heirs riding horses, now designated pack animals, were brought up for departure. As she had expected, all the men except two, who remained out on their burning mission, had congregated in the library waiting for their dinner. They expected to be on their way before long so she'd have to hurry to implement her plan and she couldn't afford any slip-ups.

She looked for anybody in the garden, the pasture, and all the way down the hill to the clump of naked sycamore trees before she dashed out across the side yard and passed through the high hedge.

When Lillian knocked, Wil threw open the door and exclaimed, "They're dead, ain't they? My sisters are both dead!" The waiting had taken its toll. The boy was frantic with worry.

Lillian reached out and caught his chin in her hand, hushing him, and whispered, "Wil, Wil, listen to me! Morgana's all right. It's Sarah, though!" There was no way she could tell him all that she knew had happened. She simply told him that Sarah had died at the hands of the enemy.

Wilson heard more in her well chosen words than she had intended him to hear, but he didn't cry. He paled, bit his lip and, unexpectedly, reached down and embraced his mother, murmuring in her ear, "Aw! Ma, you know I love you, don't you?" Though she knew it, hearing it was welcome. With his next breath, Wil declared, "Ma, I'm through with hidin'! I'm goin' to take my rifle and a couple of Papa's guns and go back up there to the house and me and Henry'll walk in while they're eatin' and—"

"No, Son, I've got a better plan than that. I saw Henry and Storm headed this way from the stream as I was coming down. Let's go meet them."

Anguish and anger fought an agonizing duel inside her and she felt she needed, desperately, to strike out! With Morgan Heirs gone, she was the head of the Heirs' family, and she had to do things the way Morgan would have done them were he still with them.

When the three of them had climbed to the top of the embankment and sat together over the entrance to the root cellar, Lillian dangled her booted feet and full skirts over the edge, burying her arm in Storm's heavy mane, sharing him with Wil while she explained her uncomplicated plan.

Starting out by looking skyward, she said a prayer aloud so Wil and Henry could hear her. "Lord, whatever You want to do with us, we're Yours to do with, but I'm aiming to clean house at

Briars, today!" Then freed from the shackles of self-recrimination, she explained painstakingly to Wil and Henry precisely what each was to do: "Now, I'm not proud of the idea of shooting any man in the back, but surprising them is the only way we're going to get them all before they can get any of us. So just you listen to what I say and we'll talk about it, after."

Henry understood, correctly, his simple instructions: Wit' Mister Morgan's prized old 1817 Flintlock musket which Miz Lillian 'as givin' t' him on th' spot because he'd always admired it so, he was t' go out by way of th' dining room's side door t' th' front corner o' th' verandah an' wait 'til all th' men were mounted an' ready t' ride out. Miz Lillian, by her own design, would be standin' in th' front doorway wit' th' young lieuten't. Morgana an' Laura Lee would be at upstairs front windows. After th' men had all mounted an' they 'as on their way down th' drive, on Miz Lillian's first shot as a signal, everybody else would fire at once takin' th' enemy by surprise startin' wit' th' ones nearer th' front so's they didn't target th' same man twice. She'd fire th' repeater pistol, takin' out as many o' th' men in th' rear as she could. That would be one Yankee each fo' Miz Laura Lee and Miss Morgana from upstairs, an' two fo' hisself downstairs, all wit' single shot guns. An', if'n she could get off that many rounds, six fo' Miz Lillian in quick succession befo' th' enemies found their wits.

As Lillian expected, Wil had not taken instruction as to his role in her plot at all well. His duty, while the invaders were eating their last meal, would be to deliver the weapons to his mother in the pantry—to leave her the pistol—then carry two rifles by the servants' stairs to Laura Lee in her own room; Morgana, in her mother's room. Then, according to his mother, he was to go straight back to the root cellar and remain there for at least two hours. Wil fumed while she went on.

Having faced the probability of her own demise, Lillian considered her decision on the pistol she had chosen for herself a wise one. It being small enough for a woman to handle and the best repeating weapon in the house. At the front door, she'd be closest and better able to fire more times and hit more targets, and though she'd given it some deliberation, she had no reservations about shooting the departing men in the back. Not after what they'd done!

Wilson completely lost his self-control at that point and cursed, "Ma, I'll be damned if I'm gonna sit down here in the root cellar, wonderin' what's goin' on, while y'all are up there shooting Hell-bound Yankees. You plan to knock off six of those bastards all by yourself? And Henry's to get two of 'em? Ain't no way in Hell you, two, gonna do that! I don't care how fast that pissin' pistol fires!"

Unexpectedly, it had been Henry, who'd quickly reprimanded the boy, saying, "That how yo' talks t' yo' Mama? Uh-uh! Somebody 'sides that puny chil', Andy, up there in th' bushes got t' be left t'carry on th' Heirs' name. Wil, you lis'en t' yo' mama!"

Pleased by Henry's loyalty almost as much as Wil's pluck and having settled the matter once and for all in her own mind, climbing back up the hill, Lillian had to admit to herself that she'd known all along, chances were she wouldn't walk away. The boy was right, of course, but she had come to view the undertaking philosophically. Morgana and Laura Lee would be upstairs at the windows, protected by the sturdy house around them, difficult targets with any gauge weapon. On the lower floor and exposed, she and Henry, both old and tired were, indeed, expendable. Henry had agreed wholeheartedly to her plan.

In truth, she believed she'd lived long enough. She had no desire to spend more years growing old as a widow. Perhaps, to grow feeble and end up burdensome to those she loved. Only days ago without warning, she'd lost her husband, her life's companion. Then, tragically, Sarah! She was consumed with grief for them. Oh, God, what was to come of the others? What of her son, Drew, away at war? Jonathan Baker, like a third son, and who was to have become Sarah's husband? If her hand wasn't fast enough and they got away, shooting her before she made her quota, she wouldn't be surprised, nor for that matter, would she really mind very much.

What was it the young lieutenant had said? "—especially, if there's liquor about—" Leaving the liquor in the house. That had been her mistake! But there could never have been time enough to have done all that should've been done, not knowing they were coming until they were there.

Then, too, she constantly worried about the babies huddled with Willow in that cave of briars. Were they still all right? At twenty feet from the driveway, were they far enough away from the target area to be out of danger? Twenty yards would have been much better. Why hadn't she known there'd be shooting when she'd sent them out? Why hadn't she guessed?

Back at the house, she went straight to Sarah's door and looked in. There was Morgana, still down on her knees scrubbing away at the blood-stained carpet where her sister's body had lain. She did not speak nor interrupt Morgana's futile energetic cleansing of the hurtful memory. Perhaps exerting such strenuous effort would spend her anger and give her respite. Nothing any of them could do would bring Sweet Sarah back. Lillian walked quickly away. Reflecting on the sad scene any more was useless. Their course was set.

Greenleaf

The Seth Thomas clock on her mantle began chiming twelve just as Lillian reached her own room, bringing her out of her meditation, and with the last chime a powerful blast rocked *Briars*, jarring the house to its very foundations. *Greenleaf!* Belching black smoke and licking red-tongued flames leapt from the site to the east that had been the Baker house until seconds ago. Thank God, Jeremiah and Hamita Baker had evacuated two days hence on the last train to Macon.

The Union Army had just burned *Greenleaf* to the ground. *Briars* had been spared by the solitary fact that the Yankee Lieutenant had chosen this hilltop estate over any other equally sited and convenient estate to shelter for the night.

The first parcel of land Morgan Heirs ever sold was to Jeremiah Baker when Atlanta was still called Terminus. Lillian was grateful that years later, when Atlanta's expansion had encroached on their land, Morgan had rightly surmised that sales and rental of the valuable property would provide security for the Heirs family after he was gone. Long standing mortgages and rental contracts, arranged by Tom Garrett, Morgan's financial advisor, poured money into the Heirs accounts. Morgan had considered all possibilities except a devastating war and his own impending demise. But Lillian thanked God that Morgan Heirs had not lived to see this day of sacrifices. How close they had come to losing *Briars*, as well as their Sweet Sarah!

Conscience

Private Carl Slade climbed the stile steps and sat atop the wooden fence to catch his breath. He looked back over his shoulder at the leaping flames and black smoke he had walked away from not five minutes before and congratulated himself. At least, that had gone right. Maybe the successful "burn" would put an end to the string of bad luck that had plagued him since he got up this morning.

They were all guilty as hell! First off, Crane, Fowler, Jenkins, Brock and Dodd had gotten hold of a woman while they were scrounging around in the pantry. She'd come downstairs from the forbidden second floor looking for a chance to get out, they said, so she was fair game and they'd dragged her off to the back bedroom. Knowing each one of them was going to get a turn with her just set the other four off! They all knew there was a whole supply of women upstairs and it had been a long dry time for everybody. Burgess and Loomis went right along upstairs with him and Black. Nobody was thinking straight by that time! If he'd been sober he never would have done what he did, but he wasn't!

The liquor had left him with a skunk in his mouth and the screaming woman upstairs had caused him to put a failed mission back in his britches. How were they supposed to know that she would be so poorly built she couldn't take a few good bangs? Even at that, they'd hurried with her. She was all bloodied up and screaming when he left her. It could have been any one of them but he'd been the last. They'd stood the door back up in its hinges hoping it would keep the noise of her wailing down a little. Hell, it was just plain bad luck, what happened, but it got to him anyway! He just hoped the woman was going to be all right; she was mighty pretty.

Sergeant Crane and Corporal Fowler had to go over orders with Lieutenant Moss and Crane didn't want any of them spilling their guts to Moss when he woke up. He assigned Burgess and Loomis immediately to the gates and sent all the others out in different directions with the simple order to burn every house within five miles, "liberate" any horses they found, and return as close to noon as possible. Dodd, Brock, and Jenkins saddled up their horses and headed off through the open field to the neighboring place to the west. Slade and Black were to go east. They kept their mouths shut about what happened upstairs, all right, but then, there'd been the cane field.

The Cane Field

At the stables, Slade determined it'd be to their advantage to rest their own horses and ordered two of the Heirs' horses saddled for their foray. Black picked a Thoroughbred the groom,

Thomas, called "Star" and Slade's choice was a handsome Tennessee Walker, the nigger called "Pal". After threatening the poor frightened stableman with cruel tortures and an uncertain death if he held back any important information, they learned of a back path to the neighboring estate to the east called *Greenleaf*. "But," the groom warned, "it ain't passable on horseback."

Slade smiled at Black and told Thomas he'd "make that judgment when and if it became a problem". Then he clicked, "Giddy-yup, horse!" to Pal, and led the way out of the stable.

Slade's and Black's route proved to be a narrow path, curving and wandering downhill half a mile or so past a small cemetery and through a copse of sycamores along a shallow rocky stream. Then all at once, it seemed to give way to a field of sugar cane. There was a wooden sign staked in the ground where the cane started and scrawled on it was the terse warning: "KEEP OUT". At some distance to their right was a waist high wooden fence with a stile for foot traffic, and away and beyond a thick grove of fir trees. Canes taller than a man confronted them and, row on crooked row, it was like a maze going off in all directions. They crossed the stream and rode into the cane. The path narrowed still more and burrowed ahead into the brake for a short distance before just disappearing.

"Damn nigger knew the path would end," Black said. "Which way do we go, now? The place is east of where we started out."

"Hell, your guess is as good as mine!" Slade spat. "The sun rises in the East, which way is that?" They looked up into a gray pall of smoke. There was no east, west, south or north. "Try that way!" He pointed off diagonally to their bearing at an angle through the canebrake.

Wil's dog, Storm, in his meandering, had come across their fresh trail and had been following his stable mates' scents for at least a quarter mile when he finally caught sight of them. The riders had neither seen nor heard him catching up to them. Flat

Ann Gray

to the ground, he skulked not ten feet behind, moving when they moved.

As the men urged their mounts on, spiked blades on tall canes whipped their faces while slender snapping jagged stalks bit into their arms and thighs and lacerating their horses' necks and haunches until they were bloody. After they had penetrated deep into the cane field and there appeared to be no way out save the way they'd come, their horses, bathed in pink lather and snorting exhaustion, finally balked.

Black who led the way, began gasping for breath as the surrounding maze loomed above and all about, closing him in. He couldn't seem to get enough air and his heart started pounding. The wind that rustled through the tall cane stalks picked up and whispered in his ears, "get out, get out, get out!". Slade mustn't know. Sweating heavily, Black stood in the stirrups, trying to peer over the dense foreboding wall. He forced himself to sound composed. "Which way, now?" he asked, over his shoulder.

"Just keep on going straight ahead," Slade said to his back. "We got to get through this mess sooner or later."

Suddenly panicked, Black shouted, "That can't be right! I'm going back! Gee, horse, gee!" Without room to complete his turn, he jerked Star's reins, forcing her to pivot. A splintered cane stalk pierced her side, and she reared, sending Black flying.

Pal, following close behind, stumbled onto Star's flank, and went down, sending Slade tumbling to the ground. Slade pulled himself up by Pal's reins and using the lengths of leather, began to lash Pal about his neck and head. The horse whinnied and struggled against the whips.

Storm gave warning before he sprang. One long guttural growl and he was on top of Slade, gnawing the arm that held the reins. Cursing, Slade fought off his attacker.

"Shoot, shoot!" Slade screamed at Black. "Kill the son o' bitch!"

By the time Storm's strong jaws released Slade, both horses had skirted the struggle and withdrawn along the trampled path, headed home. Black lay still, one red stalk thrusting up two feet out of his middle and another through his neck.

As quickly as he'd emerged, Storm disappeared back into the maze.

Gathering his senses, Slade made sure there was no major damage to his arm, searched until he found his rifle, then retraced their path out of the cane on foot. He climbed the stile and rested atop the wooden fence. *Greenleaf*'s slate roof was clearly visible from his perch. It was only then he discovered the path, plain as day, where it turned and continued on the other side of the high wood fence. Passable on foot but not on horseback, Slade thought. The nigger had told them that! Oh, well, it wouldn't take long, now, to finish up. Pity about that dumb ass, Black. What the Hell could have gotten into him? Slade promised himself he'd kill that dog next time he saw him. It would have been so easy if they had only ridden out into the stream to pass around the barrier.

It had made a fairly good sized fire, the big house with the slate roof. He watched until the un-scorched tiles fell in on the debris. Looters had been there before him. There was a scattering of furnishings and broken china leading away from the house in the rear, and marks in the soft red earth where an overloaded wagon had recently pulled away.

Yep, he thought with satisfaction, his "burn" had gone well. Crane would be pleased with that. Slade took one more backwards look at his handiwork and stepped down from the stile, heading along the path towards *Briars*. He didn't really think the lieutenant would hold him personally responsible for Black. Of course, the woman would have been a different story if the lieutenant ever found out they'd gone upstairs against orders. Then, there'd be hell to pay! But who'd tell? Nobody he knew. Black was dead and every other man of them was equally guilty.

Ann Gray

Slade began climbing the hill towards the house. Moss was a good boy, he thought. Sometimes, though, he wondered if Crane didn't live just to taunt him. Crane sure hadn't given the young fellow much of a chance this morning! Then Slade had to grin. Of course, once they got started drinking, nobody had! He smelled bacon frying. Maybe some tasty food would drive away the foul taste in his mouth.

Battle Plans

Lillian presumed the Yankees were still of the notion that all this time she had remained frightened and subdued, in her room. What fools they were! She took comfort in knowing that before the hour was out the score would be settled once and for all between one squad of Sherman's invading Union Army and the Confederacy's own *Briars* volunteers. There would be no gossip outside *Briars* hedges of the outrages they had endured.

Waiting for Wil to bring the weapons up from the root cellar, Lillian could see Henry and Rachel through the partially open pantry door. Rachel, preparing the soldiers' final meal, went about her work with a fervor Lillian hadn't seen in ages. The cook had done well up until now, finding enough to feed the additional hungry men as well as the family, but as Lillian looked at the empty larder shelves, she was amazed that the invaders had left so little. Ordinarily, shelves this empty would have called for several trips to the root cellar with wheel-barrows but not this time!

Rachel sidled up to the partially open door and said to Lillian through the crack in hushed tones, "I done stashed some dinner in th' oven fo' y'all t' have when them Yankees is gone. While ago, when they's raidin' my pantry, I tol' 'em if'n they kep' on packin' an' totin' away all my goods, they wouldn't be nothin' lef' fo' them t' eat 'fore they leave. One o' them say, 'that's so, ain't it?' Then they looks at each other an' jes' turn right aroun' an' lef'!" The women, laughing softly together, clasped hands and in so doing were both strengthened.

Lillian caught the wagging of Henry's head though, and understood she was not to discuss with Rachel any part of their plans. Knowing Rachel to be a worrier, Henry had not told his wife that he might not live to enjoy another of her 'fine, fine meals'. Rachel had enough to worry about right now, as they all did, with the children confined to the briar cave with Willow, and so close to the target area, but everybody had been warned to be doubly careful to aim true, and if they didn't have a clean shot clear of the hedges on the west side of the driveway when they were ready to fire, wait until they did.

Lillian nearly jumped out of her skin when Wilson opened the outside pantry door a crack and peeked in. When he saw his mother looking back at him he grinned handing her, one by one, three rifles and a pistol before he stepped inside. Lillian leaned each one against the pantry shelves. Henry's newly acquired flintlock would remain in the pantry until Rachel had been sent to her room for a well-timed rest and Henry deemed it safe to take the gun and go to his position on the west front corner of the verandah.

The old man, calm and deliberate in every move, loaded up the large round service tray and headed out to the guards on the gate like he had been doing all along and when he returned he told Lillian and Rachel that Willow and the children looked fine from what he could see. Then Rachel sent him to the library to say to the lieutenant that dinner was ready.

Moments later, they heard the shuffling of chairs in the dining room as the soldiers took their seats at the table, ready to gobble down what leavings they thought they hadn't already packed onto Heirs' horses to abscond with when they left. From their laughter and conversation, Rachel was noticeably relieved that the men liked her scant dinner of batter-fried fat back, mashed potatoes, biscuits and white gravy.

Strangely, Lillian appreciated the feel of the pistol's cold steel now tucked into her waistband and hidden by her shawl. The revolver had been one of Morgan's favorites, an 1843 multi-shot U.S. Martial, that was good at close range and, using both hands, she had fired it with considerable accuracy a good many times just to keep her confidence up over the years since her first, unexpected, and unprepared shooting experience with the black bear back in '38.

Standing close behind her in the small storage room, Wil balanced the Springfield Cadet single shot rifles in each hand with the Musketoon's strap slung over his shoulder. He was hoping Lillian wouldn't notice the rifle on his back, what with her concentration on the proceedings in the dining room, so he stayed behind her, urging her to go on, impatient to be moving. Despite his common sense telling him it was wrong to feel that way, hairs on the back of his neck were rising in excitement and anticipation. He'd do his part in this flaming war, yet!

"Sh, listen," Lillian whispered, "sounds like they've lost one!"

It was the lieutenant. "—and, Corporal, exactly how far into the cane field are you saying we'll have to go to find Black's body? We don't have a lot of time to spare."

"Maybe a hundred—hundred and twenty yards! If the nigger in the barn hadn't sent us up a wrong track, we'd never of hit that patch of trouble! Trying to find our way through, Black's horse threw him and he got rammed with cane stalks and a damn devil dog came out of nowhere and nearly tore my arm off! But he disappeared back into the cane and I went on and got our job done, anyways. Wasn't anybody at home to object."

The men laughed.

The corporal sounded pretty proud of himself, Lillian thought, for blowing up *Greenleaf*. One more grievance to add to her list. Even Storm had gotten in on the action. Lillian looked at Wil, who was appreciating what the man had just said.

•

"All right, men—" they heard the lieutenant say, "—eat up! We'll plant Black where he fell, put an end to our business here and get going."

When the soldiers began their meal, Lillian turned to Wil and smiled, though her eyes were sad. She held him for a moment and kissed his lips and looked at him as if it would be the last time ever, for truth be known, she didn't expect to see him again when he walked away from her this time.

"Now then, Son," she said. "You got the guns this far. I'll see they get upstairs to the girls. You get on back down to the root cellar now and, Son, put that one—" She reached out and plucked at the strap across his thin shoulder. "—right back where you got it when you get to the root cellar, you hear me?"

"But, Ma!" Wil wailed, tears brimming his eyes, "I got to do this! You don't understand! I can't just *go* and leave the fightin' to y'all women!"

Morgan Heirs, were he able to speak to her from his bier, would have looked her squarely in the eyes and said, "Now, Lilly, don't tell me you're going to deny my boy his chance at manhood." Lillian saw what it must be like for the boy. No, she could not in good conscience send him away. "All right," she relented. "You had something in mind when you strung the Muskatoon over your shoulder. What was it?"

"The other corner of the verandah! I can slip out one of the spare bedrooms and make it right up to the front corner without ever being seen. With Henry at the west corner, we got them totally covered, Ma. You go on up there with Morgana and Laura Lee. Shoot from up there! You can all shoot from up there, can't you? Ma, I don't want you to die! I couldn't handle that, Ma! Not Pa, Sarah, and you, too! Please, Ma!" When Lillian looked away, Wil said, "Mama, I ain't even said 'goodbye' to Sarah. I need to do that! Let me take the guns, Ma."

Understanding, without another word, Lillian stepped out of the pantry and moved past Henry and Rachel, giving each a reassuring pat on the shoulder as she headed up the back stairs with Wil stepping on her heels.

Having made up her mind, Lillian was growing more and more disturbed. There was so much at stake. So many lives. At this point in time, she should be assured and positive that she was doing what must be done, but there were still gray areas in her thinking that deserved closer scrutiny. That was disquieting to her. She'd be better fortified to follow the set course after the lieutenant faced up to Sarah's murder by his men, unintended though it may have been. Why hadn't he come to her, before now, to apologize for the dastardly actions of his entire detachment? He'd certainly given the impression of being well-bred. Of course, he couldn't possibly know that Lillian was aware of his unwilling participation in the drunken orgy.

Honestly, in her secret heart Lillian feared there had been goings-on earlier in the day that neither she nor the young lieutenant knew about. It was late to be having second thoughts, she knew, but even now she felt the pricking of her uneasy conscience. Would it change anything if she told Morgana and Laura Lee that she knew the young lieutenant was also a victim, himself?

When they approached Sarah's room, Wil held the weapons out to Lillian, who took them from him.

Morgana's head popped out of the open doorway to Sarah's room. "Wil, you coming in?"

"In a minute!" Lillian spoke before the boy could answer. "He'll be there in a minute." Then she bargained with her youngest and most sensible child. "You stay up here, too. Need be, we'll all shoot from the front windows! No more of us should die for this cause. We'll do the best we can from up here and if that's not good enough then it'll just be too bad. Is that agreeable with you, Son?"

"Only one thing wrong with that, Ma!" Wil said. "When the time comes for action, that would leave poor old Henry down there, all alone! We can't do that to him, now, can we?"

Lillian knew the boy was right. The plan would remain the same with the addition of Wil's rifle.

Out of the Briar Cave

It was when the rumbling sounds of an approaching wagon drifted towards them that Willow noticed the guards get up from their repose against the granite pillar nearest her and the twins, and walk out into the middle of the road for a better look. And, it was also the first time she'd seen the guards looking for any length of time in the exact opposite direction from where she and the children sheltered, let alone moving away from the gates and out into the street. With the sudden appearance of the wagon on the road, and it had to be at least a quarter mile away, she recognized the overloaded wagon and team of mules. The wagon belonged to the Johnsons and she could make out all three of the no-good Johnson boys on the wagon seat. They had stopped down the road a few feet short of the east boundary of the *Briars'* hedges and all piled down from the wagon to gather around the left rear wheel. She supposed there was a problem of some kind with the wheel.

It was not likely she'd forget the Johnsons as long as she lived. According to what she'd heard the oldest brother say last summer, they'd used her to teach the youngest one "what girls are good for". Well, the Johnson boys might just be doing something to justify their existence at last by diverting the attention of the Yankee guards long enough for her to make her move. She couldn't have said why she did it because it was in direct disobedience to her instructions from Miz Lillian but it only took a moment for her to make up her mind. She gently shook the sleeping babes into wakefulness and whispered to them, "Now, y'all crawl out of these brambles right this minute and lie flat on the ground right there beside the hedge 'til I come out, you hear? I don't want to hear a loud breath from either one of you. If you see those men even looking back towards the gates, you run hard as you can back along the hedges and head straight to the pantry door. Now, go!" She kept her eyes on the guards for a count of three before she tumbled out of the hole in the hedge and forced her legs to straighten, painful as it was. Then, unsteadily, she got to her feet and grasping their tiny hands she pulled the children along and ran to the pantry door fast as their short legs would allow.

After listening for a moment, Willow led the twins inside and slowly pushed open the inner door, looking straight into the kitchen at her mama and papa. Sounds of loud masculine voices and scraping chairs from the dining room as the men finished up their meal alarmed Willow and the twins into a terrified silence. But seeing them there, Rachel reassured them with a big smile and raised a finger to her lips. Then she tapped Henry's shoulder, whose back was to them, and he turned and saw the three ragamuffins —all soiled and scratched. Rachel whisked Alice up onto her hip, while Henry boosted Andy to a seat on the crook in his arm, and they hurried from the kitchen into their own room off the back hall, with Willow tailing after, not a spoken word between them.

Rachel cried and cried once they were inside the room. "Oh, my angel," she sobbed, embracing her daughter, "I's been so worried! But you done come back safely wif' them babies, thank th' Lord!"

Willow allowed the handling, which she detested, but it was to be expected, she knew, under the circumstances. She looked over her mother's shoulder at her papa, tears standing in his rheumy eyes, and acknowledged his great relief with a smile. He read her eyes and, knowing she'd been touchy like that since last summer, reached out and patted her on top of her head.

While Willow held Alice and Rachel held Andrew on their laps, undressing them, the twins told Rachel and Henry all about their experiences in the briar cave; and about the yelling they'd heard. Rachel wagged her head when Willow looked at her—knowing it was Sarah. They recounted the many times they'd seen Henry bringing food to the guards. Finally, they told about the Johnson's wagon they had just seen coming up the road.

Henry went away and quickly came back with a large wash tub a quarter full of cold water, which he placed on some of Mister Morgan's old newspapers spread out in the middle of the floor. Then, he went to the kitchen and brought back a kettle full of boiling water from the stove, poured it in, swished it about, and carefully deposited the children into it for Rachel to wash. Splashing was to be expected when children and water came together, so Henry went to find out how far the children's laughter could be heard. Their noise could not be heard from the kitchen, but Henry saw three uniformed men with shovels heading off on foot towards the back path towards Johnson's cane field. He knew what their mission was to be. That meant that the others were somewhere abouts preparing for their departure. Quickly, then, he went to see the wagon they said was coming and to find out what was afoot.

He didn't have to look far to find the other men. The sergeant loaded down with saddle bags, followed by four other equally burdened soldiers, stepped lively past him in the center hall. They'd be heading out the kitchen door towards the stables. He went straight down the hall to the front door and, looking out, saw the entry gates standing open but if there was a wagon on the road, it was too far away for him to see from there. But, at long last, the Yankees would be going on! In the library, he saw the lieutenant hunched over Colonel Heirs' writing desk.

The Note

When the lieutenant glimpsed Henry looking in, he picked up a paper, blew on it, folded it, and acknowledged the servant.

"You, there, Henry! I've got a note to be delivered to Mistress Heirs."

Henry felt goose bumps racing up and down his spine as he took the folded paper.

"Please deliver this and ask your mistress if she will honor me with her presence here in the library. As you can see, we are about to take our leave and I wish to thank her personally for her kind hospitality."

"Yessuh!" Henry accepted the folded paper and left the room. Had the young officer never been aware of the bloody crime committed upstairs in the early morning hours? *He hadn't been*—and th' other men knew it! Henry could tell they knew by their expressions, by their actions. They all knew and nobody had told th' boy a thing! He had no plans to go upstairs to speak t' Miz Lillian. He was calling her down! How would Miz Lillian handle this unexpected turn around?

If Henry had ever learned to read, he'd have stopped on the way down the hall and read the note. He wanted to know what the writing said before he laid more pain and suffering on Miz Lillian. Never having learned reading, he'd have to take the note to one who'd been taught!

Willow had used the water in the large wash tub, herself, in Henry's absence, and Rachel hurried upstairs to tell Miz Lillian, Miz Laura Lee, Morgana, and Wil that the children and Willow were safely back inside the house.

Rachel returned with clean clothes for Willow and the twins and Henry brought back biscuits and honey. Fed and clean, the twins were lovingly tucked into Rachel and Henry's feather bed for a nap while Henry showed the note to Willow, who read it to them both:

November 16, 1864

My dear Mistress Heirs,
I know that our use of your beautiful home has been an inconvenience to you. I do apologize for that and for

the rowdiness of this early morning, as well as the inappropriate depletion of your household liquor supply. It is by official order that we abscond with your horses and supplies. However, I can assure you that the animals will receive the best of care.

When this war is ended, I beg that you and your two daughters will honor my family with a visit. I know my own mother will be happy to receive you anytime you may be traveling in our area. The full and proper address of my parents' home is: Mister and Mistress Roger Nelson Moss, Moss Hall, Chesterfield County, Virginia. Anybody in nearby Petersburg can direct you to our farm.

Your most obedient servant,
Shane Alexander Moss,
Lieutenant, U.S.Army.

No one spoke when Willow finished reading the note until Henry took the paper from her hand and refolded it. "I's goin' up to Miz Lillian, now. Ain't no need puttin' off what's goin' to be. They goin' to talk in the lib'ry. After that, we jus' waits an' sees—"

Devil Dog

Slade led Privates Dodd and Burgess straight to the spot where Black's body laid, and they went to work. Digging through the tangle of cane roots was a backbreaking task and they grumbled as they worked. Slade found himself distracted, warily watching the cane all around.

"Come on, Slade, put your mind to it! What you looking for, anyways?" Dodd asked, tossing a shovel full of dirt and roots at Slade's feet.

Ann Gray

"That damn devil dog, that's what!" Slade replied, taking a better grip on the handle of his shovel and looking over Dodd's shoulder uneasily as he dumped a shovel full of dirt onto the pile. "I told you how he came out of the cane and bit me! He was a mean one, and he knew what he was doing—he wasn't some stray mad dog!"

Burgess, who had been doing most of the digging, laughed. "Dog's probably in the next county by now."

"Yeah? Hope you're right!" Slade said, refusing to relax his vigil.

Slade and Burgess lifted the body high enough for Dodd to reach under and cut the canes that had pierced Black's body. Then they pulled the shafts straight out the top and, betting who could throw farther, threw the spears out into the canebrake. They wrapped the man in his bedroll and lowered what had once been a Union soldier into the hole and filled it in.

"Okay, anybody want to say anything?" Slade asked. He waited a few seconds, and when neither companion volunteered, he mumbled, "Lord, this here's Yancey Black, a sinner like us, all. Amen."

As they headed out of the canebrake, if they'd looked quickly enough back along the path towards *Greenleaf* instead of towards *Briars*, they'd have seen the copper stallion and rider move off the path beyond the stile into the cover of a stand of maple trees.

When Jonathan and the Johnson boys had reached the intersection where Northside dead-ended at Briarwood Road, Milton Johnson had turned their wagon left onto the road that would take them less than a mile up the hill to *Briars* and proceeded slowly for Jonathan had to be afforded time to accomplish his objective.

With Spirit eagerly champing at the bit, Jonathan turned right and rode the last few yards that would deliver him home to *Greenleaf*—or what was left of it. Riding through the ruins of *Greenleaf* to get to the path back of *Briars* was a necessary part

Briars
The House of Heirs

of his and Milton's plan, but it had been more painful than he had expected, and as he picked his way past the charred remains, aching pain was transformed into passionate anger. The Yankees had done a thorough job of it. No structure had been left standing—stables, sheds, and the only home he'd ever known—all gone. Unfettered, some of their livestock grazed the lawns and shrubs. He'd have to round up and confine those animals that poachers hadn't picked off at *Briars* once this business was tended to. But the thing most forward in his mind right now wasn't rounding up livestock, wasn't even settling his own score for *Greenleaf*, though that was one big score to settle! It was rescuing Sarah and the other Heirs women, and the only way of doing that was to get rid of the Yankees.

He had heard the three Yankees laughing and joking, in plenty of time to duck into the small copse of trees beside the stream that separated the *Greenleaf* and Johnson properties, and when he saw the shovels, he guessed they were a burial detail and welcomed the thought that their numbers might have diminished. Good! Shortened odds would make their chore less dangerous. He watched and waited before leaving his cover until the men had gotten beyond the creek and headed up the hill towards *Briars*.

Jonathan could have forded the stream and avoided the stile fence, but he was anxious to test this horse's mettle. He walked Spirit up to the fence to show him how high it was then he rode back a ways at a brisk pace and, when he figured it was far enough, he turned and headed back at a gallop. Spirit cleared the fence with a foot to spare and Jonathan knew he had guessed right. He walked Spirit until the stallion got his wind back as he followed the creek to the Heirs' root cellar.

The sooner the impending business was over with the sooner they'd get on with living. He longed to see his Sarah—to hold her—to tell her how much he'd missed her. She'd have to agree to a wedding—soon! The time they'd waited! Four long years!

If there were no living, breathing beings inside the root cellar with Colonel Heirs, he'd have to find a way to let the family know he was back to help them.

He left Spirit to drink from the stream while he approached the cave door. Finding it locked, he pushed aside a large rock and picked up a familiar key, unlocking the heavy wooden door.

Inside, he saw Colonel Heirs resting on a bier with low burning, giant candles flickering at his head and feet. Jonathan approached the bier and looked down into Sarah's father's face. Not so all-powerfully intimidating, now, Jonathan thought, as he'd seemed when Jonathan had asked for Sarah's hand in marriage. Though the Colonel had readily approved, slapped him on the back and said how pleased he'd be to have them wed.

"I'm right sorry to see you lying here like this, Colonel," Jonathan said, "we could sure use your steady hand and true aim with what we're about." Jonathan thought about all the hunting trips they'd made together, the Colonel, Drew and himself. Later Wil had come along, too, after he'd grown enough to safely handle a rifle. Well, this was another hunting trip only this time neither the Colonel nor Drew would be in on the kill. He knew he could count on Wil's and Henry's guns if somehow he could let them know he was back. That'd be two more. With his and the Johnson's that would make six altogether. How many of them had the Johnson's guessed? Maybe, nine? Ten? More? He moved beyond the Colonel's bier to the back of the cave and, knowing where to look, loaded his pockets with ammunition before he left.

Walking Spirit up the hill to the tall hedges, Jonathan tied him loosely with reins enough to graze. With the exercise, the leg was beginning to pain him terribly, but he couldn't dwell on that. Ignoring the ache as best he could and hunkering low, he caught sight of a column of horsemen heading out from the stables up the track around the house. Hidden from view, he kept the riders in sight through chinks in the hedge as they rode up along the beaten track past the pantry and alongside the west verandah to the front. One of the last two horsemen led two unfamiliar horses, one saddled, one bridled, and the other man led two that Jonathan recognized as Heirs' fine saddle horses, loaded like pack animals. One other saddled horse! Now, at least, he knew how many they'd be up against—nine.

Then he saw the big dog Storm at a distance, nose to the ground, stealthily trailing the line of horsemen. He licked a forefinger and held it to the wind. Thankfully, the wind, what little wind there was, was carrying the men's scents back to Storm. As long as the wind didn't change and the hedge blocked him from Storm's view, he was safe from discovery by his hairy friend, but if Storm ever picked up his familiar scent he'd give him away for sure—barking and running to greet him.

Once the Yankees had made the turn around the corner of the house and were riding alongside the front verandah towards the driveway, Jonathan crawled through the pantry opening in the hedge and painfully sprinted the remaining distance to the big oak tree that graced *Briars'* front lawn.

The giant sheltering oak tree, its trunk as big around as a good-sized hay stack, had been there as long as he could remember and it offered faultless cover. Breathing easy for the first time since he'd seen the soldiers, he leaned against the tree and rested his aching leg. From his position, depending on which way he moved behind the thick trunk, he could command a view of the verandah and steps and both upstairs windows or of the driveway, entry gates, and road beyond. Knowing the oak tree was in full view from the upstairs bedrooms, he looked to the windows, hoping against hope for some sign of recognition. But he saw no familiar face—no movement—nothing.

Rounding the corner of the house, the large shepherd dog lifted his nose, sniffing the air. "No!" Jonathan whispered. "Not now, Storm!" But the dog tore out straight as an arrow across the open lawn that separated them and flung himself onto Jonathan with a low, guttural rumble of delight.

"Hey, look!" Jonathan heard one man yell, "Did you see that? That damn cane field dog just ran behind that there oak tree!"

Loud derisive laughter resounded from the other men.

Storm's hackles rose at the sound of the hated voice, and Jonathan pulled the heavy dog down on top of him, keeping a firm hold on his ruff. "Down, old buddy," he soothed, "—or you'll get us both in hot water!"

Another voice loud enough to be clearly heard, taunted, "Help! Help! Slade's seeing ghost dogs again!"

"But, I tell you, it was him!" the excited man swore, loudly. "He's stalking me! We still got these two horses of theirs, don't forget. I've heard animals do that—look out for each other—!"

"Yeah, he's just set on finishing what he started!" Another voice joined in. "Didn't see Black running alongside him, did you?"

"Okay, okay, so I'm a little edgy." Jonathan heard the man backing down over more derisive laughter. "You'd be nervous, too, if he'd tried to gnaw your arm off!"

Jonathan tousled the big dog's mane. "So that's it, big fellow? You've tied into him before!" In reply, Storm flapped his tail, inspected Jonathan's wound, gave it several cooling licks, and stretched out flat beside him, content in his company.

Jonathan turned his attention to the open gates and the vacant road beyond, and wondered how much longer it would be before the Johnson boys brought the wagon up. He hoped they hadn't changed their minds and left him there to fight the Yankees on his own. But, hell, who could tell anything about the Johnson boys?

Invitation

The rap on Lillian's door startled her, and her hand went to the butt of the revolver at her waist. Foolish woman! she

Briars
The House of Heirs

thought, what if it were Morgana or Laura Lee from the next room? She looked over her shoulder at Wil, who stood alert but apparently unruffled with the Muskatoon at the ready.

Suddenly, her heart was racing and her legs were turning to jelly under her. "Yes," she said in a clear, strong voice, belying her anxious state, "Who is it?" She reached out and placed a damp palm on the door knob, awaiting Lieutenant Shane Moss's reply.

"Miz Lillian, it's Henry. I's got a note from th' young lieuten't soldier fo' you t' read."

Lillian flung open the door. "Hen-ry! You scared the life out of me! I just knew I was going to have to confront that Yankee officer right here and now!"

"Yes'm, an' you gonna have t' do that very thing, too, I 'spects. They's down there—" he nodded towards the window, "—all set t' go, now, an' he jus' give me this here note fo' you."

While Lillian read the note, Wil chimed in, "Henry, I'm sure glad to see you!" Then he said for his mother's benefit, "I was scared you'd already be on the verandah with me up here still tied to my mama's apron strings!"

Henry gave Wil a look of disapproval. "I tol' you how I thought you'd best serve yo' mama. I sees you ain't listenin' t' nobody."

Wil walked to the window and looked down on the group of riders. "That lieutenant ain't down there, Ma!"

After she had read the note, Lillian appeared more confused than upset. She looked at the note, scanning it a second time. "Where is he, Henry?"

"He be downstairs in th' lib'ry, waitin'. Don't reckon he ever counted on comin' up here, Miz Lillian."

"Hey," Wil called, suddenly excited. "There's Johnson's wagon coming up the road. Figure that? Somethin's goin' on, Ma!" He explained, "The Johnsons—they left for Savannah early this mornin'. I saw 'em leave!" A movement off to his right caught Wil's eye. "Cripes! That's Storm over there behind the oak! He's lying so flat to the ground it looks like it's half swallowed him up, but he's got his eye on something. Damnation, Ma! It's Jonny! Down there with Storm! I just saw him!"

Lillian and Henry hurried to the window.

"See for yourself!" Wil was fairly bursting with satisfaction, making room. "If Jonny's down there, Drew must be, too! He's back, Ma! Drew's back! There's a face-off comin', can't you see?" His eyes flashed and his expression reflected a kind of excitement Lillian had never seen there before and it frightened her. "That's why the Johnson's are comin' back!" Wil explained, readily. "They ran into Drew and Jonny and *they* brung them back," Pushing past his mother, Wil said, "Come on, Henry, we got to get down there and help Drew and Jonny!"

Lillian reached out and caught the back of Wil's shirt, pulling him back. "Not so fast, young man! You just give me a minute to think this thing through before you go off half-cocked. We've got our men to think about now, too." She looked at the note in her hand. "We've got no choice. I'm going down there."

Zero Hour

On the road to—and an eighth mile from—the entry gates at *Briars*, Milton Johnson got up from squatting beside the left back wagon wheel, and checked the knots on the ropes securing the pink Queen Anne chair. He'd planned on his mama enjoying that chair for years to come. It would have even been something of value to pass on to him and his—someday—wife when his mama died, but now it looked like it would never make it intact past the next few minutes.

He'd really felt sorry for Jonny Baker coming home with a bullet wound in his leg to a burned out house and bringing back news to the ladies at *Briars* of a dead Drew Heirs. Yep, it was a sad day in all their lives. He'd lived on the little piece of land behind the two large estates all his life and been obliged to "cow-tow" to the Heirs and the Bakers for as long as he could remember. But now he saw things a little differently. They were all either burned out or suffering the loss of loved ones and they were all angry and hurting.

He pulled Daniel to his feet. "Time to move, little buddy." He'd never for a moment considered leaving Dan out of the fight. How else would the boy learn to be a man? They were all putting on a pretty good show of indifference, Milt thought, but he'd never embarrass either of his younger brothers by showing how much he cared for them. Nor how scared and worried he was that both Curt and he'd come home safely from the war only to die in a shoot-out that really wasn't even their fight! He patted Dan on his bottom, hurrying him along, and followed him onto the bench. Curt had already climbed aboard and was reaching beneath the bench, pulling out his shotgun, and laying it at his feet.

The Heirs women had always seemed pretty snooty to Milton. That was one reason he'd gotten such satisfaction out of catching the Heirs' young she nigger and learning Dan how to 'do her" last summer. Couldn't help wondering why nothing ever came of that! Anyway, here they were a year later—trying to save the Heirs women from satisfying Yankee soldiers' cravings—if it wasn't already too late! He smiled and clicked, "Giddy-yup!"

The mules ambled along and the boys sized up the place as they approached. The entry gates now stood open and unguarded. That was a bonus! As they moved closer they could see eigth horsemen, nine saddled mounts, one bridled Union horse, and the two Heirs' saddle horses, packed for travel, in front of the house. That would mean they were shy one soldier and their officer was still inside, tying up loose ends.

Right about now, Jonny should already be in place behind the big oak tree. They'd have to go on trust because there was no way they'd know if he was there until the shooting started.

Ann Gray

As Milt drove the rumbling wagon closer and closer to the open gates he just hoped to high heaven Jonny hadn't deserted them and left them with nothing between them and the damned Yankees except this wagon loaded with Jonny's mama's furniture! Milt knew what Jonny'd have done on running into thieves that had stolen his Mama's stuff before he went away to war. Yep, this war had folks seeing things from different sides, all right.

Malice

"Morgana, come away from that door," Laura Lee said, firmly. "What are you doing there, anyway?" Laura Lee knew one had to speak firmly to Morgana most of the time.

Without removing her Springfield rifle barrel from the crack between the door and the sill, Morgana glanced over her shoulder at her sister-in-law, smiling sweetly. "I'm just waiting for that Yankee lieutenant to show his handsome face above the stair well so I can shoot it right off of him."

"That's not the plan and you know it," Laura Lee reminded her, uncomfortably opening the breech of her rifle and snapping it closed again several times, practicing the unfamiliar movement before leaning the repugnant weapon, butt down, against the side of her bed.

"It's my plan," Morgana replied, not moving. She had already resumed her vigil, matching her sighting eye to the opening. "Now, please don't bother me again, Laura Lee, dear, it breaks my concentration."

Convinced of the futility of further argument, Laura Lee turned her full attention to the front window. It slid up so smoothly in its track there was not the slightest sound. She held onto the window sill and stretched out through the opening to look at the driveway beyond the roof line of the verandah. All she could see was a number of horse's rear ends; tails swishing back and forth, but nothing of benefit. The riders were still bunched too close to the steps to be seen from her position; too sheltered by the overhanging roof for her to pick her target. It would be hard deciding on only one target from the five bastards she'd been violated by, but she'd probably choose that pompous, fat sergeant with those putrid teeth and lecherous, greedy eyes. Yes, the sergeant would do nicely, once she got him in the cross hairs of that ungainly rifle.

Farther out though, squeaking and rumbling slowly up the road, she saw the Johnson's wagon with all three of the Johnson boys on the bench. What in Heaven's name were they doing riding this way? They'd be within range almost any minute, now. Shouldn't somebody let them know they were riding into danger? "Morgana, come over here and look! It's those Johnson boys in the family's wagon coming up the road. They're going to be right in those Yankees' firing range pretty soon, too. I'm afraid they're going to get shot if they keep on coming this way. If not by the Yankees, by us!"

Staying put, and remembering Willow's unfortunate experience when the brothers had pounced upon her last summer, Morgana answered, "Good! That'll be better than they rightly deserve." Now, she thought—now that Willow and she were both 'experienced', she just wished to high heaven her 'rape' itself had been less enjoyable for her! Willow's had set her to cursing men and crying for two whole days. Laura Lee and Sarah had both had the same experience and look what had happened to them! Sarah was dead from hers and Laura Lee had become a living, breathing, walking puppet until she'd seen Sarah and been shocked out of it.

Morgana hadn't told—couldn't tell—anybody what was really bothering her. She felt wretchedly wanton and unladylike. She must be a 'born whore'! Of course, she wasn't supposed to have found pleasure in the act! But try as she might, she couldn't erase the memory of the thrill of it. The man's kiss had been so warm, so tender, so delicious—and the burning desire it ignited was so unknown to her, so intriguing, that when their bodies met and combined so perfectly, she found an indescribable bliss. He was the enemy; he had raped her; and she had liked it! Not only liked it, but in responding had shown him how very *much* she'd liked it! *That* was why she was going to kill him!

When the door across the hall opened and Lillian emerged, Morgana lowered her rifle and spoke to Laura Lee. "Mama's in the hall. You keep an eye on that wagon and I'll see if she knows what's going on." Laura Lee nodded, and turned back to the window, but when Morgana stepped out to join her mother, Lillian reached past Morgana and closed Laura Lee's door.

Wil and Henry came from Lillian's room and Morgana asked sassily, hands on hips, "Mama, what's going on? Where's that Yankee lieutenant that was supposed to be coming up here any minute? Why'd Wil and Henry come up here when they're supposed to be downstairs on the verandah? The upstairs was supposed to be mine and Laura Lee's you said."

"Hush for a split second and I'll tell you," Mama answered. "Plans change, and you have to be able to change with them." Morgana couldn't abide her mama's philosophic ramblings, especially at a time like this. But Mama continued, "The lieutenant's not coming up after all, and Jonny's out front behind the oak tree—probably Drew, too."

Morgana's face lit up. "Oh, Mama, that's wonderful! I'll go tell—"

"No, wait!" Lillian grasped her arm, pulling her back. "Don't tell Laura Lee. She's waited this long, she can wait a few more minutes. We don't want her racing down there and messing things up any more than they already are. You go on back in there and don't say a word about Jonny and Drew maybe being home. I'm trusting you, Morgana."

"We already saw the Johnson's wagon coming up the road," Morgana said.

Lillian said, "So did we. You and Laura Lee keep watch, and see what those Johnson boys are up to. I'll sure feel better if you can figure out that piece of this puzzle. You girls hold off on any shooting until we see what's going on in our boys' minds—leastwise, whoever's down there."

Morgana asked, disappointment etched on her pretty face, "You really think there might be a shoot-out without us even being in on it?"

Lillian answered bluntly. "I hold that war's a man's job and I felt bad about us women having to do what needed doing to begin with! If they're here to do it for us now, Morgana, for Heaven's sake let the men do it!"

"But, *Sarah?*" Morgana felt her face flushing with anger. "Aren't we even due some getting even for Sarah's sake? Why what about Laura Lee and me? Our *honor,* Mama, what about that? You certainly have changed your attitude since this morning. What's happened?"

"What's happened is—I got this note from the lieutenant—" she offered the folded note to Morgana.

"If it's from *him*, Mama, I don't even want to see it," Morgana said evenly, looking from one face to the other. "Let's get on with this thing and finish it, can't we?" Then Morgana set her jaw, found a better grip on her rifle and walked straight-away to her previously assigned battle station at her mother's front bedroom window, leaving Lillian, Wil, and Henry still weighing the problem in the hallway.

Lillian made up her mind and spoke decisively. "It's time I got going. Both of you come on along with me in case I need you. You stay near me but out of sight in the downstairs hall while I'm conversing with the lieutenant in the library. Wil, now, Drew and Jonny have been taking care of themselves for quite a spell without your help and I don't want you fouling up anything they've got in mind to do. Do you understand what I'm saying? Wil?"

"Of course, I understand, Ma!" Wil beamed. "We're going to kill us some Yankees! Hell, let's go!"

CHAPTER NINE ~ THE SHOOTOUT

1:55 P.M., Wednesday, November 16, 1864 ~ Briars, Atlanta, Georgia

Line of Fire

Awaiting Mistress Heirs' appearance, Lieutenant Shane Moss stood restlessly beside the desk peering out the front window at his detachment gathered in relaxed assembly at the foot of the front steps. They joked and laughed among themselves. Having been excluded from their camaraderie since the assignment's beginning, Shane knew that the mood would end the moment he joined them and that a strained silence would descend on the group which would last until he left their presence again. Because of his youthfulness, he'd sensed in all of them from the beginning an intense resentment of his position of authority over them. He'd tried to pass it off as merely an overactive imagination but there had been too many instances of proof for it to be purely his imagination. No matter how he tried to blend in, Sergeant Crane especially, seemed inclined to rouse the men to roguish acts of mischief towards him such as the liquor episode, earlier. That trick had caused a large gap in his recollection of events of the early morning, and there were moments still when he worried over that fact. He knew, also, that he couldn't depend on any of the men under the Sergeant's influence to reveal themselves accountable for any misdeeds.

That, in part, was why he had requested Mistress Heirs to join him, here, away from the family floor and with the men outside, in the neutrality of the library. If there were improprieties he should know about, she would tell him. Also, he wanted her approval of the appearance of the library at the time of their departure, and her assurance that he'd had everything put back into acceptable order. He would ask her about the empty gun cabinet. What difference could disclosure of the weapons' disposition make, now? He judged Mistress Heirs to be a conscientious woman who would answer his inquiry, truthfully.

His attention was attracted to Private Slade by the man's obvious discomfort. Slade, who had been given charge of the lieutenant's own saddled horse, lingered uncomfortably on the fringe of the tight gathering of horsemen. His interest was not directed towards the other men but was, instead, locked onto something off to the west. Moss's view looking west from the library window was blocked by the expanse of the spreading oak tree.

In the other direction, looking across the sloping lawn, over the hedges, and through the bars of the high fence, a team of mules hauling an overloaded wagon labored slowly up the gradual rise of the road. The three occupants of the wagon seat seemed casually disinterested in their surroundings, typical of displaced people during these recent months of occupation by Union forces. The slowly progressing wagon would probably be of no concern but the mere fact that his men were blissfully unaware of the wagon's approach bothered him. He would go speak to them—send someone out to question the driver as to their destination.

Turning on his heel, he came face to face with Mistress Lillian Heirs. She had entered the room silently and stood not three feet from him, solemn of face and clutching her shawl tightly at her waist with both hands. Perhaps she was feeling cold as his own mother sometimes did, though it usually seemed to him—without due cause. Or, was she worried and somewhat anxious over this meeting as was he? After all, they'd burned all her neighbors' houses, occupied her own home for the better part of two days, stripped the household's pantry stores, confiscated two valuable horses, drunk all her husband's liquor and turned his attractive library into a tavern and meeting room.

Having felt his full attention come to bear on her pale and somber countenance, Lillian said, coldly, "Well, Lieutenant?"

"Mistress Heirs," he said, his gaze resting patiently on her troubled face, "thank you for coming." How exhausted and desolate she appeared. What had happened to the bold, saucy woman who had fenced with him so ably and rebuked him at their meeting only yesterday? "As you see—" he nodded toward the window, "—my men and I are ready to leave and I felt it only fitting that I bid you a personal farewell and at this time apologize for the misuse of your husband's library and ask for your approval of its restored appearance. I'd also like to emphasize my invitation to you and the Misses Heirs to visit my own family home at any time it might be convenient for you to travel to Virginia, now that hostilities are at an end."

"*Are* hostilities at an end, Lieutenant?" she asked, her weary dark circled eyes framing resentment.

"Are they *not*, Mistress Heirs?" he countered, searching for an admission of what unacknowledged circumstance troubled her. "Ma'am, war's the common enemy of us, all. Is there some further issue that you hesitate to bring to me?" A thing had happened, he was sure now, that required painful telling and he'd have the truth of it before he left these grounds. "Ma'am?" he urged, with compassion.

As he reached out to touch her clammy hand, a weapon's loud report outside broke the tension between them. The concussion's reverberation compounded by the pitch of the verandah's roof shattered the library window as well.

The officer threw the woman to her knees and secured her safely behind the sofa before dashing from the room. Entering the hallway at full stride, Moss glimpsed two armed figures racing away down the hall. The one, he recognized immediately even from the back as the servant, Henry, disappeared at a lope into the dining room. The other, whom he'd never seen before, agile and thinner, with a shock of red hair, darted through the doorway to the bedroom behind the library.

Proceeding to the front door, Moss peered out cautiously before venturing onto the verandah. Peals of laughter greeted his arrival on the scene. Private Slade sat astride his nervously dancing horse, the reins to the horses he had charge over draped loosely around his saddle pommel, a discharged weapon in his hands and the man was obviously angered by his companions' derision.

"Sorry, sir," Sergeant Crane addressed Lieutenant Moss. "It was Slade, here! Nobody knows what in Tarnation he was shooting at, right, boys?"

That, too, was probably another of Crane's lies. "What happened, Private Slade?" Lieutenant Moss asked, impatience creeping into his voice.

"It was that devil dog, sir, I saw him again. He's over there behind that oak tree. He raised his head up and I took a shot at him. I'm sorry, sir."

"So's everybody else!" Crane said, trying to restrain his laughter. "Bet I jumped two feet off my saddle!"

"If you're so sure he's there, Private," the lieutenant said, while the rest of the men chuckled, "why don't you ride on over there and take a closer look? You're armed."

"Alone, sir?" Slade asked, over the annoying laughter. "That's a mighty mean dog, sir, and a mighty big tree. And, Lieutenant, sir, he may not be alone!" His words hung in the air.

The impending attack plan formed in Lieutenant Shane Moss's mind almost as fast as the words escaped Slade's lips. There, pulling up to the open gates at this very moment was the wagon with three armed men aboard. By now, the two men he had seen running down the hall would be situated on each side of the verandah. As well as behind the oak tree—how many? There were probably also shooters upstairs, and once the riders were far enough away from the sheltering porch to be seen from above, there would be shots from all points. He leaped from the porch, took two giant steps through the disorganized unit, grabbed the pommel of his own saddle and swung into it, flipping his reins out of a startled Slade's hand.

The occupants of the wagon, before it had even stopped rolling, leapt down and moved around behind it.

The lieutenant and the worried private exchanged knowing glances. Glances that said they were all dead men. The lieutenant shouted, "Ambush!", drew his revolver, leaned in close to his snorting horse's neck and, knowing full well it was already too late, raised his weapon to fire. The dumfounded, unprepared Union soldiers—except for the suspicious Slade—hurried to secure their weapons.

From behind the oak tree a resounding holler, *"Wahoo!"* pierced the early afternoon chill, and answering echoes of the call rang out from the wagon's site as shots were fired in unison on two sides of the disorganized Union soldiers.

With the sound of multiple guns firing, Lillian crawled from the library, fighting her cumbersome skirts all the way, got to her feet in the hallway and ran to the front door. Her first heart-stopping fear had been that Wil and Henry had prematurely provoked action on the part of the soldiers. Then she realized that hearing the first single shot they, too, would have rushed to the verandah to see what had happened.

When she dashed through the front door, she saw the twisted and bloodied bodies of many men strewn over the driveway, while rider-less horses ran amok in confusion. In the driveway halfway to the gates, one armed rider on a rearing mount remained upright, looking first towards the wagon then the oak tree with no visible target.

Knowing the lieutenant was waiting—waiting for the final shot—the one that would send him to eternity along with his men, Lillian yelled, loud and clear, from the top of the steps, "Stop it! *Stop the killing, now!*" Then on the verge of nausea from the sight of such slaughter and the smell of blood and entrails, she picked her way through the broken bodies. Shot guns and forty-fours didn't make little wounds.

Ann Gray

She ran headlong towards the lone horseman. It was all over. The battle had been fought and won, praise the Lord! But not by women, an old man, and a boy. By fighting men!

Showing himself from around the corner of the verandah, shouldering his rifle and moving out slowly to the top of the steps, Wil shouted, "Ma, you get back here."

The lieutenant also called out as he rode back up the drive to meet Lillian, "Go back, ma'am, go back!" Reining in his horse so that he faced the oak tree and stood between the woman and the wagon, the source of most of the gunfire, he saw Wil clearly for the first time. "That was a foolhardy thing you just did, ma'am!" he said, looking down at her when he had come up beside her. "Do what your son says, ma'am. I don't want to take you with me!"

"You just hold on, there, Wil!" Lillian shouted back. Then, looking up at the lieutenant, she answered, sharply, "Hush up, you young jackass, I'm saving your life!"

Hanging onto the stirrup of his saddle, refusing to turn loose, she ordered, "Now hand me down that revolver!" When the lieutenant complied, still tightly gripping the stirrup, and holding up the lieutenant's weapon for all to see, Lillian looked to the wagon and then to the oak tree, and yelled at the top of her voice, *"This man's unarmed! Show yourselves, Rebels!"*

The Johnson brothers stepped out from behind the wagon, firearms in hand, while Jonathan emerged from behind the oak tree and stood leaning against it for support, holding onto Storm with one hand and Spirit's Atlanta officer's confiscated forty-four in the other. To Lillian's grievous disappointment, Drew did not step forth.

In the next instant, a shot between the ears felled the Yankee lieutenant's horse, pinning the man to the ground. He struggled out from under the horse's carcass with Lillian's help, and all eyes turned to the source of the gunfire.

Briars
The House of Heirs

The shooter shouted down from Lillian's upstairs bedroom window, "Move out of my way, Mama! Just give me a clean shot and I won't miss again!"

Once on his feet, the lieutenant looked up at the window and said to Lillian who remained, unmoving, in Morgana's line of fire. "I think the young lady means it, ma'am! I think she *really* means it!"

"Humph!" Lillian said softly to him. "My daughter, Morgana, never meant anything she ever said in her entire life for more than thirty seconds at a time, and that may be stretching it a mite." Then she shouted up to Morgana in the window, "Put the gun down, Morgana! The killing's over!"

"Not for me, Mama!" came her reply. "It's not over yet! Not while that man's still breathing! This is something I should have already done!"

Lillian placed her hands on her hips and announced loudly to Morgana, "There are seven living men and eight dead ones down here, Morgana, and I'm the only person, *living or dead*, knows what in blazes you're going on about. Now, if you want to explain what's on your mind to everybody present, and make a public spectacle of yourself, I'll move out of your way in a heartbeat. You think about that for at least one whole minute, then let me know."

Lillian turned her attention to the fourth victim of the early morning's assaults and decided that the lieutenant already knew all he needed to know. There was no need in burdening him with the sins of the men who now lay dead for their crimes against the Heirs women. Against Sweet Sarah, who had been as afraid of living as she was of dying; and against Laura Lee, who had proven herself to be a woman of strength and who would guide the Heirs' grandchildren's fortunes when Lillian, herself, was gone.

As for the hot-headed Morgana, bent on having her own way, or the victimized Union Army Lieutenant Shane Moss— which of them bore more guilt? Morgana, who'd sought out trouble by knowingly investigating downstairs against the lieutenant's direct order and deliberately disobeyed her own mother's strict instructions? Or the beleaguered young officer, who'd been unwillingly intoxicated; then had opportunity thrust upon him—and more importantly, remembered no part of it?

After a minute had passed and there was no response from Morgana, above, Lillian called out to Henry, who had moved to stand beside Wil at the top of the steps, "Henry, you're to go tell Thomas and Grady I said to round up those horses. Then they can help you bury these men. But right now I want you to unpack Pal and Star and saddle Star for Lieutenant Moss. His horse is dead and he's got a rendezvous to keep."

"But, Miss Morgana's Star, Miz Lillian?" Henry called back.

"Star," Lillian said.

Good-byes

Rousing to the sounds of the awakening household, Jonathan turned his cheek into the clean, sweet smelling feather-filled pillow on Sarah's bed and gathered his thoughts. Had it really been only yesterday he'd come back home to find his whole life in shambles? Was his darling Sarah actually lying in her grave, right next to her papa in his, down in the little family cemetery with the iron fence around it?

Only after Lillian Heirs had examined the leg wound, cleaned it, and cauterized it with a red hot poker did she allow that the leg could safely remain attached. Jonathan was mightily relieved with that pronouncement. Yes, where many a doctor would have shook his head and reached for the saw, Lillian had saved his leg, of that he had no doubt.

When he turned to the window, instead of looking out on the ruins of *Greenleaf*, he was relieved to see only the barren weedy field next door, although he knew Farley's burned out place lay just beyond. Before he reached *Briars* yesterday, it hadn't been easy riding through the skeletal remains of *Greenleaf,* now a heap of cold ashes.

Actually, Drew's mama had taken the news of his death better than Jonathan had ever expected. She'd told him she'd known her son was gone forever when he hadn't stepped out from behind the giant oak tree alongside him. Because, she'd said, she knew that if the two of them were breathing, they'd be together. They'd gone away to war together, and they'd have come home from it, together, if it had been in God's plan. While Lillian Heirs was satisfied to accept God's will, and though Jonathan appreciated her piety, he found little consolation in such thoughts, himself.

Dead though he was, Drew at least had spared his wife and mama having to see him dead and laid out—and having to watch him buried. If only they all could have been spared the torment of seeing their loved ones so and, in turn, swallowed up by the cold damp ground.

When he had told them about Drew, Laura Lee had been as brave as he'd known she'd be. Through four years of marriage, she was the glue that had held their marriage together. Jonny had always known that, in his way, Drew had tried to love Laura Lee, and he'd adored their twins and spent time most every day playing with them.

But there had been other days when Drew should have been at the depot working when he was, in fact, throwing dice in some dingy bar room with sluts hanging over both shoulders. And though he'd brought his bride home to *Briars* after his impromptu marriage at his papa's insistence, Drew had made no effort after that to build Laura Lee a home of her own. But Laura Lee had loved him with such blind devotion, she couldn't have seen his shortcomings if he'd worn a sign around his neck listing them.

Jonny supposed Stella Farley was about the worst of Drew's offenses against Laura Lee. Yep, Jonny knew Drew and his shenanigans—probably better than anybody who'd ever lived.

Gambling, drinking, brawling, and his all too frequent attraction to bawdy women like Stella. All that was just part of his flighty, self-centered nature. Hell, they'd spent so much time in similar pursuits, he should certainly understand—the only difference being, he had intended doing better by Sarah when they married. Now, his Sarah was gone.

Having no funeral parlor or mortician available, the Heirs family had done the best they could to handle unfamiliar duties thrust upon them. All of the burials had been attended to within hours of Jonathan's return. The Union soldiers were hardly cold when, just as the Yankees had done with the one that had died earlier, they were wrapped in their bed rolls and deposited without ceremony in the cane field alongside him. The Johnson boys had offered the use of their wagon and had helped in digging holes. With the three Johnson boys, Wil, Henry, Thomas and Grady, all digging, the chore was done quickly. Milton Johnson had been of the opinion that the cane in their field would lose its sweetness, now, because of all the Yankees being laid there, but he'd agreed to the arrangement, anyway, under Mistress Heirs' persuasion.

Following that, Wil and Henry brought the Colonel's body up from the root cellar on Pal's back, and laid him, head to head, with his daughter, Sarah, on the long dining room table to await burial. Because Wil had already prepared his father's body's while he rested in the root cellar, the women dressed Sweet Sarah in her prettiest blue dress and powdered her and curled her golden hair. For the whole time the bodies laid there, sounds of sawing and hammering drifted up from the barn as the handymen put together two pine boxes using the three wide boards from the Colonel's bier and siding from the barn, leaving a gaping hole to be repaired later.

Finally, Jonathan was allowed downstairs to pay his respects, alone, to Sarah and her father, and when he emerged from the dining room, Rachel took his right hand in both of hers and held it tightly, her tawny eyes boring deep into his hazel ones and she said, "You hurtin' now, Mister Jonny, but don't you lose heart. I sees much happiness still ahead fo' you." Then she released him and grinned her broad, warm grin. "Don't they look fo' th' world like they's jus' sleeping."

From the dining room doorway, Jonathan watched as father and daughter were laid tenderly on clean soft sheets within the boxes and, at twilight, they were borne down the rutted double track to the family cemetery in the back of Johnsons' wagon.

After her ministrations, it had taken all Jonathan's powers of persuasion to convince Lillian that he was fit enough to attend the graveside rites for their loved ones but against her better judgment, Lillian gave him permission to ride to the cemetery on the back of the wagon along with young Dan Johnson behind the caskets, insuring their security over bumps and potholes.

All that was left of the Heirs' family, including the servants, braved the harsh north wind to follow the wagon on foot, and to stand tearfully, shoulder to shoulder, with bowed heads, at the top of the graves of Sarah Alice and Morgan Andrew Heirs, listening as Morgana read the twenty-third Psalm from Sarah's own Bible, which Lillian, ceremoniously, placed in Sarah's coffin after the prayer and before the lid was nailed shut.

Jonathan had stood with Henry's and Thomas's support, at the foot of the graves along with Grady, and the Johnson brothers. Though their heads were bowed, Jonathan noticed the Johnson brothers' eyes weren't closed, either. He wondered if Sarah Heirs' God was watching them and if He knew or even cared that Jonathan, himself, didn't believe as his Sweet Sarah had believed with her whole heart.

Afterwards, Lillian pushed herself beyond requirement for his need, forcing him to bed and changing her medicinal poultices every few hours throughout that night and into the next morning. Jonathan had not protested her mothering because he saw it filling her need for busyness.

Ann Gray

Soon, with the rebuilding of *Greenleaf,* there would be work enough to keep him busy, and free from profitless thinking—like this.

Rallying his concentration, Jonathan pushed back the goose-down quilt, unwound the wrappings from his thigh, and lifted the thick wet poultice to look at his wound. The stench of infection was lessening, and Lillian's latest poultice bore evidence of it.

As he began re-wrapping the bandage, a simultaneous knock at the door was not unexpected. Between Lillian's frequent ministrations and under her orders, he had been succored and spoiled unceasingly by Henry's seeing to it that his every desire should be promptly fulfilled.

"Come in," he called, though the door was already opening. "Morgana!" he exclaimed, retrieving the thrown back covers, as she pranced into the room carrying a breakfast tray. "I was expecting Henry." He sat upright, self-consciously leaning against the pile of dainty, lace-trimmed pillows, which Sarah had hand-sewn for her bed.

"Henry's busy with more important chores," Morgana said. "And since I had nothing better to do, I volunteered to bring up your tray, myself." She set the tray on the bed and, pulled a pillow from behind his head which she, mercilessly, beat into submission before placing it on his lap for the tray to rest upon. "Doesn't this fried ham smell just heavenly? Wil and Henry have already made three trips to the root cellar with the wheel barrows this morning, and the pantry's fairly bulging again. Mama's even put out a sign on the front gates advertising that we've got food to spare for anybody who needs it. I told her she should have, at least, required that they work for it, but you know Mama." She picked up the knife and fork and began cutting his ham into bite size pieces. "I suppose they'll all be coming back home again, now that the Yankees have gone away, don't you?"

"I can do that, Morgana," Jonathan said, mildly amused.

Briars
The House of Heirs

"What?" Morgana paused, a luscious morsel poised on the fork in her hand.

He held up his hands. "See, two hands." He wiggled his fingers. "And they work just fine."

"Well, of course, how silly of me," she said, relinquishing the utensils and watching him attack the ham and eggs. "I just wasn't thinking, that's all." She glided across the room to stand looking out the window. "Can you imagine Mama letting that damn Yankee go, like that?"

"She must have had her reasons. Have you asked her about it?"

"Well, of course I've asked her about it." She wrote her initials in the condensation from her breath on the window. "She said she'd tell me all about it 'someday'! Can you imagine? And on my horse, too!" Morgana folded her arms and draped a wounded grimace over her pouting face. "Papa paid a fortune for Star, and I'm going to miss her. He bought her from one of the biggest breeders in Virginia. You remember that, don't you, Jonny?"

Did he remember? Could he ever forget how his Sweet Sarah had been cast into the shadows by the glow from Morgana, born the very image of Morgan Heirs, and spoiled beyond redemption by her indulgent father. Or, could he forget that, try as she might, to this very day, her practical and earnest mother had never once succeeded in planting a single noble thought or lovable quality into Morgana's pretty, stubborn head. Jonathan swallowed a tasty bite and smiled. "As I recall, that was your thirteenth birthday, wasn't it?"

Morgana exchanged the wounded air for one of mild disdain. "You know perfectly well it was! It was just before you asked Sarah to marry you." She wiped the window with her open palm. "My, that's a dismal sight out there! Not a house standing for miles around. Y'all will be staying here, won't you, while you're rebuilding *Greenleaf?*"

"We've been invited to do that," Jonathan said.

Ann Gray

"Your daddy will be glad to get back and begin re-building, I imagine," Morgana said. "I know Mama has missed Hamita terribly." Morgana frowned, prettily, "I suppose, too, you'll be up and raring to go, soon? Not that I'd blame you for wanting to be out of *Briars*, the way Mama's been clucking over you every minute like some old yard hen." She flounced back to his bedside, flopped down on the side closest to the open door and lowered her voice looking squarely at him. "Besides, there's not likely to be anything going on around here for Heaven only knows how long!"

She fastened a fretful, searching gaze upon his, suddenly, somber one. "Of all unlikely things! The three of them, all going practically at once, like that." She twiddled with a curly lock of ebony hair, wrapping and unwrapping it around a finger. "Jonny, you know I loved my papa and my sister, and for that matter, I loved my big brother, though I never really understood him. But losing them, I'm not so very hurt I want to *just stop living!* Tell me, Jonny, how long would you say it rightly takes after three people in one family die, before the poor survivors can start living their own lives again?"

Jonny wiped the corners of his mouth with the pretty lace trimmed napkin that had accompanied the breakfast tray. Undoubtedly, he thought, here was more of Sarah's admirable handiwork, and the fact of her absence freshened his heartache. He raised the napkin, again, as if her scent might still cling to it.

"Jonny? Are you listening to me?" Morgana insisted. "Is the hurt you're feeling for losing Sarah anything like the hurt Laura Lee feels, losing Drew? Or the hurt Mama feels, losing Papa? Why don't I feel the same hurt for all of them, Jonny?"

"I'd say that depends on how you felt about them before they died," Jonathan answered, becoming uncomfortable. "You're still very young, Morgana. There are things you've yet to experience before you can understand the kind of love you're talking about."

Morgana smiled, knowingly. "I don't expect there's anything of much interest I haven't 'experienced' already."

"Well," Jonny said, concluding the unwanted conversation, "I'm not one you should be talking to about this sort of thing, anyway. Go ask your mama—or Laura Lee, if you want a lesson in what married love is all about."

"Well, I swear! I never intended any such thing! You are reading an awful lot into a simple question, Jonathan Baker!" She bounced to her feet, snatching up the tray. "If you're all finished mooning over that napkin, now, you can put it on here, too, and I'll take all this back down to the kitchen."

Calling up a lighter mood, Jonathan said, "And tell Rachel I thank her for as tasty a breakfast as I've had since—since I went away."

"Humph! Tell her, yourself! You could get up and walk down there, right now, if you truly wanted to."

"Well, don't tell your mama, but that's exactly what I intend doing just as soon as you sashay back out and close that door."

Consequences

Two months later, the surviving co-owner of Heirs' Properties, reluctant holder of most of Briarwood's home mortgages, and a trustee of Atlanta's Municipal Bank, Lillian Heirs sat at her deceased husband's desk poring over pages in an open ledger. It was a new duty Tom Garrett had thrust upon her, insisting she must go over the entries at least once a month to familiarize herself with her holdings.

She frowned when Rachel, with her flickering candle, moved deliberately into the small circle of light from the oil lamp, distracting her. "Miz Lillian, we gots t' do somethin' fo' Miss Morgana. She be out back there, pukin' her very insides out. I done tol' her some o' my peppermint tea'd settle her stomach but she just shake her head, no, and keep on pukin'."

"Puking? Now what did she have to upset her like that, Rachel?" Lillian asked, closing the big record book and sliding it back into the desk drawer. "We all had the same thing, didn't we?" Lillian snuffed out the lamp and hurried from the room ahead of Rachel. From somewhere deep inside her consciousness, a fearful thought came galloping forth. "Oh, please, God, no!" she whispered.

Her candle sputtering, Rachel tagged along behind Lillian as she hurried down the dim hall. "Vittles ain't th' cause, Miz Lillian. She been eatin' like a bird, and what she do eat, she puke right back up again. Yo' girl's wit' child, Miz Lillian! I knowed it almos' soon's it happened. I could see th' change comin' on in her color an' in her eyes. I been waitin' t' tell you fo' weeks now, hopin' she'd tell you first, but she be stubborn, that one. I keeps tellin' her she need he'p! Now, I's tellin' you, Miz Lillian."

Rachel stayed inside the kitchen, listening, as Lillian dashed onto the back porch.

Morgana, startled by her mother's sudden appearance, turned away from the railing, dabbed at her mouth with her handkerchief and said, unusually subdued, "Oh, Mama, I'm so sick!"

"'Gana! Whatever is wrong?" Lillian opened her arms, and Morgana rushed into them, wracked with sobs and trembling.

"Mama, it's been two whole months since my cousin came to visit," she cried. "What am I going to do? I can't have a baby! I'm not even married! Oh, Mama, I'm going to have *his* baby! I know it! What will I do when I can't keep it a secret anymore."

Lillian held the trembling girl and soothed her. "There, there, darling 'Gana. We won't let anything happen to shame you. But you must take proper care of yourself." She held Morgana gently and walked her back into the kitchen. "Fix the tea, Rachel, and we'll see if we can't get some of it into her.

Maybe after that she'll be able to eat some soft scrambled eggs and dry toast. I always managed to keep that down."

Lillian reached for a kitchen towel and dampened it with a dipper of water. As she wiped Morgana's pasty face, she tried to console her. "Believe me, it gets better after a while. Now that you've told us, it will be even easier, I promise." Lillian couldn't remember a time when Morgana had been so docile. When she was, she was wholly likable.

Morgana drank the tea and nibbled a piece of dry toast along with it, saying that she would try the eggs later, if the toast stayed down. "You should have let me shoot him when I had the chance," Morgana said, halfway through the piece of toast.

"If you'd shot him, would that have undone your condition?" Lillian asked. With this new disclosure, Lillian knew that she must tell Morgana the entire truth regarding her encounter with the young lieutenant. Had nothing come of the affair, she would never have spoken of it, but now she proceeded to explain particulars to Morgana she'd never known about: The forced consumption of liquor the young Lieutenant had endured and it's resultant waking mental blackout—which would have passed harmlessly, Lillian felt sure, had Morgana not suddenly and inappropriately appeared in the library at a time when his judgment was impaired. She explained the gentlemanly behavior he had exhibited to her throughout the Yankees' occupation of *Briars*, and told Morgana of the note she had received from him that last fateful day, thanking Lillian and inviting her and her daughters to visit his family home in Virginia, the note Morgana had refused to read.

"He didn't even know about Sarah, Morgana. What good would it have done to tell him?"

Soon she had told Morgana all that had led up to her saving the life of Morgana's antagonist—himself a victim of circumstances.

Recalling the rush of passion Shane Moss had awakened in her, Morgana asked finally. "You're sure he didn't remember any of what happened, Mama? He didn't remember me even being there?"

"I'm positive, he didn't," Lillian answered, brushing back a stray ebony curl from Morgana's brow and kissing her pale lips.

"But," Morgana said, thoughtfully, "—I do." Her eyes brightened. "Rachel, I'd like to try some of those scrambled eggs. I think your tea has done its job. I feel ever so much better, now."

Rachel put the skillet on the stove to heat and whipped up two fresh eggs.

The next day, Morgana felt even better and managed to keep down a little more food. Her color improved and, thereafter, Rachel bent every effort to cook Morgana's very favorite dishes.

Lillian wrote to her mother in Richmond asking if a visit might be well received, but because of the war's winding down another few weeks passed without reply, and she was getting terribly anxious for Morgana.

Briars
The House of Heirs

CHAPTER TEN ~ SURRENDER

3:00 p.m., Thursday, April 27, 1865 ~ Briars, Atlanta, Georgia

Three Letters

On Sunday, April ninth, General Robert E. Lee surrendered 27,800 Confederate troops to General Grant at Appomattox Court House, Virginia. On Friday, April fourteenth, President Lincoln was shot by John Wilkes Booth in Ford's Theater in Washington and died the next day. Over April seventeenth and eighteenth, the Confederacy's General J. E. Johnson surrendered 31,200 more men to Sherman at Durham Station in North Carolina and the war was officially over. On Wednesday, April twenty-sixth, Booth was reported dead.

Thursday, the following day, as Lillian sat in her parlor with Hamita Baker, conversing over a cup of hot tea, she rather wished Hamita would find an urgent need to leave so that she could read the three letters which Henry had just brought in to her on a little silver tray. The mails had been so undependable and so far behind, there was no telling how long the communications had been in transit. She glimpsed the one on top which was from Richmond and addressed to both herself and Morgan and recognized Winifred Courtland's small neat handwriting. Morgan's spinster aunt could not have known of Morgan's demise since Lillian hated writing bad news and was terrible about postponing such duties long as possible. But then, she didn't expect the letter from Winifred would contain good news, either. According to Winifred's last correspondence four years ago, Constance, Morgan's mother had gradually lost touch with the world around her and had been living in a tight little cocoon of her own making over those years.

The other two letters were hidden from view and Lillian fought the urge to check them for return addresses, lest Hamita think her glaringly rude.

"—spending a great deal of time together lately, haven't you. Lilly?" Hamita was asking her a question. "Lilly? Lillian Heirs, where are you? You're certainly not here with me. I doubt you've heard a single word I've said!"

"I'm sorry, Hamita. Here, let me freshen your tea." She leaned forward and laid aside the teapot cozy, then poured a stream of fragrant amber liquid into Hamita's cup. "What *were* you saying?" Lillian smiled, focusing her full attention on Hamita. "Milk?"

Hamita nodded. "And two sugars, thank you. I was saying that I've been noticing Jonathan and Laura Lee spending a great deal of time together lately, haven't you?" She stirred the mixture until it was appropriately pale then took a dainty sip. "Mm, perfect! I'll have another of those delicious scones, too, if I may."

Lillian passed the scones. "Rachel will be complimented that you enjoy her new recipe for peach scones. She made it up right out of thin air. They are delicious, aren't they? I'll have another, too."

"Where is Morgana hiding these days?" Hamita asked, bluntly. "I haven't seen her since I returned from Samantha's three weeks ago.

Lillian's relaxed posture became rigid. "Here," she said, disguising her uneasiness, "let me wrap the rest of these scones for you to take home. Jeremiah and Jonathan will enjoy them, too." She scooped up the remaining scones and folded them into a napkin.

Hamita took the scones with one hand and grasped her best friend's arm as she spoke.

"Now, Lillian, if you don't want to talk about Morgana, it's all right with me, but if there is something wrong, it might be better just to get it out. I might be able to help."

Briars
The House of Heirs

Lillian looked into Hamita's dear face and weighed her options. Then she smiled. "There's nothing wrong with Morgana that a visit to my mother in Richmond won't cure, Hamita. She's become moody and reclusive as a hermit what with the whole household in mourning. Also, having six long months still to go before the mourning period ends, the girl is suffering the ache of smothered youthful exuberance and a stifled desire for gaiety. There are no outlets for her energies. She absolutely refuses to ride since I've deprived her of Star. She sits in her room alone, and reads or shares her free time with Willow. I expect one of those letters—" She nodded towards the small silver tray on the table beside the sofa. "—is an answer to my inquiry of my mother as to the suitability of a visit if travel North is safe again by now. The war appears all over but the shouting, and the Yankees are prepared to do enough of that, I'm sure." She shook her head, remembering her own heartache. "What a waste of lives this useless hostility has been." Then, she sighed. "Anyway, I think Morgana's old enough, now, to appreciate such a trip. She'll be eighteen in August and she'll love the hustle and bustle of Richmond. She needs some excitement in her life." Lillian took a sip of her tea, leaned back in her chair, and having chosen her direction, relaxed. It was the first time she'd ever deliberately lied to Hamita.

Hamita placed her empty cup on the tea tray. "I probably have mail from my sister, Samantha, waiting for me at home, too. I hope so. I miss seeing her since I've been back home, and Macon's too far away to run back and forth to every day like the two of us always do." She stood and hugged Lillian. "Answer me, though, before I leave. Do you think Laura Lee and Jonathan will possibly consider marriage in time? Wouldn't a union between those two be just Heaven sent?"

Lillian cocked her head and looked askance at Hamita, smiling. "Now, Hamita, aren't you being a bit over-anxious? I do know that Jonny cherishes the twins because he's always making toys for them. Did you see the doll-house he built for

Alice? It's a beautiful piece of work, and he's making Andy a pony cart, right now. I don't know where he finds the time when he's so busy rebuilding *Greenleaf*."

"You see! That's what I'm talking about," Hamita said. "Still, I think Sarah and Drew would have wanted it. Oh, Lilly, Jeremiah and I were never blessed with children after Jonathan and I've always envied your large family. And you should know by now I've never been one to mind my own business."

Lillian smiled. "Yes, I do know that, Hamita, and I have always valued your opinions, and you know that, too." Lillian walked Hamita to the front door and watched her pass through the hedge arch and down the hill towards home. *Greenleaf* was barely livable at this point of re-construction but Jeremiah and Jonathan had no choice but to finish re-building it around her, because Hamita had wanted to come home.

Lillian hurried back into the parlor where she picked up all three letters and fanned them out. Immediately recognizing her mother's flowing script on the next envelope she moved the one from Winifred Courtland to the bottom. The third was addressed in a rather large studied handwriting, only vaguely familiar. This one she slipped behind Winifred's.

She opened her mother's letter, immediately. In it, as she had hoped, her mother insisted that Lillian bring Morgana to Richmond at the very first opportunity as they were eagerly looking forward to meeting their only remaining granddaughter at last. Her mother expressed their shock and grief at learning of the tragic losses of three of their family at once but, she wrote: "God's will is unpredictable. So be it."

Lillian blotted tears with her tea napkin while she read the letter from Winifred. Constance Heirs had passed away on November twelfth. The same day as her only son, Morgan. There must have been such a celebration in Heaven when those two souls arrived, Lillian thought, knowing the depth of love shared by mother and son.

Briars
The House of Heirs

What a shame it was that none of her own children had ever gotten to know their grandparents. She had always intended that they should meet someday. At last, she was about to see to it that Morgana met at least one set of her ancestors. When Wil was a little older they'd make the same journey to visit her parents, but there was no way under the sun she would have wrestled both of them at once. Every parent's nightmare, she imagined, must be having to pry one's teenage children away from home, friends, and animals to make excursions to meet people they have only heard from at Christmas and on birthdays. Morgana's case would be the exception.

She laid the two open letters back on the tray and examined the third envelope. It bore no postmark and though it was of fine linen paper it showed signs of mishandling, having been wrinkled and wet before arriving at her post office box. She tore open the envelope, noted the long past date on the folded sheet of writing paper, and read:

November 30, 1864

My dear Mistress Heirs,

General Sherman has been met here in Madison, Georgia by a Mister Hill, the acquaintance of a mutual friend and because of his entreaty, has not ordered anything burned except the train depot, a cotton gin and a clothing factory. A Mister Bennet also has kindly extended hospitality to our troops in furnishing food and refreshment and the use of pen and paper to some of us so that we may write overlong delayed letters.

Having been much distressed by the loss of my entire detail, and too urgent in my leave-taking to thank you properly, this letter is proposed to remedy that oversight. I do, herewith, gratefully thank you for your noble act of saving my hide while exposing yourself to great danger.

Today having been my only chance to write my parents, also, I have explained my debt to you. They

> *would never have forgiven me on reading the report of my war experience at Briars, if an invitation had not been issued to you and your family to visit us in Moss Hall. They will welcome an opportunity to show their appreciation for your having saved the much overvalued skin of their younger son. Please do not disappoint me.*
>
> *Your most beholden servant,*
> *Shane   Alexander   Moss,*
> *Lieutenant, U.S. Army*

Lillian read and reread the letter. The phrase: *"reading the report of my war experience at Briars"* leapt out at her. *He didn't even know the truth of his war experience at Briars!* Moreover, she had hoped with all her heart there'd never be reason for him to know it, but Morgana's pregnancy changed everything. She folded his letter, slipped it into her pocket with the others, and crossed the hall to the library. Now there were letters of her own to be written. Important letters. She had barely sat down at the desk and reached for stationery when Morgana stormed into the room.

"Mama!" Morgana cried, tears of frustration and aggravation brimming. "Look at this!" She yanked at the gaping waistband of her skirt, trying to button it. "Nothing, absolutely nothing fits anymore! What am I going to do for clothes?"

"I was about to write to your grandmother O'Donnell saying we are coming for a visit. What do you think of that? While we're there we'll buy you some suitable clothes."

Morgana's face reflected a new optimism. "Richmond?" Lillian sensed Morgana's changing attitude in the lilt of her voice. "Yes, Richmond! Oh, Mama, I shall stay there until this horrible nightmare is over. The lieutenant's family home, as he said, is nearby to Richmond. We'll get in touch with them. Maybe they'll offer to take his child and raise it. If not, some worthy Richmond couple will come forward to adopt it. People are always wanting children when they can't have them."

Morgana whirled around, laughing. "Oh, Mama, what a wonderful idea!"

"Try to be sensible, Morgana. Adoption agencies require more information than you'd wish to become public knowledge. Nor must you count on the lieutenant's family for anything. There's no proof this child is his."

Morgana looked down and smoothed the front of her ankle length bouffant skirts. "I hate this! He should have to pay *some price* for what he's done to me! My condition will soon be obvious even to the casual observer."

"Nonsense," Lillian assured her. "You have a while yet before your physical state will be evident 'to the casual observer'. Now, if you'll go through your closet *patiently*, I'm sure you'll find at least one nice outfit that will serve for travel. In any event my fingers are still nimble enough with a needle and thread to make any minor alterations you may require." Lillian looked away, thoughtfully. As Morgana turned to leave the room, Lillian said, almost as an after-thought. "There is, however, yet another promising alternative to your suppositions. If Laura Lee and Jonathan married, they could take the child and raise it as their own."

"Laura Lee and Jonathan *marry?* Oh, no!" Morgana wailed. "Not Jonathan and Laura Lee! If Laura Lee marries Jonathan, I'll just *die!*"

Ann Gray

CHAPTER ELEVEN ~ SHANE

9:00 a.m., Tuesday, May 2, 1865 ~ Near Petersburg, Virginia

Fateful Journey

    Her nose buried in a delicately perfumed handkerchief against the abundance of varying unpleasant odors, Morgana cast disdainful glances about the crowded railroad coach, eyed her mother and said not quite loud enough to be overheard, "Thank heavens this tiresome journey is nearly over!" She turned her saucy nose back into her handkerchief and sniffed. "I've never been so humiliated in my life! First, the damn Yankees kill my brother and defeat the *entire* Confederate army. They invade our home, rape us, and kill a member of our family. Now, to further embarrass us as defeated Southerners, we are forced to travel all the way to Virginia tucked between a car full of rowdy homeward bound Union soldiers and their war wounded. I know we must make this horrible journey but must we be subjected to the stench and overcrowding of this noisy, reeking, *overwhelmingly* Yankee-occupied, northward bound conveyance? I'd have thought with all the years of Papa's working for the railroad—and considering the shares of stock we own—you'd have been able to acquire better accommodations for us, Mama!"

    Lillian returned the pleasant smile of the heavy-set, florid-faced, obviously well-to-do gentleman across the aisle and laid critical eyes on her petulant daughter. "It's for those very same reasons that we were allowed on this train at all, dear girl, and were it not for those *very favorable reasons*, we'd still be in Atlanta weeks from now patting our feet and whistling "Dixie" waiting for such an opportunity. While you, in the meanwhile, would have ballooned into an unmistakably expectant unwed mother. Now stop this carping and count your blessings,

Briars
The House of Heirs

Morgana, and for Heaven's sake, take that handkerchief away from your face and smile at the nice people. You've managed to survive the stench thus far, and I don't relish this lot of faces scowling in my direction the rest of the way into Richmond because I happen to be in your company."

When, in answer, Morgana turned to gaze out the window, Lillian smiled at the little girl with blue ribbons in her pale blond hair who had been playing hide and seek with her over the forward seat all the way from Raleigh. How like Sweet Sarah at that age she is, Lillian thought, before the child was hauled down into her seat once again by her mother.

Looking from the pretty little blonde girl to her own darkly beautiful but volatile Morgana, so unlike her demure and proper departed sister, Lillian wished she could feel confident the outcome of this dismal journey would be pleasantly concluded. But the unfortunate circumstances of this journey, Lillian feared, precluded a happy outcome for any one of the three innocent lives concerned. Certainly not for Lieutenant Shane Moss who, having no memory of the event, would surely deny Morgana's accusation. Nor for Morgana, who would always carry the disgrace of having given birth, illegitimately. Most unfortunate of all, their bastard child, who would bear the stigma of their carnal sin throughout a lifetime.

In search of less disturbing thoughts, Lillian's mind reverted to the hated subject of politics. She worried for everyone's safety, including their own, because she had heard it rumored that a few days ago, immediately following the surrender of the last of the Confederate forces at Durham Station, North Carolina, Confederate renegades, refusing to acknowledge defeat, had formed outlaw bands and were striking targets throughout the federally occupied Southern states, crippling and hampering governmental operations wherever possible. Innocent victims of their actions included civilians, Northerners and Southerners, alike. She worried about their safety in making this necessary journey on this particular train at this critical time but she would not voice her fears to Morgana, for whom the journey was essential.

Leaving Atlanta, the train had originally been designated as a hospital train. It was only after Lillian had contacted every important person Morgan Heirs had known who was still active on the railroad and bought a thousand additional shares of railroad stock, that the civilian coach had been added and their passage assured. Despite arguments by those railroad authorities who were against adding a civilian coach, it was already practically full on departing Atlanta. In Raleigh, the troop car, overfilled with soldiers fresh from mustering out and eager to get home, had been added and more civilian passengers had boarded, filling the civilian coach to its absolute capacity of sixty.

Looking past Morgana, Lillian concentrated on the passing scenery and tried to focus her mental energy on what reactions her letters might have inspired when they reached their destinations. The one thanking her mother for her open invitation would probably have aroused a great deal of curiosity and speculation. Lillian had said they would be coming for an extended stay but without explanation as to why or for how long. The one to Lieutenant Shane Moss's mother, Patricia, announcing hers and her daughter's availability from tomorrow's date forward at her parent's address in Richmond must have caused some shock and consternation. Especially, if the young lieutenant had been exaggerating his case when recently he wrote: *"Today having been my only chance to write my parents, also, I have explained my debt to you."*

Even if an invitation should be forthcoming from the Mosses in response to Lillian's noble act towards their beloved son, how did one go about proclaiming to doting parents that a chance encounter between their son, a victimized, stone-blind drunk young man and an impudent, overly adventuresome young girl had ended so dramatically. Especially when the act could not be characterized otherwise than "rape". Would they open their arms and say to her, "Welcome to the family"? Of that one outcome, Lillian was quite certain! They would not! Assuredly, there had to be a more subtle way of introducing Morgana. But whatever means that might be fully escaped her.

The short stopover in Petersburg had been dismal. The war-ravaged city had appeared a ghostly skeleton of its former self. Only a few people had detrained and, mercifully, fewer still had boarded, Richmond being the primary focus for the majority of passengers much as it was their own.

Once the train had resumed full speed, the swaying porter quickly made his way down the aisle, grabbing onto the top of each seat as he progressed. Pale-faced, and red-eyed, he called out, "Richmond in forty-five minutes. Next stop, Richmond in forty-five minutes. Passengers for Richmond, forty-five minutes." There followed a hum of animated conversations and bustling activity as passengers, motivated by his announcement, straightened clothing and gathered belongings. Lillian could tell it had been a difficult run for the porter. It took a lot of stamina to be a railroad man. She knew, because she'd married a railroad man.

Almost Home

In the bright light of morning, Shane Moss stood on the south bank of the Appamattox River at the base of the bridge, waiting for Star to drink her fill. There'd be no more watering places once they crossed the bridge and headed up the road into Chesterfield County—not until they got home. He had spent a restless night in his bedroll in a field south of Petersburg and ridden straight through, so anxious was he for the sight of home. Hard tack and river water would hold him just fine until then.

At the pace Star had been setting for herself he could be home by mid-day but he wouldn't push the filly. She was too fine an animal for that. It had been his choice to ride Star back though it was a longer trip, by far, than it would have been by train. At the end of their campaign, most horse soldiers in Sherman's Army had turned in their mounts and opted for the faster, more comfortable train. But he'd pampered Star ever since he'd ridden her out of *Briars* at Mistress Heirs' insistence, and he'd see the filly was well cared for until such time as he could return her to her rightful owner, Miss Morgana Heirs.

The only time he remembered seeing the vengeful Miss Heirs, she had been aiming a rifle at him from an upstairs window at *Briars*. They'd never even spoken nor ever been in actual physical contact. But, somehow, her image had embedded itself deep in his imagination. Time and time again, like last night, he had found himself waking out of a deep sleep with her in his mind's eye—sensual, alluring and so close that her scent was in his nostrils; her taste on his lips; her soft and eager body yielding in his arms, so tangible to his touch he'd awakened in a state of excitement he'd always consciously reserved for his favorite ladies at Mistress Lydia Campbell's House. Even thinking of her now aroused the same excitement and he doused his head in river water, sending the conjured up image of Miss Morgana Heirs back to wherever she belonged. But the fact of the matter was, and it was becoming exceedingly clear to him that despite all his efforts, the hauntingly beautiful raven haired vision was escaping confinement more and more frequently. Someday, he'd unravel these too frequent mysterious dreams of Morgana Heirs. Of that he was sure.

Shane would be happy to shed his Yankee blue uniform. Maybe then, he could go back to being just another Virginian, and not "that damned Yankee son of Roger Moss". He was sorry for that. But at the war's beginning, having been called forth from military school to serve, he'd argued against his parents, his brother, Luke, and all his other relatives and friends that to his mind slavery was downright wrong. His contrary opinion had put him out of step with the majority of people he'd known growing up. It wasn't easy, being on *the other side* in a war where everybody knew where you came from and how much you weighed when you were born. But principles were principles and Shane refused to deny his inner voice in order to please anybody else. And despite the rebuffs and hostility he'd encountered, he'd held true to his belief that no man should have the right to own another. That strong conviction had been responsible for his political leaning towards Lincoln. He'd been schooled, after all, in the military—a far more political atmosphere than existed in rural Virginia among the livestock and tobacco farmers.

Besides getting home to *Moss Hall*, there was only one other thing on his mind right now, and that had been worrying him off and on since the damned war started. That was: what had happened to his brother, Luke? When they'd gone off in different directions at the war's beginning, he had felt anger and resentment towards Luke. They'd always been at odds over one thing or another. Luke being older always had the advantage of size over Shane when they fought, and Luke tended to be rambunctious and trouble seeking. The final break had come when Luke had taken the side of the big slave owners and had shamed Shane for his admiration of Abe Lincoln.

Then after his own experience with the people in the South, he'd mellowed some in his own view of their attitudes about slavery, which to his mind was their main concern. Slavery, though an unjust practice, was not necessarily an unkind custom, for most Southerners were generally upstanding, took good care of their own, and most had carried the same fears and reservations about the war just ended that he'd felt from the beginning. He just hoped that Luke had fared well during these past four years, and would be coming home all in one piece, too. Yep, he thought, he and Luke more than likely would be able to hold a civilized conversation when they both got back home—a little older now—a little wiser. If Luke had learned to curb his hotheadedness during these four years that, too, would be a blessing.

After Star finished drinking Shane tightened her girth and, looking towards the deep green of the tall pines across the river, he whispered in her ear, "Hell, Star, we're almost there!"

How would *Moss Hall* have changed? The growth of the near-by cities of Richmond and Petersburg and the changing faces of Chesterfield and Dinwiddie Counties had long been a festering barb in his father's side. The senior Moss had spent a lifetime building *Moss Hall*'s reputation for good breeding stock and though it was far from being Virginia's largest horse breeding farm, it was well respected among the cream of Kentucky's buyers and traders. While Shane knew it wouldn't be long before the farm would have to give way to the area's urban growth and progress, he had always hoped that his father would never have to see the change in his lifetime.

Fifty yards farther downstream from where Shane stood with Star at the river's edge and rising out of the tangle of undergrowth, was the trestle that carried trains back and forth across the Appomattox river's broad waters. Railroad companies had to be straining every effort to get back into normal operation in the few weeks since hostilities ended. He already knew trains were getting through. He'd seen several loaded with Union soldiers headed north since he'd started riding for home. Sure enough, he heard the whistle of an approaching northbound train and smiled. There'd be a lot of happy men aboard who were, like him, heading back home. After another four or five toots, the train was noisily rattling onto the trestle. Shane watched the train pass and when the engineer waved at him, he waved back. Following the locomotive and tender, he counted two Union army hospital cars, one civilian passenger coach, and a troop car where a caboose would normally have been attached. Happy homebound soldiers hung out of every window of the troop car, laughing and singing and waving at anything that moved. Shane waved back at them, too. Damn, it was good to see some merry-making again!

Appomattox Crossing

The train with Lillian and Morgana aboard rattled onto the trestle above the Appamattox river. The view from Morgana's window was finally unobstructed by trees. Scanning the scene, she pulled on Lillian's sleeve, crying out, "Mama! Mama, look! There! Down there on the river bank by that bridge. That's Star! I'd recognize her anywhere. See? That's her!" She leaned back, trying to flatten herself against the seat, making room for Lillian, who stretched across her daughter to look out.

It did look like Star, Lillian had to agree. She squinted to see more clearly as the train moved forward across the trestle taking them farther away from their point of interest.

Morgana continued to examine the scene for a likely rider as the train progressed on the trestle. Then she saw a man in the dark blue of a Yankee uniform step out around the horse and start waving at the train. "There, Mama, do you see him?" she asked Lillian, who shaded her eyes against the bright morning sunlight, trying to follow Morgana's pointing finger. "That's got to be *him*," Morgana hissed.

"Perhaps," Lillian said, "but then, at such a distance—"

The train was making its way onto land again, and watching the greenery outside the coach come closer, Lillian breathed a sigh of relief. Not only had she not liked being on the narrow, complaining trestle, but the motion of the fast flowing water beneath the moving train had been unsettling to her. She'd never been required to learn to swim, and she'd never before been so acutely aware of that deficiency. As a younger woman, nothing had been daunting in her eyes, but as age had crept upon her, more and more, she weighed situations with an eye to her ability to cope.

Calamity

 Shane had watched the train's progress almost all the way across the expansive trestle when an ear-splitting blast at its southernmost foundation sent the trestle crumbling. Struts collapsed. Crossties peeled away from sections of rail and splashed into the river like oversized toothpicks. The unsupported rails hung like untied boot laces until, by force of their own weight, they began separating and falling, one by one, into the roiling waters of the Appamattox. He felt relieved when at first it appeared that all four cars had made it safely to the other side. But then he saw that the last two cars had jumped the tracks. Only then did he realize that the last car—the troop car—was beginning to grate backwards pulling the preceding derailed passenger coach, skidding sideways on its belly, along with it into a precarious jack-knifed position along the track. The troop car broke loose and tumbled off the splintered end of the remaining trestle into the shallows on the far side of the river. The cries of those trapped within the car rivaled those of a battlefield and he watched, transfixed, from the opposite bank of the river as the car pitched backward, overturned, and sank into the murky waters. Open windows afforded a way out for many, and swimmers swarmed away from the sinking wooden coffin. Shane's attention was immediately drawn to and riveted on the trestle's demolished foundation at the south end. Quickly, he mounted Star and rode headlong through the tangle of high weeds on the riverbank towards the site of the blast.
 The locomotive, its tender, two hospital cars, and the passenger coach Morgana and Lillian occupied had barely cleared the wooden trestle onto solid ground when the occupants heard and felt the force of a catastrophic explosion. It sent shock waves vibrating along the rails, up through the wheels and into

the very core of every human being trapped inside the conveyance.

Morgana screamed as she was catapulted from her seat and flung across the back of the seat in front of them by a tremendous force. Lillian, forced to her knees in the aisle by the magnitude of the blast, held onto an arm rest. When the coach abruptly changed directions, Morgana's momentum propelled her sideways into the aisle, where she tumbled over her mother and slammed against the arm rest of the seat across the aisle. Lillian held onto Morgana, the two of them tumbling down the aisle as the car screeched sideways along the rails in the direction from which they'd just come.

Confusion reigned, and the sound of it merged with the horrible grinding that erupted as the body of the car skidded along the rails. The little girl with the blue ribbon in her hair, jolted from her seat, went hurtling through space over their heads. Lillian reached up for her with one hand while trying to hold onto Morgana with the other, but she'd reacted too late. The man who had occupied the opposite seat across the aisle, reached out from his new position, wedged against the wall of the car between seats, grabbed the child in mid-air, and held her firmly against his chest as the coach careened crazily into an even more extreme sideways position before it finally glided to a stop.

The sudden silence when the coach stopped was overpowering. Lillian could see out the coach's side windows, now facing back along the track, the ends of the remaining rails swinging free not ten feet away. Beyond, was open space. Below, the roaring river.

The formerly pleasant smiling man, his once florid face now white with shock, returned the child, unharmed, to her mother who, having come to rest across Lillian's and Morgana's legs, scrambled to her feet.

Morgana lay still, face down.

Lillian pulled her right arm free from beneath her daughter and got to her knees, gently rolling over the unconscious Morgana. She felt for a pulse at the base of Morgana's throat. The pulse was there, strong and overly fast. Everyone on the train had been terribly frightened, the pounding of her own heart left no doubt of that.

The gallant gentleman was most accommodating as he helped Lillian lift her limp daughter back into her window seat. Sitting down beside Morgana, supporting her, Lillian looked down at the troop car mired in the murky shallows below the remainder of the trestle. Already she saw able swimmers converging on the scene from out of nowhere wading out into the water from the riverbank. Self-sufficient survivors, like a school of surfacing blue-gills, rose to the top and swam alongside rescuers with the fortunate ones being towed to safety.

Her attention was drawn back to the furor in the coach as occupants scrambled over one another in their frenzy to get out the open doors and onto solid ground.

Morgana groaned and Lillian gave her full attention to the girl.

"What happened?" Morgana asked, her hands going immediately to her abdomen. "Oh, it hurts, Mama, it hurts terribly!" she said, softly in Lillian's ear. Then she sank back into unconsciousness.

In one movement, Lillian removed her wedding band and slipped it onto Morgana's third finger, left hand. Then she reached and caught the sleeve of the benevolent gentleman, who sat rigidly in his seat, now looking in awed fascination at the frantic clamoring of hysterical passengers.

"Sir, I realize there are many in distress here but—since I can't leave her alone, would you please be so kind as to see if you can find a doctor from the forward hospital car who might look at my daughter soon? I'm afraid she's losing her baby. I've recently been deprived of three members of my family—

two by this damnable war—and now that it's supposedly over, I simply cannot bear losing another two."

"Oh, dear lady, of course, I'll go immediately!" he said, patting her hand, before forcing his bulk up the crowded aisle.

Lillian hugged her limp daughter to her and kissed her full lips. How beautiful she was, her face in repose. Why must they always be at odds, Morgana and herself, when she loved her more than life, itself? "Don't worry, 'Gana' darling, Mama's here for you," she said, soothingly, into Morgana's oblivious ear. Without warning, she began shaking violently, and above the din, an odd buzzing sound assaulted her ears, and for the first time in her life, Lillian Heirs swooned.

Renegades

As Shane reached the site of the explosion, he was joined by two other uniformed horsemen who had struck out towards the thicket from the road at about the same time he had left the riverbank. The three of them arrived on the scene while the smell of powder still hung in the air. At once, Shane was off Star and by the side of a man lying crumpled on the trampled ground at the water's edge. Another two horsemen, followed by a rider-less horse, were making their getaway into a nearby stand of pines across the railroad tracks. The other two uniformed riders never came to a full stop, but took out after the fleeing riders, leaving Shane to deal with the fallen man.

He only needed to approach the injured man to see the sliver of flying wood that had pierced his back before he could get cleanly away. Kneeling to cradle the dying man's head, Shane carefully turned him over and opened the collar of his blood-splattered Confederate gray uniform void of insignia.

"Who helped you do this?" Shane asked, leaning close to hear the dying man's response.

"Do what?" was the smirking, bitter, whispered reply. He coughed blood, his eyes glazed, and he died in Shane's arms.

Shane went through the dead man's pockets, but found no identification.

The two uniformed riders returned from their futile chase and saw that the wounded man had died.

Looking across the river at the end result of the renegades' handiwork, the three mustered out soldiers exchanged looks. Not a single word was spoken between them, each man merely nodding to the other, yet it seemed to Shane that at once they shared a profound understanding and mutual respect. Though both of the other men wore Confederate gray, they rode with Shane across the bridge to do what they could for the victims of the derailment. For these three, the war was truly over.

Shane tied Star to a low branch on a maple sapling some distance from the riverbank, and waded in alongside other rescuers to pull three struggling swimmers to safety before he tracked down a Union Army Major and told him what he'd found on the other side of the river.

The recovered dead—too many—were lined up row on row and covered with blankets.

In shock and chilled to the bone, coughing soldiers sat shivering on open ground in the crudely prepared receiving area near the water's edge while two army doctors worked feverishly over the surviving victims. Civilian passengers from the coach had been herded into a group apart from the military, and Shane heard one of the overburdened doctors say that those injuries—mostly bumps and bruises—would have to wait for treatment until the more seriously injured army personnel had been attended.

After reporting his findings to the major, Shane rode back into Petersburg as fast as Star would carry him with news of the disaster. Every wagon that could be rounded up would be needed to transport the train's occupants back into Petersburg, where they would have to pass the night with wherever shelter could be found for them. The Sheriff would send somebody to haul away the renegade's body and look into the act of sabotage along with railroad authorities and army officers, too, no doubt.

Renegades!   Shameless bastards!   Anybody'd play hell finding them, now!

Moss Hall

"Hm! What do you make of this?" The proper Mistress Patricia Moss asked from her place in the front porch swing, passing the letter she had just finished reading to her husband for his scrutiny. "Who in the world is this Mistress Heirs? Have we met? She says she and her daughter will be temporarily residing with the Michael O'Donnells in Richmond and she looks forward to hearing from me. Do we know any O'Donnells in Richmond?" Tightly coiled braids encircled her ears and her small dark head bobbed up and down as she spoke. Her eyes, wide set and round, looked out from a sharply defined countenance. "She says she is writing to me in reference to an invitation to visit *Moss Hall* from Shane? Since when does our son invite people to visit *Moss Hall* when he's not in residence?"

"What's that? Shane's invited someone here without your knowledge? That's not like him, is it?" Her husband, Roger, seated at a small wicker table with his Solitaire card game in progress, adjusted his spectacles over his slender nose, held the letter at arm's length, and quickly read it. "Brief enough, isn't it? And to the point, I must say. I have no memory of a Mistress Heirs, myself. Perhaps this Heirs woman is someone Shane met while in the army. I expect if he's invited her here it's for a very good reason."

"She makes mention of Shane's having invited both her and her daughter but there's no mention of the daughter's age. You don't suppose—?" Patricia's eyes grew rounder.

Ann Gray

"Certainly not!" He stroked his short, neatly trimmed white beard contemplating his next card play. "Surely, we'll hear something from Shane, himself, regarding this invitation before long. You know how damned undependable the mails have been! Perhaps he expected to be home by the time this letter arrived. Don't get upset without cause, my dear. You become so excited over little things, often needlessly."

"Little things? What if it's some woman he's met who has designs on him? He's been away so long, I only hope he hasn't made such a commitment without telling us. He's just a boy. He wouldn't do such a thing, would he, Roger?" Worry wrinkles crept into their accustomed place between her brows.

"Dismiss the thought, my dear. Shane is much too level-headed. He's not likely to have made any promises he's bound to keep. You must realize he's no longer a boy. He's been to war. He'll soon be twenty-two, and he's been away four year, after all."

"I certainly know how old my own child is, Roger. And, I know exactly how long he's been away." She pouted, eyeing her husband who was again intent on his card game, as she lifted a small glass of sherry to her lips, half emptying it. Then she patted her pursed lips with a lacy handkerchief and quickly refilled the glass from a decanter on the banister at her elbow. "After all, I was there when he was born. You were not." Another sip of sherry. "I know how long *both* my boys have been away. It's heart breaking—shameful, the way the two of them fought all their lives and argued over this horrible war. It wasn't enough to have the North and South at one another, we had to have a small war in our very own home. I have worried terribly about their having gone off in opposite directions and at such odds with each other, too."

"Yes, my dear, so I've been told a million times or more," Roger answered without looking up. "It hasn't been long since dinner, Patsy, so if you intend emptying that entire decanter before suppertime, perhaps you should inform Bessie there will only be one at table again this evening. You know that wine you drink always puts you to sleep."

"What difference does it make? I declare, our days are so dull, it's unrewarding even getting up mornings anymore, and sherry dulls the pain, Roger. *You know* that's the only reason I drink it!"

"So you've said, Patsy, so you've said." He placed the last King on the Queen of Diamonds and scooped up the four piles of cards to reshuffle and play again.

"Roger, I have this terrible sense of impending dread, you know? It's like something appalling is about to happen and I'm to have no control over it."

"Nonsense! You've let the letter from the Heirs woman unnerve you. I'm sure there'll be a simple explanation for it soon."

"I do so hate being put into this type of situation, though, don't you see?" She sipped her Sherry. "I mean, it would have been more fitting had I written to her first if such a visit were to be, but only after hearing of its nature from Shane. Now, I'm put into the unenviable position of responding to an unknown party about an unanticipated visit. I shall, most certainly, have to think this over for a few days before answering."

"As you will, Patsy. Perhaps we'll hear something from Shane in the meanwhile." Roger laid aside his cards, reached for his broad-brimmed hat, got up and ambled to the steps, yawning. "I think I'll take a walk. Clear out a few mental cobwebs, and such. Care to join me?"

"No, thank you, dear," Patricia answered, eyeing the decanter. "I'll just sit here a little while longer."

The same question. The same answer. It happened every afternoon at the same time. Roger stretched out his long legs and loped away down the winding drive.

Years ago, he had designed the drive to ramble through a thick stand of Virginia pines, completely shielding the house from the road. It satisfied his need for privacy, having the house sit so far back from the road to Petersburg. The long winding drive might, also, have been partly responsible for their having been spared a lot of attention during Grant's hostile passage. They'd only lost some horses. Others had lost a lot more. A few miles to the east, Petersburg had become a battlefield, its railroads seized by the invading Army. Large sections in neighboring Richmond, seat of the Confederacy, had been evacuated and businesses burned in anticipation of Grant's arrival. Now that the war was over, there'd be a lot of reconstruction going on.

He set a steady pace down the main road alongside the low rock wall that marked the entire two mile frontage of the farm. When he reached the end of the wall he would retrace his steps, and by the time he reached his front steps again he would have completed a five mile walk. Out of sheer boredom, he'd play another two or three games of Solitaire before supper and then he'd sit down to table and, against his own better judgment, eat heartily. His waistline was already straining at his trousers from the inequity of intake to activity.

There was not enough to do around the farm to keep a man fit in mind nor body. Not enough work. Not enough profit. Certainly, not enough time left for him to start over, what with all but one old mare and one stallion having been seized by Grant. Still, it could have been worse. They had heard the sounds of actual fighting in the distance from their own front porch. At least they'd been spared that. Petersburg had fallen to Grant on April second. The capture of Richmond followed shortly after and so—the war's end. Now, he lived only for the safe return of his two sons. God, how he hoped they'd let go of their personal war, now the country's was over!

Briars
The House of Heirs

Jacob Garner

Roger heard the pounding hoof beats long before the horseman riding towards him became visible. Topping the slight rise of the road and kicking up a cloud of dust, he was riding hard from Petersburg. He recognized Jacob Garner, owner of the city's public stables, by his mane of wildly flying white hair, even from such a distance. Jacob waved as he came closer and slowed his mount, finally, to a snorting halt.

"Somebody blew up the south end of the trestle at Appamattox crossing with a northbound Yankee train on it!" Jacob sputtered, trying to contain his excitement. "A carload of Union soldiers went into the river. By damn, the war may be over, but the renegades ain't quitting. Not yet!" He patted his horse's lathered neck. "Doc Wilkins has more'n he can handle and wondered if you'd come and help out."

"I've doctored horses, Jacob, but never people," Roger protested. "Abel Wilkins knows that."

"Things sure are in an uproar in town right now," Jacob said, spitting a stream of brown juice onto the road on the other side of his horse. "Doc says they need all the help they can get!" When he saw Roger's hesitation, he added, "Well, I got to hurry back! My rig's needed down at the river. Give you a ride back to your place?"

"Thanks, Jacob, thanks a lot!" Roger said, and taking hold of his friend's arm, he swung up onto the horse's back behind Jacob's saddle, mulling over Doc's request.

"There's been some drownings down there. Lots of injuries. Sure hope your Yankee boy wasn't on that train, Roger," Jacob said over his shoulder, as they cantered smoothly along. "I can understand how troublesome it must have been for y'all, having boys on both sides like that," Jacob said. "But every man's

Ann Gray

entitled to his own opinion, I always say and nobody's ever held it against you, having a Yankee soldier in your family and all."

"That's good to know, Jacob, seeing that the war's over, now!" Roger said, a flare of agitation coloring his cheeks. "But there's no way *in Hell* you, or anybody else could possibly know how it's been for us! Though I appreciate your concern, Jacob, I'm sure our Shane won't be among them." When they got back to the entrance to the drive, Roger slid off and said, "You can tell Abel Wilkins, I'll be along." Then he slapped Jacob's horse on his rump and watched the horseman ride off the way he'd come, in a pall of gray dust.

At the driveway's end, both Patsy and the decanter were gone from the porch. Roger hesitated before mounting the steps and, instead, went directly around the side of the house. By now, Patsy would be sound asleep. There'd be no advantage in waking her to explain his hurried departure, and leaving her awake and worried the whole while, unquestionably, would only lead her to consume more spirits.

He entered the small stable at the far end of the show corral, saddled the stallion, Victor, and rode him out, latching the stable door from his saddle. He averted his eyes from the main stables, standing empty along with the handlers' quarters, working corrals and empty pastures, beyond. It was a sorry sight, anyway. A waste. All his hired hands had long since quit to fight the war. "Bleak" was the word, Roger thought, that best described his life.

He rode straight to the back porch and called for Bessie. Cook and housekeeper, Bessie remained the only servant in the house. She understood Patsy and had cared for her conscientiously these past four years since her "health" had become unstable. Roger had no doubt that it had been his wife's worry over her sons' having argued and left home to fight on opposite sides in the war that had nibbled away at her until she had succumbed to the lure of drink. It was only recently she had begun using excuses of illness to mask her inclination to imbibe to excess.

"Bessie!" he shouted, and when the woman's face appeared in the doorway, "I've been summoned into town. There's been an train derailment at the Appamattox trestle crossing, but don't tell Mistress, I don't want her upset. If I'm not back by the time she wakes in the morning, tell her I left early to take Victor in for shoeing."

"Yessuh," Bessie answered, and Roger heard the bolt slide as the door closed.

Yes, Roger would go to Petersburg and do what he could to help his friend, Abel Wilkins, but he didn't expect that his son who'd joined the Union army would be coming home on that train. Shane was much too resourceful to depend on the army to get him back home. Especially not on a train. Not if he could have a horse under him. But, Roger thought, since he'd be going into Petersburg anyway, he'd just check the train's manifest of passengers for Shane's name.

Wonder of Wonders

"Ma'am? Ma'am?" Lillian wished the voice would go away. For the first time in weeks her mind was unoccupied by worry, floating free in a cloud of forgetfulness, serene and comfortable. "Ma'am, are you awake?" Coming into focus the young face with the old eyes was unshaven. An army doctor was kneeling beside her. "Ma'am, the young lady who was with you is about to be transported into Petersburg. I thought you should know."

Tucking her legs under her, Lillian sat up and fastened her gaze onto his. "Yes, yes, I'm fine." Seated on an army blanket on the ground, she was surrounded by other civilians from the train. "She's my daughter. Where is she? Is she conscious? May I ride along with her?" she asked anxiously. When he helped her to her feet, her legs were shaky but they supported her as she looked around for the wagon with Morgana aboard.

"She's going to be all right, but her pregnancy was already terminated when I got to her. I'm sorry. The father—he's in service?"

"The same army as you. Only he didn't know she was expecting," Lillian answered, honestly.

"That will make it easier on him, at least. Last time I was home, I left a wife with a baby on the way, myself. Still don't know what we got. But I know how I'd feel if this were my wife." As the young doctor spoke, he supported Lillian, guiding her around others who rested and waited for transport. "I've given your daughter a sedative so she'll sleep a while. She'll require at least a day's rest before continuing her journey. I wish I could have done more." Lillian could see that he was overly tired and equally distressed. "She's over there," he said, pointing towards a wagon where the driver, an old man with shoulder length white hair, was climbing onto the driver's bench.

Lillian approached the wagon and caught hold of the brake handle, looking up at the driver. "The young woman in back is my daughter. I'll ride the bench with you if it's all right." The driver nodded. "May I have a word with the doctor, here, before we leave?" The old man's white head bobbed again. The doctor walked her around to the other side of the wagon to help her up.

Buoyed by relief in hearing that Morgana was going to be all right, a wave of gratitude swept over her and before she climbed up Lillian said to the doctor, "My daughter will bear other children, God willing. You've just told me that *my* child will be all right, and for that, Sir, I humbly thank you." Then, on tiptoes, she kissed his rough cheek and he smiled and helped her up onto the wagon.

As the driver worked his way into the wagon procession for Petersburg, Lillian realized that she and the Union Army doctor had never even swapped names.

She leaned down behind the old man to look at Morgana, lying under an army blanket in the bed of the wagon closest to the bench. Though drugged, she appeared to be sleeping naturally. Beyond her, wrapped like babies after their ordeal in the muddy waters, four pale youthful soldiers slept in exhaustion. Lillian gently took hold of Morgana's wrist with one hand and with the other found a regular, strong pulse. Without Morgana's ever having known it had been there, Lillian slipped her wedding band off Morgana's finger, and returned it to it's customary place. There was not the slightest doubt in Lillian's mind as she raised a silent prayer on Morgana's behalf that the day's agenda of events had been written in Heaven. Time had been called for some; the trusting faithful had been rewarded; the innocent, redeemed; and a gracious God had provided unbelievers another chance for redemption. He did, indeed, work in strange and wondrous ways.

She turned and smiled at the driver sitting next to her and, attempting to make casual conversation said, "I'm Lillian Heirs. That's my daughter, Morgana, in back."

The driver nodded and said, around his fat wad of tobacco, "Pleasure, ma'am. Jacob Garner."

Lillian went on, "I've been through Petersburg on the train between Richmond and Atlanta before. It's shocking to see the difference this war has made. Matter of fact, my husband and I used to live in Richmond. I was taking our daughter to visit my parents back there when this horrible accident happened. You lived in Petersburg long?" The wagon rumbled onto the better road and turned towards the bridge.

"Yep, all my life." He flicked the reins over the team of mules' broad backs. "And—it weren't no accident."

Jacob had Lillian's full attention. "You think the trestle was tampered with?"

"Blowed up! Union soldier found a man dying and evidence of dynamite the other side of the river." The old man spat a stream of tobacco juice with the wind. "Renegades!"

"My daughter almost died in that wreck." Lillian looked back at Morgana who was beginning to rouse a bit from her drug-induced sleep. "I hope they find out who did it and punish them to the letter of the law."

Jacob turned his blood-shot eyes on her. "They'll be long gone by now. It's going to take a while for some hot-heads to simmer down. War don't necessarily end with the signing of a paper," the old man said.

Lillian nodded in agreement. There was certainly truth in that remark.

She turned her thoughts to more personal matters with a lightness of spirit long absent. There was really no reason to contact the Mosses of Chesterfield County, now. No reason at all. Morgana would rest the next day in Petersburg and, hopefully, by then the railroad crew would have righted the cars and they could resume their travel to Richmond. They'd make the visit with her parents a short one and return home with renewed vitality.

As far as Lillian was concerned the personal business with Shane Moss on Morgana's account was ended except for the return of Morgana's horse. She could breathe freely again and when she awakened, Morgana would be jumping for joy at the turn of events. So why, she wondered, did she hear herself inquiring: "I'm told there's a family near Petersburg name of Moss. You know them?"

"Known Roger Moss my whole life," the driver said, eyeing her with different interest.

"How far out of town might their place be?" Lillian asked, perplexed at her own need to pursue the subject.

Jacob spat off the side of the wagon, again. "If it's him you're wanting to see, Roger's in town helping Doc Wilkins with these injured folks from the wreck."

Lillian felt a surge of apprehension. "He's a doctor?"

"Nope, but he knows horses. Ain't much difference whether you're fixing broken parts on horses or on people, I'd guess.

Anyways, they run out of rooms down at the hotel so they're using Mistress Campbell's house, now. That's where we're headed and that's where he'll be." He laughed out loud, showing his snaggled teeth. "Bet Lydie Campbell never expected so many people'd be happy to see the inside of her big old bawdy house."

Lillian pointedly overlooked the inclination of his humor and said, unsmiling, "If Mister Moss is busy with the injured, I won't bother him. It was only to be a courtesy, anyway. His son, Shane, asked me to look up his parents if I should have occasion to be in this vicinity." She smiled, remembering Shane's last letter. "He said anybody in Petersburg would know the Moss name, and as fate would have it, here we are."

"Shane, huh?" The old man cocked his head, and looked at Lillian with renewed interest. "He's their youngest—turned out to be a Lincoln man! Surprised everybody when he went with the North. Older brother, Luke, now—," and with satisfaction, "—he fought for the South. Brother against brother, that's the shame of it!" After a moment's reflection, he spoke again. "Y'all're from Atlanta, eh?"

"Um-hum," Lillian said, looking out at the desolate battlefield that had once been a beautiful countryside, "moved there in thirty-eight from Richmond."

"Y'all were in Atlanta, then, when Sherman went through. I've heard tell Shane was with Sherman. All that burning and—"

"Please, I'd rather not talk about the war any more if you don't mind," Lillian said.

She turned to look at Morgana. First, the twitching of a hand, then the slow rolling of her head from side to side, eyes still tightly closed.

"That where you met Shane? Him being with Sherman, and all?" Jacob's gaze was steadfast, expectant, eager for details.

"Tell me more about the Moss boys," Lillian countered.

"Well—," He used his tongue to move his chewing tobacco to the other cheek and spat again. "—both of them's good with horses." An overloaded wagon with a black family aboard passed, going the other way at a good clip. "Humph! Look at that! Niggers flocking north, now! They ain't going to find it any better up there than they did down here."

Lillian doubted that any of her own five faithful servants would ever feel the urge to leave *Briars* in a search for freedom in the North.

Jacob flicked his reins and clicked to the mules. "Shane's got some crazy Yankee ideas! Probably from all that schooling he got! Now, Luke, there's a whole different story! Never wanted any schooling at all if he could get out of it. Quit, too, once he got past reading, writing, and numbers. When the war came along and it looked like he couldn't get out of it, he joined up. Well, he's a natural born Rebel, anyway. Always in hot water for one thing or 'nother."

Having no interest in Shane's brother, Luke, with Jacob's words still droning in her ears, Lillian rode on in silence. Her muscles were aching from the pummeling she had taken and she was terribly tired. She'd welcome the rest when they reached their destination. Lillian looked back again at a slowly awakening Morgana. Wonder of wonders, after the battering the girl had sustained in the derailment and the resultant miscarriage, she was more than fortunate to be alive; she was blessed.

Mistress Campbell's House

An intermittent, high-pitched rasping squeak penetrated the darkness of Morgana's unconsciousness and soon evolved into the unmistakable groan of a grease-starved wheel. Then there was the sound of indistinct voices, and she became aware of motion, of being jostled by an uneven ride. Hard as she tried, she couldn't open her eyes, and her limited perceptions were strained as she struggled to put her impressions together to form some recognizable design.

Immediately, she accepted that she was on a wagon's firm bed, and one of the nearby muddled voices belonged to her mother. That within itself was comforting. She forced her eyes open to slits when the motion stopped and made out, looming overhead, a large white two story house. More voices joined in unintelligible conversations and the wagon bed rocked back and forth and side to side. Bringing her sensibility to focus on closer objects, by the time she was fully aware of the presence of the four silent blanket-wrapped soldiers who shared her space, they were being off-loaded, one by one, onto stretchers by Union Army personnel.

For Morgana, past and present warped into oneness, and as two young servicemen climbed aboard the wagon and reached to move her to the back of the wagon for transfer into the house, Morgana fended off their helping hands, exclaiming loudly and in typical Morgana temper, *"Take your hands off me this instant, you damned clumsy Yankees! I do not intend to be man-handled by your kind—ever again! What have you done with my mother?"*

Lillian, who had climbed down alone and walked around the wagon to watch Morgana being removed by the stretcher bearers, was startled to hear Morgana's outcry. "Morgana, please! I'm right here," Lillian called to her from the rear of the wagon.

Through her wakening dream state, her eyes still dull and heavy-lidded from the effects of the sedative, Morgana searched for Lillian's face. "Mama?"

Lillian turned her back to the interested and curious throng beginning to gather around the wagon and concentrating her attention on Morgana, whose wan countenance wore an expression of utter confusion, she soothed, "Let them help you, darling! You've been hurt and they're only trying to get you inside where you can rest and recover."

"I'll rest and recover a lot better, Mama, without Yankee hands all over me!" Morgana sang out, hugging the blanket that covered her bloody clothes tightly about her as she eased along on her bottom to the rear of the wagon. When she reached the dropped tail gate, she held out one unsteady hand to Lillian. "Help me down, please, Mama."

"Mistress Heirs, let me!" The familiar voice came from directly behind Lillian, who looked over her shoulder in stunned disbelief as Shane Moss stepped up beside her. Undisturbed by Morgana's continuing insults, he competently scooped the blanket-wrapped combatant into his arms.

Morgana beat her fists against his chest, wailing, "You? Not you, again! Damn you—!" Her voice rose to a higher pitch as Shane carried her, squirming, up the steps and across the porch to the wide double doors of the house. An embarrassed Lillian followed close on Shane's heels, trying all the while to appear indifferent, as if Morgana's behavioral display was a fact of daily life.

When Shane stepped through the doors into the busy hallway with his burden, Morgana lowered her voice to a stinging whisper in his ear. "My mama says you didn't even remember what you did! Considering I was there, I find that very unlikely!" She looked over his shoulder at her mother. "Mama, you tell him to put me down or I'm telling everybody what he did!"

With the tone of that threat, Shane stopped still and lowered Morgana's feet to the floor. "I took the horse with your mother's permission, and you know it!" he said, confidentially, lowering his forthright gaze to her scowl. "Was there something else, Miss Heirs?"

"No, Morgana!" Lillian protested, closing in on them and smiling up at Shane. "There's really nothing else—now!"

Following her mother's gaze, Morgana slipped a hand through the fold of the blanket and ran it smoothly down the front of her limp dress. Expressions on her face progressed from purely naked anger to confused astonishment to sheer joy. "Well, I'll just be!" Morgana exclaimed. In a less impertinent tone, looking incredulously at her mother, she added, "I do believe that horrible wreck has knocked the sense right out of me."

"I only hope it has knocked some sense *into* you," Lillian whispered, moving quickly to stand between Morgana and Shane.

Morgana grinned broadly at Lillian. Then, drawing the blanket closer around her, she eyed Shane Moss's face over her mother's head. "I thank you, Sir," she said, quite civilized, "for your gracious assistance, and I do apologize for my shameful behavior. But you must realize we still do have differences!" Smiling decorously, she glanced about the crowded corridor as most people, suddenly disinterested, began to move around again pursuing their own interests.

There was still, however, the gathering of painted young ladies huddled on the staircase, who continued to watch their exchange with unwavering interest, punctuated by an occasional giggle or titter.

Containing her animosity, Morgana inquired privately, "Star, Lieutenant? How much longer do you plan to hold my mare a prisoner of war?"

"Don't worry, Miss Heirs," Shane assured her, just as exclusively. "I intend to return Star soon enough after I get back home and see my folks. With a *Moss Hall* Thoroughbred under me, I'll probably have Star safely at *Briars* long before you arrive back from your own journey."

Thus dismissing Morgana, Shane placed both hands gently on Lillian's shoulders and looked into her weary eyes. "Mistress Heirs, may I be of further service to you?"

Painfully aware of the depth of warm regard that flowed between them, Morgana found it absolutely shameful the way her mother was hanging on every word Shane Moss spoke. Also, Morgana had to wonder, why he seemed to tower so over

Mama? She'd not noticed him being of extraordinary height before. Nor had his shoulders seemed so broad before that they strained the seams of his uniform, as now.

"I think we'll do fine, now, thanks, Lieutenant," Mama was saying. "I could say '*Mister* Moss' now the war's over, couldn't I? Should I?"

"No, ma'am," the meddler replied. "Just call me 'Shane' from now on."

From now on? Morgan thought, angrily. As if there were going to be a 'from now on'! Despite herself, Morgana stared, captivated by his natural, unadulterated appeal. Handsome even beneath the stubble of at least a week's growth of beard, he was purposely avoiding eye contact with her. She wanted to look away—desperately—but whenever she tried, she was drawn right back by his amiable, resonant voice.

The painted ladies on the staircase had not missed one single gesture by any of the three of them, and Morgana found it absolutely humiliating that Shane Moss's total focus had been so long on Mama. She watched her mother openly reach up and take hold of both Shane's hands at her shoulders as they talked. Her own mother, shaming her publicly with such a forward display of partiality towards—and she thought it, angrily—the man who had *raped* her own daughter, no less! Damn the fact that she, herself, had provided the opportunity! Double damn the fact that she, guiltily and with titillation, remembered it—and Mama swore to her—he didn't! Now there were all these vulgar painted women hanging over the banisters on the staircase staring at him with expressions of—what? Appreciation? No! Remembrance! How many times before had he sexually known which ones—or all of them?

Her mother was saying, "It's good to see you and Star have made it safely together this far. There's really no reason to be concerned about her immediate return. I know you're taking good care of her. But now that you're this close to home, I'm sure you're most anxious to be on your way. Don't let us hold you up. I should be seeing about getting Morgana settled, anyway."

Lillian nodded towards the open doorway on her right through which the stretcher cases from the wagon had disappeared. "There's where we have to register, I believe." Then to Morgana's eternal embarrassment, Mama grasped her blanket-covered elbow firmly as if to guide her like an unruly child into the room.

Drawing the blanket closer around her as she pulled free of her mother's grip, Morgana turned to Shane Moss. "I think your 'lady friends' there on the stairs are eagerly seeking your attention. They've been watching your every move since you entered this house."

Shane glanced towards the staircase, and a broad smile swept across his face. "Miss Violet. Miss Myrtle. Miss Charlotte. It's my pure pleasure to see all your pretty faces, again."

"Well, really!" Morgana seethed.

Leaving him to his admirers, Morgana glanced back momentarily at the young women who had rushed down the stairs to surround a grinning Shane. Without a doubt, one of her curiosities about Shane Moss had just been answered. Hugging her blanket closer, she tossed her curly black head and walked ahead of her mother into the large pink room that was Mistress Campbell's parlor.

Morgana and Lillian approached a table where a young man sat recording names of the newly arrived in a large book. Beyond the registrar, a bearded man in a blood-splattered white coat went routinely from one occupied stretcher to the next listening to each incoming patient's chest with a stethoscope, checking pulses and noting injuries. He moved to stand beside the nearest stretcher.

Lillian leaned down to sign the book, and Morgana's interest was again drawn towards the open doorway to the hall where laughter punctuated Shane's conversation with the women of the house. It was not difficult to understand their attraction to him. She had been altogether at home in his arms and felt strangely abandoned when he had released her. Fate had not been fair to her. Her first experience with a man should not have been one so crudely begun nor so sadly memorable for the occasion as had been that day last November. She could have—would have—welcomed this man's attentions at another time and under other circumstances. But, she reminded herself, she was once again free of encumbrance. Dared she give just a little? Perhaps, a smile, an open invitation to a truce between them.

Shane had followed them into the room with his eyes. Then, all at once, he had walked quickly away from the joyous reunion with his old flames and entered the room as if summoned, moving quickly towards them. Morgana caught her breath as a grinning Shane moved silently towards her. But then he passed right by her and by Mama to approach the white-coated man bending over one of the unconscious soldiers from the wagon not three feet away.

"Pa?" Shane asked, the single word ringing with emotion.

At the sound of Shane's voice the white-coated man straightened up, and after a long moment he turned slowly. "Shane? Shane, my boy!" He opened his arms and father and son embraced. "You look good, son," Shane's father smiled, tears standing in his eyes as they embraced.

"How's Mother? Is she well?" Shane asked, wrapping his arm comfortably around the other man's shoulders.

"Well, son, you know your mother—" Roger Moss hesitated. "She'll be much better when she sees you, I'm sure."

A shadow fell across Shane's face as he asked, "Luke back?"

The older man's eyes saddened. "Not yet. Haven't heard a word from him either, since—"

Morgana's breast throbbed with resentment. Every newfound ounce of civility and politeness evaporated inside her as she viewed the tender scene. Moving forward three paces to stand before Shane Moss's father and trembling with raw emotion, Morgana erupted, "What a delightful family scene! I lost an older brother in the war. An older sister, too—!" She drew one hand free from her blanket and pointed an accusing finger at Shane. "Your son—this man—!"

"Morgana!" Lillian said sharply, "That's enough!"

Morgana read in Lillian's face, a combination of disbelief and alarm that asked: "Why must you badger this innocent man?" Why? *Why, Mama?* Why, because the men who killed Sarah were under his command, of course! *Also, Mama, he raped me! Remember?*

No, the quiet little voice inside chided her. *No,* Morgana, the reason—*the real reason is simple enough*—*he does not remember!* He had taught her passion, but he had not even remembered her. Teetering momentarily, Morgana burst into tears, then she fell into a heap on the fine rose carpet of Mistress Campbell's parlor.

Shane reached down and picked up the blanket wrapped Morgana again as lightly as if she were a feather, and he held her in his arms as he said to Lillian, "Ma'am, meet my father, Roger Moss." Then nodding towards Lillian, "Pa, that lady is Mistress Lillian Heirs and this bundle of spent anger is her daughter, Miss Morgana, who was injured in the train derailment and, unfortunately, from all appearances, she's been talking out of her head ever since."

"Completely out of her head," Lillian affirmed, nodding. "The sedative she was given is wearing off and it's affecting her badly, I'm afraid."

Under Lillian's caustic glare, Morgana's head bobbed upon Shane's shoulder and her eyes closed as she sought sanctuary in depths of silence, deliciously aware of Shane's closeness. In all her years of loving Jonathan, she'd never felt currents such as these that passed between herself and this man in merely touching. How bizarre!

Roger Moss's voice was warm and friendly as he said to Mama, "Mistress Heirs! Yes, of course! We received your letter.

Ann Gray

You're on your way to Richmond to visit your own parents, I believe."

"Yes, that's right," Mama acknowledged. "Morgana's had a terrible experience, as have many who were aboard the train, but the army doctor who attended her has said she'll be all right after she's rested. Please don't bother about us further," Mama told Roger Moss through her embarrassment. "If you'll excuse me, I'll see she gets to a room."

As Mama spoke, Morgana drank in Shane's appeal and she sensed his expressive blue eyes on her face, inspecting, admiring, as she lay uncommonly quiet in his arms.

"Here?" Roger Moss was asking Mama, with some consternation. "Not here! I wouldn't think of allowing you and your daughter to stay here, Mistress Heirs," he said, confidentially. "Furthermore, my dear wife would never hear of it—your spending a night in a brothel! We'll get you both to *Moss Hall* at once. It's not far. You'll be there by supper time. Shane," he said, turning to his son, "see to it, won't you?" When Lillian appeared taken aback, Roger Moss said, "No, really, I insist, Mistress Heirs." He placed an open hand on Morgana's forehead. "This poor girl is feverish. She needs fluids, caring for, and a long rest. You're welcome to stay at *Moss Hall* as long as you feel comfortable there."

"Well, if you're sure, thank you!" Mama said, graciously, to Roger Moss.

"Pa, I couldn't have said it nicer," Shane said, admiring Morgana's sweeping black eyelashes.

"And—," Roger said, gently smacking Shane on his back, "—needless to say, the sooner Shane gets home, the happier we'll all be. Especially his mother!"

Readjusting his burden, Shane said, "We'd better get a move on to catch Jacob before he leaves for the river again. Besides, this armload is every bit as heavy as a bag of oats!"

Not daring to lift her head lest he put her down, Morgana's mind raced wildly! *A bag of oats, indeed! Star loved oats!* Oh, how glad she would be to see Star again. Would Star love Shane more than her, now?

Shane called to his father over his shoulder, mischief dancing in his eyes as he strode quickly towards the door. "I can't wait to see Mother's face when she finds out what I'm bringing home."

When Shane carried Morgana out past the gathering of Mistress Campbell's painted ladies, Morgana's liquid black eyes opened wide and flashed unusually bright in their direction. Afterwards, an uncharacteristically subdued Morgana rested quietly in Shane's arms.

It was not until the three of them had almost reached Jacob's wagon that Morgana cast a sly, calculated glance at her mother over Shane's broad shoulder. Now just where, she wondered, would this new twist of fate possibly lead? Aloud, so that Shane would be sure to hear—smiling jubilantly—Morgana exclaimed to Lillian, "My goodness, Mama, isn't this unexpected hospitality most welcome? And, here, I don't have a thing to wear!"

Vaguely aware of droning of voices Morgana slept fitfully all the way to *Moss Hall*. Had she been fully awake she would have heard her mother explaining to Shane Moss the sad story of her sister Sarah's rape and subsequent death during his liquor induced sleep.

Never once were Laura Lee's or Morgana's names mentioned. For it had been against Shane's orders and at Lillian's direction that they had ventured out of their rooms and been accosted before they could reach the root cellar. Those sad atrocities had been the outcome of her own decision making and were not his responsibility.

CHAPTER TWELVE ~ MOSS HALL

6:00 a.m., Wednesday, May 3, 1865 ~ Moss Farm, Chesterfield County, Virginia

Mistress Patricia Moss

The Moss men left the house at first light. Morgana knew because when she roused from her long therapeutic sleep wondering where she was, she had smelled the mingled aromas of coffee brewing and bacon frying and heard murmuring voices through the closed door to the kitchen—a woman's high humming one and two men's, low pitched. Shortly after, she'd heard the sound of muted laughter and the back door opening and closing quietly.

Mama sighed in her sleep, and Morgana turned on her pillow to face the older woman, suddenly aware that they were lying side by side in a strange bed in a small bedroom within a farmhouse. Gathering her thoughts, she remembered she'd entered the bedroom by another door from the hallway. They were in the home of the former Lieutenant of the Union Army Shane Moss and his family in rural Virginia.

Recognition of Shane Moss's voice had sent currents, messengers of instantly recalled intimacy, pulsing through Morgana. Freed from the consequences of their fateful misdeed by circumstances over which she'd had absolutely no control, Morgana was sadly unprepared for life's disturbing and ambivalent emotional responses. When, exactly, had the hatred she'd carried for Lieutenant Shane Moss all these months dissolved into this peculiar, urgent and demanding hunger for him? Why should the women in Mistress Campbell's house by merely looking at him with familiarity as they had done have aroused such tides of jealousy in her? How could she possibly be *in love* with Shane Moss, anyway, when all her life she had secretly adored Jonathan Baker?

Unexpectedly, deep stabbing pangs of grief and loss swept away her reverie and she realized the child she'd carried—Shane's child—was no more. Doubtless, Mama would soon be telling her it was God's mercy that had recalled the child home and spared her the ultimate humiliation. Perhaps. But she'd prayed to God for Drew and he was gone. Sarah had prayed night and day, and Morgana had seen what piety had gotten Sarah. No, since Sarah's tragic death Morgana had put aside any budding belief in such a God. Brushing away grief's hot tears, Morgana lay quietly, watching the gentle rise and fall of her mother's breast. Gazing on the older woman's countenance with unaccustomed tenderness, at once Morgana realized how old Mama appeared—up close. How careworn. Actually, quite gaunt and haggard.

With Sarah, Drew, and Papa gone, Morgana felt she had become the primary focus of Mama's misplaced need to worry rather than Wil who, being a boy and two years younger, would have seemed to Morgana to be the more likely candidate for it. Suddenly, Morgana felt nagging concern for this dear woman whom she lovingly called "Mama". This same Mama, who urged Wil onward toward adulthood every single day, but who steadfastly reproached Morgana for every step she took towards the same goal. Why? Was it because she felt Morgana wasn't prepared for the responsibilities of adulthood?

Morgana remembered that all her life Mama had remarked almost daily that she was her father's daughter because she was so like him. Could it be Papa's strong personality that still bound the two of them together? Was it Papa, whom Mama still saw in Morgana, and could not let go? Or was it actually Morgana?

Yet why, Morgana wondered, must she so tenaciously resist Mama's every directive to her? Argue Mama's every word of

Ann Gray

advice? Ignore Mama's every warning? Wasn't that because she was an independent thinker—just like Papa?

In that moment, a window of understanding opened to Morgana, and she reached out and smoothed a stray lock of graying, faded red hair from her mother's tranquil face. "I *do* love you, Mama," she whispered, "Truly, I do."

"Circumstances change," Mama had encouraged her in those dark days before their journey to Richmond when it had looked like there would be no train seats available. "—always be prepared for change." Of course, how right she had been. Because Mama had bought more railroad stocks and used Papa's influence to pull company strings, she had made it happen. Morgana smiled. It wasn't so hard, after all, giving Mama her just deserts. Morgana vowed, thereafter, to be more thoughtful, more amenable, and though eager to get on with the new day—this new adventure in Shane Moss's world—she waited patiently for Mama to awaken.

After breakfast the three ladies sat sipping coffee in the fresh early morning air on the Moss's front porch. Morgana was pleasantly aware of the symphony of bird songs, the smell of burning firewood on the air from a backyard wash-pot, and the utter peacefulness of the rural scene. She found these new surroundings most appealing and relaxing. So many things had changed. So very many things—and so very, very fast.

The squeaking wicker of Mistress Moss's chair as she fidgeted was the only obtrusive sound Morgana was aware of in the whole of Shane Moss's world.

Across the round table from her, Mama was saying to the restless Mistress Moss, "It was so gracious of you to open your house to us like this. I can't tell you how grateful we are for your kind hospitality."

Mistress Moss nodded. In the long, silence that followed, Mistress Moss's silent response and the unbroken, strained expression on her colorless face led Morgana to wonder if Mama's comment had even penetrated the 'peacock-ish' woman's consciousness. Morgana thought Mistress Moss looked anything other than gracious, and hard as she tried, since their first meeting last evening she could not seem to like the woman who, covertly, eyed her while presumably conversing with Mama.

Mistress Moss carried herself with an air of arrogance, stiffly erect, and when she spoke her voice was sharp and piercing. She exhibited little concern for whomever might be talking, interjecting complete changes of subject and leading conversation in her own direction, usually reverting to her own poor health or the sad condition of *Moss Hall*'s stables since the Yankees had passed through.

Yesterday on their unexpectedly arrival from Petersburg, bad off as Morgana had been, she was aware of Mistress Moss's exceptional concern with the appearance of her parlor. In the short time before Morgana was spirited away to bed, Mistress Moss had seemed exceedingly inattentive to her company's comfort, while she had shown herself to be an overly fond and doting mother. It was evident even to Morgana in her ill state that Mistress Moss' constant patting and caressing of her grown son was an embarrassment to him.

In the room quickly prepared for them, Mama had undressed and bathed a lethargic Morgana and the servant had taken away her blood soaked dress to try to salvage it. Morgana had lain, naked, under a light coverlet, waiting an hour or more before the woman of the house had finally succeeded in finding a clean garment for her. Much too tall and thin for anything in her own wardrobe to fit the curvaceous Morgana, Mistress Moss, a lone woman among a family of three men had finally produced one of the servant Bessie's clean and ample flour sack nightgowns.

Thus clothed, Morgana had rested abed that entire night, drifting in and out of wakefulness, the result of a carefully measured draft of Mistress Moss's sherry wine. Mama, at bedside, kept cold compresses on Morgana's forehead and urged cold tea and clear broth into her each time she awakened. So totally spent was Morgana, only vaguely did she remember Mama's saying that she was leaving for a while to partake of supper at the Moss's family table. Later, Morgana had been aware of Mama, in her petticoat, reaching to snuff out the candle before crawling into bed beside her.

This morning, until Bessie had Morgana's clothing clean and wearable again, Mistress Moss had outfitted her in over-large clothing from Shane's own wardrobe. Her new apparel, consisting of a red checkered flannel shirt and a pair of heavy work pants made snug around her shrinking waist by a tightly buckled belt, even after having been laundered and stored for four years in his chest of drawers, still carried the appealing scent of the man.

From her chair at the table with her mother and Mistress Moss, Morgana had forced smiles and feigned attention to the on-going conversation between the two older women until her patience was strained beyond endurance.

"Mistress Moss," she inquired finally, "would it be permissible for me to visit the stables? I understand that my horse, Star, is there; and although the Lieutenant—that is, Shane tied her to the wagon coming here last night, I haven't seen her up close since he rode her away from *Briars* to join that demon Yankee, Sherman on his cruel march through Georgia. I'm sure Mama has regaled you with that story by now." The familiar Morgana smiled arrogantly in Mistress Moss's direction, while Mama's cordial smile congealed on her lips.

"Miss Heirs, let us understand one another," Mistress Moss sat taller in her chair and answered bluntly. "You should know my two sons, Luke and Shane, each served his country in the army where he saw his duty lie. The fact that they served on opposite sides in the war just ended is not pertinent to me nor should it be to you. That they served—is, and should be. It was by order of the President of the United States that my younger son, Shane was pressed into service under General Sherman whose army devastated your city and killed Georgians. We

Briars
The House of Heirs

Virginians suffered under his heavy hand, too! My son was not the culprit, but an eager young student called fresh from the classroom to the soldier's saddle by order of the President. He was not lured by the saber's rattle. I easily understand and agree with your resentment against the Union army, but I advise you to channel that resentment in the proper direction." Color enlivened her features, and Mistress Moss's unblinking vivid blue eyes bored into Morgana's black ones. "I'm sorry, my dear, if I have spoken harshly. I'm sure your mother will agree with me that emotions are easily confused in one as young as you, therefore I take no offense." From a stoppered, cut glass decanter on a silver tray perched nearby on the porch railing, she poured amber liquid into her empty coffee cup. "My morning medication," she explained, then continued, "Of course you are free to go to the stables and if you feel up to it, by all means, ride your horse. Use my sidesaddle—it should make the ride more comfortable considering your recent injuries. Our boundaries are all marked by low rock walls. You'll find no fences here. Dinner is at noon. The gong will summon you if you lose track of time in your wanderings." Unsmiling still, Mistress Moss tippled her 'morning medicine'. "I do suggest, however, that you remain clear of the east field where the men are working. I fear your unexpected appearance might produce too much of a distraction. The oats must be sown and they are late going in, already."

"Thank you, ma'am. I've never been on a farm before. I'm sure I will find the jaunt most educational. May I?" Morgana asked, as she took two sugar cubes from the bowl on the wicker table. When Mistress Moss nodded, Morgana turned to her mother. "If I may be excused, now, Mama—"

Incredulous of the undercurrent in the exchange, and Morgana's apparent submission, Lillian nodded. No, this was not the genuine Morgana! Something unpredictable and calculating must be brewing in that lovely head of dark, bouncing curls, Lillian thought as she watched Morgana walk quickly away.

Morgana glanced back over her shoulder just as Mistress Moss turned back to Mama and asked in her assertive manner, "Now, where were we, my dear?" Though Mistress Moss's hand shook only slightly as she picked up her cup, giving away her agitation, in that moment, Morgana sensed that she had clashed for the first time with the one woman in all the world with whom she would henceforth engage in never-ending conflict. Just as Mistress Moss had most certainly recognized in Morgana a rival for her beloved younger son's affection. How could the possessive woman possibly have known? Morgana mused.

Star

Morgana's mare whinnied recognition of her and came prancing immediately from across the large, clean, straw-strewn stall. The old mare in the next stall neighed for attention, but Morgana's eyes were only for her own beautiful Star.

"You haven't forgotten me, have you, Star?" Morgana reached over the stall gate to stroke Star's graceful neck with one hand, allowing the mare to pry open her other closed fist with a velvet muzzle. "There, girl, there's your sugar."

She opened the gate and entered the stall, running her hands along the sleek black body of the animal. "My, you *are* in fine condition. Let's not let Mister Shane Moss know, now that he's home from the war, that I have complimented you on his care of you all these months." She ran her hand down a foreleg and lifted it to examine the hoof and shoe. "It would only serve to swell his head even more than the ladies of Mistress Campbell's house have already." Finding no fault with the mare, she saddled up and rode out of the stables.

Morgana looked up into the expanse of azure sky and caught sight of a lazy hawk riding gracefully on the upper winds. It had been a long time since she had ridden and her recent accident had left her less than sure of herself, physically, but she was determined so Morgana rode slowly away from the stables. Mistress Moss's sidesaddle did make her ride a lot more comfortable.

She let Star amble to the back of the farmhouse where she paused to speak to the servant stirring her wash pot on a bed of glowing coals. Crisp, clean sheets hung from a clothesline, flapping and snapping in the wind, the line's sagging middle propped upon a stubby nub of a branch on a tall sapling stick that swayed to the changing winds. "Good morning, er—"

"Bessie, ma'am." The woman looked up with wide set eyes from under a heavy sweat-beaded brow. She paused in her stirring and wiped her forehead with the hem of her apron.

"Bessie, then! Have you tried your hand yet with my dress? Do you think you'll be able to save it?" Morgana tried to sound friendly as possible. Considering Mistress Moss's obvious dislike for her, she would welcome any ally in this house.

Bessie cocked her head and frowned. "Th' dress been done a long time ago. Miz Moss, she ain't give it back t' you, yet?"

"Perhaps it slipped her mind. I'll ask when I return from my ride. Thank you, Bessie." Morgana, feeling a new, unexplored zest for life, eyed the hawk still leisurely riding the winds aloft, and cried excitedly, "Isn't it a perfectly beautiful day, Bessie?"

Star stomped the ground, urging Morgana to finish her conversation, and Morgana wished she had not spoken so freely to the woman when Bessie replied, "From up there, I guess it be. From down here, it be jus' another day."

"Oh, Bessie, that was thoughtless of me, wasn't it?" Morgana said, earnestly. "I had no such intention. I hope you won't think me unkind. You remind me of my own sweet Rachel, who practically raised me and my brothers and sister. I've been gone for just ages it seems, and I miss her." Morgana smiled and clicked to Star, turning towards the rock lined path that led away towards the pastures to the west.

Ann Gray

Bessie stood looking after Morgana, hands on hips—appraising, judging—before she called after her while pointing the other way. "You'll be wantin' to ride off yonder, Miss, beyond that cypress windbreak. Th' oat field's on t'other side. That's where they be."

As she caught Bessie's meaning, Morgana turned and rode back. "Why, Bessie! Mistress Moss has only minutes ago warned me away from the field where the men are working. I wouldn't want to displease my hostess. Perhaps I should avoid that direction, altogether."

"Lady, when young Mister Shane walk in carryin' you, Miz Moss be your own worst enemy startin' then. Nothin' you do goin' change that." Bessie moved towards Star and folded her arms, looking up at Morgana. "Mister Shane, he oughta be like that hawk—flyin' free. I been Miz Moss's housekeeper too long not t' know her ways. She'll hold onto that boy 'til he be old and she be dyin' if'n she can." Bessie looked back at the house. "I best get on back t' my washin'."

"My name is Morgana Heirs, Bessie," Morgana said. "I thank you for your honesty, and I promise I'll not betray your confidence." With that, Morgana rode off towards the cypress windbreak and the field, beyond.

Luke

Flat on his stomach in the irrigation ditch that ran along the border of the east grain field, Luke Moss watched the women's discussion through the low-slung thick branches of the full cypress trees on one side and on the other, kept an eye on his father and brother tilling and sowing at the far end of the open field. A wallow too far to the right and he could be seen from the field, and if the horsewoman decided to ride in his direction she'd be right on top of him any minute now.

Briars
The House of Heirs

Yesterday, after the blast he'd managed to elude his pursuers by crawling into a hollow log in a stand of pines near the tracks. Later, in the safety of the town stables, he'd removed the narrow pointed chunk of wood the explosion had blown into his shoulder. And, still later, after dark he'd made it to this well-remembered line of cypress trees. From here he could watch the farmhouse without being seen.

Though hurting and bloody, it had never been part of Luke's plans to have a family reunion. Should his parents learn of his seditious activity, Ma would be shocked but she'd never turn him in. Pa, on the other hand, would—in a wink! And, little brother? It was enough to see he'd gotten home whole. There'd been bad blood between them too long for them to ever kiss and make up. Given half a chance, too, he knew Bessie would plant a cleaver in his head since he'd "borrowed" her paltry savings when he'd left home four years ago. Bessie never forgot and never forgave. But now, there was the added complication of having company in the house.

Yesterday, hours after the blast, when he'd finally walked all the way home, he'd only planned to sneak in, pick up a change of clothes, two day's supplies from Bessie's pantry, any new savings she'd collected, along with a significant amount from the parents' safe box—and Victor. Then better prepared for his journey west, to leave again—undiscovered.

But everything that could go wrong had gone wrong! When he'd arrived late yesterday afternoon, he'd tried the kitchen door and found it locked. Usually, the door was left open unless Pa wasn't on the place so he figured Pa had gone into town. Probably having to do with the derailment.

He couldn't afford to leave evidence of a break-in, so he'd slept until dark, planning to enter by the window in his own room. But by then there was a light in there, meaning that the room was occupied. All night long, chilled to the bone and aching from the deep flesh wound in his shoulder, he'd waited for morning and a chance to enter through the kitchen door unobserved and unannounced.

Then at daybreak he'd watched his father and brother head out to the east field, passing along the path at the end of the windbreak not fifteen feet from where he lay—hurt, cold and hungry. Bessie had started her wash-pot fire only minutes later, and now this strange young woman, clad in Shane's clothing, was riding slowly towards him. Who was she and where had she come from? Her sleek black Thoroughbred mount was not one of theirs. Had little brother Shane taken himself a wife?

The horsewoman veered onto the path his father and brother had taken earlier to the field and passed clear of Luke, though still close enough for him to clearly determine her fine lines. He watched with interest as she rode slowly and deliberately, never once allowing her horse to break gait, along the path on the outer border of the grain field towards the far side, and the men working there.

After having ridden the path almost the length of the field, she paused, apparently unsure as to whether or not to continue. She raised her hand and hailed the men in the field, "Hel-lo!" Her voice was pleasing to Luke's ear.

Both men straightened from their toil to wave, Shane gesturing for her to wait where she was. Luke smiled. She wasn't a farm woman or she would have known without question that riding into the field would disturb the freshly sewn seed. Shane spoke to his father and they laughed. Then he untied the kerchief from around his head, wiped his face with it and, still carrying his hoe, walked along the furrow towards the woman. From the look of anticipation Luke saw on her face it was clear this was Shane's woman, all right. Too bad, Luke thought, he wouldn't be around long enough to argue that point with his younger brother.

It happened too fast to sort out exactly what had caused it but, suddenly, the woman's horse whinnied and reared. At the same time, Shane started running towards the misbehaving

Briars
The House of Heirs

animal, hoe in hand. The mount reared again. The woman sat the horse. No inexperienced rider, this one. The mare whinnied, reared and pivoted, coming down in a full gallop headed back along the path.

Shane lifted his hoe and brought it down, over and over again, striking the ground with force.

Luke lay still as one of the trees' shadows.

Calming, stroking, talking to her mount until she had the animal back under control, the woman rode to within several feet of his prone position under the cypress windbreak. Concentrating as she was on soothing her horse, there was very little likelihood she had caught sight of him in his bloody, gray uniform under the heavy green boughs of the cypress trees. Still—she was that close. Close enough, that before she turned the mare and started back along the path, he heard her coax, "Whoa now, Star, easy girl."

When the horse quieted, the woman rode back along the path to where Shane held up the writhing carcass of a three foot long headless snake—from its markings, a deadly copperhead.

Pa hurried to join them, and after they came together and the woman dismounted, Pa examined the horse's legs. Luke knew by the way Pa stood gently patting the mare, he had found her frightened, but un-bitten.

The woman had not thrown her arms around Shane's neck in appreciation. Perfectly restrained, she had offered her hand. Maybe, Luke thought smiling, he'd been too swift to conclude the attractive woman belonged to his kid brother, Shane. But if not that, then what could possibly have brought this beauty to *Moss Hall*?

Surely not that damned train derailment! Those northbound passengers had been held in town overnight and were to continue on to Richmond tomorrow. He knew, because he had overheard a conversation between Jacob Garner and Doc Wilkins from his hiding place in the town stables yesterday before beginning his trek to *Moss Hall*. This lovely creature must be the present occupant of his room but how many others were there and how long would they be staying? How much time could he afford to waste just waiting?

Hardly five minutes elapsed before the men returned to their work and the rider mounted her horse. She rode back up the path at a good pace and when she had reached the path's end, without pause she cut behind the thick barrier of cypress trees, unseen from the field, and rode straight as an arrow to the very trees covering his retreat. Dismounting, she checked her horse's girth and walked around the animal to adjust the stirrup on the side next to the cypress boughs above Luke.

Without looking towards him, she said, "Now, you there, soldier! If I scream, they'll hear me." Leaning down, she held back a sheltering cypress limb and looked in at him. "You know that, don't you?"

Luke nodded and groaned. "Yes, ma'am, I do." He grimaced, pitifully, and lay looking up at her through tired, ice blue eyes.

"If you feel you must hide on your own land, you should wear a mask as well. You're Luke Moss, Shane's brother." Morgana knelt on the meadow grass an arm's length from the row of cypress trees, allowing Star a reins' reach of grazing room. She winced, eyeing his bloody tunic. "How badly are you hurt?"

"Not too bad, but it does prick a mite" Luke answered, taken aback by her fearlessness and forward manner. Here was a woman he could appreciate. "Are we that much alike—me and my brother?" he asked.

"You are. Though you are older, heftier—and dirtier, by far." She laid a nearby rock on the springy cypress limb and sat down, wrapping her arms around her knees, completely relaxed. "So why don't you go on to the house? Your mother will be anxious to see you and your wound needs dressing."

"Well, ma'am," Luke moved as if to crawl out of the ditch and through the trees to sit beside her.

Briars
The House of Heirs

"No! You stay right where you are," Morgana insisted. "I prefer talking with you flat on your stomach, down there. What have you done, anyway, that you can't let your presence be known?"

Luke calculated his risk. Then, knowing truth to sometimes be more unbelievable than a well-spun tale, he replied, "I blew up the trestle that derailed the train yesterday." He watched for alarm to register on her soft refined features.

"You didn't!" Morgana's eyes became round, like saucers. But it wasn't shock that her expression reflected. It was sheer admiration. She flushed, and smiled. "While I do deplore the loss of life your act caused—after all, all acts of war are aimed at killing, aren't they?—I am disgusted by the way this whole war business has turned out! Now they have put us, all, in Georgia under military jurisdiction and disallowed our money and our slaves. Where will it end?"

"Exactly, ma'am, where will it end?" Luke looked up, pleased with the reward for his honesty. Only moments ago, he'd been wondering what to do? Where to turn? Now, here, with her jet eyes gazing down on him through thick sweeping lashes, was the made-to-order answer to his quandary. Luke could hardly believe his good fortune! "Ma'am," he said, mournfully, "I've been waiting in this ditch all night for a chance to get into my house, unseen. Just long enough to gather a few personal things, I swear—and then, so help me—to be on my way!" He watched her face as he opened his canteen, turning it upside down. "As you can see, my canteen's empty. I sure could use a drink of water, ma'am, and a bite to eat. I'm weak, too, from loss of blood, I guess."

"You haven't even asked who I am," Morgana said, ignoring his well-aimed hints. "Nor have you asked how I came to be here. Aren't you the least bit curious?"

"Yes, ma'am, I am! But I figure you'll tell me sooner or later, given reason to." Luke gripped his shoulder and tried to moan convincingly. "Sorry, ma'am, but the pain seems to come in waves. Like the thirst and hunger!"

"I'm Morgana Heirs. My mother and I are here from Atlanta. We are *very* close acquaintances of your brother, Shane, and we *were* on our way to visit my grandparents in Richmond. It's at your father's invitation that we enjoy the hospitality of your parents' home due to an injury I suffered in the very same derailment you *say* you're guilty of perpetrating. Now, are you *still* guilty of the crime?"

"Yes, ma'am, I'm still guilty as sin! Though I'm sorry you were hurt—" Luke cocked his head, obviously admiring her shape, and smiled, "—though your injury doesn't appear to have been too serious. That is compared to my own, of course."

Drew's antics came immediately to Morgana's mind. She was used to dealing with ne'er-do-wells. "You are a crude and obvious rascal, Luke Moss."

"Yes, ma'am, but I'm still awfully thirsty, ma'am, and hungry. Without anybody knowing, do you think you could finagle me a few personal items from my room—the one closest to the kitchen? And maybe enough eats for a two day journey? That, with a few Yankee dollars in my pocket and Victor under me and I'll be gone. Believe me, any one of them would turn me in—in a heart beat if they knew I was this close."

"Surely not your mother!" Morgana gasped, shocked at the thought of a mother turning a child over to the authorities—for anything!

"Yes, ma'am, 'fraid so! Ma never was one for sentiment 'cept where my little brother was concerned. Many's the time she's given me the licking when it was him at fault."

"No!"

"Yes, ma'am."

Medicine Bottle

Morgana rode Star back to the stables and returned the mare to her stall. Then Morgana moved past Bessie hidden from view by flapping sheets. Quietly, she slipped through the kitchen door and, looking down the hall, she could see clear through to the front porch where Mama and Mistress Moss still sat at the wicker table, their chairs turned away from the house.

In the kitchen, Morgana found a clean, dry flour sack Bessie had been using for a dish towel and dumped into it several already partially used items from the pantry she figured Bessie would be slow to miss—like half a jar of honey, and a crock of soft cheese. From a high shelf, she took an unopened box of crackers and a tin of beans. Then, on looking around and finding no suitable container for water, she found and took down from the corner of the same high shelf, a large half-full bottle labeled sherry wine. This, she hurriedly stuffed into the flour sack, too.

Morgana carried the sack into bedroom she and Mama occupied—Luke's room—and sat it down. In a chest of drawers, she found and folded into a small parcel, a pair of work pants and a flannel shirt, much like the ones she was wearing. She took from her own purse the few federal dollars Mama had given her before leaving home for shopping in Richmond. She stuffed the money into one pocket of the work pants and wrapped the bundle around the wine bottle in the sack. These few acts of assistance were the least she could do for a *true* Southern hero, whom everyone else called "renegade" for continuing to fight on in an unjust world.

Mama would never have approved had she known what Morgana was doing, because Mama had accepted the distasteful fact that the war was over and the South had lost! That— according to Mama—was that! Remembering Drew and Sarah, Morgana thought angrily, *No!* That *need not* be that!

Ann Gray

As she and Luke had conspired, Morgana opened the window and lowered the parcel to the ground behind the hydrangea bushes growing there.

Luke had wanted her to leave the window in their room open tonight for him to get into the house while all were sleeping so that he might rifle the safe box belonging to his parents, but Morgana, shocked that he would even think of robbing his own parents, had refused to be drawn into this act of family betrayal. Still, she felt sure Luke would be pleasantly surprised when he found the little gift of cash she had planted in his pants pocket.

With an eye on Bessie, Morgana, left the house as quickly and as quietly as she had entered, returning to the stables to resume her ride.

In the west pasture, Morgana spied a carved rock marker standing some two feet high in the grassy field. She walked Star up close to it and read the carving on it, which read simply: Prince. A strange tombstone, that one, with no dates.

It had to be nearing the noon dinner hour so she would inquire about the peculiar marker when she got back to *Moss Hall*. Within sight of the house, she heard the loud outcry. It was Mistress Moss's voice. Of that, she was certain. Morgana hurried ahead, eager to learn what had provoked such an emotional outcry from the overtly well-composed and somber woman.

By the time Morgana arrived from the stables, Mistress Moss, in an angry temper, was tossing items from the pantry shelves, left and right, through the pantry door into the cluttered kitchen.

Bessie—and Mama—who had apparently come upon the scene unexpectedly—gawked in wonderment at the display of sheer panic that possessed the woman.

"Where is it, Bessie? Where have you misplaced my medicine bottle? You know I require it for my ailments!" Mistress Moss appeared to be in great physical discomfort. "I must have it! Give it to me." She came out of the pantry then,

Briars
The House of Heirs

her long plaits of hair unwinding and hanging, disheveled, about her face. "Bessie, where have you hidden it?"

"I done tol' you, ma'am, it 'as there this mornin'. I put it right back where it come from after I filled yo' medicine bottle."

"Medicine bottle?" Mama asked, noting Morgana's arrival. "I haven't seen any medicine bottles, have you, Morgana?"

"No, I'm sorry to say, I have not!" Morgana answered, a flicker of recognition lighting her eyes as she remembered the half-full bottle of sherry wine she had spirited away for Luke. So, Mistress Moss was a slave to alcohol! That knowledge would come in handy someday, no doubt, but right now Morgana had to think of a way to recover the wine for the woman before she became insufferable.

"Now, now," Morgana soothed, reaching out to Mistress Moss. "You're all upset. Why don't you and Mama take a short walk. It will help to calm your nerves. Bessie and I will find your medicine," Morgana promised. "Won't we, Bessie?" she asked, turning to the servant, who stood shaking her head as she observed the disorder in the room." Morgana bustled the agitated woman out the kitchen door and started her walking along beside Mama down the hall before she could object further.

"I done tol' her, ma'am, it 'as there this mornin'. I put it right back where it come from after I filled her medicine bottle." Bessie's face mirrored her distress.

"I know!" Morgana said, softly. "I took the bottle of wine, myself!" She waited until the others were out the front door before continuing, "I may as well confess to you, Bessie, somebody besides me needs to know what's going on. It was for Luke."

"Lawdy! Mister Luke's back?" Bessie's eyes grew wide and troubled. "How you know Mister Luke, ma'am?"

"He's hiding by the east field windbreak, Bessie, and he's wounded. I saw him there while I was riding and we spoke. He blew up the trestle that caused the derailment of the train, Bessie.

Now, we have to help him get away before he's discovered and turned in." Morgana felt better already, having shared her knowledge with somebody.

"Um-um! He done got t' you, all right! That one, he be good at that!" Bessie shook her head. "Now, ma'am, you tell Bessie what you done." Morgana told Bessie about the wine, food, and clothes-filled flour sack, and her gift of money which she had hidden behind the hydrangea bushes.

Then Bessie told Morgana about Luke! About how conniving and thieving and mean he'd *always* been and for Morgana's own sake, lest she be scolded for helping him, they went and fetched the parcel back into the house.

"But, Bessie?" Morgana asked, when they had returned the items to the shelves. "What happens tonight when he comes for them and they're not there?"

"Then if'n he knows what's good fo' him, he'll go on away like he should of done t' start with," Bessie said. "Mister Moss, he say he done tol' that boy fo' th' las' time t' straighten up or stay away. Now, it look like he ain't done neither one!"

Morgana couldn't bring herself to tell Bessie about Luke's plans to rob his parents' safe box.

Challenge

Despite Morgana's assurance that her mama would not touch the glass intended for her use, Bessie carried a small silver tray holding a decanter of the found wine—filled to the brim—along with two dainty sherry glasses and set it in its accustomed place on the wide banister near the swing so that it would be there when Mistress Moss returned from her walk with Mistress Heirs.

Morgana had been simply amazed when Mama had agreed to have even one tiny glassful of wine before noon dinner, having been lured into the consumption of it at her hostess's perseverance and, at that, only in an effort to be polite. But, unexpectedly for Morgana, there followed a glass at table with dinner; one sipped slowly along with afternoon conversation; another with supper, and at Mistress Moss' insistence, a final sip before bedtime.

After they had said a polite "goodnight" and returned to their bedroom, Morgana admonished Mama while she undressed her and poured her into bed. All the while, Mama smiled and smiled. Mama, who had always found it difficult to tolerate the use of spirits in men, let alone in any woman, fairly reeked of the sweetish smell of sherry wine as she drifted into deep, besotted sleep.

Morgana lay, sleepless, listening to Mama's heavy snoring under the influence of the juice of the vine. Unprepared for the parenting role Morgana didn't care for it one little bit. In her eyes, Mama's stature had shrunk in direct proportion to the amount of drink she had consumed as the day wore on. By bedtime, Mama had tumbled from her lofty pedestal and become merely mortal—tempted, tested, and fallible. Morgana would never see Mama the same—ever again.

It was the proximity of their sleeping quarters—Luke's room—to the kitchen that enabled Morgana to hear the scrape and creak when the outside kitchen door was pried open. Her eyes popped open and she lay still as a mouse when their bedroom door creaked open and, by moonlight slanting through the window, she watched Luke's dark figure move to the chest of drawers from whence she had removed clothing earlier in the day. She watched as Luke took out several garments, stuffing them into his buttoned tunic, then he threw the bundle over his shoulder, tiptoeing back into the kitchen, but leaving the squeaky door off its latch.

Chilled by the late hour, Morgana, in Bessie's flimsy night gown, tip-toed to peer into the kitchen through the narrow crack.

Luke had laid his bundle of clothing on Bessie's small wooden work table in the center of the kitchen and pushed the table aside. He'd rolled back the braided rug the table ordinarily stood upon and by light from the candle Bessie used to reseal the wine bottle's cork, he was chiseling away with his hunting knife at the flooring around a metal ring embedded in a small trap door, undoubtedly, his father's safe box.

Morgana almost cried out when Shane, bare-footed and in his union suit, came stumbling into the kitchen from the hallway. To her amazement, upon discovering his brother there, Shane grinned and said softly, "Hell, I was only coming in for water, but just look what I found me—a thief! Still up to your old tricks, I see, Luke!"

"Don't get any bright ideas about being a hero, little brother," Luke said, holding out the hunting knife towards Shane so that it gleamed in the candle's light. "I'm only taking my share of the money and then I'll be gone! There's no need for there to be any trouble between us, here. You just get your water and go on back to bed like a good little boy!"

"No, Luke, not this time! You've taken your share of the money a couple of times, already now. What's left is all Pa's got." Shane stepped quickly forward and crouching catlike, reached out towards Luke's knife-wielding hand. "You know what, big brother? I think I can take you, now." He took two quick steps around the table.

"You'd better call Pa, little brother," Luke smiled, backing away as he flicked the knife back and forth in Shane's direction. "See, even with just one hand, you're going to need some help." Luke waved the knife, keeping his left arm folded against his chest.

"You're hurt, big brother," Shane observed. "That wound might slow you down a mite. How'd you get hurt, anyway? The war's over, Luke, and that's a fresh wound."

The two men circled Bessie's worktable, eyeing one another.

Morgana bit her lip and watched, mesmerized, as the contest between the estranged brothers commenced. Should she go for help, now, or allow the scene to play itself out? Surely, the armed older brother would never actually do bodily harm to the younger unarmed one?

"It was you on the riverbank, wasn't it, Luke?" Shane talked slowly and deliberately as he walked Luke backwards around the table. "It was you and the other two blew up the trestle, wasn't it?" Shane said, remembering the glimpse of riders through the tangle of undergrowth. "I pulled a spear out of one of your sidekicks. It had gone straight through him. He died on the spot, Luke. Didn't you even wonder about him after you left him there to die?" Shane held out his hand. "Give me the knife, Luke. You know you're going to have to give up! Your face will be plastered on every wanted poster from here to hell and back. God, Luke! All those people dead, and the war being over! I'm going to have to turn you in!"

"You're right, little brother, I sure as hell did it! And you say *you're* going to turn me in? Look at me, little brother, I'm laughing! Hey, look here—I'm the one with the blade! That's my advantage! The advantage is always mine because I plan it that way! Let me show you—" Luke lunged, dragging the sharp edge of his knife across Bessie's work table and leaving a deep gouge in it. If the knife had found its mark, Shane would have been deeply cut. "Damn you, Shane! I should have drowned you in the creek when you were eight and I had the chance instead of tying you up to Prince's tail!" Luke laughed. "He *almost* did the job for me, though, didn't he?"

"Yeah, that's true, I did nearly die back then, Luke. Pa shot Prince for that!" Shane moved a step closer to Luke, picking up the pace of their dueling dance. "He was the best stallion we ever had. Took a long time to recoup that loss—I remember that, too—all because of you, Luke!"

"But, loyal little brother never told, did you? I see you're still wearing Prince's shoe print! God, little brother—" Luke fumed, "—you've been a damn pain in my butt for as long as I can remember! It looks like now may be my chance to finally fix that."

Ann Gray

Shane, silent now, took a quick step towards Luke. Backing up, Luke almost tripped over the rolled up rug.

Morgana saw and remembered the crescent shaped scar on Shane's chest from their fateful encounter in November. Even that cruel mark had been of Luke's doing! Charming, misunderstood Luke of the irrigation ditch! Confederate renegade and thief Luke, attempting to kill his own brother, now.

Luke slashed out at Shane, barely missing his mark, and Morgana cried out, *"Shane!"*

Both men turned to face the bedroom door as Morgana pitched forward into the room, running quickly to Shane's side. "Oh, please, Shane, let him go!" she cried, tugging at his arm, trying to drag him away from the conflict.

"Morgana!" Shane warned, pulling free of her, "Get out of here!" But she stood firm, anchored to the floor between the warring brothers until Shane took hold of the back of Bessie's nightgown and flung Morgana behind him.

"So I was right!" Luke said. "You *have* taken yourself a woman. Well, now, little brother, aren't you the lucky one? You'll have a pretty young woman to mourn you!" Luke threw himself forward, lunging at Shane, the knife cutting thin air as it came down.

Shane grabbed Luke's bundled clothing from the tabletop and held it before him to take the knife's thrust, twisting the bundle as the knife plunged into it, prying the blade from Luke's grasp. Then Shane planted a left fist firmly into Luke's belly followed by a sharp right blow to his jaw and Luke folded into an unconscious heap on the kitchen floor.

Sobbing softly in an emotional state she had never known before, Morgana threw herself against Shane, clinging to him and trembling.

Shane held her in shaky arms, stroking her hair and whispering in her ear, "Now, now, it's all over. I'm sorry if I hurt you."

Shane released her to pick up Luke's knife lying at his feet and placed it on the table.

"Good man, Son," Roger Moss exclaimed from the hall doorway. "I knew someday, you'd even the odds. I just didn't know how long it would take."

Morgana quickly collected herself and moved to hide her thin apparel behind the bedroom door and to watch the scene play out.

Having arrived late on the scene, her eyes full of pain at the sight, Mistress Moss turned and walked slowly back down the hall to her room.

"Shane," Roger Moss said. "Tie him up. We'll tend his wound and lock him in the stable for the rest of the night. Tomorrow, we'll take him into town, together!"

Morning After

The next morning when Lillian awakened, Morgana sat beside her on the bed and told her, excitedly, of the events of the night she had slept through. "Oh, Mama, Shane was so brave! I wish you could have seen him! You might well have seen Luke Moss, too, but for all the wine you drank, because he came into our room."

"Whatever do you mean, Morgana? I drank one little glass of sherry, and that only for Mistress Moss's pleasure."

"Oh, Mama!" Morgana laughed, realizing at once that mama, being unaccustomed to the effects of spirits, retained no memory of the remainder of yesterday, just as had happened with Shane at *Briars*. Morgana went on to tell Mama of the violent set-to between the Moss brothers. How, of all things, Luke Moss—admittedly, guilty of the train's derailment and who was being held for the authorities, was nowhere to be found this morning. His knife was missing from the kitchen table, and his bindings were discovered, cut, in the stall he had occupied in the stables.

It had to be assumed that someone had freed him during the wee hours of the morning. Roger Moss and Shane appeared to be wondering who could have—would have—done such a thing?

As Morgana told Mama, the men would believe there could be only two possible suspects who might have performed that deed in order to get Luke out of the vicinity—herself, for Shane's sake, and Patricia Moss—for Luke's. Morgana confided to Lillian that Luke had told her of his intention to steal the stallion, Victor. Therefore, when Jasmine, the old mare, had been discovered missing instead, she told Mama that only Patricia Moss could have persuaded Luke to leave the stallion for the good of the farm in exchange for his freedom.

They agreed to keep the truth between them.

The Stables

Morgana quickly planted a kiss on her mother's lips. "Mama," Morgana said. "Mama, I am in love with Shane Moss. I think I may have always been."

"Oh, I suspected that." Lillian smiled. "I recognized the signs. If I were pressed to seek a suitable mate for you, I would look no further than Shane Moss. Hard as it may be for you to imagine, my darling, I was young once. I shared a wondrous love affair with your father."

"Papa? Not the Papa I remember, Mama!"

"No, not that gruff, successful business man, but another Morgan Heirs. A young, vigorous, loving, touchable man." Lillian sensed Morgana's excitement. "Oh, go on, now! See your Shane before we leave."

Morgana was already hurrying from the room. She tried desperately and repeatedly to manage a quiet liaison between herself and Shane during the remainder of that last day only to be out-maneuvered at every turn by Mistress Moss, who could suddenly appear from out of nowhere to engage her in flippant, banal trivialities. It wasn't until just before Jacob's wagon arrived to transport them back to the train that Morgana, discouraged by Shane's apparent inaccessibility, hurried to the stables to bid a tearful good-bye to Star.

Knowing that she would come, Shane watched from the shadows of Jasmine's vacant stall as Morgana, once more clad in traveling clothes, entered the stable and walked down the straw-strewn center aisle until she reached Star's stall. Just watching her graceful movements in the dim light aroused passion in him, the same urgent desire that had stirred him last night when she had flung herself into his arms after he had beaten Luke. It had been all he could do to resist kissing her trembling lips then, even with his father looking on. Now would be his only chance to declare his feelings until he returned Star to *Briars*. In the shadowy half-light of the stable, Morgana was the most beautiful, the most sensuous woman he had ever laid eyes upon. Unlike his self-assured encounters with the ladies at Mistress Lydia Campbell's house, Shane sensed mounting tension as his palms dampened and anxiety dried his mouth. What if she wouldn't have him? What if she spurned him and turned away, amused? Always, in his dreams, they were drawn inescapably into each others arms, coming together in wordless, burning passion and rising to the heights. Now, in reality—what?

While Star nuzzled Morgana's neck and Morgana, tears rolling down her cheeks, spoke affectionately to the mare, Shane stole quietly from Jasmine's stall and came to stand behind Morgana.

"I know you're there, Shane Moss," she said, softly. "I feel your presence, but I shall not turn around and let you see me cry again so soon." She stroked Star's smooth muzzle. "I have missed her so. But now I'm to give her up to you once more. What if she forgets me?"

Gently wrapping his arms around Morgana's slender waist, Shane buried his face in her sweet scented hair and whispered in her ear, "Could any living creature having loved you, Morgana, ever forget you?" He moved one hand to stroke Star's blaze. "It won't be for long, and then there'll be our foal to love, too. I'll bring your Star and the colt to *Briars* as soon as he's old enough to travel."

"How do you know the foal will be a colt?" she asked, kissing Star's twitching velvet muzzle, a smile creeping into her voice as Shane's arms enfolded her once more. "Perhaps Star will produce a precious little filly." Within the circle of his arms, Morgana turned to face him.

"Marry me, Morgana." Shane whispered, drawing her even closer, fiery thobbing passions of past sultry dreams becoming reality.

And, she answered, "Oh, yes, Shane."

With the exchange of so few words, Shane secured Morgana forever in his heart.

It seemed to Morgana their eyes met and held for an eternity before his lips sought hers. But when they did kiss—eagerly, passionately—sweet memories swelled within her. Someday, she would disclose their secret past to him and, together, they would explore wild new horizons. But for now she would linger in his arms and delight in shared words of affection and tender kisses.

CHAPTER THIRTEEN ~ RETURN TO *BRIARS*

10:45 a.m.., May 5, 1865 ~ Moss Hall, Chesterfield County, Virginia

Michael Wilson O'Donnell

As had been anticipated, after the train's derailed cars had been righted on the tracks, passengers for Richmond and points north were gathered together and conveyed by wagon to the location for boarding. After promises of reciprocal letter writing and lengthy leave-taking between the harmonious older generation and a bittersweet parting for Morgana and Shane, the Heirs women bid farewell to the Moss family and resumed their journey to Richmond.

In his references to *Moss Hall*, either intentionally or inadvertently, Shane Moss had led Lillian Heirs to believe *Moss Hall* to be a much larger and richer estate than she had found it to be. However, after their limited stay at the Moss farm Lillian believed the farm to be well worth redemption. She had struck a fair bargain with Roger Moss whereby sufficient funds for the refurbishing of the horse breeding stables would be forthcoming after a satisfactory coupling of Morgana's Star and Roger's stallion, Victor, was assured. Combining the highly respected Thoroughbred blood lines, would undoubtedly produce a prize foal. Actually, Lillian was prepared to go even higher in future should Roger's present calculations of overall costs prove to be underestimated.

Upon their arrival at her parents' home in Richmond, Lillian discovered her mother, Catherine, had died suddenly of heart failure only two weeks before. A letter had been posted but had not arrived before their departure.

Ann Gray

Morgana felt a smattering of guilt for not experiencing more empathy for her grandfather's and her mother's loss of the grandmother she had never known. But she was so full of future plans, any grief she might have evoked was smothered beneath joy and elation as she flitted about with her trousseau in mind from emporium to emporium in a shopping frenzy accompanied by her grandfather's recently engaged young nurse and housekeeper. Cassandra was only a few years Morgana's senior, and white.

Lillian's father, Michael O'Donnell of the glib Irish tongue and hardy laugh lay shriveled and forgotten inside the emaciated man whose world had shrunk to the four walls of his room. His only diversion was Catherine's music box, which played one little tune, "Greensleeves", and he listened to it hour after hour after hour.

Accustomed to Cassandra's strict regime and apprehensive of the nurse's critical eye, the old man smiled and patted Lillian's hand whenever she recommended a minor change in his routine, thus casually dismissing her very best intentions. Her every word of advice to the younger woman regarding her father's care was rudely shunned as being too old-fashioned. Her well meaning suggestions towards improving his diet so as to add meat to his bare bones were over-ridden—much too gaseous—too binding—too laxative. Lillian was so disheartened by the environment that existed within the household, she cut their visit short. On Monday, May 15, 1865, Lillian wrote to Hamita Baker:

My dear Hamita,
  We have arrived too late. My mother has died and Father is held prisoner of cruel disease, a living corpse. Though it pains me to see my father in such a state, my presence is not wanted here. I have spoken to my father's lawyer and arrangements have been made for his interment. That is all I can do.

I have no doubt his youthful and calculating nurse expects to inherit this house, my childhood home, when Father goes, and probably rightfully so since she has been his caretaker in my absence, though I had always envisioned it as Morgana's wedding gift someday. Is that selfish of me?

Please have Jonathan meet us at the terminal on our return, which I am advised will be late afternoon of Wednesday, the seventeenth of May.

A fish out of water cannot long survive. It is May, is it not, dear friend, or have I lost all powers of reasoning? It will be so good to be home again.

Morgana sends her love to everyone, as do I.

Lillian

Good news

There had been a heavy rainfall earlier in the day, and as Jonathan Baker's carriage bounced from Atlanta's railroad terminal towards *Briars* through numerous puddles along muddied roads, Jonathan cocked his head and smiled at Morgana Heirs seated beside him on the driver's bench. "You're mighty quiet for a young lady just back from the big city. I'd have expected the Morgana I know to be so full of tales of the sights she'd seen and the folks she'd met, she'd be hopping up and down and talking a mile a minute."

"Really?" Morgana looked sidelong at him. Jonathan had somehow grown older, fleshy, and somewhat ordinary-looking in the time she had been away. Certainly, in comparison to Shane Moss, he was portly and ancient. Actually, on such close inspection, Morgana wondered what she'd ever seen in the man who was her deceased brother's age. "Was I so brash and childish?" Morgana asked. "I suppose, then, the journey has been broadening for me." Morgana glanced back at Lillian, sandwiched between several large valises and holding one of Morgana's shopping bags filled with gaily wrapped packages on her lap. "Would you say so, Mama?"

"Definitely broadening," Lillian agreed, remembering the many misadventures of their journey. They had agreed not to expound upon the train derailment beyond the fact that it had interrupted their journey, Morgana having sustained a minor injury. "How are things at home, Jonny? Quiet and restful, I hope, for I am worn to a frazzle and in need of a good rest."

"Tolerable," Jonathan smiled. "There is some news. For one thing, Laura Lee has convicted me for the omissions of religious learning in my bachelor days and I have joined the church."

"Hallelujah!" Lillian cried aloud.

Morgana remained silent, letting her eyes rest upon her folded hands on her lap.

Jonathan went on, "I might add, it was a revelation to me, bringing with it a peace of mind I've never known before." He looked sidelong at Morgana, so still, so unlike her old self. "Then, too, we've finished reconstruction of our house. There is other news, too, but I should probably wait and let Laura Lee be the one to tell—"

"You've finally found your tongue, have you?" Lillian interrupted, reaching forward to slap his back. "I wondered how long it would take. Where and when is the wedding to be?"

"At Greenleaf. A quiet one. Just our two families. Laura Lee thought you'd feel better about having it there. As to when? Whenever you are rested enough to help with the preparations, I've been told." Without looking back, a grinning Jonathan asked, "Would tomorrow be too soon?" Then he allowed his gaze to return to Morgana who sat, unmoving, quietly pensive.

Morgana finally spoke, unsmiling. "Laura Lee's and Drew's wedding was the most beautiful wedding this town has ever seen. At least, we will always have that cherished memory of my brother. Nothing can take that away from us—or change it."

She leaned to kiss Jonathan's cheek. "I'm truly glad you and Laura Lee have decided to marry, Jonny. I think Drew would approve, too. Don't you, Mama?"

Lillian's expression sobered. "I'm as sure Drew approves of this union between his widow and his best friend, as I'm sure God's looking down on us, right now, and smiling."

Morgana rolled her eyes in Jonathan's direction, and said, "Mama, must you always talk so much like Sarah? Sarah prayed all the time and I saw what happened to her. Where was God then, Mama?"

Jonathan, pricked by the memory of having lost Sarah whom he had dearly loved before Laura Lee, looked away.

Catching the essence of rancor in Morgana's voice, Lillian answered almost as lightly as if she were commenting on the weather, "Someday, young lady, you will come to call upon God. Until then, I'll thank you to keep your callow criticism of my religious nature to yourself."

Just as the carriage ground to a halt in *Briars'* driveway, Storm came racing round the side of the house, barking and howling and wagging a greeting before anybody inside even knew they had arrived. Storm's noisy salutation caused the front door to fly open and Wil, who'd grown a foot; Laura Lee, prettier than ever; and Hamita Baker, who'd added a few pounds, all rushed down the verandah steps to welcome the travelers home.

The household staff, Henry, Rachel, and Willow followed them out, waiting respectfully on the porch.

"What a sight for sore eyes you, all, are!" Lillian exclaimed, patting the big shepherd dog on his broad head. She reached for Wil, kissing and squeezing him until he was embarrassed, then Laura Lee and Hamita, before climbing the steps to hug Rachel and Willow, and shake Henry's big, rough hand.

Resigned, Lillian said to one and all, "Remind me of this worrisome journey if ever I say another word about traveling again—anywhere, for any reason!"

Morgana tolerated the hugging and kissing, much as Wil had done. She passed out her presents and excused herself, quickly, dragging Willow away, eager to disclose the recent momentous events in her life. The dangerous outcome of her unwelcome pregnancy. Gruesome details of the train derailment, at least, as much of it as she had been told. And saving the best for last, about her engagement to Shane Moss.

"Yes, the *same* Shane Moss," she had to admit. "The Lieutenant from the Yankee occupation."

Willow grimaced, ashamed of Morgana for consorting with the enemy.

But Morgana laughed. "No, Willow, it wasn't like that, at all, really it wasn't. He's a *Virginian*, and he's wonderful—simply wonderful!"

Bad Turns

When Henry brought Lillian's valise upstairs and set it upon her bed, she heard his labored breathing from across the room. She turned from the window where she'd been drinking in the sights of home and looked long and hard into her old friend's face. "My God, Henry, you're almost white! You sure you're all right?"

"I's been poorly some of late, Miz Lillian, but not 'nough t' complain 'bout out loud, I reckon," the old man smiled, pleased that she had noticed. "Rachel, she be takin' good care o'me though, and I's not lettin' up any on my chores. Like ever'thin' else—in time, it'll pass."

"Not likely!" Lillian said, patting his arm. "It's old age, Henry. You and I are just getting old! I've been having a few bad turns, myself. Recently, I was surprised to find myself in a pile on the floor, having slid from my chair while putting on my shoes and stockings—in a faint, I suppose. It's happened before though and I'm still here but, for heaven's sake, don't breathe a word about it—," she looked towards the open door, "—to any of them or I'll end up in some new-fangled doctor's office." She looked accusingly at him. "You tell, and so help me, Henry, I'll make you go, too!"

"Yes'm, you can trust me, Miz Lillian. I ain't goin' tell *nobody!*"

Over one of Rachel's sumptuous spreads, both Laura Lee and Morgana talked on and on, excitedly, about their coming weddings, and Lillian was glad when she saw happiness sparkling in Laura Lee's eyes. Happiness, she had feared Laura Lee might never know again. She remembered finding her daughter-in-law after the Yankee soldiers had left her dazed and brutalized. Had it only been six months? Had her beloved Morgan, Drew, and Sweet Sarah, all been gone only six short months? Impossible. Normally, a mourning period would have lasted a year before the war, but these were not normal times. Pshaw! Lillian thought. Let folks find happiness whenever and wherever they can.

When supper dishes were cleaned and stored and the house had quieted, Lillian stole out onto the back porch to sit in her favorite bent wood rocker alone in the fresh Spring night air, to collect her thoughts and to meditate a spell. She never intended to overhear the conversation from Rachel's and Henry's room, but the wooden walls were not thick on the added-on back portions of the old house as they were on the rock-faced front and sides, and the raised voices of her servants, mother and daughter, came through clearly audible.

"Don't say that, Mama!" Willow wailed, "I've told you over and over again, you've got to stop saying, 'I's goin' to' do this and that. It's 'I'm going to', Mama! *'I'm'* not *'I's'!* Can't you remember that?" Willow's tone was less than patient. "How am I ever going to get anywhere in this town with you and Papa dragging me back down every time you open your mouths? I can't help you, Mama, if you won't even try to learn. I don't want to be a household servant all my life like you and Papa.

I'm educated. I want to be a teacher. I want to teach Negro children to read and write and do numbers. They can learn as well as white children can, but somebody's got to *teach* them. There's a new age upon us, Mama, a Reconstruction, and I want to be a part of progress."

"Reconstruction? So tha's what you calls it when chil'ren talks down t' they mamas and papas, and breaks they hearts? An' gets highfalutin' ideas 'bout theirselves."

"*'Themselves!'* Mama. *'Themselves!'*"

Lillian felt responsibility for this quarrel fell unmistakably on her shoulders. It had been she, who'd insisted on schooling Willow. Not for Willow's sake, but for Morgana's! Perhaps, it would have been better for everyone, Lillian thought, had she not drawn Willow into Morgana's white world at all. But it was too late now for second thoughts. Too late to mend rifts between generations. The War Between the States and, now, this new Reconstruction had changed all that.

Lillian stole back into the house, took down and lit a lamp from the shelf in the kitchen and, quietly passing Rachel's and Henry's closed bedroom door, climbed the back stairs to the upstairs hall. Her lamp scattered shadows as she walked the length of the hallway to her own room, passing Wil's and Morgana's bedrooms and, empty now, the ones that had belonged to her dearest Morgan and to Sweet Sarah. Soon, there would be two more empty rooms upstairs when Drew's wife, Laura Lee, took their twins and moved to their new home after the wedding at *Greenleaf*. Wil, Morgana, and Lillian—only the three of them remaining. Later, with Morgana's marriage, there'd be only two of the family left in the big, quiet house that once had rung with all the joyful noises and occasional turmoil that went with a family of nine.

Perhaps the servant's *would* be better off if they claimed the freedom they'd been offered years ago and sought outside opportunities during this Reconstruction so highly spoken of by

Willow. Tomorrow, Lillian would have to remind them to think on that choice, again.

The lamplight illuminating the corridor a few paces ahead of Lillian reached into the darkness to reveal the tall, gangling man sprawled on the floor just outside her bedroom door. With no lamp other than her own evident, Lillian judged Henry'd been lying there since before nightfall. Hurriedly, she set her lamp on the floor beside Henry's still form and felt for a pulse. Henry's pulse was weak and thready but it was there—just the same. Beside him, she found the letter that had fallen from his hand as he collapsed. Lillian breathed a sigh of relief and quickly retraced her steps to Wil's room.

"Henry's fallen ill. Help me to get him into your father's room," she urged, soberly. "We can't carry him all the way back downstairs."

"Pa's room, Ma?" Wil's eyes opened wide as he followed her up the hall.

Scowling, Lillian answered, "Stop gaping, and take hold of that other arm, Wil Heirs!" Together, they pulled Henry the few feet back down the hall to Morgan Ayer's bedroom, where Lillian threw back the coverlet on the bed to receive their trusted servant.

"Your father would have done no less," she said emphatically to Wil as they heaved the long thin form onto the bed. "—and don't you start getting *yourself* any highfalutin' ideas, either!"

"I don't know what you're talkin' about, Ma," Wil protested.

Of course, Lillian knew that he didn't, but she sent him downstairs to bring back Rachel, who *would have* caught her meaning, to minister to Henry. Wil was also to bid Willow to come, too. Lillian was determined that Willow should see her father, at least once, in far better circumstances than she had *ever* known.

While Wil was gone, Lillian opened the envelope Henry had been trying to deliver when he fell, and read it by her lamplight.

Ann Gray

It was a telegram from her father's lawyer containing the unwelcome but not unexpected news of her father's passing. Her instructions for his burial had been followed to the letter. According to her father's Last Will and Testament, the house and all of its contents had been left to Lillian. Papers would follow. Cassandra Cochran had been bequeathed a generous annuity, which would sustain her comfortably until she found another position. It was as Lillian had dared hope. Michael Wilson O'Donnell had not lost his senses along with his health, and Morgana's wedding gift, the O'Donnell's Richmond house, was assured.

Later, when Henry regained consciousness, despite his vehement protests, Lillian insisted that he sleep the night in Morgan Heirs' bed—a privilege Willow would someday tell his grandchildren about.

CHAPTER FOURTEEN ~ MARRIAGE

1:00 p.m., Monday, August 12, 1867 ~ Atlanta, Georgia

Something Old, Something New

Because slaves in the South, remembering no other surnames, often adopted the family surnames of their owners, so it had been in the beginning with the Heirs' slaves, Henry and Rachel. Willow, in turn, had come by the surname naturally. Without prior knowledge, on introduction to the two beautiful young Heirs women, Morgana and Willow, a stranger would be hard pressed to discern either beauty's blood line.

An unintentional inheritance from her grandmother's lecherous white owner, and passed down to her through her own Mulatto mother, Willow's flawless complexion was exquisite. Strolling down Atlanta's Peachtree Street, her jaunty step in rhythm with Morgana's, the tilt of her chin, her chocolate brown eyes, narrow cinched waist—nothing about Willow Heirs' appearance suggested anything less than aristocracy.

One week after Morgana and Willow had quietly observed their shared twentieth birthdays, and one short month before the eagerly anticipated arrival of the Moss family from Virginia for Morgana's wedding to Shane Moss, the young women had left Henry dozing in the Heirs' carriage on a downtown street while they went shopping.

Willow stopped to look in a store window. "There! Oh, 'Gana, look at that beautiful scarf. It would make a perfect gift for your Mistress Moss, wouldn't it? Shall we go in and ask to see it? Maybe we'll find your blue garter in here, too."

When the saleslady produced it, Willow draped the lighter than air fashion accessory over her outstretched arm. "Gana, how do you like the scarf?"

The scarf was pale blue silk shot through with gold threads much like Mistress Moss's eyes, Morgana thought. Smiling, and without ever looking at the price tag, Morgana said to the saleslady, "We'll take it."

On the next aisle, optimistic after the sale of the expensive scarf, the saleslady started with the most extravagant, fanciest blue garters in the display, showing them seven before Morgana found the very one she wanted.

When the sale was accomplished, Willow made note that Morgana had chosen for herself the simplest, least expensive lace trimmed blue garter of the lot. Then Willow pulled out her own small purse and bought the matching garter. "You haven't said yet what you'll have that's 'old' but when you are dressing for your wedding, let me lend you this new blue garter of mine. Then, you'll have 'something new, something borrowed, and something blue', all in these two garters." She grinned and winked at Morgana. "That way I can guarantee both your stockings will stay up—at least until the reception is over." Morgana hugged Willow in thanks for her gift and they left the store, arm in arm.

Walking towards the waiting carriage, when conversation turned to Willow's floundering plans for her Negro children's school, Willow stopped talking mid-sentence to stare at a young Negro man approaching them.

"Well? Go on! Then what did you say to Mistress Clark?" Morgana prodded.

"What could I say?" Willow replied, her eyes following the tall cocoa-brown man in the fine tailored suit as he passed. "I said, 'thank you, ma'am,' and just walked away like any subservient, obedient colored girl would do." Resentment and anger flared in Willow's eyes. "Morgana, let it be! My teaching classes were doomed before they ever began."

"I won't have you talking that way," Morgana countered. "It's not doomed until *you* give up the fight! And I'll never let you do that! We'll find a way to make it happen, believe me we will. We, Heirs, don't quit! You should know that by now!" She waited a moment to allow Willow to reflect upon her words then asked, "Well, who is he? Don't tell me you don't know. I can tell by the way you looked at him you do, so who is he?"

"He's Calvin Tubbs. That's all I know." Morgana suspected that Willow knew more about this Calvin Tubbs than just his name. Today was the first time Morgana had seen Willow look with interest upon any man's face other than her own father's since the summer when she was sixteen and the three Johnson boys viciously raped her in their cane field. Morgana certainly intended to find out more about Calvin Tubbs. Perhaps he could help in Willow's cause.

While slavery might ostensibly be dead by decree, the opinion still prevailed among the local gentry where Willow's parentage was well known, that Negro servants and freedmen's families were, and always would be, subordinate to whites. And since it was whites who determined which ventures succeeded and which ones failed, Willow had petitioned nearby manor houses to allow the Negro children of their servants to populate her teaching classes.

Willow's pleas had fallen on deaf ears. While never named aloud, the "uppity white nigger with the highfalutin' ideas" was daily tongue-lashed in whispers over morning coffee and afternoon tea along with other morsels of malicious gossip throughout the better part of Atlanta's racially bigoted high society. Stimulating those insults was the *scandalous* fact that the matriarch of the wealthy Heirs family had actually consented to allow her spoiled daughter Morgana to include the colored girl along with her former sister-in-law, Laura Lee Baker, as her only attendants in her forthcoming marriage.

This time the eccentric Mistress Heirs had gone *too far!* Nowhere in greater Atlanta's inner circle of society would an established family admit to having plans to attend the Heirs' wedding even if invited. Nor would they allow their servants to send their children to the Heirs' servant girl's Negro classes which were be conducted in the Heirs' old barn commencing in middle September.

Though she was yet to realize it's ultimate cost, Willow knew that the unalterable fact of her Negro blood was the basis for the white community's refusal to approve of her school. Overcoming *that* obstacle would be Willow's unremitting goal for the betterment of colored children's circumstances.

Two controversial bills had received congressional approval in early 1866 on behalf of Negroes everywhere. One bill concerned the Freedmen's Bureau, which offered economic assistance and legal protection to Negroes making the transition from slavery to freedom. It was immediately vetoed by President Johnson, who believed no such assistance was necessary. Further, Johnson also vetoed the second proposal, the Civil Rights Bill, expressing his concern that giving Negroes civil rights would result in reverse discrimination against whites. For the first time in U.S. history, Congress overrode a presidential veto on a matter of significance.

The Southern states suffered as political upheaval continued unabated. The influx of ambitious politicians and would-be humanitarians from the Northern states dubbed "Carpetbaggers" by Southerners, joined with Southern Unionists called "Scalawags" to promote their own political agendas and both groups were fiercely resented by the general public.

Ku Klux Klan

A social organization calling themselves the Ku Klux Klan sprang up in Pulaski, Tennessee in the winter of 1865 to 1866. The Klan's sole aim in the beginning was to drive out the "Carpetbaggers", and the Klan's wrathful acts were primarily directed at Republican Reconstruction government leaders, both Caucasians and Negroes. But with the withdrawal of federal troops from Southern states the local Klaverns began taking

Briars
The House of Heirs

"justice" into their own hands declaring it their intention to "protect the weak, the innocent and the defenseless; to relieve the injured and oppressed; [and] to succor the suffering..." The Klan's infamy would quickly spread throughout the South.

Facts such as these were of no interest to Morgana. She was ecstatic. Other than those converstations concerning Willow's unsettled plans for her school, Morgana's discussions of late revolved solely around her forthcoming marriage.

Morgana had thoroughly immersed Willow in talk about her romance with Shane Moss, which had blossomed and grown ever deeper and richer through their letters. The Moss family was expected to arrive from Petersburg on the tenth of September. Their visit was to last through the eighteenth. The wedding, itself, was scheduled to take place in Briarwood's Nondenominational Community Church on Sunday afternoon, September fifteenth.

Ages ago in May of 1866, Shane had written the good news that exactly eleven months after a successful coupling with the Mosses' stallion, Victor, Star had dropped her foal. He had written to Morgana of his great joy when it had been a colt which he described as *"the prize"* Thoroughbred colt in *Moss Hall* history—maybe, in all Kentucky and Virginia's Thoroughbred history." Shane promised that until Morgana named him, the colt would be called "Boy".

Under Shane's watchful eye, the youngster, old enough to travel on a lead but too young for the saddle—by nearly nine months—would accompany his dam, Star, on her expected return to *Briars*. The animals were to be transported in one of the livestock conveyances on the train along with the Moss family. Shane had written Morgana: "When you are ready to leave *Briars* without regret, we will bring our prize stock back home again to *Moss Hall*."

Shane Moss loved her. Life was good. From that day forward, Morgana lived for their future. She wrote to Shane that she had always wanted to *see* New Orleans and riverboat

Ann Gray

cruising *was* the latest craze. Therefore, as chance would have it, the groom made arrangements weeks ahead for their honeymoon travel to New Orleans by train, anticipating a leisurely river boat cruise up the Mississippi. Their journey was to start in the late afternoon after their wedding reception at *Briars*.

"Won't it be just heavenly, Willow? I can hardly wait to be married though I shall miss you, terribly. You will come to visit us in Virginia, won't you? Say you will."

"That will be for your mama to determine, 'Gana. Don't forget, I am still a servant at *Briars*."

"Oh, poo," Morgana sniffed at Willow's retort. "You know Mama would never refuse us if we asked together. She never has."

And they laughed, for it was true.

It was not until they were almost home from their shopping excursion that Morgana, having fortified herself so that she would not cry with the telling, confided in Willow the 'old' token that she had chosen for her wedding. It was to be the white linen wedding dress Sarah had begun sewing before the war for her own ill-fated wedding to Jonathan Baker.

In over six years of storage the white linen had aged to a mellow ivory. And to Morgana's delight, Mama had succeeded in matching the material and added a flounce of ivory linen and lace to lengthen the dress for Morgana. Mama was absolutely ruining her eyes, adding seed pearls to the generously cut bodice. The dress was utterly beautiful, and it was, finally, to be worn in a wedding.

Willow was pleased to know that Morgana was honoring her sister's memory in such a loving way.

As Henry prodded Mary Belle up the long hill, the returning shoppers caught sight of flames leaping skyward from behind the manor house and heard Storm's loud voice, wailing.

"Faster, Henry, faster," Morgana cried, leaping to her feet as soon as she saw the flames and smelled the acrid smoke.

"We's goin' fast old Mary Belle can climb this hill," Henry answered over his shoulder, urging Mary Belle on. "Miss Morgana, you sit down, now, 'for you falls!"

"Why, that's just Papa's old barn going up in flames!" Morgana said, turning to look at Willow. "Good heavens! That old thing hasn't been used in years except for storage. Why would anyone fire up that old pile of boards and backyard chickens' nests?"

"You know why the old barn's burning," Willow declared angrily, pulling Morgana back down into her seat. "It's because I wanted to use it for my classes." Then she pointed, "Look! Look, it's them!"

A dozen silent ghosts—hooded riders in white garb—rode boldly from behind the west side of the stone house, cutting across the lawn below the massive old oak tree. They entered the driveway at an angle and rode out through the open gates, showering loose gravel onto the red clay roadway. When the hooded leader leaned forward in his saddle, pointing a finger at the approaching carriage the pack of horsemen split into two columns and rode towards the carriage, half on one side, half on the other.

"Oh, God," Willow whispered, as they neared. "Let's not say anything! Please! Just let them pass!"

But Morgana, incensed, would not hold her tongue and at the exact moment the leader reached her side of the carriage, she leaned out and said to him, "I do believe that is decidedly the *dingiest* sheet I have *ever* seen! You should be *ashamed* to be seen out and about in that!"

The hooded rider held up one arm, signaling the columns to stop and, as if he would have words with her, the ghostly figure bent towards Morgana. The fingers of his right hand gripped the pommel of his finely-tooled saddle and steely gray eyes narrowed behind round holes cut into the pointed hood, but he didn't speak.

His troupe rode around him as Henry began to advance the wagon forward ever so slowly, and Willow pinched Morgana's thigh through her skirts. But Morgana, the tone of her voice rising, continued to prod even as the gap grew wider between the carriage and the mounted specter.

"Our old barn surely *did* need razing," Morgana quipped, "and I suppose we should be grateful to you for the favor. *Whom* are we to thank, sir?" Leaning out her window when the man trotted silently away, Morgana called after him, "You're afraid I'll recognize your voice, aren't you?"

"Please, 'Gana, hush your mouth!" Willow pleaded, just as she'd done when they were children. She peered over her shoulder, making sure the departing horsemen were not turning back to assault them. "You can't toy with those men! Surely, you've heard of the Ku Klux Klan?"

Morgana looked straight ahead at the column of black smoke, thinning now, and folded her hands in her lap. "Humph! Only cowards would disguise themselves and do devilment like the burning of our old barn. We've survived one *real* war. We can't sit idly by and allow a bunch of cowardly ruffians to rise up from the ashes of our shameful loss and bully the whole South to its knees again, now can we?"

Henry had listened to the young women and held his peace, but in the driveway once his feet reached the ground his knees shook so that he held onto the carriage for support.

When they ran back to the site of the fire, Jeremiah and Jonathan Baker, Thomas and Grady had done an admirable job of containing the flames to the barn and only a small circle of brush had been singed outside the structure.

Wil sat cradling his injured dog, Storm, in his arms and called out when he saw Morgana approaching, "The bastards ran Storm down! He'll be all right though, I think it's just a pulled muscle. Y'all all right?"

"As 'all right' as can be—considering—" Morgana answered, rushing to where Hamita tried in vain to calm Mama down in her rage over their old barn's being burned. Adding to Mama's anger, Morgana told about her confrontation with the robed men.

To Willow's great satisfaction, after listening to her own account of their encounter with the Ku Klux Klan, Mistress Lillian reprimanded Morgana for her 'foolishness' in trying to provoke the Klansman into speaking. If he had been someone whose voice she recognized, Mistress Lillian had told Morgana, she would have been in far greater danger than she was, now, in not knowing.

Then Willow revealed the ugly gossip making the rounds concerning Morgana's "mixed company" wedding, and about her own unkind reception by Mistress Lillian's acquaintances when Willow had mentioned her planned teaching project for colored children. Well, now, with the barn's burning that was no longer an achievable goal.

"Don't worry," Morgana encouraged a tearful Willow. "We'll find another place. I'm sure we'll find one, somewhere."

Lillian sent Wil immediately with a note to Tom Garrett, her banker and financial advisor, requesting that he call by *Briars* tomorrow afternoon at four o'clock. There were important financial and family matters that required attention.

The Colt

Though it was barely two years since the end of the war, Atlanta's railroad yards were burgeoning again with activity. On the Tuesday afternoon of September 10, 1867, the terminal building echoed with strident voices as newly arrived and soon-to-be departing travelers crowded through widely separated colonnades in opposite directions. When the Heirs family finally found their platform it, too, was overcrowded with baggage carts and impatient people.

Ann Gray

The Mosses' train was thirty minutes late and Morgana nervously paced the platform, stopping finally to stare at Lillian who sat quietly on a bench beside the busy doorway to the terminal, unperturbed. "How can you be so calm, Mama?" Morgana asked, beginning to pace once again.

"'Gana," Lillian scolded from her seat, "you're going to cut a trough there if you don't come over here and sit down." Lillian observed that she was having less success in pacifying Morgana than in dealing with her seven year old twin grandchildren who sat obediently between herself and Wil, having been allowed to come along to watch the trains and see the new colt.

Wil, who had reluctantly agreed to don a coat and tie for the occasion, squirmed uncomfortably. At least, he wouldn't have to be in torture long, as he and the twins would ride back to *Briars* with Thomas, hauling luggage in the slower work wagon, the two extra horses tied on behind. Henry would drive the remainder of the group in the carriage.

Minutes later, when the eagerly awaited train puffed to a halt, the platform was transformed into a shouting, jostling, scrambling multitude—some arriving, some leaving, some searching for lost baggage or lost people—all bent on getting from one point to another.

Worming her way through the throng, Morgana caught sight of Roger Moss's trim white beard and hailed him as he helped Mistress Moss down the steps from the car. Even Mistress Moss, who fussed with her jabot as she stepped down, was a welcome sight to Morgana. "Mistress Moss, how lovely you look!" Morgana said, quickly putting Shane's mother at ease. "And, Mister Moss, I am so glad to see you looking so handsome. I do believe you've thinned down considerably since I saw you last."

Roger Moss answered over the uproar, "Work, Miss Heirs! It's hard work keeps a man fit and trim. And you are prettier than ever, dear girl, if that were possible."

Briars
The House of Heirs

Morgana quickly stepped aside when a stout lady with a garishly designed floral carpetbag forced her way from the car's exit and grumbled past the three of them. Southerners were finding that Carpetbaggers came in all shapes and sizes, and they were none too considerate of others.

When Shane did not immediately appear, Morgana's disappointment was evident for Roger Moss said, laughing, "Shane went to check on the horses at the last stop. Let's hope he's still in the livestock car with them and not plodding along behind, trying to catch up to the train."

Morgana laughed, and her eyes sparkled with anticipation. "Please let me show you to my mother. She's anxious to see you both." As they worked their way through the throng, Morgana said, "I'm so excited! I can hardly wait to see our colt!" She pointed. "There's Mama."

"Go on, child," Roger Moss chided, playfully, "go find what you're looking for! And I don't believe for one moment it's that scrawny little colt that you're so anxious to see. I think it's the larger stallion!"

"Roger!" Mistress Moss admonished, smiling in her proud way, as she made her way to Lillian Heirs.

Morgana ran past clusters of weary detraining passengers towards the livestock car farther down the tracks.

"Oh, he's magnificent!" she cried from a distance, catching sight of the long-legged bay colt, his black mane and tail flying in the breeze as Shane led him down the ramp from the railroad car. Running to Shane, Morgana threw herself into his open arms, their lips seeking, and remembering.

"I've missed you so," Shane whispered, holding her close. "Tell me you'll never leave me again." He held her away and looked into her black eyes. "Promise!"

Morgana tip-toed to kiss his lips again. "Oh, I do promise," she said, clinging to him for a moment, his closeness whetting again her deep desire for him. "Nothing will ever separate us again, my darling. Nothing!"

Shane shortened the colt's lead and brought the youngster up close for Morgana's inspection. "Now, what do you think of our colt," Shane asked, proudly.

Morgana admired the colt's stature. His short, slightly concave back and his lean fine body. His neck arched majestically and his jaw was wide and rounded. "What a fine head he has," she said, running her fingers appreciatively down to his velvet muzzle. "His eyes are beautiful—so large and wide. And, look, Shane, his blaze—a perfect star! You didn't tell me!"

"I wanted to surprise you," Shane admitted. "But we can't call him 'Star', can we?"

"We *must* call him 'Blaze' then, mustn't we, Shane?"

"That is yours to decide," Shane laughed, as he pulled her close again. "My own Morgana! I can't believe you're really mine!" he said, and separated from the crowds, they kissed again and again.

Wedding Plans

It was truly amazing to Lillian how smoothly preparations for the wedding had proceeded after the Mosses' arrival. Mistress Moss had to have been most impressed with the efficiency and thoroughness of Lillian's planning. Lillian, of course, knew full well that she couldn't have managed without Hamita's exquisite good taste to guide her in the planning of the reception, and Rachel's scrumptious menu for the big day, which could only to be eclipsed by her light as a cloud, white wedding cake with the fluffy white icing.

Laura Lee made herself indispensable in entertaining their guests with stories from Morgana's frivolous youth much to Morgana's chagrin, including the episode of her having wangled a large portion of Laura Lee's own wedding cake, which she later learned Morgana had given to the kitchen maid, though Willow's name was not spoken.

On the front verandah the evening before the wedding after everyone else had gone inside, Mistress Moss sat in a wicker rocker with a small glass of sherry wine in her hand while Morgana and Shane sat, side by side, on the top step at her feet and watched the gaslights twinkle on down the hill in the city.

"Are you *sure* you'll be happy living on a farm after the convenience of living your whole life so close to the city?" Shane asked Morgana. Having asked the question a hundred times before, Shane still needed the reassurance of hearing her say it again.

"I am," Morgana said, reaching to place her other hand over their intertwined two on his knee. "All my life, there's been somebody to wait on me hand and foot, and I've been spoiled to the comforts of Papa's wealth and Mama's social standing. The time I spent at *Moss Hall* was the first time I'd ever realized there could be a life for me other than the absurdly pampered one I've known. When I was there on the farm riding free, unencumbered by tight clothes and corsets—," She giggled.

"—and I listened to nature's wondrous music and saw that lazy old hawk soaring leisurely over your grain fields, I knew then *that* was the life I truly wanted."

Shane grinned, pleased by her answer. "I've drawn up rough plans I want to show you later of the house I want to build for us near the road in the far western pasture. But you mustn't think farm life will always be as leisurely as it was at the time of your visit," Shane reminded her. "Horse breeding is a business. There'll be times when we'll all have to work—!" Shane smiled when Wil, who had been listening at the front door, slipped out and settled down beside him on the steps. "—harder, even, than you might ever have imagined but—" he continued, "—in the end, the pay is unbelievably good."

"And can I come and help out, too, sometimes?" Wil interjected. "I won't be any trouble, and 'Gana can tell you, I'm real good with horses. Ain't I, 'Gana?"

"The very best," Morgana said. "And don't say *'ain't'!* Have you rubbed down the colt, as you promised you would?" Morgana asked, leaning across Shane to speak to her younger brother.

"I was just goin' to do that," Wil lied, getting up. "Shane, you want to come along and take a ride down the back path on my horse? You haven't been on Pal, yet, and you did say you'd like to give him a try. I'm thinkin' this'll be your last chance before the weddin'. And after that—"

Shane stood and gave Wil a good-natured slap on his back. Morgana could see right away that the two of them would become the best of friends. "You know, Wil," Shane said, "I was just thinking about doing that very thing. Why don't we go on down there, now, and leave these ladies to their woman's talk."

After Shane and Wil had gone, Patricia Moss held out her cold, thin hands to Morgana. "My dear Morgana, I was hoping to have this opportunity to speak to you privately. And, though I am not accustomed to apologizing—" Considering her words carefully, the older woman looked away, her eyes misting, then she spoke again, mindfully. "—My dear, I realize I have not been altogether kind to you. Sometimes mothers of strong desirable men, in a sense, experience a possessive love of their sons—but now that you're to be my son's wife—and I do realize I must step aside—at least, may I offer one little snippet of advice?"

"Tell me first," Morgana asked, looking squarely into Mistress Moss's teary eyes. "May I call you 'Mother Moss'?"

Patricia Moss's face registered surprise and she said, "Of course that would please me, Morgana, though I tell you now that regardless of any fondness we may develop for one another, I expect we shall always have our differences."

"Of course, we shall!" Morgana laughed. "Loving the same man, mothers and wives most always *do!* Now, what is your advice? I want to know anything that you believe will make me a better wife to Shane. You must know, by now, that I love him with every fiber of my being." Morgana waited patiently for her future mother-in-law to compose herself.

Patricia Moss sipped the last of her sherry, setting the empty glass on the floor beside her chair then she said, "Shane will make you happy, Morgana—of that, I'm sure. But if you want to make him happy in return, use my example, dear. I did practically everything *wrong!* My three men have one remarkable family trait in common which I understand now, but when it would have counted most, unfortunately, I didn't." Mother Moss placed her hand under Morgana's chin and lifted it, leaning closer to make her point. Her eyes looked deep into Morgana's. "Listen to me carefully. As a horsewoman, Morgana, you'll surely understand that like any robust stallion, he'll test the bit at the very start! Never try to rein him in too tightly nor drive him to run against his will—he'll surely buck! But give him his head. Let him set the pace and wholly trust him. Then, my dear—he'll run his very heart out for you!"

Realizing how difficult it must have been for her to speak so frankly concerning her own failings, Morgana looked upon her future mother-in-law's taut face with a new understanding and felt compassion for her. "I will do that, Mother Moss. I promise you, I will," Morgana said, rising and holding out her hands to help the older woman to her feet.

"Oh, dear, I'd almost forgotten," Mother Moss said, picking up her empty wine glass. "I should return this to the kitchen." They entered the hall and when they reached the staircase, she kissed Morgana's cheek, her eyes still teary, "You run on along, dear. You must get your beauty sleep. After all, tomorrow is going to be a very big day for you."

Before Morgana started up the stairs, she leaned over the banister. "Goodnight, dear Mother Moss. And, if you'd like just a touch more of that sherry, look on the third shelf in the pantry. You can't miss it. I put it there, myself."

"Bless you, my dear," Mother Moss smiled.

The Wedding

On Sunday, September fifteenth, in Briarwood's Community Church, Reverend Hoyt Wylie stood, starched and nervous, behind the organ greenery waiting to walk out and perform the solemn ceremony of marriage. Ever grateful to the community and to Morgan Heirs in particular for the endowment that established his church, he had dutifully spent two hours the previous Saturday afternoon interviewing the happy couple, making doubly sure that they were entering into the holy state of matrimony, unencumbered, and with integrity.

In the sanctuary murmuring voices competed with strains of familiar melodies being played by the church organist, hired for the occasion. Each pew had been mysteriously filled to capacity with Atlanta's curious elite, dressed in their finest and awaiting the appearance of the bride and groom. Weeks before, around the second week in August word had *somehow* leaked out that attendance to the most lavish wedding in Atlanta since the war's end was to be by invitation only. But as the engraved invitations went out a few at a time, a large segment of Atlanta's gentry began to worry. Many having earlier professed indifference to the event mainly associated with the "mixed company" aspect of the planned ceremony had begun to rethink their attitudes. Suddenly, admitting to not having received an Heirs' wedding invitation was tantamount to social suicide.

The mother of the groom, Mistress Moss in violet and lace sat before him alone on the first pew. Red eyed and tearful behind her dainty handkerchief, she awaited the groom's best man, her husband, Roger Moss, who would join her after presentation of the ring.

Briars
The House of Heirs

Reverend Wylie glanced up into the balcony usually bulging with coloreds and saw only the Heirs' servants, Rachel and Henry, Thomas and Grady, spick and span in their Sunday best, seated quietly on the front row. Well, that was a mercy!

A miniature bouquet of ivory, lavender, and white chrysanthemums decorated the end of each pew on the center aisle. In Atlanta, still recovering from the ravages of war, flower shops were non-existent therefore Mistress Heirs had stripped *Briars'* own Fall gardens as well as those being painstakingly resurrected at Bakers' *Greenleaf,* of every blooming chrysanthemum, cape jasmine, pink, ivory, and white rose for today's attendants and bride.

At the Reverend's own suggestion, on each side of the alter, ivory candles burned in five foot high ornate silver candle sticks, borrowed from the new mortuary next door. To the Reverend Hoyt Wylie' eye, his church had never looked more beautiful.

In the room directly behind the sanctuary, Lillian Heirs was adamant, her face only slightly less flushed than her deep rose dress. "Morgana, how could you have left her last night with a half bottle of wine? You know how Patricia is when there's sherry about!" She tugged at Morgana's corset strings.

"Ow, that's tight enough, Mama!" Morgana protested. "She was nervous and upset and I knew it would pacify her. Besides, how was I to know she'd drink the rest of it?" Morgana asked, laughing at her mother's consternation. "I seem to remember you had a little problem with sherry wine, yourself, or have you forgotten that?" Morgana pulled on her hose and slipped her new blue garter in place. Willow, in her pale lavender bridesmaid's dress, held out the other blue garter she had purchased to Morgana mouthing, "something borrowed", then, watched with pleasure as Morgana slipped it into place.

While Lillian rattled on and on, Morgana eased into the petticoat Lillian was holding over her head. "She'll be fine, Mama. Don't worry about Mother Moss. She's been drinking like that so long, she's accustomed to it. She only does it to build up her confidence. Why, she'll be charming as all outdoors this afternoon at the reception, you just watch."

In the next room, Morgana knew Shane being attended by his best man, his father, and Jonathan Baker, who would give her away in her own father's absence. She wondered if Shane was having second thoughts. She'd heard marriage often affected men so.

Poor Jonny, undoubtedly quaking in his shiny dress slippers. Being of a naturally shy nature, Jonathan had resisted taking part in the wedding from the beginning, but Morgana had three unspoken reasons for wanting Jonny to give her away. One, Wil had said he'd kill himself first and thus Morgana had excused him, saying she really preferred not to be given away by someone younger than herself, anyway. And two, after having lost her own father and older brother, while she could have asked Jeremiah Baker, whom she loved dearly, Jonathan had been the one man she'd ever been "in love with" before Shane. Therefore, the third and most important reason in Morgana's mind for having Jonny give her away was to prove to herself, once and for all, that her long held attraction to him had been founded merely on adolescent infatuation.

Willow turned from the door where she'd been peeking out. "I can't believe my eyes!" she said. "Everybody in town is out there. I just saw Mistress Clark, big as life! And after what she had to say about your 'mixed company' wedding, too! I never expected to see her sour old face today!"

Lillian had been attentively buttoning Morgana's dress up the back, all thirty-eight tiny pearl buttons and loops, and they'd come out even. "Shows you just how much credence you can put in folk's empty pronouncements when they bad-mouth and censure other people for doing things differently than themselves. Spend enough money, put on a good enough show, buy enough French champagne and Russian caviar, and the devil, himself, will find his way to your reception table."

"Mama, you made that up!" Morgana laughed. "But I guess if *you* invited him, he'd feel obliged to come!"

Laura Lee settled the tiny sweetheart roses and cape jasmine tiara into Morgana's ebony curls, its ivory train, caught up immediately in Willow's arms; then Laura Lee handed her former sister-in-law the sweet-smelling cape jasmine and rose bud bridal bouquet with the narrow lavender and ice blue ribbons streaming from it.

"Now," Lillian said, stepping away, already wet-eyed, "turn away from the mirror and let's have a look at you."

In the room next door, pale and shaking, Jonathan Baker attempted to tie his own cravat for the third time. "God, Shane, you get to stand there—cool as a cucumber! I have to walk down that long aisle out there with all those eyes glued to my back."

"Here!" Shane said, taking the ends of Jonathan's necktie into his own steady hands and tying a smart knot. "It's all in the wrist, see!"

Jonathan looked in the mirror. Perfect.

"They won't be looking at you, anyway!" Shane informed him. "They're only going to be looking at Morgana. Men are merely incidental accessories in weddings. Weddings are all about brides—always have been—always will be. Why, Pa and I'll be standing there watching Morgana, too. And like everybody else, we'll be thinking what a lucky bastard I am. And wondering, no doubt, how out of all the other bastards in the whole wide world, she chose me! Right, Pa?"

"She chose you with good reason, Shane." Roger Moss laid his hand on his son's shoulder and looked him squarely in the eyes. "I can't think of a better man I've ever known, living or dead, and I'm honored to be your best man. Morgana Heirs is fortunate to have won your admiration, though I feel for the grieving hearts of all the young ladies at Mistress Campbell's House."

"You knew about that?" Shane asked, a shy grin creeping across his face.

"Petersburg is not so large a town that a boy of fifteen—or in later years, freshly home on school vacations isn't noticed slipping into the town's only brothel.

"You never said a word!" Shane laughed, reddening.

"No, and your mother never knew, of course," Roger Moss said. "Unless human nature has changed mightily since I was a young pup, I should think that genteel behavior on the part of her lover is still highly desired by any young lady of breeding who might be contemplating marriage. And, likewise, any young stud worth his salt should prize a good education in lovemaking. I can only assume that in all these years, you've learned your lessons well."

Through his own nervousness, Jonathan beamed, watching father and son in perfect harmony and understanding.

At the stroke of one, the strains of Wagner's wedding march filled the church. The groom and best man, standing atop the altar steps looked to the back of the church and saw Laura Lee's Alice strewing rose petals in the aisle while her brother, Andy, walked beside her carefully balancing a narrow circle of gold on a delicate blue silk pillow. Next, Laura Lee Baker and Willow Heirs walked side by side, each carrying a small nosegay of fragrant cape jasmine blossoms tied up with lavender and blue ribbons.

Following at a precisely determined distance, Jonathan Baker stepped through the double doors with Morgana on his arm. Necks craned on both sides of the aisle as Jonathan quickly found the tempo and led Morgana forward to the alter, step by step, in perfect time with the music.

When Morgana reached Shane's side and they stood together ready to take their sacred vows a venerating silence filled the church. Not a cough. Not a sneeze. It was then that Reverend Wylie opened his Bible and solemnly began, "Dearly beloved, we are gathered here, today, in the presence of God and of men, to join together in the bonds of holy matrimony this man and this woman—"

The Honeymoon

Apart from of the four hundred present in church for the wedding, at the more intimate reception that followed, one hundred and forty-two honored guests spilled over from *Briars'* wraparound verandah where the food service had been situated onto the tattered gardens, the driveway, and the lawns. Toasts having been raised, Rachel's lighter than air white wedding cake having been cut and enjoyed, gorged and giddy honored guests sipped the last of the French champagne.

"It wasn't nearly as bad as you thought it would be, now, was it?" Morgana asked Shane as they shared private words beneath the giant spreading oak, apart from the chattering company.

"In an hour it'll be even better," Shane said, handling the small meerschaum pipe he had recently begun to enjoy. "We'll be on our way to New Orleans—finally just the two of us."

Morgana laughed. "I think Mama has outdone herself, don't you? Our wedding has been all—no, more—than I could have ever wished for." Her eyes shimmered with unshed tears. "I've thought of my sister, Sarah, so many times today. It should have been her wedding, you know. First hers—then mine. I've even worn her wedding dress. Do you think she knows, Shane? I've never put much stock in Heaven and all that holy-holy talk, but today I think I've been closer to such feelings than ever before."

"Weddings do that to people," Shane said, looking away. "I believe she's in Heaven. I have to. I'd never be able to live with myself, if I didn't. I still feel a gnawing guilt every time I hear your sister's name. If I'd been awake and alert, that shameful crime would never have happened."

"I won't have you talking like that, Shane Moss! Mama has already told you how it happened. Why, Mama says you were as much a victim of those crimes as we were."

"We?" Shane searched Morgana's eyes. "Sarah—that would be *'she'*. Why did you say *'we'*, Morgana?"

Morgana would have answered, willingly, except for the intrusion of Mistress Clark. She forced a smile as the woman neared. "Thank you for coming to our wedding and reception, Mistress Clark. I understand from Willow, you have mentioned to her today that you're willing to consider allowing your servants' children to attend her 'colored children's classroom' once she has it going. That would be very decent of you."

"Teaching young coloreds to read and count may lead to more problems than she—or you, Morgana—could ever dream of! But, since times are changing so fast, if schooling for 'coloreds' must come, then I want mine to be among the first to learn. Mister Clark is not of that opinion, however, and I cannot say definitely yet, you understand."

Feeling her resentment rise, Morgana opened her mouth to say more, but reading her, Shane interrupted, "It was my distinct pleasure to have made your acquaintance earlier, Mistress Clark. However, if you'll excuse us, ma'am, it's time we prepared for our departure."

"I *do* hope Mister Clark is well," Morgana said, pointedly. "I have not seen him about at all, today."

"Mister Clark is unwell and forced abed, I'm afraid," she replied. "Thank you, though, my dear, for asking."

"Good afternoon, Mistress Clark," Morgana said. "And I am *so* honored that you have favored us with your presence today." Morgana executed a deep curtsy, before Shane dragged her off her stance, leading her away towards the house.

"That wasn't really necessary, was it?" Shane asked, laughing quietly as they ran.

Morgana glanced over her shoulder at the look of wonderment still etched on Mistress Clark's face. "It should give that intolerant old social climber puzzlement enough to last a while!"

"Until our return, at least, I'll bet!" Shane said, and when they reached the steps, he urged Morgana, "Hurry and change, 'Gana. We can't be late for our honeymoon."

"You called me 'Gana'!" Morgana said, pleased. "Only members of my family have ever called me 'Gana' before."

"I am your family, now," Shane said.

Confession

Comfortably settled in their sleeping car as darkness fell, the gaslight having been lowered; the only sound that of the clicking rails; an exhausted Morgana, in her prettiest silk peignoir and gown nestled in Shane's arms, sighed, and said, "Tell me I'm not dreaming."

"Ah, but you *are* dreaming," Shane said, "—and so am I! I have dreamed this dream so many times before."

"You have? Of me?" Morgana asked, pouting impishly. "Or, perhaps, of one of Mistress Campbell's painted ladies in Petersburg? You can't know how jealous I was when I saw you exchanging words with them in such accustomed familiarity."

"You mustn't worry about those dear ladies. They were essential to making you appreciate me all the more."

"Oh, you are so conceited, Shane Moss!" she said, pretending anger.

Shane kissed her then, passionately, and Morgana, reminded of their past together and aware of his rising excitement, felt her own physical urgings pulse with impatience.

Once again, as in his dreams of her, Shane was enraptured by Morgana's sensuality—her sweet scent—her luscious lips—her soft and eager body arching to his touch. The hauntingly beautiful Morgana Heirs of his dreams had escaped confinement

Ann Gray

tonight for all time. N*ow*, tonight—he would unravel the mystery of Morgana Heirs—no, of Morgana Heirs Moss.

As they stood facing each other, swaying with the movement of the train, when Shane began unbuttoning his shirt Morgana reached out and caught his hands. "Wait!" she said. "Before you disrobe, there's something I must say, my darling."

"Oh, God, Morgana! Must you—now?" Shane caught her up in his arms again and kissed her with fiery passion.

"Shane, I am not virgin," she said. As the words penetrated his fervor, Shane paled. "I know I should have told you before we married," Morgana said. "—but there were reasons why I couldn't. Tonight, you would soon have found out for yourself, anyway, so I wanted to tell you—first."

She watched him sway under the shock of her blunt statement, then he turned away and ran his fingers through his sun-streaked hair.

Morgana continued. "It happened that morning last November to Laura Lee and me—as well as to Sarah. But we—that is, Laura Lee and I, *both,* had left our rooms against your orders, I'm afraid."

"That's what you were trying to tell me when that Clark woman came along, then?" Shane slammed his fist against the closed door of the compartment.

Morgana kissed his bruised knuckles. "Yes, my darling." It was then she was certain she would never tell him of the child lost in the train derailment.

"Which one was it? I must know! Did he hurt you?"

"On the contrary, he was the perfect gentleman. It was my first and only coupling with a man, you see, and I'm ashamed to say I found it absolutely thrilling."

"My God, Morgana, what are you saying? You were *raped* and you enjoyed it?"

"Oh, I must confess, I'm afraid I did." She untied the strings of her dressing gown and continued, "I can describe the man." As she spoke, Morgana slowly unbuttoned Shane's shirt. "He has a distinguishing mark. Not a mark that would normally be seen by anyone unless they were quite intimately engaged. An old scar—a crescent shaped scar—on his breast bone." When she opened the fourth button of his shirt she said, "There it is." She leaned forward and kissed the mark as she let her silken finery fall in a heap around her bare feet. "There is so much to tell, my darling," Morgana said, standing before him in unabashed natural beauty. "So very much more!"

"Later," Shane said, for Morgana's confession had dispelled the mystery behind her haunting presence in his thoughts, waking or sleeping. Eagerly he kissed her lips, her breasts, her belly, and after he lifted her onto the swaying berth, the clicking of the rails droned on and on, unnoticed.

Motive

Mistress Althea Clark paced the floor, watching her husband, Ezra, don his freshly washed, starched and ironed white robes.

"Tell me you won't do this, Ezra!" she pleaded. "I was there, and it was no different from any other wedding. Maybe a little fancier but not like you say, 'unholy'. I'd give anything to have seen our girl married in a church like that." Althea Clark turned accusing eyes on her husband. "Don't you ever wonder where she is, Ezra? Don't you ever worry what happened to Carla after she ran away? She was just a child, Ezra."

"*Never!*" the Klansman answered. "It was her choice to leave us! Now, don't let me hear you say her name again—ever! And that wedding *was* different! There was niggers mixing with white folks publicly, defilin' a holy weddin' in the sight of *God!*"

"Only one, Ezra, and she was white as you and me," Mistress Clark explained.

His hand flashed across her face and left its crimson imprint on her cheek. "White as *who?*" he said. "You watch your mouth, woman!"

"I only meant—oh, please, don't do this! Back off, now! You've let all the 'nigger talk' down there in that old meeting house get you all keyed up. Please, Ezra, don't go tonight! Tell them you're sick!"

"Don't go and say I'm sick? I'm sick, all right. Sick of seeing Morgan Heirs' family enjoying wealth rightfully should have been mine all these years! Sick of watching the whole damn town cater to them."

"It's been twenty years, Ezra! Over time, you've butchered his bird dog, stole from his root cellar, wrecked his office and left that disgusting dead weasel; you even burned his barn! Ezra, the man's dead."

"I should've killed th' son-of-a-bitch long ago! I thought about it enough times—"

"You weren't cut out to be a killer, Ezra, and I thank the good Lord every day for that!" She stood back and watched as Ezra pulled the clean, white sheet down over his shoulders.

"Everything they've got should've been mine! Just like that land was mine! What you're talkin' about was nuisance stuff compared to this, Allie! The she-nigger was going to school picaninnies there in that barn! School them picaninnies and they'll think they're good as whites when they grow up!" He pulled the pointed hood down over his head and fitted the eye holes so that his steely gray eyes peered out. "Use your head, Allie? The she-nigger's been the bait I used to get the Klavern all riled up!" He posed before the mirror. "If it hadn't been for the Klan I'd still be a nobody! Hell, Allie, they've just made me Nighthawk of the whole damn Klavern! I'm somebody! Tonight, I'm in control of a major operation, and I like it!"

The door slammed behind him and Althea Clark fell across her bed and wept tears of regret and despair.

CHAPTER FIFTEEN ~ LOYALTY

5:30 p.m., September 15, 1867 ~ Briars, Atlanta, Georgia

Adversity

Lillian Heirs had seen the last of the reception guests pass through the gates a little after five o'clock, and by six-thirty, Rachel, Willow, and Henry had the verandah cleared and everything on the outside back to normal again. Lillian had sent the Baker families back to their respective homes with baskets full of leftovers. The soup kettle, containing the meaty bones from hams and vegetable odds and ends, was already on the stove where it would simmer all night.

Lillian closed her bedroom door as the clock on her mantle chimed ten. It had been a grueling day, but a satisfying one.

As she took down her braids and brushed out her snowy hair, she reflected: Never had she seen Morgana more vital, more beautiful. She smiled, going back in memory to the day Rachel had come chasing after her to 'see to' the child who had gathered her clothes from her mother's chest of drawers and moved into her own room down the hall. How could that toddler have grown so quickly into the strong-willed and perceptive woman wed today. Through shame that might easily have thwarted a weaker spirit, Morgana—a victim of rape, pregnant and unwed, had found courage and endurance sufficient to deliver her to this happy day. If anyone had asked Lillian how this miraculous destiny had come to pass, she would have told them to ask God for she truly had not one earthly clue, herself.

It was nearing midnight when Storm's barking outside her window aroused Lillian from a deep, sound sleep. Before her thoughts could take form, shots rang out, and Storm's barking ceased. A brilliance reflected onto her bedroom wall casting her shadow, tall and angular, as she ran to the window. By the light of the flaming cross on her lawn, she saw the body swinging from the lowest limb of the oak tree.

Barefoot, her nightgown flapping, Lillian ran fast as she could down the stairs, out the front door, and across the lawn, past the burning cross and the motionless animal lying beneath it, to the oak tree. Following after an hysterical Rachel, who had gotten there moments before, Lillian cried out in shock and horror at the sight of Henry, his neck broken, his long legs dangling two feet above the ground.

But he could not hear their cries.

Rachel reached out and caught Henry's dancing feet, crying bitter tears. "He hear'd Storm barkin'!" she rasped as Lillian approached. "And thought he hear'd th' front gates squeakin' open, Miz Lillian! I tol' him he 'as jus' dreamin', but he 'as goin' t' check did he remember t' close 'em this afte'noon, anyway."

Wil plunged through the front door next. He saw Storm lying motionless and bloody in the flare from the cross and he sickened, knowing his dog was dead, but being followed closely by Roger Moss, Wil ran on to help bring Henry down.

"They 'as goin' set fire t' th' house wit' torches!" Rachel cried, holding Henry's dead body and rocking. "They must o' be'd twelve o' 'em! Oh, my po' Henry! My po' *dead* Henry! Oh, Lord God, *please* let me come wit' him!"

Disbelieving the scene before her, Willow stopped on the top step of the verandah, but coming behind her, Mistress Moss embraced the shaking and woeful young woman and whispered words of consolation to her.

Lillian reached down and lifted Rachel to her feet and held the round woman's wretched anguish in her arms, and when she looked back at the house, in the firelight she saw the dripping words emblazoned in Storm's blood on the front door: "NIGGER LOVERS".

Lillian gave Rachel a heavy dose of Laudanum and put her back to bed but not another living soul in *Briars* slept the rest of

Briars
The House of Heirs

that night. She had Grady and Thomas bring Henry's body to the dining room table, where she and Patricia Moss prepared it for burial.

With Grady's borrowed shovel, Wil stole away in the wee hours packing Storm's body across Pal's saddle and he laid their good companion to rest in a secret place known only to the three of them. When he returned from his private mission, he dragged the smoldering cross around back and chopped it into firewood.

The sun was barely peeking above the horizon when a tearful Willow scrubbed the offensive words from the front door.

At six o'clock sharp, Lillian Heirs summoned every living soul on the Heirs' estate together on *Briars*' front verandah. Then, to the wonderment of all present, she ordered Grady and Thomas to bring down *Briars*' giant old oak tree in homage to their beloved Henry.

The first chopping blows echoed from the hilltop bringing neighbors and their servants to stand outside the iron gates to watch. In the first hour, Lillian bade Willow to go fetch a pail of water and a dipper and to bring back churned butter and fresh baked bread to strengthen the two hard working men for it would take time to fell the tree. Volunteers offered to spell Henry's good friends in their enormous task but Thomas and Grady waved them away. They remained at their labor the eight solid hours it took to fell the great oak tree where Henry Heirs had met his violent end.

At twilight, in a pinewood casket handmade by Jeremiah Baker, Henry was laid to rest in a corner of the pasture cemetery not too far from where Morgan and Sweet Sarah Heirs slept. Willow sang her papa's favorite hymn "Swing Low, Sweet Chariot" and Lillian supported Rachel through the short family graveside service.

Afterwards, Grady and Thomas, fearful for their own lives, packed up their meager belongings from their room in the stable and, in the middle of the night, with a month's wages and Miz Lillian's blessings left *Briars* for good and always.

Willow laid aside her plans for the 'colored children's classroom'. That dream had died along with her father and now her sole concern would be keeping her grieving mother sane and occupied, for Rachel refused from that day forward to leave the confines of the house even for the gardens.

The law had given Henry's demise only cursory attention. Of more concern to the local peacekeepers was the burning of the Heirs' old barn, a far greater value being placed on white folk's property than on a Negro man's life. By the acerbic nature of responses Lillian received, she had no doubt that some of the very men whom she'd called upon for justice were members of the organization that had forged the family Heirs' adversity. Amid multiple offers to buy the Heirs' property Lillian was outspoken, refusing to be driven from her home of thirty years by a band of cowardly hate-mongers hiding their identities beneath hoods. If, she informed them, she could expect no punishment to be forthcoming for the culprits, at least, she would not give them the satisfaction of leaving *Briars*. In the next few days, Lillian's every effort to hire new workers, white or black, met with rejection.

On September eighteenth, as planned earlier, Roger and Patricia Moss left *Briars* for home. Lillian decided that under present conditions it would be best to send Star back again to the Moss farm along with the fine young colt, Blaze. In vain, the Mosses argued with Lillian that she and Wil should go at once, with Rachel and Willow, to the O'Donnell house in Richmond for safety's sake. But Lillian would not to be moved.

Between them, Wil and Roger loaded the luggage onto the wagon and tied the mare and colt on behind. They followed the carriage into town. With Lillian driving and Patricia on the bench beside her, people they passed on the road looked away. Lillian reckoned they all knew of the Klan's crimes at *Briars* and seeing nothing had been done to find and punish the guilty, folks were fearful to acknowledge her lest the Klan act against them, too.

"Oh, Lillian, my dear," Patricia said, when they were parting. "It hurts me to see you in such straits. Won't you please reconsider and leave *Briars* just until this storm blows over?"

Lillian's usually gentle voice grew adamant. "I'll *never* abandon *Briars!* Morgan Heirs didn't build that house for me so that in bad times I could walk away and leave it for those zealots in bed sheets to burn down."

In late afternoon, after Lillian and Wil returned home from the terminal, they sat down in the kitchen with Rachel and Willow and divided up the chores. Wil would keep the grounds and stables, tend the horses, and chop wood. Rachel would milk the cow, gather eggs, bake, cook, and clean the kitchen. Willow would wash clothes and iron, polish silver, and clean downstairs. Lillian would clean the upper rooms, sew whatever needed patching, do shopping and run errands into town where she would keep up with Tom Garrett's handling of her finances. Such an arduous routine would work out, she deemed, only if they all tried very, very hard.

They would test the new schedule for the remaining three weeks and five days until Morgana and Shane returned from their honeymoon. So many events had taken place at *Briars* in the young married couple's absence! Only two days, and already another soul had gone on, and those remaining had changed beyond imagining.

After Morgana and Shane's return, what then? Lillian refused even to think beyond that point.

Natchez

The grand old Rob't E. Lee steamed sluggishly up the middle of the broad Mississippi river, its paddles slapping the muddy water in rhythmic tempo. Every table in the buffet area on the open deck had been filled but now satisfied diners were seeking other activities.

"I cannot eat another bite," Morgana sighed, leaning back in her chair and looking out beyond the railing of the slow moving riverboat. "And, I've never tasted such deliciously different cuisine," she added, watching a graceful white bird on stilts walking through the high weeds on the shallows of the distant riverbank. "If I'm not careful, I shall begin to look like that pregnant woman over there with those two small children hanging onto her skirts. Traveling while pregnant and with two small children cannot be for pleasure! The older of the children doesn't appear to be more than two. Imagine! Suddenly, I'm very aware of the pitfalls of family life I've heard Mama talk about so often. Do you want a large family, Shane? We've never discussed such things."

Shane filled his pipe and took a deep puff as he lit it. The smoke smelled of cherry as it wafted up and away. "Two," he said, finally, cradling the bowl of the small pipe in his hand. "Preferably, one of each. If we should get two of one kind, we'll send one back."

Morgana laughed. "Oh? Don't count on that!"

The woman looked their way and quickly hastened to leave her table, disappearing with her energetic charges into the lounge. Suddenly, the woman's face re-appeared, peeking through the curtained glass of the closed lounge doors and this time she looked squarely at Morgana before disappearing again into the room.

"That's strange," Morgana said. "That woman! She came back to look at me again through the glass of the door, there."

"Nothing strange about it, darling," Shane said, perfectly convinced of his reasoning. "It's common knowledge aboard that we're honeymooning, you know. As you say, she was probably envying your youth and good looks."

"No, I'm sure it was more than that," Morgana answered, unsmiling. "She recognized me! And she wasn't pleased at seeing me, either. Strange, I have the peculiar feeling that I should know her, too. But, honestly, right now, I can't remember from where!"

"You're imagining things, my love." He pulled her to her feet and withdrew a small pamphlet from his pocket, peering at it. "Natchez is just ahead. Are you interested in going ashore? Or shall we retire to our stateroom and allow the afternoon to pass without notice?"

The gist of his unspoken message flew past her as, eyeing the entrance to the lounge, Morgana repeated, thoughtfully, "— Going ashore? I don't think so. There's only so much space in our luggage for souvenirs, and I have already filled that beyond its limits. If you'd care to browse about ashore, however, feel free to do so. I think for a change I should like to spend some time in the lounge. Perhaps make a few acquaintances. Would you like that, dear?"

"I can't think of anything I'd dislike more!" Shane said, allowing his disappointment to show. "I'm running quite low on tobacco, though. There must be a tobacco shop near the docks where I'll find my cure."

Morgana smiled, warming his disposition. "The aroma is delightful by the way, and I've been meaning to comment on it." She frowned, playfully. "Darling, we have taken every step together since we boarded. Perhaps we will survive without each other's company for an hour or two if you will promise not to be gone too long?"

Shane grinned, realizing the truth of her words. "Promise. Now let me escort you to a chair in the lounge. I see we're heading in already."

Looking around the large room filled with plush settees, chairs, and writing tables, Morgana was not surprised to see that, although the room was occupied by many others, the staring woman was no longer present. She had passed through with her small troupe and gone on to some other part of the floating hotel.

Ann Gray

Her comfortable seat by a window in the lounge overlooked the deck and commanded a view of the gangplank, thus Morgana could watch Shane leaving and returning from her chair. She waved "good-bye" to him through the glass and when he had gone ashore, she smiled at a woman sitting on a nearby settee. After they had chatted for a reasonable time, Morgana inquired of her, "There was an expectant woman with two adorable small children dining near our table earlier. I shouldn't think there'd be too many passengers aboard with such a retinue. She seemed very familiar to me but for the world her name escapes me. Would you know her name, by chance?"

"You would be talking about Mistress Andrews. An interesting woman, if too brash at times. She and her husband are returning home to Natchez from New Orleans, where he's been in hospital." She smiled, having produced the information so readily, then qualified it: "Oh, my dear, you know how people like to talk to strangers when traveling. Not at all unusual. She spoke to me about her husband's illness. Poor dear, she's so distraught. He has left her alone with those children most of the time while, according to my own husband, he's spent his time in the Grand Saloon drinking and, no doubt, gambling."

"That is such a shame," Morgana said, losing interest at once. Relieved that the peering woman's name meant absolutely nothing to her.

"Oh, there go the Andrews, now," the talkative lady said, looking out the window and back again to Morgana as the family headed down the gangplank. Morgana paled and leapt from her chair, running towards the lounge's closed doors. "My goodness, dear girl, what is it?" the lady asked, shaken.

"Excuse me!" Morgana threw the words back over her shoulder. "I'm sorry! I just remembered who she is! I have to catch them before they disappear!"

Morgana left the boat and climbed the wickedly steep embankment to reach the busy roadway where she paused to catch her breath beneath a sign that read: Silver Street. She followed a few feet behind the family as they made their way slowly along amidst other discharged passengers to the carriage station above the busy dock.

The father obviously cared for his children, lifting the smallest of the two onto his shoulders, and bouncing him as they waited their turn for an empty cab. Then, as Morgana watched, he settled his wife and two children inside the carriage, paid the driver proper fares, and sent them on their way, turning his attention immediately to a nearby pub. As he walked towards the establishment, Morgana chased after him.

"Mr. Andrews!" she called. "Wait, *please*, I must speak to you!"

Without turning, he hastened his pace and Morgana was forced to run to catch up to him. "She told you she recognized me, didn't she?" she called out, breathlessly, to the man's back when he refused to wait for her. "It *was* Stella. I remember, now! She told you she'd seen me and you chose to run away without *ever* even speaking to me! *Why, Drew?*"

"Leave it alone, Morgana!" He shook her off when she grabbed his sleeve. "I was *dead!* Just let me *stay* dead!"

"You are my *brother*, Drew, and you will always be my brother!" Morgana sobbed, tears bursting forth, as she watched him walk away.

Mister Andrews stopped, and returned to take the tearful Morgana in his arms. "My God, 'Gana, you're a woman!" he said, and he embraced her and kissed her cheek.

"A *married* woman!" Morgana corrected him. "Oh, Drew, I can't believe it's really you! Where can we talk?"

"Not here," Drew said, directing her away from the pub's entrance. "I'll walk you back to the boat. You had no business leaving without an escort. Where's your husband?"

"He went in search of a tobacco shop." Morgana wiped her eyes. "Oh, Drew, why did you do this to us? Why—why—why?"

Minutes later, back aboard the riverboat, they sat at a writing table in a corner of the deserted lounge. Drew had chosen this spot away from conversational groupings in the event that the room might become occupied by others during their talk, but with most of the passengers ashore and Morgana's recent companion having departed, the room was theirs.

Morgana dried her eyes and waited anxiously for Drew to speak.

His face was strained as he began, "You're old enough now to understand my predicament. Also, in being married yourself, you will know what I mean when I say, I could not endure marriage to a woman I did not love."

Morgana drew in her breath quickly, so shocked was she at his declaration.

"Bear with me, 'Gana," Drew said, reaching for her hand. "The marriage to Laura Lee was a mistake to begin with—an arrangement between our father and hers. Morgana, it was a business deal! I would marry Laura Lee and give her security. And marriage to her would, supposedly, contain my foolishness with women, liquor and money. Sad to say, it didn't! The twins came, and then the war, and—"

"No, I can't believe what you're saying," Morgana frowned and looked away.

Drew gently turned her chin and continued, his eyes burning into hers. "When Stella Farley left Atlanta, my world shattered into a million pieces. Can you understand what I mean when I say, I *tried* to forget her? Can you understand when I say, I knew from the first time she lured me into the hay loft of her father's barn, I was in love with her? Can you understand, too, that when the difference in her station in life and ours grew so far apart, I hated myself for my weakness and my need for her? 'Gana, no matter how I pretended that I was happy in my marriage to Laura Lee, it wasn't true, and it wasn't enough! It was never enough. I never stopped seeing Stella. Laura Lee was far too proper, too genteel for me, 'Gana." As he talked the words came easier. "And then, when Jonny and I went away to war, and the opportunity presented itself for me to disappear at Mobile Bay—well, I took it! Jonny and I had been assigned separately and I knew he saw the barrage we were under. I knew, too, that when he came looking for me later and didn't find me, he'd go back and report me dead or, at least, missing. The rest you can guess. I knew where Stella had gone and I followed her here."

Morgana looked away again, unwilling to see the depth of pain mirrored in his eyes. "Laura Lee mourned you, Drew! We all did. And all this time we thought you dead, you were here—here, and happy in your new life!"

"Not wholly happy! Ours is a common law marriage. The children are ours, but they bear the name of Andrews. Their father, being known as James Andrews since August of 1864, has no background, no past, no family other than the one you saw here aboard the riverboat."

"How do you live?" Morgana asked, candidly.

"Honestly? From hand to mouth. I manage a small dry goods store. And I put back each morning what I borrow from the till for gambling the night before. So far, I've kept my family fairly well fed and the owner off my back. Stella's managed to save a little from my winnings." He winked, grinning. "Occasionally, there are dry spells."

"And your health is bad, too, I understand."

Drew looked puzzled.

"A passenger who spent time with Stella related it to me." Morgana's tone softened. "You have inherited our father's poor health as well as his passion for gambling and drinking. That *is* unfortunate."

"Isn't it?" he laughed. "I must stop drinking and control my temper, though, or they tell me I shall soon die. That wouldn't be fair to Stella. I was about to have my last drink when you encountered me."

"Your *last* drink? Can I truly believe that, Drew?" Morgana asked. "For the good of your family, I hope so. How is Stella? She looked worn out when I saw her, earlier, on deck. I didn't even recognize her though she did know me, obviously."

"She is due to deliver our third child in a month. After that, I have promised to modify my demands for her health's sake." He laughed. "Tell me about my twins, and Laura Lee. Are they doing well? Ma and Pa? How are my other sister and brother?"

Drew was pleased when Morgana told him about the twins' recent spurt of growth, and glad to learn of Laura Lee's blissful re-marriage to Jonathan Baker. Happy, with Morgana's account of Wil's maturing into a fine young man. Intrigued, when she told of Mama's and her own travels. And, finally, saddened, when she told him of his father's passing and his sister's awful fate.

While they talked, time had flown and passengers were starting to come aboard again. When Drew said, regretfully, that he must leave, Morgana swiftly penned a note on a piece of stationery bearing a miniature trademark of the riverboat, and laid it before him on the writing table.

"I must ask that you sign this statement before you go, Drew. I hope that you will understand its purpose and not hold this action against me. It's to protect the rights of those you abandoned to pursue your present course."

Drew read the paper and, looking about, asked two gentlemen passengers entering the lounge to witness his signature, adding their names and addresses to the document. "There, now," he said, laying down the pen after signing his proper name to it, "—there can never be any doubt that this statement was properly taken." He thanked the witnesses and when they were alone again he said, "I understand your feelings but, on my honor, there was never any reason to fear. I would never have come back to Atlanta."

"Now, that you have signed away your birthright, the entire inheritance passes to Wil and me. We will always see that Laura

Lee and the twins are well cared for. You've done the right thing, and though I admire your professed good intentions, Drew, I do not feel that you are trustworthy after all that has gone before."

"You've grown shrewd as well as beautiful," Drew said, rising from his chair.

Morgana got to her feet and, folding the paper, slipped it into her purse as Shane entered the lounge and walked towards them.

"Hello, darling, did you find your tobacco?" Morgana greeted Shane, lightly. And when he said that he had, she said to Drew, "This is my husband, Shane Moss." And to Shane, "Darling, let me introduce Mister James Andrews. We've just had the most interesting conversation about life here on the Mississippi. Haven't we, Mister Andrews?" She held out her hand to Drew. "I've so enjoyed meeting you, sir, and I do hope you will fare well in future."

Drew brushed his lips ever so lightly across Morgana's hand, his eyes meeting hers, as he said, "A pleasure meeting you, Mistress Moss." He turned to Shane and said, "You are a most fortunate man, sir, to have won such a lovely and intelligent woman for your own."

"True, sir, every word," Shane said, smiling with pride.

As Drew hurried away, Morgana moved again to the window overlooking the gangplank. Shane followed and together they watched as James Andrews, never once looking back, made his way down the gangplank and climbed the steep embankment to Silver Street, the ribald district which lies below the tall cliffs of Mississippi's prestigious port of Natchez.

"That was a stroke of luck, wasn't it—your finding someone interesting to talk with while I was gone?"

"An extraordinary stroke of luck!" Morgana agreed.

Homecoming

"Hurry, Wil, drive faster!" Lillian called anxiously from inside the carriage. "They'll be wondering what's happened to us."

"Ma, we've got plenty of time, and Mary Belle won't go no faster! You know that good as I do!"

Lillian leaned forward so that Wil wouldn't miss the warning in her tone. "Not a word to 'Gana about the way things are. I'll try to break it to her about poor Henry and Storm, and about Star and the colt being gone as easy as I can. No need to upset her soon as she steps off the train."

"She'll know something's wrong when she don't see the oak tree from the road," Wil said.

"I want to have it all said by the time we get that far." Lillian sat back and folded her hands. "If I can remember my speech in proper order, it will all be told by then. Gently told, and with no tears on my part."

"Tell her it's the damned Ku Klux Klan we got to do battle with now! She's already had a taste of them. At least, if we take them on this time Shane will be fighting on our side." Wil looked away into the distance. "I remember a time when you had Henry, and Laura Lee and 'Gana and me, all, ready to do battle with them damn Yankees. Now you say we got to sit still and wait on the law to punish our damn enemies. Them being Southerners to boot! And, Ma, the law ain't going to do 'doodle-dee-squat'!" Wil looked sheepishly over his shoulder at his mother. "I'm sorry, Ma, but I get so confounded mad with the way things keep happening!"

"I know, son," she said. "But you've just got to realize, there's too many of them, and too few of us. At least, with the Yankees we knew how many we would be dealing with. With the Klan? Well, God only knows how many of them live in

Briars
The House of Heirs

Atlanta acting like just regular folks. And they'll be like hornets—step on one and the whole swarm will be on you in a wink. We can't take on the whole Klan by ourselves, Wil, I only wish we could." Lillian reached out to pat him on his back and she smiled with pride at her son's unmistakable courage. "Now, let's put all this kind of talk back on the shelf and get our best faces on for the returning bride and groom. Not one word out of you about the Klan, Wil, do you understand?"

Wil did. He'd tied Mary Belle to the hitching post and had barely helped Lillian from the carriage, when three short blasts of the train's whistle announced its imminent arrival. They reached the platform, all smiles and happiness, as arriving passengers began emerging from openings the length of the train.

"Shane, over here!" Lillian called out over the noise of the bustling crowds, waving her handkerchief above her head when she saw him. "Hurry, Wil, go help Shane with those bundles. My stars, Morgana must have bought out New Orleans!"

Morgana leapt from the step and plowed through the throng running into Lillian's open arms and she kissed her mother's lips. "Oh, Mama, it was such fun," Morgana said, breathlessly, "You have never seen such sights!"

"Let me look at you!" Lillian said. "Never imagined I'd ever miss anybody so much in such a short time. So, you've enjoyed your honeymoon? And how is my son-in-law?" Lillian asked.

"Shane?" Morgana grinned, reading the hidden question in her mother's eyes. "I adore him, Mama. You will never regret your choice of son-in-law." When Lillian smiled, a faint but comprehending smile, Morgana continued, "When you spared him in the battle at *Briars*—I knew that you valued him, Mama. And rightly so, though I swear I could not see it then." Morgana hugged her mother, and noticing her thinness, looked again, deeper into Lillian's eyes. "You don't look well, Mama. Tell me what's wrong."

Lillian felt what little strength she had mustered for their meeting flow from her and her wretchedness poured forth as Morgana supported her and they walked back to the carriage some distance ahead of Shane and Wil.

"Henry's down in the cemetery," Lillian lamented, tears flowing for the first time since Morgana's wedding. "The Klan tried to burn *Briars* the night you left, and Henry came upon them, and they shot Storm and hung Henry from our oak tree. Oh, 'Gana, I made Grady and Thomas chop down the oak tree! Then I let them go, and now it's just Willow and Rachel, and Wil and me. I'm sorry, dear, but I had to send Star and Blaze back to Virginia with the Mosses to insure their safety. Oh, 'Gana, it's been just awful!"

Listening to her mother's concise report, Morgana's tears surged to the surface and by the time the men reached the carriage with the valises and packages—inside, the two women clung to one another and wept.

Shane looked quizzically at Wil, so while they loaded the carriage's luggage rack, Wil told Shane all of what had happened in their absence.

Back at *Briars*, Morgana's and Shane's luggage was brought to the West bedroom which had been Drew's and Laura Lee's, at the front of the house, opposite Lillian's.

After Lillian, Wil, and Shane had gone back downstairs, Willow took the opportunity to speak to Morgana in confidence about her mother.

"Morgana," Willow began, "your mother's been having spells of swooning."

"Swooning?" Morgana repeated. "Mama? Whatever do you mean, Willow?"

"I don't know. Mama says she's been trying to hide them, but one time she was just standing beside her bed and fell down and Mama heard the bump and found her. Twice now, she's slid right out of her chair in the parlor while sewing and Mama has found her on the floor, the same. All three times, Mama's revived her with smelling salts. When she would get back to herself, she'd say, 'Now, Rachel, you know how I dislike doctors. Forget what just happened!' And she would, but first she'd tell me."

"Mama mustn't know you have told me." Morgana looked away towards the open door. "Does Wil know?"

"Not from me! But I can guarantee you, your mama'd be mad right now if she had any idea you knew!"

"Thank you, Willow. She'll never know I heard it from you, I promise. I'll have to find an excuse, though, to get her to a doctor's office, won't I? Let me think about it for a day or so. We don't want to be too obvious, do we? After all, we just got home." Morgana hugged Willow and handed her a gift box. "Here! This is for you, Willow! It's from the French Quarter in New Orleans!"

Willow ran her fingers over the small white box tied with a pale blue ribbon. "Now what have you done?"

"Open it! How else will you ever know what's inside?"

Willow carefully removed the pale blue ribbon and opened the box, reaching in to withdraw the small oddly shaped blue bottle of perfume."

"It's called *Nuit Enchanté*. It's French. And it means 'enchanted night'! You simply must try it out on Mister Tubbs—"

"I thank you for the gift, but—Mister Tubbs?" Willow looked askance at Morgana. "Now, *whatever do you* mean?"

"—Never mind! Open it! You'll love it, I promise."

Before Willow could open the bottle the sound of excited voices in the hallway brought both of them flying to the door. Wil, pale and anxious, called to Morgana as he ran alongside Shane, who carried an unconscious Lillian in his arms, "Turn down Mama's bed, 'Gana, something terrible's happened!"

Morgana hurried across the hall to Lillian's room, and Willow, who ran to look for the smelling salts, met Rachel puffing up the stairs with the bottle in her hand.

"She done lef' it in th' parlor," Rachel explained, handing the bottle to Willow. "Lordy, Lordy, please he'p us, God! Don't take Miz Lillian away from us, too!" Rachel prayed, hurrying toward the front of the house behind Willow.

Before Rachel reached the room, Wil passed her heading for the back stairs. "Rachel, tell Morgana I'm going for a doctor. I ought to be back with one in an hour or so!" From the other end of the house at the top of the back stairs, Wil paused to shout back down the corridor, "If Ma comes awake and asks for me, tell her I've gone fishing! Tell her anything but that I'm getting a doctor for her! You understand?"

"Yessuh! I sho' do!" And knowing the reasoning behind his words, in spite of her fears, Rachel chuckled.

Something!

The darkened room swarmed with people. Hushed voices murmured, too low to be understood—too loud to be ignored. In her delirium, Lillian strained to make out faces—words.

All at once, she found herself standing on the back porch in bright afternoon sunlight. A younger, slimmer Rachel, stood at her elbow while they watched a crew of Morgan's workmen digging up a long row of the hawthorn hedge. Rachel, disturbed, was speaking quite forcefully, "It 'as bad enough when they cut th'ough th' hedges t' th' stables, Miz Lillian. I knowed when Mister Morgan had them hedges chopped out it 'as goin' to bring on trouble. But now, I's really perturbed 'cause fo' this garden, he done had them make a big, gaping hole in th' circle of protection th' Lord done set about this house like he done for Job."

"Rachel," Lillian heard herself saying with a heavy heart as she watched her efforts come to ruin, "don't forget, it was also by God's own hand that Job's protection was removed. You mustn't worry about it. It's Mister Morgan's property to do with as he sees fit, after all."

Then, it was her own voice and that of Hamita Baker's buzzing in her ears as they sat, together, in the parlor over an afternoon's tea and scones. "I suggested she invite one of her young friends from school, today." Lillian heard herself saying. "The little Cabot girl is quiet and attractive, but Morgana insisted on bringing Willow along. Of course, I agreed. I doubt I could separate the two of them for very long, anyway. They are the best of friends."

Hamita nodded. "A more well-spoken Negro, I've never come across—thanks to your schooling. But do you think that's appropriate? Allowing Willow to go along with you, shopping? Literally, everywhere you go? Especially, in the better stores? After all, she is *still* a Negro and she certainly doesn't fit one's usual mental picture of a 'Mammy'. And, even if you don't fancy calling Willow and her parents 'slaves', she's still a servant girl."

Lillian blinked her away.

Next, it was Drew, leaning down to kiss her lips, and promising to say his prayers, to take care of himself, and to come home safely from the war. Then, somehow, from her bed she watched him halfway down the driveway, turning back to seek her face in the window, and lifting a flying kiss to her.

But then, there beside her bed, she saw Wil's big dog, Storm, being held in check by Henry, who stood with one hand buried in the shepherd's mane, holding firmly onto Storm's collar.

"Storm, old boy," Lillian said, and his plumed tail wagged. "Wil's been looking everywhere for you." Then, she examined Henry's anxious, wrinkled old face. "Henry, you look just awful."

"Yes'm, I's been th' whole night listenin' outside yo' door. Folks is all upset you be so poorly, Miz Lillian!"

"I know, Henry. I'm keeping y'all on tenterhooks, I guess." Lillian frowned. "I'm trying to make up my mind, you see!"

"Yes'm. You go on an' do that, Miz Lillian. Best, we talks later." And when she looked again, Henry and Storm had gone.

Wil came, then, and leaned down to slide a cool, moist kiss across her dry, creased cheek. "Ma, you seen old Storm around?"

"Henry's got him. If you go looking for them, though, promise you'll not go farther than the hedges!" Lillian said, half telling—half asking.

"I can't do that, Ma. I'm going to join the military, now I'm old enough. Give me your blessing, Ma?"

And she sighed and nodded. "Go! Have your way—! I always knew someday you would." And he grinned his crooked little grin and kissed her lips before he left.

"Willow—? Do you hear me, girl? Look alive!"

"Yes'm, I'm here," a mature and lovely Willow answered respectfully, standing in Wil's place beside Lillian's bed.

"Quickly, now—dress the children! Take them, and run along the hedges to the briar cave—" She frowned, worry creasing her brow. "—you understand?"

Willow nodded. "Yes'm, they still play there, now and then." And she moved quickly away.

But Sarah came, at once. Sarah sat, then, on the side of Lillian's bed and peered down into her mother's pained face. "Oh, Mama, I felt so guilty! I was just such a horrible person, I know. But, Mama, I couldn't have married Jonny and had him go off to war to get killed and leave me—maybe pregnant—like Morgana! Who'd have wanted to marry me then?"

Lillian heard herself answering: "Sarah, Jonny married Laura Lee! And they are happy together, now. Your sister, Morgana, married the young Union Army Lieutenant, Shane Moss. You know that, don't you, dear?"

Sarah cried, "Oh, Mama, I love you," and kissed her, hurrying away.

Then, a young and vital Morgan stood at ease peering lovingly into her face. He bent to kiss her warmly before he spoke. "Lilly, Lilly, my love, you've got to do this thing, you know!" Morgan's black eyes gleamed with a familiar light, and he winked at her. "There's really nothing to it!"

"But, Morrey, I've never done it before!" Lillian argued.

"You'd never shot a bear, either, but you did that on your first try!" Morgan cajoled.

"I'm not sure I really want to do it right now, though! There's something—"

"You're waiting for—?"

"I can't rightly remember! But I know it's important—*very* important!" Lillian closed her eyes and struggled to remember. "Something—!" And when she looked again, he was gone. "Morrey? Where are you, Morrey?—*Morrey?*"

"Sh-h-h-h!" Morgana's face filled the vacant space when Lillian opened her eyes. "'Gana's here for you, Mama." Morgana's voice, soft and comforting; her touch, warm and gentle, as she stroked Lillian's brow. "You must have some of this delicious broth Rachel has made for you. Here, let me raise your head a little." Morgana tucked another pillow beneath Lillian's head.

"Where—?" Lillian asked, opening her eyes wide enough to peer about the shadowy room for the first time. None of the other intended words seemed to form properly on her tongue.

"—have they all gone?" Morgana finished the question for her. "To bed," Morgana answered softly, spooning some of the warm broth into Lillian's mouth. "It's late, very late." Lillian coughed, and Morgana wiped the broth from her mother's chin. "You've given us quite a turn, you know. We thought you were going to leave us for a while."

"Why—?" Again the word struggled for form in her mind.

"There's no need trying to fool you, Mama. I've told them, I intend telling you everything. It's no less than I'd expect from you if our positions were reversed."

Lillian nodded, watching Morgana's expression intently for signs of a lie.

Morgana went on. "The doctor says you've had a stroke. You've had others before, little ones, but without knowing about them, how could we help you? You are a long way from being well, Mama. And now that you are in my care, you must eat, take your medicine on time, and rest until you're strong again." Lillian pushed away the spoon, but Morgana remained resolute until the bowl was empty.

The warmth of broth, followed by a spoonful of bitter medicine, soothed Lillian into quiet, restful drowsiness. When, between heavy lids, she saw Morgana set aside the bowl and spoon, she gave in, again, to the ghosts of hallucination.

They were in the carriage with Jonathan and Morgana was asking, sassily, "Mama, must you always talk so much like Sarah? Sarah prayed all the time and I saw what happened to her. Where was God then, Mama?"

And Lillian, had answered almost as lightly as if she were commenting on the weather, "Someday, you will come to call on God, young lady—"

Confused in time, somewhere in the labyrinth between sleep and wakefulness, she heard Morgana's voice, again...

"Please, God, if You are there—" Was it truly Morgana's voice, soft as a whisper, near her ear, praying plaintively? Was it Morgana kneeling, now, beside her bed? Was it Morgana, whose hands tightly grasped both of hers? "God, if You hear me, please don't take my mother away. I'll do anything You say, God, but let us keep her for a little while longer. I wouldn't blame You if You didn't listen to me, now, after all my doubts and accusations but Mama always says You're there for anyone who calls upon Your name. And I do, now. Hear my prayer, please, Lord. But, God—if You need her there, I'll try to understand. *Thy will be done*. Amen."

Something—!

Morgana leaned forward, then, and gently kissed her mother's lips as always.

Amen! Lillian's inner voice sang out, joyfully. Amen, and *hallelujah!* And Lillian Heirs slept—never to waken in this world again.

Funeral Rites

It was bright and clear that Saturday morning, October 19, 1867, when Lillian Heirs' funeral service was celebrated in Briarwood's Community Church. The sanctuary, under the watchful eye of a neatly dressed Reverend Hoyt Wylie, had gradually filled to capacity with loyal friends and admirers of the Heirs' family matriarch. Reverend Wylie looked up and saw that the balcony was already crowded with Negroes, despite the widespread fear of an unannounced appearance by the KKK, as the dreaded Ku Klux Klan had come to be broadly known. The Heirs' older servant woman Rachel, surrounded by solicitous friends, sat throbbing with emotion in the front row next to the rail.

Oh, that the daughter were up there with her!

The nervous Reverend mulled over the obvious risk to his church in holding the Heirs' funeral there. He owed an awful lot to the Heirs family. After all, old Morgan Heirs had funded the building of the church, himself. But, on each of the four days since Lillian Heirs' death, an unsigned letter had been found in the Heirs family's mail box. Two, had even been left in the church's lobby. Warning letters in a feminine hand, imploring that the mulatto Negress not be allowed onto the white folks' floor of the church that day or—God forbid—the letters said, there would be more suffering for the community's first family.

Other unsolved crimes against the Heirs' family—including the root cellar theft and locking up of the Negro, the vandalism at Heirs' office, the barn burning, the Negro's lynching, the boy's dog being shot—all, having gone unpunished to date, officers in civilian dress, hopelessly conspicuous, had been posted inside and outside the church sanctuary. In case further injury to the unfortunate family might be contemplated by the seemingly uncontrollable KKK, other officers had been dispatched to the Heirs family's residence.

The grieving extended family—Heirs, Mosses, and Bakers, together—innocently unaware of the police's covert precautions, sat in the first two pews. Standing beside the flower bedecked casket, Willow Heirs' clear, sweet soprano voice, a cappella, sang the closing words of *Amazing Grace*: "'Tis grace has brought me safe thus far. And grace will lead me home."

All good works of the deceased having been recited in elegies spoken in reverent tones, the last hymn having lovingly ended even as he checked his watch, the Reverend Wylie stepped forward to close the service with a prayer. The church still stood—untouched—praise God!

Entombment was to follow at Crestview Cemetery in a new eight vault family crypt purchased on the day following the elder Heirs woman's demise. Whereupon, on orders from Mistress Morgana Moss, daughter of the recently deceased, coffins of three pre-deceased family members had already been disinterred from the Heirs' private cemetery and removed to the new crypt. Mistress Lillian Heirs' remains would occupy the fourth vault, leaving yet another four unsealed.

Condolences passed from mouth to ear as grieving family and friends filed from the church to awaiting carriages for the trip to the cemetery. Mistress Althea Clark hesitated, then making up her mind, gently clasped Morgana Moss's elbow and pulled her aside. "I'm sorry for your losing your mother," she said, from behind a lacy handkerchief.

"Thank you, Mistress Clark, I appreciate your sympathy," a tearfully sincere Morgana replied, turning to face the smaller woman. Above the handkerchief, Morgana saw a harsh blue tint on Mistress Clark's swollen left eye. "My goodness, you poor woman!" Morgana said, "I can't believe that was an accident!"

Briars
The House of Heirs

Mistress Clark, lowering the handkerchief, displayed a bruised and swollen jaw. "It'll be all right! I'm used to it. He's always sorry—after, but my Ezra's a man with a devil inside!" She kissed Morgana's cheek. "My own daughter, Carla, ran away years ago. I'd love to have seen her married. I—I've owed your mama a debt for a long, long time. I've tried to make it up—a little." Mistress Clark turned then, and walked swiftly away, mingling with other departing mourners. Watching her leave, Morgana felt compassion for Mistress Clark, an unfortunate prisoner of a long and bitter marriage.

Shane came quickly to Morgana's side and as he guided her out to the Baker's carriages, he said, "I've put Rachel and Willow in the carriage with the elder Bakers. You're to ride to the cemetery with Laura Lee and the twins. Jonny, Wil and I are leaving now to ride back by *Briars*—just to make sure—"

"No, Shane, come with me!" Morgana pleaded, concern furrowing her brow. "You never told me you were planning this! If you go now you might not get back in time for Mama's entombment."

"Don't worry, we won't be long. Fast as we'll be going, we'll probably get to the cemetery ahead of the funeral procession!" Shane kissed Morgana's lips, swollen and hot from crying, and helped her into the carriage beside Laura Lee before he hurried to join Jonathan and Wil, on the bench of the Heirs' carriage.

Wil picked up the reins and Mary Belle stepped out at a good fast trot, moving quickly away from the line of carriages in front of the church.

Three blocks away, Wil guided Mary Belle into a stable that housed Milton Johnson's blacksmith shop. The Johnson brothers, Milton, Curtis, and Daniel, dressed in their finest, fresh from the funeral service for Lillian Heirs awaited them there on horseback, holding the reins of three more horses.

Wil produced three pistols from his father's gun collection from beneath the bench of the Heirs' carriage and handed two of them to Shane and Jonathan, holding for himself, the U. S. Marshall's pistol his mother had worn at her waist in the Yankee confrontation three years ago.

After Jonathan had mounted his own horse, Spirit, and Wil had mounted Pal, Shane quickly examined the third horse, mounting, also. "Decent of you to loan me a horse," he said to Milton Johnson. "When Wil said you'd help us, I was a little afraid after our last meeting you might just want another try at blowing *my* head off!"

"I would have, too, the first time—" Milton grinned, watching as the late arrivals loaded and checked their weapons. "—if Mistress Heirs, God rest her soul, hadn't come out of the house yelling, '*Stop the killing!*' Don't kid yourself, Yankee—," Milton spat, scanning the faces of Jonathan, Wil, and his two brothers, all of whom had been present for the battle at *Briars* that day. "—we, all, would have—to a man!"

"Good thing for me, then, I guess—" Shane said, grinning, as he tucked the weapon under his belt, "—that that was *then*— and this is *now!* Gentlemen, shall we—?"

Six men rode out of the blacksmith's stable together, leaving an old mare still harnessed in the traces of an unoccupied carriage, contentedly nibbling at a rack of sweet feed.

It being a weekend, they made good time through lightly trafficked city streets finally allowing their horses to stretch out on the road that would take them in the direction of *Briars* and *Greenleaf*.

From Northside Drive they saw smoke billowing skyward. First there was wispy light gray smoke, climbing like a single smoke signal. But as they rode nearer and faster, it changed to a dense black column dropping ash on them as they neared. At the intersection where Northside dead-ended into Briarwood Road, the newly restored *Greenleaf* to the right, stood unharmed but up the hill to the left *Briars* was afire, flames licking out of windows and climbing its granite walls.

Briars
The House of Heirs

Thundering into view around the east side of the burning house and down the driveway toward the road, Wil counted a column of eleven white-sheeted horsemen, headed onto the road before scattering quickly in all directions through open terrain, riding fast away.

"No!" Wil screamed. Leaving the others behind, he urged Pal into a full gallop, puffing up the hill towards *Briars*. Seeing Wil's distress and realizing the futility of his cause, Shane left Jonathan and the Johnson boys to chase down the Klansmen and took out after the boy. With drawn weapons, the remaining four spread out following the outlaws, blasting away at fast disappearing figures as they went.

"Wil!" Shane called, his horse clattering up the gravel driveway. "Wil, wait! Don't go in there!" But if Wil heard him, he ignored Shane's warning. Reaching the house, Wil leapt from his saddle and slapped Pal on his flank, sending him back down the drive away from danger and topping the stairs in two bounds. Crossing the porch, he ran straight to the library window puffing acrid black smoke, and crawled through the opening over shards of broken glass.

Shane sent his borrowed horse after Pal, and cleared the stairs, darting though the opening after Wil, calling into the pitch black darkness, "Wil—Wil, where are you?" With one hand over his nose and mouth, the other feeling for Wil, he moved ahead slowly. "Answer me, damn it! Where are you?"

"Right here!" Wil shouted at his elbow, over the roaring fire. "Now, let's get the hell out of here!"

"You go first!" Shane yelled in Wil's ear over the roar of the inferno. "What a damned fool thing to do!"

"Here, hold this!" Wil said, before climbing through the window.

"What is it?" Shane asked, irritably, taking the large round pasty ball from Wil while the younger man climbed through the window.

Ann Gray

Once outside, Wil reached to retrieve his trophy, and Shane, still admonishing, crawled through the opening behind him.

It wasn't until they had tramped back down the driveway to their horses, and were standing at the gates looking back at the fiery remains of *Briars* that Wil unrolled his trophy.

"It's Ma's bearskin rug," Wil said, holding onto the marble-eyed, heavy head and stroking the soft black fur. "Getting right down to it, this was about the only thing left in there I really gave a damn about—she killed it, you know!"

Shane wrapped his arm around Wil's shoulders, and for the first time since his mother's death, Wil leaned against Shane and wept.

When they saw the others coming back, Wil rolled the bearskin rug back into a compact bundle and tied it to his saddle.

The Johnson boys all took turns telling Wil how sorry they were that the white devils had gotten away.

Jonathan swung down from his saddle, grabbed Wil and hugged him. "Sorry, Wil," Jonathan said, "We just got here too damned late! The way they scattered we didn't have much hope of catching any of them."

People were coming, then from all directions to stand in the middle of the road and watch the unquenchable fire burn. From away down Northside towards town they finally heard the clanging of the fire wagons' bells.

"I'd better get on back to the cemetery," Jonathan said. "Somebody's got to break the news to Morgana. It might as well be me." He grinned at Shane. "I've been helping her handle her problems longer than you have."

Shane returned Jonathan's grin. "It's all right. We've talked about this happening. She's known *Briars* was in danger ever since we got back. Maybe you could say a few words about Mother Heirs yourself at the entombment—you know, stretch it out a bit—give us time to wind things up here? Shouldn't take long." Shane checked his pocket watch.

Briars
The House of Heirs

"I'll do what I can," Jonathan said, reluctantly, "I'm not naturally talkative."

Knowing Jonathan's natural shyness, Wil grinned. There was pure truth in Jonny's words, but he always did love and respect Mama and he would do just fine.

After Jonathan had ridden out, the youngest of the Johnsons, Dan said to Wil, "I found some fresh tracks upstream behind Farley's place heading back down towards y'all's root cellar! Looked like a single rider, though!"

"Probably not Klan!" Milt Johnson said, "Unless one doubled back for some reason." Milt turned to Shane. "You don't suppose anybody, Klan or otherwise, would be foolhardy enough to take a chance on getting caught in that root cellar, do you?"

"Root cellar? Where is there a root cellar?" Shane asked Wil, straight out.

"That's right. Nobody ever showed you, did they?" Wil said, breaking into a half grin. "Come on, Shane—!" he said, eager to get away from the fire scene. "It's high time you knew! Maybe we'll catch ourselves a thief, besides!"

They stopped at the rocky stream, and Curtis Johnson asked Wil, "Y'all want us to go with you the rest of the way?"

"No need! The two of us ought to be able to handle one lousy thief!" Wil answered. "The way I feel right now—if there is anybody near the cellar when we get there—well, I'm damn sure itching for a fight!"

Then they all shook hands and the Johnson boys rode off single file into their cane field. When the Johnson boys came to the place where the Yankee soldiers had been buried, Wil told Shane to watch and just as he knew they would, all three spat on a different Yankee's grave.

Wil led Shane along the stream to the root cellar. When they got there, there was no sign of tampering with the door to the cave. Remembering Henry's admonition for his father to put locks on it, Wil pulled out his key ring and unlocked the heavy squeaking oak door while Shane watched, amazed.

Wil lit a lantern mounted to a timber near the entrance and gestured for Shane to enter. "I don't like coming down here much, anymore, but this is the cave where I hid out with my dead Papa while you Yankees had use of our house. Between Mama, Henry, and me, we must have all been up and down that hill from the house to here—seven, eight, maybe ten times or more, and none of y'all ever knew it."

Shane looked around the cold clay room, crammed from wall to wall with stored food, arms and ammunition. "Why are you just now showing me this?"

"Never thought about it," Wil said, honestly. "Actually, never saw any reason to."

"It's a virtual arsenal!" Shane realized a truth. "This was here all that time?"

"Yep, all the time!" Wil nodded, and produced a wan smile. "These are Papa's weapons. He usually kept them in the cabinet in the library. I brought them back down weeks ago. Wanted to be sure nothing happened to them. Reckon, they're all mine, now."

Shane took one more look around before Wil doused the lantern and they left the cave. Wil let Pal lead Shane's borrowed mount up the rugged path in the vacant field towards the high hedges.

Shane still grinned with admiration over just how successfully he and his entire detachment had been outwitted by a full house of women, a boy, and one old Negro man.

It was as they neared the top of the hill that they saw the single white-robed Klansman. Lying prone on the path at the narrow opening in the hawthorn hedge that led to the pantry door, he was intently watching the fire. He had tethered his horse, a handsome sorrel, to the prickly hedges nearby—the whole weedy area completely hidden from the road by the rise of the hill.

Briars
The House of Heirs

Tethering their own horses to a scrub oak a good forty feet downhill, Shane and Wil went ahead on hands and knees over rocky terrain until they were no more than fifteen feet behind the hooded man.

"Burn, damn you, burn!" he sang out, laughing and smacking the ground with his fists as he enjoyed his band's handiwork.

Seeing the skeletal remains of Mama's favorite bent wood rocker fall into the hot ashes of the caved in back porch, Wil lunged for the man, who turned to look too late to fend off his assailant.

With a loud cry, "Damn you to Hell!" Wil was on him.

Shane got to his feet and stood by quietly while Wil walloped the man until his anger was spent.

"Damn you to Hell and back!" Wil yelled, as he landed one fist after another to the Klansman's white-hooded jaw. "That's for Henry! That's for Storm! That's for *Briars!* That's for Mama! *And, this one's for me!"* he said, finally, landing one more telling blow to the beaten man's jaw before crawling off him. Then he reached down and ripped off the bloody hood and whooped in downright astonishment, "My God! It's Ezra Clark!"

"Get up!" Shane said, booting the man, when Wil stepped away nursing his wounded knuckles.

"There were two police guards on the gates—" Shane said.

"They're over there," Clark nodded towards the open field. "But I didn't kill them! It was—"

"Save it for the law!" Shane said.

They trussed Ezra Clark with his own belt and put him on his horse. Then Wil walked to the place where the Klansman had pointed, and found the guards shot dead.

"Wil?" Shane asked, as they were bringing their prisoner back to where the pumper wagons stood idle, and the law was waiting, "Why didn't you just shoot him? I already had my finger on the trigger."

"Too quick!" Wil said. "He needs to die hanging—like poor Henry did."

When they reached the road and looked back, B*riars* lay smoking—a gutted gray stone skeleton. An angry mob had gathered in the road and exclaimed among themselves over Ezra Clark's having been discovered at the scene in Ku Klux Klan apparel.

Shane stood quietly by, watching, while Wil handed his prisoner over to the Chief Magistrate.

Wil blew on his raw knuckles. "You'll find two of your men up there in that open field. I'm afraid they're dead."

"Clark's pretty beat up," the lawman observed.

"Yep, pretty much! I gave him a good beating, I guess!" Wil answered. "Not nearly as much as he deserves."

"Won't argue that point with you, Mister Heirs," the lawman said.

When they were riding away, Wil said, "Did you hear what he said, Shane? He called me Mister Heirs."

Shane reached and tousled Wil's hair. "A man gets the respect he earns, Wil."

Cocking his head to look at Shane through a shock of mussed-up red hair, Wil grinned his shy smile. "Yeah, Mister Moss, you're absolutely right."

Then Shane checked his pocket watch. Impossible! It had actually been a little less than an hour since Jonathan had left them. If they picked up their pace, they'd be at the cemetery in another thirty minutes. They'd be mighty late, but they knew they'd be present for Lillian Heirs' entombment.

Jonathan Baker had said he'd talk awhile, and Jonathan Baker was a man of his word.

CHAPTER SIXTEEN ~ THE HEART OF *BRIARS*

1:30 a.m., October 20, 1867 ~ Briars, Atlanta, Georgia

Yesterdays and Tomorrows

Its hot gray stones encompassing glowing embers, *Briars'* charred remains still radiated heat. In that circle of warmth on the barren hilltop, Morgana and Shane lay together on a pallet of blankets looking up at the star-strewn October sky.

"Hamita has always been a dear friend to Mama," Morgana said, snuggling on her husband's shoulder. "And it is no less than I would have expected of her, offering us shelter until we are able to leave for *Moss Hall*, but I could not have endured one more hour of her gushing, sentimental reminiscences. Don't ask me why, but I had to be here—right here at home tonight. Thank you for understanding."

Shane kissed the top of her curly head, breathing in her sweetness. How comfortable they were together. "Wil says he's leaving Monday to join the Marines. He asked me to keep the rescued bearskin rug and his gun collection at Moss Hall until he has a suitable place for them. The news came out of the blue to me. Did you know he had these plans?" Shane asked.

"As for the bearskin rug—that comes as something of a surprise. But a welcome one, nonetheless. Actually, I shall find it rather consoling to have old Bruin with us until Wil comes to collect him. After all, Bruin is all we have left of *Briars*, now." Morgana paused, realization of the sad truth bringing stinging tears. She blinked them away, and continued, "And, as to Wil's desire for a military career! Heavens, yes, I've known about that for years! Mama and Papa had to practically lock him up during the last year of the war, even though he was only fifteen when it ended. He always swore when he came of age he'd join the Marines. I guess it's only fair he gets his wish at last."

"I was in military school at fifteen," Shane said. "I haven't regretted it. It'll be good for him."

"My brother, Wil—God love him, will still be telling the story as we, children, heard it from Jeremiah Baker of Mama's killing that bear to our grandchildren and his grandchildren. And he'll be cleaning and polishing Papa's guns when he's an old, retired military man."

"If that's what pleases him," Shane said, "it shouldn't be a bad life." He was silent for a moment thinking, then he said, "Pa got word before we left home that Luke was caught robbing a bank in Tulsa, Oklahoma. He won't be back. He got life. We haven't told Ma. Probably never will."

Morgana sighed. "I'm so sorry, Shane."

"Me, too," Shane answered. "I can't understand what makes a man think that way."

"I, for one, am glad, darling!" Morgana said. She rolled over onto her elbows and looked down at him in the pale moonlight. "I'm happy to say, I have good news! I haven't had a chance to tell you! It's been the farthest thing from my mind until right now, but since Wil will be leaving soon, we talked to Willow yesterday, and promised her money to start her school. She has her eye on an old house on Ashby Street. I think we can get it for 'a song'. There's this man, Calvin Tubbs—he's a black educator from New York, and he's interested in her project. She's been talking to him about it for weeks now, without saying a word to a soul."

"Not even to you?" Shane asked. "I thought you and Willow shared everything."

"Not *everything*, darling!" Morgana giggled, flopping down to nestle closer to him. "I couldn't get over Rachel's response when I told her we were going to be living in Richmond in the O'Donnell house part of the time, and that it was to be her home if she wanted it to be for as long as she wanted to live there. She stopped crying immediately and said she'd always wanted to see 'that Richmond house!'. Then, she wanted to know how far it was from the farm and when I told her it was only a few miles she said, 'All right, so long as she could come visit 'if'n' she got lonesome.' I really think she was afraid we were going to turn her out. Imagine!" Morgana laughed softly. "Can you conceive of the uproar it will cause if those bigots at the cemetery ever discover that one of the Heirs bodies they removed from our family plot to the new Heirs' family mausoleum was a Negro's? Dear old Henry, it makes me so happy, his still being right there with Mama and Papa and Sarah. I'll tell you a secret, too. When Rachel dies, there's a vault there for her, too."

"That's only five," Shane eyed her, puzzled. "What about the others?" There was a familiar sparkle in his eye when he added, "Did you have somebody in particular in mind when you bought an eight vault tomb?"

"Silly!" Morgana answered, lightly. "Now don't laugh, but one will be for Willow if she ever wants it. Or Wil, if he never marries. Or for us, if you so desire. Also, one will be kept as a spare. You never know when you may need a resting place for some long lost relative who might turn up sick, lonely, and insolvent."

Night sounds surrounded them. Listening to the whippoorwill and the crickets' noisy drone, as if silence were painful, Morgana looked towards *Briars*' burnt remains, with sad eyes and said, "I can see it—I can smell it—still, I can't believe it's gone! Papa started building *Briars* on this beautiful hilltop graced only by a great oak tree, because it overlooked the little village of Terminus back in 1838. He added to *Briars* when Terminus was renamed Marthasville, and finished building it when Marthasville became Atlanta. It remained standing, thanks to you, while everything around it was destroyed during those fearful days of Yankee occupation. You couldn't have known then that it had sheltered our family for so many years. But in a matter of minutes today—a dozen fanatical Southerners burned it to the ground! Isn't that ironic?"

Suddenly, she turned her head on his shoulder. "Shane, I just realized—there is yet another part of *Briars* they have left us! They have only destroyed the shell of Briars, the heart of Briars still lives in everyone of us who lived within her hedges. Tomorrow I shall find time to take some cuttings from *Briars'* hawthorns to bring with us to Virginia."

"We have hawthorns in Virginia," Shane said. "I'll help you gather some."

"Not *just* hawthorns— *Briars'* hawthorns!" Morgana explained, sitting up. "I'll take enough to keep Mama's hedges alive and growing there. She'd like that. In time, too, we'll come back and build again, *right here*."

Determination shone anew in her jet eyes and she gestured with open arms as she described the image in her mind: "It must be something extraordinary if it's to take our precious old *Briars'* place! Maybe a hotel—a grand hotel, teeming with interesting vibrant people and activity, sparkling and exciting—like my father. And it must have a firm, strong foundation, be well-crafted, well-disposed and comfortable—like my mother. Handsome, like Drew. Ethereal, like Sarah. But never some stodgy old vacuous, echoing museum. That would *never do* for my family. Yes, a fine hotel on the top of this hill! We could call it *'Briarcrest'*. Now, isn't *that* a splendid idea?"

"Oh, a wonderful idea!" Shane said, hesitancy in his voice. "Are you serious?"

"I'm quite serious," Morgana insisted, lying back down beside him. "The idea came to me right after the fire, and it's been persistently nudging me ever since. I am determined to do something substantial with this land, darling, and it's an obvious fact that Atlanta's growing so fast it will soon need more accommodations for weary travelers. Ours is a perfect location. It has a natural overview of the city, and it's far enough out from mid-town to be—you know, exclusive."

Briars
The House of Heirs

"You'll need somebody dependable to be in charge of your hotel once it's built?" He frowned. "Not you. You'll be happily occupied on the farm or in Richmond—with me, naturally."

"Oh, naturally," Morgana agreed, and Shane was relieved to have her accord.

"Not Wil, he'll be in the military," Shane added, thoughtfully.

Laughing, Morgana replied quickly, "Jonny and Laura Lee, of course! The twins will be away at school, and I know Jonny and Laura Lee will support such an endeavor because Hamita and Jeremiah already plan to move to Macon to be near Hamita's sister, Samantha, who is in poor health. Why, with their collaboration, we can even convert *Greenleaf* into a beautiful garden teahouse and restaurant on our hotel's lush, rolling grounds."

"'Gana!" Shane looked incredulously at her. "What's gotten into you?"

"It must be my dear Papa!" Morgana laughed. "How sad you never knew him! You would have found him inspiring!" Shane grinned, thoughtfully, as she continued, "Even now he must be whispering in my ear. He was always building something or investing in promising ventures. All I know is that thanks to him and to circumstances of fate, I am a very wealthy woman, these things are possible, and I'm able to do them."

"And, your older brother who died in the war—wouldn't he have been ideal for this exciting new enterprise? What a shame he's gone."

"Isn't it?" Morgana said, smiling faintly. "Poor Drew—always so selfish! Though it's sad, I can honestly say that, like your brother, Luke, Drew never really gave a damn about anybody but himself. What a shame he'll never know how much he's missing. But let's not talk about Drew!"

Morgana fell silent, wondering if her brother would keep his word never to return to Atlanta. Wondering how he was controlling his health problems inherited from their father.

Wondering if he had beaten the unfavorable odds of his illness and remained alive? If not, what of Stella and his children? How had Stella managed with three small children if he had continued to sicken and died. Perhaps in years to come Morgana would seek answers to such questions but now her heart was much too full of sadness and grief to search out more.

She sat up again and looked thoughtfully towards *Briars'* smoldering ruins. "Now tell me, darling, that you thoroughly approve of my new scheme and that you're not just coddling me. In this absurd world, it seems women must be totally dependent on their men if they're to get things done. Say you'll help me!"

Shane pulled her back down and kissed her soundly. "Do I have a choice?" he teased, knowing he would go to the ends of the earth for her.

"Not really," Morgana replied, knowing she could depend on him, always, and that she'd trust him with her fortune or her life—anywhere—any time—anyway.

Shane said, looking up into the blue-black canopy of endless stars, "My God, it's a beautiful night! How long has it been since you've slept out under the stars, like this?"

"Honestly?"

"Of course, honestly."

"Never," Morgana admitted, giggling. "Why should I?"

"Everyone should spend at least one or two nights sleeping outside under the stars," Shane explained, wrapping her in his warm embrace. "It's a good reminder of just how fleeting our lives really are."

Closing her eyes in a feeling of déjà vu inspired by Shane's profound statement, Morgana could feel Mama kissing her lips and smoothing her hair like she always did. Suddenly, her composure gave way to great jarring sobs denying the playfulness, the busyness, the rush of words that had masked her grief since losing her mother. At last, Morgana released the crushing heartache that had been closeted in her heart.

"But, Shane," Morgana cried out, clinging to him, "I wasn't *ready* to let her go!"

"'Gana, darling, we're *never ready!*" Shane whispered, understanding. He held her tenderly in his arms while, trembling in utter wretchedness, she wept bitter tears.

When the wrenching sobs had passed and she was quiet once again, seeking her husband's lips, Morgana whispered, "I want a baby. Make me a baby, Shane."

Ann Gray

CAST OF CHARACTERS

INSIDE *BRIARS*

Morgan Andrew Heirs, (Born Sat., January 5, 1817—died Sat., November 12, 1864). Son of **Glenn Arthur Heirs** (died 10/29/1848), a grocery store chain (The Grocery) owner in Virginia and Maryland. Mother, **Constance Marie Courtland Heirs**, (died November 12,1864) eldest daughter of Jerome (a gentleman banker) and Madeline Hayes Courtland, (a lady of distinction). Family home in Richmond called **Heirs House.** Married, Wednesday, March 21, 1838 at 21 to **Lillian Maureen O'Donnell.** Owner of *Briars,* begun August 29, 1838.

Lillian Maureen O'Donnell Heirs, (born September 10, 1820—died October 16, 1867) Daughter of **Michael Wilson O'Donnell,** supervisor on Virginia Rail Road, and **Catherine Hall O'Donnell,** both of Richmond, Virginia. **Wife** of **Morgan Andrew Heirs, I,** and mother of four **Heirs** children.

Morgan Andrew (Drew) Heirs, II, (born Sunday, February 10, 1839) Married **Laura Lee Hill Heirs** on March 3, 1860. Father of twins, **Martha Alice** and **Morgan Andrew, III.** Alias, **James Andrews, Natchez, Miss.** common law husband of **Stella Farley,** dry goods store manager.

Sarah Alice Heirs, (born November 2, 1844; died November 15, 1864), Eldest daughter of **Morgan** and **Lillian Heirs**, engaged four years to **Jonathan Baker**.

Morgana ('Gana) Irene Heirs, (born August 6, 1847), Younger daughter of **Morgan** and **Lillian Heirs**. Married September 15, 1867 to **Shane Alexander Moss**.

Michael Wilson (Wil) Heirs, (born July 27, 1849), Youngest child of **Morgan** and **Lillian Heirs**. Joined Marines at eighteen.

Laura Lee Hill Heirs, married **Morgan Andrew Heirs, II** on March 3, 1860. Mother of twins, **Martha Alice** and **Morgan Andrew, III** (born November 5, 1860).

Rachel and Henry Heirs, Bought from **Charley Rose**, plantation owner. 20 years faithful servants, as former slaves, to **Heirs** family, and **Willow**'s parents.

Willow Heirs, (born August 6, 1847) daughter of house servants, **Rachel** and **Henry**, reared and schooled along with **Morgana**.

Grady, gardener, former slave.

Thomas, groom, former slave.

Heirs' **Animals**: **Morgan**'s horses, Ambler, Rex, **Morgan**'s bird dog **Freckles** in **Terminus; Morgana**'s Thoroughbred black horse, **Star; Star's** foal, a colt, **Blaze**; **Wil**'s horse, a Tennessee Walker, **Pal, Wil's** dogs, female shepherd dog, **Daisy, Daisy's** son, **Storm**. Family cow, **Flossy**. Carriage horse, **Mary Belle**.

Ann Gray

UNION ARMY CHARACTERS inside *BRIARS*

(1) Lieutenant Shane Alexander Moss, (born July 20, 1843), Home, *Moss Hall* near **Petersburg,** south of **Richmond, Virginia**. Younger son of **Roger Moss** and **Patricia Moss**. Brother of **Luke**.

Other Nine Union Army soldiers, (2) **Sergeant Crane**, (3) **Corporals Brock** and (4) **Fowler**, **Privates** (5)**Emmett Jenkins**, (6) **George Dodd**, (7) **James Burgess**, (8) **Harold Loomis**, (9) **Carl Slade** and (10) **Yancey Black** died in cane field.

OUTSIDE BRIARS in ATLANTA

Jonathan (Jonny) Baker, (born Friday, February 15, 1839) son of **Jeremiah** and **Hamita Baker** at neighboring *Greenleaf* estate, east of *Briars,* engaged four years to **Sarah Heirs;** owner of copper stallion horse, **Spirit;** Later marries **Drew's widow, Laura Lee Heirs.**

Jeremiah and Hamita Baker, best friends of **Heirs** family since 1838. Owners of *Greenleaf,* and **Baker's Lumber Mill**.

Tom Garrett, unmarried, Railroad worker and family friend. **Morgan**'s and **Jeremiah**'s drinking buddy. In later years, banker and financial advisor to **Lillian**.

Stella Farley, Drew's favorite prostitute. Later common-law wife of **James Andrews**.

Milton, Curtis, and Daniel Johnson, sons of **Mr. and Mrs. Homer Johnson,** neighbors behind *Briars,* cousin, **Earl**, in Savannah.

Briars
The House of Heirs

Daniel (Dan) Goddard, Railroad doctor in **Terminus** - tended **Morgan's** bear wounds.

Reverend Hoyt Wiley, Minister of **Briarwood Church.**

Ezra Clark, local **Ku Klux Klan Klavern Nighthawk.**

Mistress Althea (Allie) Clark, wife of **Ezra** sent warning notes. **Lillian** helped her as part of church work.

Calvin Tubbs - **Negro educator** from **New York.**

Charles Watson Davis, Cotton plantation owner down by **Savannah**. Previous owner of **Henry, Rachel, Grady, Thomas.**

Woody and Frank, Black market slave kidnappers of **Henry and Rachel.**

Stewart and Margaret Farley, neighbors, west of *Briars,* parents of **Stella.**

Linus, Farley's groom.

CHARACTERS in RICHMOND

Glenn Arthur Heirs, father of **Morgan Andrew Heirs**, (died 11/21/1848), a grocery store chain owner (**The Grocery**) in Virginia and Maryland. Husband of **Constance Heirs**.

Constance Marie Courtland Heirs, (died November 12, 1864), wife of **Glenn Arthur Heirs** and mother of **Morgan Andrew Heirs**.

Michael Wilson O'Donnell, **Lillian's** father. Lived in Richmond.

Ann Gray

Cassandra Cochran, Nurse to Michael O'Donnell.

Carl, Constance Heirs' driver.

Chesterfield County, Petersburg, Virginia

<u>**Roger Nelson Moss and Patricia Thomas Moss**</u>, **Shane Moss' parents, and owners of *Moss Hall.***

<u>**Luke Moss**</u>, Shane Moss' brother, **Confederate Army Renegade**.

Bessie, Moss' Cook and Housekeeper at *Moss Hall.*

Moss Hall's stallion, **Victor**, old mare, **Jasmine.**

Abel Wilkins, MD, Petersburg doctor.

Jacob Garner, Owner of the **Petersburg Public Stables**.

Mistress Lydia (Lydie) Campbell, **Madam** of **Petersburg's** bordello.

Violet, Myrtle, Charlotte, Girls in **Mistress Lydia Campbell's House**.

Un-named kind gentleman on train.

Un-named Young Doctor with **Union Army.**

ABOUT THE AUTHOR

How lucky can one "little ole Southern girl" get to be? Quite frankly, when these events occurred, I couldn't believe they were actually happening to me!

There I was wearing a svelte black evening gown with ostrich feathers, sipping cocktails across the table from Lucille Ball and Gary Morton, her producer husband. Later that same evening, I was sitting with them alongside Jack Donohue, distinguished motion picture and television director and dear friend, watching a Las Vegas MGM Grand Hotel stage show. I'd spent the entire week watching these fabulous people rehearsing and taping a *Lucy Special* on which my husband, Norm Gray, was Jack's First Assistant Director. The year was 1974, and the show was about Lucy going to Las Vegas. Dean Martin was her special guest star.

On another occasion, imagine the kick I got from giving "The Fonz" his biggest laugh line in a *Happy Days* television program that my husband was directing called, "The Dance Contest."

One cold winter's day, I remember the fun of watching Robin Williams and Pam Dawber frolicking in eight inches of fresh fallen snow in Boulder, Colorado during the making of the titles for "Mork and Mindy".

Another perk came each year during hiatus when the shows were down. Then, Norm and I traveled the islands of the Pacific. We started by visiting Majuro in the Marshall Islands where Norm had served in the USMC during WWII. Inspired by the beauty and tranquillity of the islands, year after year we expanded our explorations, until we had visited Tahiti, Moorea, Bora Bora, American Samoa, Western Samoa, The Kingdom of Tonga, Rarotonga in the Cook Islands and, naturally, Hawaii was always our point of departure.

Have I mentioned yet, that my husband made all these events possible by deciding early in our marriage that it would be advantageous to his career if we settled in Los Angeles? It was. He gave thirty-five years of his life to the entertainment industry.

Though I'd been writing since I was editor of the West Fulton High School weekly newspaper in Northwest Atlanta many years before, my first real sale was to *Happy Days*. I was hooked. After that encouraging beginning, I studied writing for two years under Maren Elwood in beautiful Royce Hall at UCLA. My short stories began selling.

Many years later, inspired by family genealogy buffs who searched my ancestors and those of my husband, I was bewildered to learn that both our Southern families go back farther than five generations. I learned about ancestors who lived even before the days of the War Between the States (as we Southerners prefer to call the Civil War of 1861-1865). My great-great grandfather, James Alexander White fought in the Confederate Army's Company A of the 8th Georgia Battalion of Volunteers, and was captured in 1864 and imprisoned in Illinois until the war's end in 1865.

Proud of my Southern heritage, I found the courage to undertake the task of painstakingly researching and faithfully depicting the times and turmoil surrounding a fictional Southern family from 1838 through 1867. Welcome, y'all, to *BRIARS, The House of Heirs*, my labor of love.

Printed in the United States
777900001B